AND SO IT BEGINS...

Charlaine stood. "Master Rurlan, to what do I owe the honour of this meeting?"

The Dwarf smiled back, though a hint of sadness lingered in his eyes. "Why, correspondence, of course." He dug through his satchel, retrieved a sealed letter, and placed it on the table. "This comes from the Royal Court of Hadenfeld."

"From Prince Ludwig?"

Rurlan lowered his voice. "That's King Ludwig now." He snatched up the missive. "My apologies. In my haste, I almost forgot to unseal it." He touched his phoenix ring to the seal, then broke it open, revealing another sealed document, which he placed directly into Charlaine's hand.

"Please," she replied. "Have a seat. Would you like something to eat?"

"I should be delighted. Do I just help myself?"

"Grab a platter and line up over yonder." Danica nodded towards the food line. "The sisters on duty will look after you." The Dwarf headed to the front of the room while she turned to Charlaine, who was reading over the letter. "News?" she asked once her friend finished.

"Much has happened in Hadenfeld," replied Charlaine. "Ludwig has seized the Throne, and he and Charlotte were crowned king and queen."

"Any word of Frederick?"

"Yes. He's doing fine, although I expect it'll take time to adjust to life in the capital."

"Anything else I should know?"

"The Temple Knights of Saint Mathew supported his claim. According to Ludwig, the previous king, Morgan, grew paranoid and began executing people as traitors."

"And you trust his accounting of events?"

"I have no reason not to. Ludwig has never been the type to covet power, and I harbour no doubt that Lady Charlotte wouldn't put up with such nonsense if he did."

"You only met her for a short time."

"True, but I've been told I possess a knack for quickly taking the measure of a person, and she seemed a most earnest and forthright individual."

ALSO BY PAUL J BENNETT

<u>**HEIR TO THE CROWN SERIES**</u>

SERVANT OF THE CROWN

SWORD OF THE CROWN

MERCERIAN TALES: STORIES OF THE PAST

HEART OF THE CROWN

SHADOW OF THE CROWN

MERCERIAN TALES: THE CALL OF MAGIC

FATE OF THE CROWN

BURDEN OF THE CROWN

MERCERIAN TALES: THE MAKING OF A MAN

DEFENDER OF THE CROWN

FURY OF THE CROWN

MERCERIAN TALES: HONOUR THY ANCESTORS

WAR OF THE CROWN

TRIUMPH OF THE CROWN

MERCERIAN TALES: INTO THE FORGE

GUARDIAN OF THE CROWN

ENEMY OF THE CROWN

MERCERIAN TALES: THE SPARK OF CHANGE

PERIL OF THE CROWN

SAVIOUR OF THE CROWN

VICTORY OF THE CROWN

Power Ascending Series

Tempered Steel: Prequel

Temple Knight | Warrior Knight

Temple Captain | Warrior Lord

Temple Commander | Warrior Prince

Temple General | Warrior King

The Frozen Flame Series

Awakening - Prequels

Ashes | Embers | Flames | Inferno

Maelstrom | Vortex | Torrent | Cataclysm

Duality of Magic Series - Coming Spring 2026

Voices From the Past

The Chronicles of Cyric

Into the Maelstrom: Prequel

Midwinter Murder

The Beast of Brunhausen

A Plague on Zeiderbruch

TEMPLE GENERAL

POWER ASCENDING: BOOK SEVEN

PAUL J BENNETT

DEDICATION

To my wife, Carol, who gave me wings to let my imagination fly.

Map of Eiddenwerthe

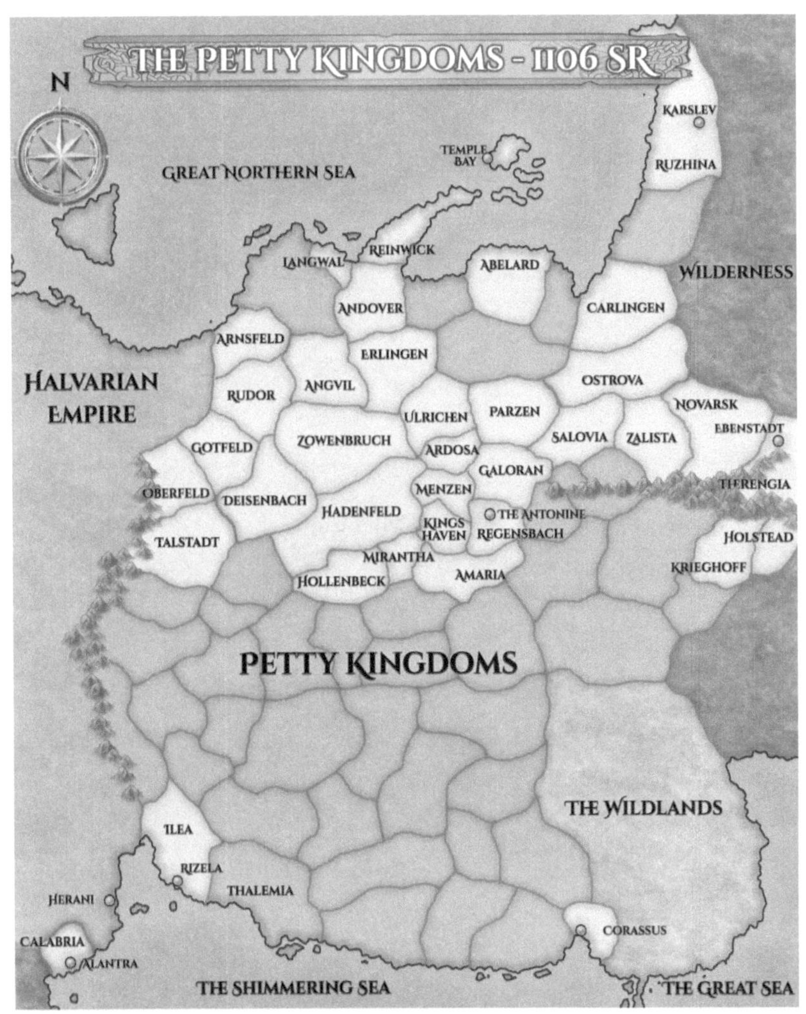

Map of Petty Kingdoms

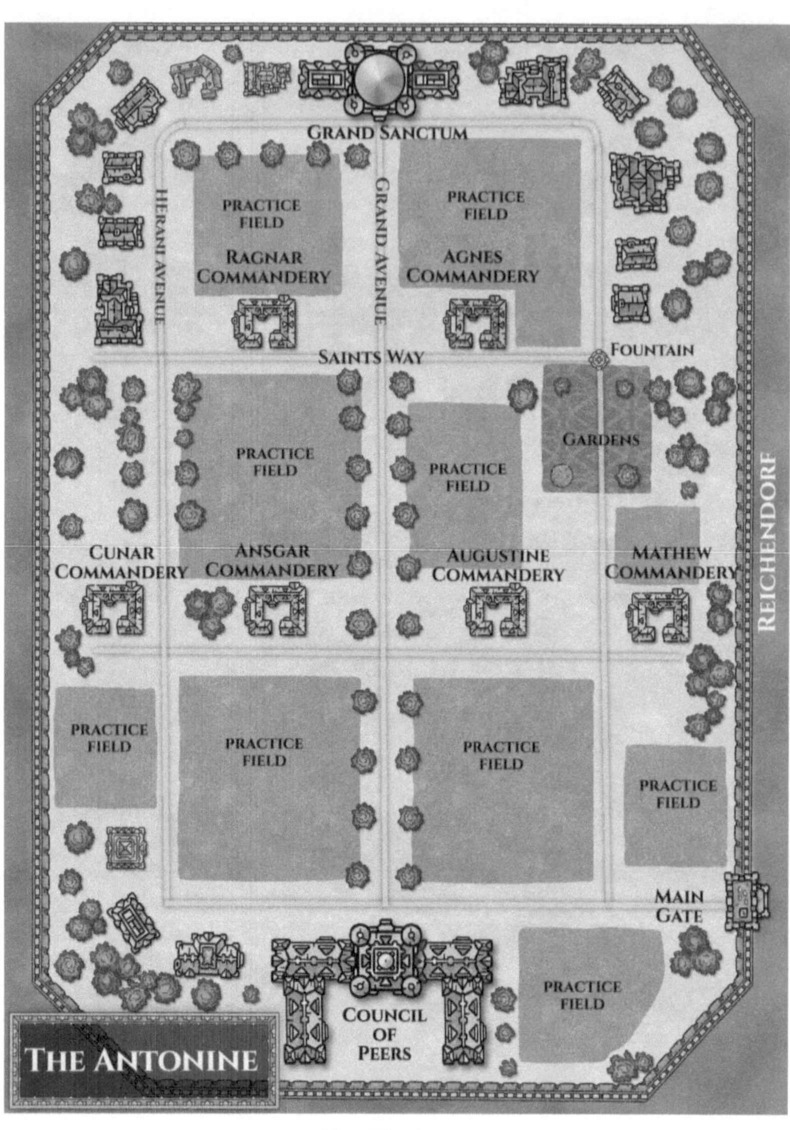

Map of The Antonine

1

BEGINNINGS

SUMMER 1105 SR* (SAINTS RECKONING)

Charlaine stood, staring out the window of her office. Most days, the magnificent view of the harbour greeted her, but today's overcast sky brought rain and rough seas. Her grand mistress had sent her to Lidenbach three years ago to assume command of the region, but no one had foreseen Halvaria attempting an invasion.

With the empire's defeat came peace, and the kingdom now prospered, but a dark cloud hung over them, everyone knowing the old enemy would one day return.

A knock at the door interrupted her musings. "Who's there?" she called out.

"Danica."

"Come in," replied Charlaine, returning to her desk. She waited for her friend to sit before continuing. "How are repairs going on *Fearless*?"

"They're progressing, though not nearly as fast as I'd like."

"Why's that?"

"The ship's been leaking more than usual. We discovered shoddy workmanship when we pulled her ashore to examine the hull."

"You're not suggesting the shipyards in Temple Bay are responsible?"

"No. The poor construction is from the Halvarians. They rushed building her, and the timber warped over time."

"Warped?"

"Yes," replied Danica. "They could've prevented that with more ribs but took shortcuts to get her to sea faster."

"That sounds serious."

"It is. It's meant tearing down the hull to add additional supports. Thankfully, the shipbuilders in Lidenbach can handle it."

"How things have changed," said Charlaine. "Not so long ago, shipbuilding had come to a standstill here, but with the empire's defeat, sea traders have returned in droves."

"Speaking of the empire, any news on them?"

"The border's been quiet, if that's what you're asking."

"You're the regional commander," said Danica, "which means you have ears in Rudor and here in Arnsfeld. You must have heard something?"

"There's no sign any of their legions are mustering on our borders, but I wouldn't expect there to be."

"You don't think they've given up, do you?"

"Not at all. When the time comes to launch their next invasion, it'll be farther south, in Gotfeld or Oberfeld. And those, my friend, do not fall under my supervision."

"Do we have Temple Knights in either place?"

"I don't know. Admittedly, the order is somewhat lacking in keeping its Temple Commanders informed about other regions. Come to think of it, the grand mistress has been quiet of late; something must be keeping her busy."

"Perhaps there's nothing to report?"

"That would make for a nice change, and under other circumstances, I'd be glad of the respite."

"But?"

"I wrote some months ago asking her for more Temple Knights to be sent to the border kingdoms and have received no reply."

"You don't suppose we got ourselves a new grand mistress, do you?"

"I certainly hope not," replied Charlaine. "Now is not the time for a timid leader."

"What makes you think anyone new would be timid?"

"Have you forgotten what happened when we visited the Antonine?"

"Not at all," said Danica. "However, that threat is over and done with, isn't it?"

"I wish it were. Unfortunately, there are others like Temple Commander Hjordis still out there."

"I don't know about you, but all this thinking has given me an appetite."

Charlaine smiled. "And here I am, keeping you from your breakfast. You should have said something earlier."

"There was much to discuss."

"There's no reason we couldn't talk while we eat." Charlaine stood. "Come on. Let's get some food into that belly of yours."

"Are you proposing we eat in the mess hall? I'm surprised you don't have someone bring it to you."

"How long have we known each other?"

"Ten years. Why?"

"In all that time, have I ever given the impression of someone who enjoys lording their position over others?"

"No, of course not."

"Then let us humble ourselves by eating with the other sisters of the order."

The morning patrols had risen early to be on the streets of Lidenbach before dawn, leaving the dining room half-empty. Charlaine and Danica got their food and then sat near the back, the better to hear each other over the friendly banter of the other sister knights.

Danica dug in, relishing the freshly baked bread in particular, but Charlaine picked at her food, her thoughts elsewhere. Things had been calm of late, particularly regarding the Empire of Halvaria, but she couldn't shake a sense of foreboding. It'd been two years since she'd commanded the army that defeated the invasion, and it wasn't like the empire to sit back and do nothing. A storm was gathering somewhere, and she wouldn't rest until she knew where.

"Can I have that?" said Danica.

Her words brought Charlaine out of her musings. "I'm sorry?"

"That bread. You're obviously not going to eat it."

"It's all yours."

"Something on your mind?"

"I was thinking about the empire."

"Ah, politics. The world would be a better place without it."

"Politics happens when one group of people decides to force their will on others."

"An interesting concept," said Danica, "but necessary, unless you want the Petty Kingdoms to fall into chaos. Even our order is political when you think about it. After all, we use our strength to protect women, which is another way of forcing our will on others."

"I suppose it is, now that you mention it."

Sister Maeve entered, glancing around the room, then set her sights on the two of them, moving to stand at the edge of their table. "Temple Commander, you have a visitor."

"Who is it?"

"A Dwarf. He claims to be carrying letters for you."

"And does this Dwarf have a name?"

"Rurlan," replied Maeve.

"Bring him in here."

"Here? To the dining hall?"

"Yes. Why? Are you confused about where we are?"

"No, Commander, but…" She paused. "He's a male."

"And that's a problem because…?"

Maeve stood, mouth agape, at a loss for words.

"Sister," said Danica. "You're not suggesting he's going to ravage our fellow knights?"

"Go and fetch him," insisted Charlaine, keen to quell Maeve's rising panic. "I think you'll find him a most civilized visitor."

Maeve hurried off, eager to be about her business.

"Some things never change," said Danica.

"It wasn't so long ago we were that young."

"Were we so full of ourselves at that age?"

"Don't be too eager to dismiss the passion of youth; you're not much older yourself."

Danica grinned. "In amongst all these sisters, I feel positively ancient."

"You're twenty-seven!" replied Charlaine. "Hardly what I'd call old. For a Temple Captain, you're young, and that's not even considering your position as Admiral of the Temple Fleet!"

"Still, you can't deny our recent recruits look younger."

"As young as you were when we first met?"

"I'll admit I may be overdoing it a bit, but I feel like we've been through so much."

"No one ever said service to the order would be boring."

Danica chuckled. "That's putting it mildly. I wonder what our instructors would say if they knew the path we've walked?"

"They'd probably say we were exactly where we were needed most."

Sister Maeve returned with the Dwarf in tow.

Charlaine stood. "Master Rurlan, to what do I owe the honour of this meeting?"

He smiled back, though a hint of sadness lingered in his eyes. "Why, correspondence, of course." He dug through his satchel, retrieved a sealed letter, and placed it on the table. "This comes from the Royal Court of Hadenfeld."

"From Prince Ludwig?"

Rurlan lowered his voice. "That's King Ludwig now." He snatched up the missive. "My apologies. In my haste, I almost forgot to unseal it." He touched his phoenix ring to the seal, then broke it open, revealing another sealed document, which he placed directly into Charlaine's hand.

"Please," she replied. "Have a seat. Would you like something to eat?"

"I should be delighted. Do I just help myself?"

"Grab a platter and line up over yonder." Danica nodded towards the food line. "The sisters on duty will look after you." The Dwarf headed to the front of the room while she turned to Charlaine, who was reading over the letter. "News?" she asked once her friend finished.

"Much has happened in Hadenfeld," replied Charlaine. "Ludwig has seized the Throne, and he and Charlotte were crowned king and queen."

"Any word of Frederick?"

"Yes. He's doing fine, although I expect it'll take time to adjust to life in the capital."

"Anything else I should know?"

"The Temple Knights of Saint Mathew supported his claim. According to Ludwig, the previous king, Morgan, grew paranoid and began executing people as traitors."

"And you trust his accounting of events?"

"I have no reason not to. Ludwig has never been the type to covet power, and I harbour no doubt that Lady Charlotte wouldn't put up with such nonsense if he did."

"You only met her for a short time."

"True, but I've been told I possess a knack for quickly taking the measure of a person, and she seemed a most earnest and forthright individual."

"I trust your instincts."

"There's more," continued Charlaine. "Someone named Koldan Sartellian was involved. Ludwig assures me that Stormwinds and Sartellians are no longer welcome in Hadenfeld."

Rurlan returned, his plate filled high with bread and cheese. "Good news?" he asked.

"From all accounts, King Ludwig is thriving, but I'm not certain I can say the same about Hadenfeld. It's experienced a great deal of strife in recent years."

"Ah, I was hoping it would prove cheerful."

"Why?"

"I'm afraid I bear a second letter for you, one more sombre in tone." He placed his plate on the table, then pulled another note from his satchel, unsealed it with his ring, and handed it over.

Charlaine carefully unfolded it, then began reading. The more she read, the more the colour fled her cheeks.

"Charlaine?" said Danica. "What's wrong?"

"It's my father," she replied. "He's dead."

"Dead? How?"

"He led Malburg's militia in the uprising that put Ludwig on the Throne. It says here he saved them from disaster."

"He died a hero," said Rurlan, "although I doubt that gives you any solace."

"What else can you tell me?" asked Charlaine.

"King Morgan sent Ludwig east to a place called Eisen, which lies in the territory formerly part of Neuhafen. Officially, he went to punish the eastern barons but took it upon himself to forgive them their past transgressions. Morgan didn't take kindly to that and ordered him to make arrests. It soon became apparent the two didn't see eye to eye, and the result was… well, I'm sure you know the rest."

"Where did the battle happen that claimed my father's life?"

"Northwest of Verfeld Keep, at Erhard's Folly. Are you familiar with it?"

Charlaine nodded, too overcome to reply.

"I think you need some time to absorb this," said Rurlan.

"Good idea," agreed Danica. "Come, Charlaine. Let's go to your office. Master Rurlan, could you remain here for a while longer? There may be letters to carry back to Erlingen."

"Of course." He turned to Charlaine. "Commander, please accept my most sincere condolences. I know this comes as a shock."

Charlaine stood unsteadily. "A question, if you would," she said.

"By all means," replied the Dwarf.

"There was no mention of my mother?"

"She lives still. Don't you worry. The guild will look after her, and rumour is, the new king awarded her a widow's stipend as well."

"I must compose a letter of thanks."

Danica took Charlaine's arm, guiding her from the room.

That evening, Charlaine stood, once more staring out her office windows. The storm had subsided, and the lights of the bay now flickered in the darkness. "We must do something to celebrate my father's life."

"What about a memorial service?" suggested Danica. "Are you familiar with Calabrian customs in that regard?"

"I am. When news arrived that a good friend of my father's had died, he held a gathering where we all ate, drank, and celebrated his life."

"Calabria was by the sea. What if we gathered aboard a ship and committed his soul to the depths?"

"Yes! He would've liked that. Perhaps we could invite Orlina Day? He'd be tickled pink if he knew a sacred mother of the old Gods was involved."

"I'll get started on it first thing tomorrow, but it will take a while to send word to her."

"There's no hurry," replied Charlaine. "I'd prefer we take our time and do things properly."

"Understood. Anyone else you'd care to invite? The king, perhaps?"

"No. I'd prefer to keep this as informal as possible. Maybe Brother Gatan, and as you're going all that way to find Orlina, you might see if Bethiel would be interested."

"The Elf? That will raise some eyebrows."

"It's time we Humans stopped pretending they don't exist. Now, what about the ship? It's not as if *Fearless* will be done with its repairs, unless there's something you're not telling me?"

"No secrets here. *Fearless* is unavailable for the next few weeks, but *Illustrious* is due any day. I'm sure Zivka wouldn't mind us using her for the ceremony."

"Good. Oh, and ensure Marlena gets an invitation, will you? It feels like ages since we last saw each other."

"You're the one who sent her company to the border."

"Only because I needed someone I could trust to report the truth."

"Speaking of which, don't you think it's time you acquired a new aide?"

"I'm more than capable of doing this by myself."

"It's not that you aren't capable," replied Danica. "However, having somebody to assist you would give you someone to bounce ideas off of."

"Isn't that what you do?"

"When I'm in town, yes, but I spend most of my time out at sea or up at Temple Bay."

"I keep meaning to visit, it's just that my duties keep me too busy."

"Even more reason to get yourself an aide."

"You're one to talk. Whatever happened to Sister Grace?"

"I gave her command of the *Redoubtable*."

"That's not even built yet."

"True," said Danica, "but it takes time to assemble a crew. She's sailing around with Grazynia to learn more about commanding a warship."

"I would think you'd post a more senior captain to such a large vessel."

"Oh, I tried, believe me, but you know how possessive our captains can be when it comes to their ships."

"That reminds me, in my last message to the grand mistress, I suggested she promote you to Temple Commander. It's a little strange having you serve as admiral when you're only a captain."

"I'm more concerned with my fleet captains being ranked as knights. I've never been one to worry too much about titles, yet it's difficult for them to be taken seriously when they go ashore on fleet business."

Charlaine laughed. "You're a victim of your own success. When she sent you north to assemble a fleet, she never imagined how effective you'd be."

"What can I say? I'm an overachiever, not that the same couldn't be said of you."

"Thank you."

"For what?"

"For always being there for me," replied Charlaine. "You're the only family I've had these last ten years."

"Your mother's still alive."

"My mother and I never really got along. I always saw myself as my father's daughter."

"You must have had something in common?"

"I wish I could say we did. She never liked the idea of me becoming a smith. It's not that she disliked a woman working a trade; it was more that she felt I could do better."

"And by better, you mean getting married?"

"How did you know?"

"It's an old tale. Sometimes, it feels like half the fleet joined the order to avoid marriage." She hesitated. "Sorry. I didn't mean to imply anything."

"No. It's fine," said Charlaine. "And to be accurate, I joined because I wasn't allowed to marry, not the other way around. Still, I can't complain. I found my calling."

"If you had it to do all over again, would you change anything?"

Charlaine shook her head. "No. I am who I am today because of the choices I made." She smiled. "Besides, if I'd remained in Malburg, I never would've met you!"

2

AT SEA

SUMMER 1105 SR

The Great Northern Sea was calm as if Akosia herself had seen fit to honour the occasion. Charlaine stood on the starboard side of *Illustrious* as Orlina Day spread herbs over the water.

"We all come from nature," said the sacred mother, "and when our time upon this mortal world ends, we return to it." Her ceremony complete, she turned to Charlaine and offered a bow before joining the others at the stern.

Gideon, the Holy Father of Saint Mathew, moved to take up his position beside the ship's railing. He cleared his throat, looking around at those assembled. "We are gathered here today in remembrance of Tomas deShandria, master smith and Elector of Malburg. I know many here never met Tomas, but we are all connected in Eiddenwerthe, a chain of life stretching from the Shimmering Sea in the south to the Great Northern Sea, where we find ourselves today."

He paused, considering his words before continuing. "Tomas was an accomplished smith and advisor to Eugenia, the last Queen of Calabria. He and his wife, Estelle, fled the realm following the Halvarian invasion, settling in Hadenfeld, where they raised their daughter, Charlaine. I shan't go into why she joined the Temple Knights of Saint Agnes, but I will say, without her presence in Arnsfeld, we, too, may have fallen under the oppression of Halvarian rule."

Once more, a pause, and then he looked skyward. "Oh, blessed Saint Mathew, guide thy faithful servant Tomas deShandria to the Afterlife and embrace him as your own." He lowered his arms and gazed out to sea. "Saints be with us."

"Saints be with us all," echoed those gathered.

Father Gideon turned to face Charlaine, standing directly before her. "May the blessings of Saint Agnes guide you this day, and may you find comfort in the knowledge your father led a good life."

"Thank you," she replied.

"Would you like to say a few words?"

"I would." Charlaine stepped up to the ship's railing and then faced everyone. "Thank you all for coming. I understand this may seem strange to some of you, but we Calabrians have our own customs for celebrating life and mourning those who make the ultimate journey to the Afterlife. Although my father's passing brings me great sadness, I am heartened by the love and support of my friends, both new and old, who've embraced me for who I am. He has always been a part of me, and without his presence, I wouldn't be the person I am today."

Finding herself tearing up, she turned to face the water. A hand touched her shoulder.

"We're here for you, Charlaine," said Danica.

"Thank you. You'll never know how much that means to me."

"I'll always have your back. Let's get inside, shall we? You can take a little break while Zivka brings the food out on deck."

Charlaine nodded, then let her dearest friend guide her aft, towards the captain's cabin.

Charlaine returned to a quiet and sombre gathering of her friends.

"This is a celebration of life," she said, "not a day for mourning. Let us partake of this food and remember my father for his contributions. I would have happy thoughts of him on my mind this day."

"Your father would be proud of your accomplishments," said Orlina Day. "Was he a religious man?"

"He was. He read a passage from the Book of Saint Mathew every day before opening the smithy, a habit he acquired while serving at the Royal Court in Alantra."

"His faith served him well."

"I'm surprised to hear you say so. Most worshippers of the old religion look down upon those who follow the teachings of the Saints."

"That's your influence," said Orlina. "Before you came along, I would've agreed, but you've taught us there's room in Eiddenwerthe for both our religions, and that when we work together, we accomplish great things. Perhaps that is your legacy, Temple Commander."

"Please, call me Charlaine."

"I'd be honoured to do so." Orlina plucked a morsel of meat from a passing crewman carrying a tray. "I rather like this custom of feasting in honour of the fallen. You say this is Calabrian?"

"It is, although it's not typically done at sea."

"What convinced you to add that particular flourish?"

"My father's love for open water. He grew up on the coast and often went to the docks to see what the morning catch brought in."

"Yet he fled to Hadenfeld, a realm in the middle of the Continent?"

"He wanted to get as far away from the empire as possible."

"Why not go farther east?"

"My parents didn't talk about it, but I got the impression they were short of coins once they reached Hadenfeld and had to settle down."

"Lucky for us, they did," replied Orlina, "otherwise you wouldn't be here today. Father Gideon may have been long-winded, but he made a good point—we are all connected somehow. Take your father, for example. When he and your mother settled in Hadenfeld after fleeing Calabria, he set in motion a chain of events that led to you coming to Arnsfeld precisely when you were needed most."

"Are you suggesting my parents' misfortune benefited everyone here?"

"It's a lot to absorb, but the Gods, or the Saints, for that matter, are said to move in mysterious ways. Ask yourself this: would you have been so dedicated to defeating the empire had they not driven your father from his home?"

"His faith convinced me to read the words of Saint Agnes, not his hatred of Halvaria."

"Yet the two are entwined. I suggest that a man with less faith would've remained in Calabria despite its being under the empire's rule. Instead, he believed he and your mother could build a new life elsewhere. Perhaps your Saints guided him, or maybe he needed the strength of will to make the effort?"

"Perhaps he, too, went where he was needed most," said Charlaine. "I'm told he played a crucial part in the recent civil war back home."

"Did he, indeed? How interesting. Might I ask how he was involved?"

"He supported the new king's claim to the Throne, leading the militia of Malburg to help out at a crucial point in the battle."

"So he supported the usurper?"

"Is one truly a usurper when they are victorious?"

"That's an interesting observation," noted Orlina. "I assume you agree with King Ludwig seizing the Throne?"

"I do. From the accounts I received, there was little choice."

"I'm surprised you still take an interest in such things. I've been told that most Temple Knights leave their past behind when they join an order."

Charlaine shrugged her shoulders. "I'm not like most members of my order. As for Hadenfeld, I did not choose to leave."

"And with a new king on the Throne, will you return now that your work here is done?"

"My devotion to the cause is as strong as ever, and I shan't rest until the empire is defeated."

"As a sister of Saint Agnes, aren't you free to leave the order at any time?"

"While some women choose to leave, others remain to serve our blessed Saint for the rest of their days."

Orlina Day nodded. "You show a wisdom far greater than I expect for one of your modest years, but it serves you well." The old woman glanced around the deck of the *Illustrious*. "If you'll excuse me, I wish to speak with Father Gideon about matters of faith."

"You want to argue with a Holy Father?"

"No. I seek only to find common ground." She wandered off.

Charlaine focused on Temple Captain Gatan. The Mathewite soon noticed her attention and moved closer.

"My condolences," he offered before he realized what he'd said. "Sorry. I forgot that is not the Calabrian custom."

"It's fine," she replied. "I've had ample time to mourn his loss, and celebrations like this are for the living, not the dead."

"I like the idea of celebrating the life of the departed; it helps us remember the good people have done, don't you think?"

"It does."

"I sense something else is on your mind."

"It is," replied Charlaine. "I hoped you might give me some insight."

"Into what, may I ask?"

"Are you familiar with recent events in Hadenfeld?"

"Ah," said Gatan. "I assume you refer to the civil war?"

"I do."

"And you're wondering why we supported Ludwig's claim to the Throne?"

"I am. I'm not complaining, but I am curious why your order defied Church doctrine."

"Not so long ago, both our orders defied the Church to fight the empire."

"True," replied Charlaine, "but that was for the common good. This was a civil war in Hadenfeld. Taking sides in such a conflict could be seen as a grievous breach of protocol."

"I agree, but there were extenuating circumstances that our regional commander addressed in a recent correspondence. King Morgan was displaying signs of mental decline, and whether that was his natural state or outside interference is still up for debate. However, my superiors felt something had to be done to avoid needless suffering on behalf of our followers."

"You speak of outside interference. Does that mean they suspect the empire of meddling?"

"They never explicitly acknowledged that, but that was my impression. It would make sense, given that Hadenfeld traditionally had one of the larger armies in the Petty Kingdoms. There's also the proven battle record of Ludwig Altenburg, one of the more seasoned army commanders of the Continent."

"While I might not always agree with how the Church handles things, I believe they made the correct decision."

"Oh, it wasn't the Church," replied Gatan. "In fact, the Antonine was most displeased."

"But I thought your order supported his claim?"

"The regional commander of that area made the decision. Our grand master wasn't even consulted until after the fact, but he agreed with them, which did not please the Council of Peers."

"This bodes ill," said Charlaine. "Back when Danica and I visited the Antonine, forces were at work seeking to reduce the role of the temple orders."

"That doesn't surprise me, especially considering the actions of our brother knights, the Cunars. It's one thing to remain apart from secular matters, quite another to actively interfere in another order's pursuits."

"Do you refer to my order's trouble with them, or is this something newer?"

"This is much more recent," replied Gatan. "A movement is afoot to place all orders under the command of the Temple Knights of Saint Cunar. A case could be made that a unified command would benefit the Holy Army, but I can't help feeling it would be detrimental to us as an organization."

"How would that work? What would happen to our grand mistress?"

"Presumably, she'd be removed from her position, as would our grand master. Not that it's likely to be a problem in the short term. The Cunars are one of six orders of Temple Knights, and a majority vote from the Council of Peers is required to make a change of that magnitude." He glanced around. "I fear I have taken up too much of your time. You have other guests to see to."

"I thank you for your opinion, Brother. It has proven most insightful."

He offered a slight bow. "I live to serve, Commander."

That evening, Charlaine and Danica sat aboard the *Fearless*. With her repairs almost complete, the ship was now afloat in the bay, though it was still awaiting its new rigging and sails.

"She's getting old," said Danica, "and the sea has not been kind to her."

"I'm surprised to hear you say that," replied Charlaine. "I thought she'd be good for a while with these repairs."

"Over the last few years, I've come to the conclusion Halvarian ship designs have some serious shortcomings."

"Which are?"

"Their ships are not intended for life on the Great Northern Sea."

"Isn't that where the empire uses them?"

"Oh, they're fine for hugging the coast, but leave sight of land, and the waves are too rough. Unfortunately, that's where the Temple Fleet spends most of its time."

"What about the non-Halvarian ships in our service?"

"You mean like the *Valiant*? They're fine. In fact, they thrive in the open waters."

"Then what's your answer to the problem?"

"The *Redoubtable* and her sister ships. Our shipwrights have learned what makes the *Valiant* a good ship and melded that with some of the Halvarian techniques."

"So the empire ships possess some redeeming qualities?"

"They work fine when considering Halvaria's seaborne strategy. They're primarily a land-based power, so in their eyes, the fleet is only there to augment the army."

"Like they did at Lidenbach?"

"Precisely. Our strategy, however, is more focused on controlling the sea lanes, including tracking down pirates who try to sail into deeper water to avoid getting caught."

Charlaine chuckled. "So we need to thank piracy for making our ships better than the empire's?"

"I suppose that's one way of looking at it. I prefer to think we spent more time studying the past and identifying shortcomings."

"You've learned so much about ships."

"I have, but there's so much more to know. If we weren't so busy watching for the empire, I'd return to the Antonine and meet with the naval architect, Temple Captain Leamund."

"Even though he's a Cunar?"

"He never impressed me as someone interested in Church politics. If you recall, he refused a promotion to concentrate on ship design. He also helped me plan out the Temple Fleet despite his own order's opposition to it."

"My apologies. I've grown so accustomed to considering them our opponents that I now assume the entire order is corrupt."

"Our own order wasn't immune," Danica reminded her. "I wonder whatever happened to Hjordis? When we last saw her, she was under arrest."

"She was presumably dismissed, although she might have spent some time in a prison first."

"The Antonine has a prison?"

"How else would they punish those who abuse their power?"

"I assumed they banished them."

"That's only for less-serious infractions," replied Charlaine. "I'm surprised you didn't know about the prison. It was part of our training."

"Was it? I don't remember anyone mentioning it."

"Didn't you read the books the grand mistress gave us?"

"No," said Danica. "I was never a strong reader."

"But you read reports all day."

"I do, but those are pertinent to the day-to-day running of the fleet."

Charlaine chuckled. "I'll admit some of those books make for dry reading, but they hold a wealth of information."

"Such as?"

"They explain the entire structure of the Church, along with everyone's responsibilities."

"How does that help a Temple Captain?"

"I'm not certain it does," replied Charlaine, "but now that I'm a Temple Commander, I've found it useful. That, in turn, would seem to suggest you should learn it. After all, they won't keep you a Temple Captain forever."

"I was all right with you teasing me with that once, but it's becoming a habit."

"Sorry. I just think you deserve recognition. I know no other admiral who defeated two enemy fleets."

"Temple Bay was hardly even a flotilla, let alone a fleet."

"You still defeated them. You're also responsible for building the Temple Fleet into what it is today. How many ships do you have now?"

"I'm not entirely certain."

"Liar," said Charlaine, although her tone was friendly. "You know exactly how many ships sail under our banner."

"Thirteen," replied Danica, "not including those currently under construction. However, the fleet won't be getting larger any time soon."

"But you're building new ones."

"Those are to replace the ones aging out. You could always take a little trip to Temple Bay and see them yourself."

"I'd love to, I really would, but I'm needed here. Regional commanders don't have the luxury of taking trips just because they feel like it."

"Fair enough," said Danica. "But I tell you what; I'll have Grace bring the *Redoubtable* down here to Lidenbach on its maiden voyage, then you can see her for yourself. I think you'll be impressed!"

3

ORDERS

SPRING 1106 SR

After a harsh winter, the reprieve of the warmer spring weather was welcomed by all, especially the Great Northern Sea, which offered calm waters for weeks, a most unusual experience for those traders who chanced an early season.

Charlaine watched the *Fearless* enter the harbour from her office and used it as an excuse to see Danica. Thus, she waited as the ship's boat pulled up to the dock. "Greetings, Admiral. I hope all is well?"

"That depends," replied Danica.

"On what?"

"The contents of these sealed orders." Danica held a large envelope covered in sealskin to ward off the water. "They're from the grand mistress via Korvoran." She glanced around, noting the presence of others on the dock. "Best open them back at the commandery, I think."

"That sounds ominous."

"I was given a message indicating I should deliver them with all haste and be present when they're opened."

"This grows more interesting with each breath," noted Charlaine. "Is there anything else I should be aware of?"

"Not that I can think of."

"Let's return to my office, where we'll have more privacy."

Danica called back to the boat crew. "You can go back aboard the *Fearless*. I'll send word when I need you."

"Yes, Admiral," replied the Temple Knight commanding the boat.

Charlaine and Danica headed east on the road running along the edge of the bay.

"Any news on when that new ship of yours will visit?" asked Charlaine.

"I'm afraid it won't be anytime soon. We've run into a bit of a problem."

"What sort of problem?"

"We need to enlarge our shipyard to accommodate her sister ships."

"How does that affect *Redoubtable*?"

"We're using her as a framework for the others, so she needs to stay in the shipyard for reference."

"Don't you have plans for her?"

"We do," said Danica, "but we made adjustments as we built her, and we don't want to miss out on applying them to the rest of her class."

"That sounds complicated."

"It is, but they'll be the finest ships on the Great Northern Sea when they finally launch."

"You're enjoying being an admiral far too much."

Danica grinned. "Is it that obvious?"

They turned onto a side street, heading towards the commandery. "I can't imagine what's in that letter," said Charlaine. "Surely it's not a reassignment?"

"Isn't a normal assignment for a Temple Commander five to ten years?"

"Ah. I see you've finally gotten around to reading those books."

"Some, but they give no clue why someone would go to the trouble of sending a message to the two of us. And why send it through me? You're the senior member of the order."

The guards on the commandery doors acknowledged their arrival with a simple nod as they passed through. They were soon upstairs in the regional commander's office, where Charlaine wasted no time breaking open the sealskin bag to peruse its contents.

She looked up at Danica. "We've been summoned to the Antonine."

"Does it say why?"

"No, but it stresses we should proceed with all haste."

"You don't think this is the doing of Hjordis, do you?"

"No," replied Charlaine. "Grand Mistress Kaylene signed it, with Temple Captain Nicola as a witness."

"Witness? That's a little unusual, isn't it?"

"Very much so."

"Any word on who's to command in our absence?"

"She left that to our discretion. Have you someone in mind as acting admiral?"

"Yes, Grazynia. She'll complain about it, but she's the most suitable candidate. How about yourself? Will you put Marlena in charge?"

"No. I have no doubt she'll make a fine Temple Commander eventually, but she's still struggling to come to grips with her role as Temple Captain. Florence will take over in my absence."

Danica nodded. "A good choice, but that leaves us with a difficult decision."

"That being?"

"What route will we take? The Antonine is far from here, and we must cross half the Continent to get there."

"That's true."

"What if we sailed back to Reinwick and then headed south?"

"I'm not certain that would save us much time. I thought we'd leave from here, then head east, through Angvil and Erlingen, eventually turning south."

"We could go south and cross through Hadenfeld if you like?"

"No," said Charlaine. "The grand mistress used the phrase 'with all haste', so we'd be wise not to take unnecessary detours."

"I'm not opposed to travelling through Angvil and Erlingen; it's what comes afterwards that worries me."

"Why? Have you heard something?"

"Only rumours of unrest in the Five Kingdoms."

"Five Kingdoms?"

"Yes: Ardosa, Galoran, Menzen, Kingshaven, and Regensbach. We travelled through a few of them to our assignment in Reinwick. If you recall, the Antonine is in Regensbach."

"Yes, but we saw little of those other realms. The road we travelled was mostly wilderness, and I never took the time to learn about their politics. When you say unrest, what does that mean? Are they rising up against their rulers?"

"No," said Danica. "From what I understand, they're arguing over their borders, which appears to be a common problem in many Petty Kingdoms."

"I doubt a border dispute would threaten members of the Church."

"True, but it could clog the roads with refugees."

"You're overthinking things," said Charlaine. "And they're only rumours. Let's wait until we get closer; then, we can decide based on facts."

"When do we leave?"

"Did you want to ship your horse here?"

"Spirit? No, she's far too comfortable running around the pasture back in Temple Bay. If it's all right with you, I'll take one of your spares."

"Of course. There are several to choose from, although none are as fast as Stormcloud."

"Are you suggesting it's a contest to see who can get to the Antonine first?"

"No," replied Charlaine with a smirk. "That wouldn't be a fair race."

"Then I'll need to be content with having a fast ship." Danica's breath caught in her throat. "You don't think they're going to take away my fleet, do you?"

"After all the work you've put into it? That would be the height of folly."

"I agree, but you know as well as I that a new grand mistress could change the direction of the order."

"Nothing in that letter indicates Sister Kaylene might be replaced."

"Nor is there anything to suggest another subject requiring our presence."

"Let's indulge that a little, shall we?" said Charlaine. "Suppose we have a new grand mistress, or one will be appointed soon. How does that require our presence in the Antonine?"

"The new appointee might see fit to replace us."

"True, but why summon us there to do it? Wouldn't sending orders to that effect be far simpler?"

"Yes, but if that's not the case, then why?"

"You tell me."

Danica sat in silence while she considered the possibilities. "It's likely related to the corruption we uncovered."

"That was my thought. I think the grand mistress needs someone she can trust for something. The question is, what might that something be?"

"Could it be trouble with another order?"

Charlaine chuckled. "You know, you can just say Cunars. It's not like any others have ever given us trouble."

"My question still stands."

"We've definitely had our troubles with them, even before the Halvarian incursion, but they've been quiet of late, at least in Arnsfeld. However, they no longer maintain a garrison here, which might have something to do with it. Your fleet is always on the lookout for news. Are there any updates on that score?"

"They say Therengia has risen from the ashes in the east."

"Truly? Where?"

"Near a place called Ebenstadt. Ever heard of it?"

"No," replied Charlaine.

"Neither had I."

"Do we have a presence there?"

"I couldn't say," replied Danica, "but it's too distant to worry about right now."

"Still, it might be worth mentioning to the grand mistress."

"To what end?"

"For her to send a company of Temple Knights."

"To Therengia? I doubt that would be well-received by the other Petty Kingdoms. Not when they fear a resurgence of the Old Kingdom."

"Has this new Therengia threatened retaliation for the fall of the Old Kingdom?"

"Not that I'm aware of," replied Danica.

"Then they're worrying over nothing. Right now, I'm more interested in the actions of the Temple Knights of Saint Cunar, not a new kingdom to the east."

"You asked if I'd heard anything."

"Yes, I did," said Charlaine, "and I value what you've learned; I just don't think it's of immediate concern."

"Fair enough. On a different topic, how long do you need to make arrangements?"

"At least a week, I'm afraid. I must gather all my captains stationed in Arnsfeld, not to mention send dispatches to the neighbouring realms which fall under my jurisdiction."

"I can help you with that. I'll take *Fearless* down to Braunfel and bring back Temple Captain Florence."

"That would help immensely. Thank you."

Danica rose. "I'd best be on my way, then. See you in a few days."

The *Fearless* returned in less than a week, the summoned officers assembling in the dining hall in the old Cunar commandery. Three Temple Knight companies protected the kingdom: two in Lidenbach, commanded by Florence and Bernelle, and the third, commanded by Marlena, responsible for watching the border in Braunfel. Danica and Zivka, captain of *Fearless*, added to their numbers.

Charlaine waited until all were seated before beginning. "Doubtless, you've all heard the rumours, so I'll get straight to the point. Yes, the grand mistress has called Admiral Danica and I to the Antonine, so I am appointing Temple Captain Florence to temporary command of the region. A new commander typically receives training, but unfortunately, our presence is urgently required. Florence will eventually travel to the Antonine to receive the necessary instruction, but I'm afraid you'll have to make do for now."

She let her words sink in before continuing. "There is the possibility the Church will assign a new regional commander."

"Does that mean you're not coming back?" asked Bernelle.

"That's impossible to say. Certainly, Admiral Danica will be needed to continue her work with the fleet, but they might see fit to send me else-where." This statement brought grumbles from everyone.

She let them voice their complaints, then cleared her throat, silencing them. "I've spent the last few years securing this kingdom from the Halvarian Empire. I expect you all to do your part to ensure the region's safety."

"Will the fleet remain here?" asked Florence.

"At least one temple ship will remain in port at all times," replied Danica. "My current instructions call for a second to be out at sea watching for any signs of Halvarian intrusions. Since we cannot predict how long Charlaine and I will be gone, I've issued orders that the fleet liaise with acting Temple Commander Florence regularly. Captain Zivka is to be your advisor on naval matters." This last statement was directed towards Florence, who looked a little nervous.

"You all know what needs to be done," continued Charlaine. "You've done an exemplary job since the empire's incursion, and I have complete confidence you will continue to be vigilant." She consulted her notes. "Seeing as how Florence is new to the position, Captain Marlena will return to Lidenbach to act as the order's representative at the court of King Handrik. She has the advantage of working with him before, so I expect it to be a smooth transition. Bernelle, you'll assume command of the company in Braunfel. Are there any questions?"

"Yes," said Florence. "What if the empire returns?"

"I doubt that will happen, but if it does, you do whatever it takes to safe-guard this kingdom. If that entails fighting, then so be it, but if you're outnumbered, conserve your strength for when you can stop them. Remember, you're the regional commander, which means there are three other kingdoms to draw support from. There are also our brothers, the Temple Knights of Saint Mathew, to lean on, if necessary, so don't hesitate to contact them if trouble is brewing."

She scanned the room, confident these experienced captains could look after things in her absence.

"Will you require an escort to the Antonine?" asked Marlena.

"The admiral and I are more than capable of making the trip on our own."

"You should at least allow us to escort you to the border."

Charlaine nodded. "I will accede to that request, but let's make it small, shall we? I don't want anyone getting carried away."

"And if a Halvarian ship enters the bay?"

"That won't be a problem," replied Zivka. "The king already banned the empire from seeking shelter here and gave his blessing to detain or repulse any attempt to anchor their ships in his waters."

"Even if it means war?" pressed Bernelle.

"Yes," replied Danica. "When word reaches the Halvarians that there's been a change of command in Arnsfeld, they'll seek to gain the advantage, which could mean encounters at sea or people crossing the border in small groups. Whatever they do, take decisive action to address it before it gets out of hand. Remember, you have the king's backing, and unlike his predecessor, King Handrik has a large standing army at his beck and call."

"That's all well and good," said Florence, "but what if they try something in Rudor or a seaborne assault on Langwal? Those are still under my jurisdiction."

"We can't predict every eventuality," replied Charlaine, "but considering the loss they suffered in oh-three, I doubt they'll be back."

"What makes you so certain?"

"If I were in charge of their legions, I'd attack through Gotfeld or even Oberfeld. Attacking there allows them to drive deep into the heart of the Petty Kingdoms."

"But that's not their way," insisted Bernelle. "They've always gone after one kingdom at a time."

"That's been true in the past, but with the Temple Knights of Saint Cunar no longer protecting the frontier, the situation has changed dramatically. While we have a presence here in Arnsfeld, I doubt it's the same farther south."

"Surely the order would've reinforced the area as they did here?"

"We're not a large order," replied Charlaine, "at least not on the scale of the Cunars. Reinforcing this region took a great effort, and most of those who came here during the emergency were recent recruits. I don't think we have enough spare Temple Knights to do the same in Gotfeld. If an invasion seems probable farther south, confer with King Handrik. Remember, you can't be everywhere at once, so you must balance your responsibilities here with the desire to help our sisters in the bordering realms."

She looked at each in turn, noting their sadness, and it touched her. She struggled to maintain her composure in the face of such devotion. "I leave knowing this command is in good hands," she said at last. "I wish you all well."

"You're all dismissed," added Danica, saving Charlaine the heartache.

With much to discuss, the three captains moved towards the other end of the room, where food was laid out.

"Thank you," said Charlaine. "I couldn't take much more of that."

"That's what friends are for," replied Danica. She paused, watching her comrade's features. "You don't believe you're coming back, do you?"

"Is it that obvious?"

"Only to me."

Charlaine lowered her voice. "I've been thinking about this ever since we received that letter. I can't imagine the grand mistress summoning me to the Antonine simply to send me back here, can you?"

"We talked about this; it's probably something to do with the corruption in the Church."

"Maybe, but what if she's sending me somewhere else where I'm needed more?"

"Such as?"

"You tell me," said Charlaine. "You're the one with ears in every port."

"I know of no place currently threatened by the empire."

"The crusade in the east failed. What if she sends me there?"

"That's been over for a while," replied Danica. "The Cunars were given a thrashing at the Battle of the Wilderness about a year and a half ago. Their losses were said to be great."

"But wouldn't that make the Church eager to see them revenged?"

"Quite possibly, but you're an Agnesite; no Cunar will agree to put you in charge of a Holy Army. I'm afraid it's looking more and more like we're heading to the Antonine to deal with trouble within the order."

4

THE JOURNEY BEGINS
SPRING 1106 SR

A cloudless sky hung over them as they set off from Lidenbach with their escort. The trip to the border would take ten days, a little less if they hurried, but Charlaine was more concerned with setting a steady pace for the sake of their mounts. Temple Captain Marlena insisted on commanding the escort, a recognition of all her mentor had taught her.

Three days of riding brought them to Dubrow, where Charlaine had first encountered the Royal Army of Arnsfeld while it was still mustering. She'd taken command of it there, leading them to the edge of the Brinwald, where they made their stand to repel the Halvarians. The battle had been close, and had it not been for the defences Orlina Day had prepared, it might have ended much differently.

Another four days brought them to Kurtzenberg, one of the larger cities of Arnsfeld. It reminded Charlaine of Malburg, particularly when they passed through the artisan district. Then it was on to Meirshoff and the border with Angvil, the trip ending up being eleven days in total instead of the ten they'd estimated.

A stone engraved with the duchy's name was the only indication they were about to cross into Angvil. They halted here to say their goodbyes to their escort.

"You've served me well," said Charlaine, speaking to Marlena. "But perhaps even more importantly, you are a good friend. I hope that we will meet again."

"As do I," replied the Temple Captain. "You've taught me so much and promoted me despite my fears."

"You have a bright career ahead of you, I'm certain."

"Any last words of advice?"

"Yes," said Charlaine. "When making hard decisions, let your heart guide you."

"And there's no way I can convince you to allow us to accompany you to the Antonine?"

"You're needed here. It may not seem like it now, but great changes are coming to Eiddenwerthe. The Kingdom of Therengia has been reborn, and the empire will one day return. In days such as these, we must be as vigilant as ever."

"I shall remember your words," replied Marlena.

"Goodbye," said Danica, "and keep an eye out for Zivka. She'll be spending a lot of time in the region."

"I will."

Marlena called out, and the Temple Knights drew swords, offering a salute. Charlaine acknowledged it with a nod, then turned Stormcloud south, heading down the road into Angvil.

"Don't worry," said Danica. "I'll look after her." She then trotted her own horse after her comrade.

The countryside was pleasant, the sky clear, and the afternoon sun warmed them as they rode.

"This is getting harder and harder," said Charlaine.

"You mean the road?" replied Danica.

"No, leaving friends. It seems as if all we do is go somewhere, meet people, then get shipped off."

"Except we're on horses, not a ship."

"Spoken like a true admiral. Remind me again how long we were in Ilea?"

"I arrived late in ninety-four, but you didn't show up until the summer of ninety-five."

"And when did we leave?"

"Winter of ninety-six."

"Was that all?" said Charlaine. "It feels like longer."

"Well, we did travel to the Antonine, and that alone took almost six months."

"And here we are doing it all over again."

"You're the expert in these things," said Danica. "What's the usual length of an assignment?"

"For Temple Knights, typically ten years. Captains and commanders, however, tend to move around much more frequently."

"How frequently?"

"Generally, any time after five years."

"That's how long you were in Reinwick."

"Was I? Funny, now that I look back, it feels like less. Still, Arnsfeld was a shorter posting, only three years."

"That's what you get for being so successful. Had you not defeated an invasion, you'd likely still be back in your old office, watching over Lidenbach Bay."

"You can blame that on the Halvarians. I wouldn't have interfered if they'd minded their own business."

"Fair enough."

"And what about you?"

"Me?" replied Danica. "I don't know what you're talking about. I've been Admiral of the Temple Fleet since we arrived in Reinwick. That makes my current assignment longer than yours."

Charlaine laughed. "All right, it's not a competition."

"Nervous?"

"Who, me? I'm an accomplished Temple Commander. What have I got to be worried about?"

"Plenty, chief amongst them, where the grand mistress will send you."

"What are your thoughts? Aside from troubles in the Church, I mean."

"My guess is somewhere where they expect trouble. Thanks to our recent success, the northern border with the empire is pretty secure, so you'll likely go south to the Shimmering Sea. I wonder if Halvaria has begun rebuilding a fleet there."

"The Holy Fleet would be more than capable of dealing with it if they have."

"Perhaps east? After all, Therengia represents a potential threat, especially considering they defeated a Holy Crusade."

"They're a young realm," replied Charlaine. "I doubt they represent much of a threat."

"Tell that to the Cunars."

"The Temple Knights of Saint Cunar had no right to invade their land. Only the primus has the authority to order a Holy Crusade, and even then, he needs the support of the Council of Peers."

"True," said Danica, "but it's easier to beg forgiveness after the fact than get permission beforehand. They likely believed the Church would be happy with them after a successful campaign."

"Except that they failed," replied Charlaine. "And from what I've heard, there wasn't much support for it. The Mathewites certainly weren't happy, failure or not, and I agree. What message does it send if you invade your neighbours whenever you feel like it?"

"You're talking about Halvaria."

"Exactly. There's no point in opposing the empire if we're just going to adopt their methods."

"My goodness, you've become outspoken of late."

"Only with you," said Charlaine. "This isn't the sort of thing one discusses with Church superiors."

"Well, for the record, I'm in complete agreement. To my mind, the Church should have spoken out sooner against Halvaria rather than trying to maintain a neutral position, especially the followers of Saint Agnes. Our oath is to protect women. For Saint's sake, we can't do that if we look away whenever a kingdom is threatened." She drew in a quick breath. "You don't suppose we're being called to task for interfering in Arnsfeld, do you?"

"No. If that were the case, she would've summoned us sooner. Besides, we both know the grand mistress supported our choices."

"What I don't understand is why her summons was so secretive. Surely she could have given us some hint about what to expect upon our arrival?"

"That's an excellent point," replied Charlaine, "and one I hadn't considered before. How was the summons delivered?"

"The Prior of Korvoran placed it into my hands himself."

"Not a courier?"

"No," said Danica, "but we can trust him; he's a Mathewite."

"Unfortunately, we don't know whose hands it passed through before him. Church correspondence isn't protected like that of the smiths guild."

"So you think the grand mistress feared someone getting hold of it?"

"When I was assigned to Arnsfeld, my orders were clear. That's completely the opposite of what we got this time."

"An interesting point."

"Yes," continued Charlaine, "and who would have access to Church couriers?"

"Other members of the Church."

"Precisely."

"If what you're saying is true, it means the old serpent has raised its head again."

"You have a strange way of saying things."

"Sorry," replied Danica. "It comes from spending so much time at sea. Aside from that, though, it appears our original fear was correct; Hjordis has reared her head again, or at least her faction. We need to figure out what the grand mistress expects us to do."

"That's difficult when we don't know the details. There's also the time involved in travelling to the Antonine. It'll be months before we get there, during which this so-called faction could cause untold damage. We don't even know if Kaylene is still the grand mistress or when these orders were issued. They could be months out of date."

"Yes. I noticed there was no date on them, which is unusual, to say the least. Then again, this whole situation is unusual."

"Well," said Charlaine. "There's plenty of time to think it over."

"What's our next stop?"

"We pass through Neiburg, the capital of Angvil."

"Do we stop to pay our respects to the duke?"

"I'd prefer not," said Charlaine. "If we are heading into bad news in the Antonine, I'd like to deal with it sooner rather than later."

The sun was throwing long shadows across the landscape when they spotted a roadside inn. They tied their horses up out front and entered the place. Judging by the numbers within, a village must be nearby, although they'd spotted no sign of it on the way here. Conversations halted as they entered, for the sight of a Temple Knight, let alone two, was rare in these parts.

The barkeep, however, had no reservations concerning visitors. "Would you be looking for a room, Sisters?"

"Yes," replied Charlaine. "And stabling for our horses, if you would be so kind."

"I'll get the stable boy to look after them. Charlie!" His shout filled the room. Outside, a youthful voice responded as the fellow waved them over to a table. "I'm afraid we're busy tonight, but if you don't mind sharing a table, I can bring you some food."

"That would be nice," replied Charlaine. "Thank you." They moved over to the proffered table, where two men and a woman sat, but one man rose as the Temple Knights took their seats.

"You'll excuse me," he said, "but I've lost my appetite."

"Not on our account, I hope?" asked Danica.

His sneer indicated his true feelings. "I'll not break bread with troublemakers."

"Troublemakers? My order helped save Arnsfeld from Halvarian aggression. Were it not for us, the empire would be breathing down your necks."

"And you think standing up to them was wise? They'll be back in even greater numbers next time. All you've done is delay the inevitable, which makes them all the nastier."

"Are you suggesting you'd prefer that Arnsfeld had surrendered?"

"You sisters should leave military matters to the Cunars. At least they're trained for such things."

Danica opened her mouth to respond, but Charlaine placed her hand on her companion's forearm, forestalling her. "People should be free to express their opinions."

The fellow moved to another table, dragging his chair with him.

"Never mind him," said the woman. "He thinks he knows everything."

"Is that a common attitude around here?" asked Charlaine.

"People fear what they don't understand."

"And what do you think?"

"The empire is coming whether we want it or not. I'd prefer it be in the distant future, but it's not as if I've got any control over such things."

"Do you fear Halvaria?"

The woman shook her head. "I doubt the lot of us commoners would be all that different under their rule. We still farm the land, while nobles take the greater portion of our crops. What difference does it make whether those in charge are the nobles of Angvil or the empire?"

Charlaine directed her gaze to the remaining fellow. "What do you think?"

He hesitated before answering. "I don't know enough about the Halvarians to have much of an opinion. Do they conscript locals to fight their wars?"

"They do," supplied Danica.

He lowered his voice. "Then they can rot in the Underworld, as far as I'm concerned."

"I assume that's not a popular opinion?"

"Folks around here don't much like the idea of women doing our fighting for us."

"Plenty of men were on the battlefield," replied Danica.

"Still, it's unsettling."

"So they'd prefer all their men died in battle?"

"I doubt they've given it that much thought," he said. "To most of us, the empire was a distant threat, but having them on our borders is too hard for us to take in."

"Then it's a good thing these sister knights stepped up," said the woman.

"What I'd like to know," added her companion, "is when the Holy Army's going to show up."

"What makes you think they're coming here?" asked Charlaine.

"It's pretty obvious, isn't it? They pulled back from the empire's border so they could respond to any invasion with the full might of their order." He looked at his companion. "What did that fellow call it?"

"Defence in depth," she replied.

"Aye, that was it."

"What fellow was this?" asked Danica.

"He were a tall one, dressed much like you two, but in grey, rather than red."

"Was there a sword emblazoned on his surcoat?"

"There was—in white."

"That means he was a Temple Knight of Saint Cunar. I'm surprised he didn't announce himself as such."

The woman elbowed her companion. "I told you he was someone important."

He shrugged. "How am I supposed to tell the difference between the duke's men and a Temple Knight? It's not as if they pass through here every day."

"How long ago was this?" asked Charlaine.

"Three days."

"Four," corrected the woman. "It was just after you got kicked by that mule."

"Yes, that's right. He came down the road from the north."

Charlaine looked at Danica. "That's the one we came down. It leads to Arnsfeld."

"The Cunars don't maintain a presence there, do they?"

"No, not officially, but that doesn't mean they can't send people across the border." Charlaine sat back in her chair. "I can think of only one reason why a Cunar might be heading along this road."

"Let me guess," said Danica. "He's bringing word that we're on the move?"

"Precisely."

"We shall have to be careful, going forward."

"Why?" asked the woman. "Does this fellow mean you harm?"

Charlaine stared back, unsure how much she should say. Revealing Church problems to a local would do little good, but how else could she explain herself? The day she was sworn in as a full-fledged Temple Knight, she'd taken an oath to be truthful, yet the truth here could only damage the Church. How, then, should she proceed?

Danica answered for her. "We're not aware who this fellow is, but it appears he's been spying on us."

The woman knitted her brows. "But I thought you said he was a Temple Knight?"

"From your description, he wore the garb of one," added Charlaine, "but there's always the possibility he was an imposter."

"You think he's working for the empire?"

"That is unlikely." At that point, the barkeep appeared, setting down two bowls of pottage and spoons.

"Here you go," he said. "Nice and hot. Dig in and warm your innards."

"Thank you," replied Charlaine. "It smells delicious. Might I ask how far it is to Neiburg?"

"Two days, maybe three," answered the barkeep. "Just take this road east, and it will lead you straight there."

"Are there any towns along the way?"

"A few villages and a couple of roadside inns, but I doubt you'll see much traffic. Folks seldom come out this far."

"Why's that?" asked Charlaine.

"They say most traders prefer the road farther to the south that heads into Rudor."

"You're here?"

"That can't be helped," he replied. "My family's been here for generations. My great-grandfather built this tavern."

"You must have a few tales to tell."

"Who, me? No. I keep to myself."

"You have travellers here, surely?"

"On occasion, but most of my business is from the local village."

"And that would be?"

"Sternhelm, about two miles south of the road."

"Sternhelm?" said Danica. "That sounds Dwarvish."

The barkeep chuckled. "Dwarvish? No. It dates back to the Old Kingdom. Grey-eyed folk still live there."

"And how do people take to that?"

He shrugged. "Us common folk couldn't care less. They work the fields, same as us. Treating them differently because of the colour of their eyes seems a mite silly."

"Sensible words," said Charlaine. "If only the ruling classes saw it that way. I am curious, though. Have you heard of what happened in the east?"

"East? You mean Neiburg?"

"No, much farther, on the other side of the Continent. They say a new Therengia has risen."

"On the other side of the Continent? That's hardly going to cause much excitement around here."

"So you don't fear the rebirth of the Old Kingdom?"

"Why should I? I never did them any harm, and as far as I'm concerned, they're welcome to the east. I hear it's nothing but wilderness, anyway." With that, he left to look after his other patrons.

"You know," said Charlaine, "I often take solace in the sensibility of the common folk. It tells me there is hope for the Continent after all."

"Agreed," replied Danica. "Now, if only we could convince the ruling classes of that approach."

5

NEIBURG

SPRING 1106 SR

With summer around the corner, the folk of Neiburg were eager to soak up the sun and enjoy the unseasonably warm weather. No walls surrounded the city, as it had seen little war over the years, allowing it to grow immeasurably since its founding, now sprawling miles across mostly flat terrain, with many fields seemingly placed at random locations amongst the city's twisting streets.

"There it is," said Danica, pointing. "The Ducal Palace. Quite the sight, isn't it?"

"Indeed," replied Charlaine. "I've corresponded with the commandery here many times over the last few years, but Temple Captain Georgia never saw fit to mention it."

"It's hardly the type of thing that would come up in official correspondence."

"No. I suppose not."

"Did you want to visit the commandery while we're here? We could spend the night?"

"I'd rather push on. The good captain might feel it necessary to host a dinner to celebrate her superior, which is the last thing we need. We'll stay at a roadside inn once we pass through Neiburg, saving us time in the long run."

"Don't look now," said Danica, "but it appears we have company." A knight had ridden into the street and turned side-on to them, blocking their way. "Oh, great," she continued. "Just what we need—a Cunar."

"Let's not panic quite yet. Perhaps he simply wishes to offer us his best regards?"

"Temple Commander Charlaine," called out the knight. "My name is Brother Roydin. I have been ordered to bring you before my captain."

"And if I refuse?"

His lips curled up, but his smile did not reach his eyes. "It would be in your best interest to comply with my request."

She looked at Danica. "He's suddenly become polite. Now it's a request."

He stiffened in the saddle. "Are you mocking me, Commander?"

"No," replied Charlaine. "I am merely curious whether it is a demand or invitation. Wait. How did you know I'd be on this road today?"

"You are travelling to the Antonine on a matter of some urgency, are you not? And the Royal thoroughfare is the only road you would logically take, as it's the fastest way to cross through the city."

"That doesn't explain how you know I'd be here, in Neiburg."

"True, it doesn't," replied Roydin. "In my defence, I can only say I was informed that you would be here at some point today."

"And have you been waiting long?"

"Half the morning."

"Well then," said Charlaine. "We'd best not keep the good Temple Captain waiting." She slowed Stormcloud as she advanced. "Might I know the name of your superior?"

"Temple Captain Guthrie. He awaits your presence at the Cunar commandery."

"Then lead on, Brother Roydin. I am unfamiliar with the way."

He turned his horse and advanced up the street, moving slowly, glancing over his shoulder occasionally to ensure they followed him.

"I don't like this," said Danica, keeping her voice low.

"Nor do I," replied Charlaine, "but if we don't face this head-on, it may come back to bite us."

"A good point, even if we don't know what 'this' is."

"Look on the bright side; they only sent one Temple Knight to intercept us."

"That we're aware of. For all we know, there could be a dozen more waiting down side streets."

"I'm surprised there's any here at all," said Charlaine. "Their order supposedly pulled back from the frontier. From what I read, that meant Angvil as well."

"Clearly, that isn't the case; otherwise, we wouldn't be riding to the Cunar commandery."

They turned a corner to see a familiar-looking building. Temple Commanderies all followed the same layout, with a hollow square surrounded by two floors of rooms to house the knights. By tradition, the captain's window faced west, towards the Holy City, although, technically speaking, Herani was more south than west.

The guards stood to attention as they approached, and then one opened the double doors that led into the courtyard. Brother Roydin dismounted and passed his reins to another knight wearing a simple cassock. He waited while Charlaine and Danica did likewise, then led them into the building.

The dark grey banners, bearing the white sword of the order, hanging in the hallway were the only thing that made this building different from those back in Lidenbach. They passed several empty rooms, indicating this commandery was not at its full capacity. They ascended the stairs only to find two more knights standing guard outside the captain's office.

"Wait here," said Roydin before he disappeared through the door. The two guards remained motionless, staring straight ahead, reminding Charlaine of the Cunar's rigid and inflexible discipline.

"Come," came a voice.

One guard opened the door, allowing them entry. Inside sat a Temple Captain, his short hair common amongst the Cunars. However, his snowy white beard stood in stark contrast to his dark features, proclaiming him as a man of advanced years.

"Greetings," he began. "I am Temple Captain Guthrie. I'm glad you accepted my invitation to visit, Commander."

"I am Temple Commander Charlaine, and this is Temple Captain Danica."

"Oh, I'm fully aware of who you are. My question is, why are you here in Angvil?"

"We were travelling through."

"Yes. On your way to the Antonine, if I'm not mistaken."

"News travels quickly," remarked Charlaine.

"So it does, especially when it concerns someone of your stature."

"I am but a humble servant of Saint Agnes."

"Don't be so modest, Commander. You're much more than that; you and I both know it. And as for you…" His gaze swivelled to Danica. "Well, that can wait for later."

"What is it you want, Captain?"

He leaned forward, placing his hands on his desk. "My order is well-acquainted with your accomplishments, Commander. Why has your grand mistress summoned you to the Antonine?"

"What business is that of yours?"

"My order is tasked with the safety and security of the Church."

"As is ours," replied Charlaine.

"I'll admit you sister knights are responsible for guarding some of the

Church's temples, but we are tasked with training and maintaining the Holy Army."

"Your point being?"

"Your presence here in Angvil raises questions about your loyalties."

"I took a vow to serve my order and my Saint."

"Yes, but does that include blindly obeying the orders of your grand mistress?"

"Do you not obey the orders of your own grand master?"

The Temple Captain smiled. "I see your reputation is well-merited, Commander."

"My reputation?"

"Yes. It's said you have a keen intellect and a flair for tactics."

"I'm unsure whether I should be flattered or troubled, Captain. Do you spend your time reading about the Temple Commanders of all the orders or only Saint Agnes?"

"I'm only interested in you because my superiors ordered us to watch for you."

"To what end?" asked Charlaine.

"We're looking out for your best interests, I assure you."

"You'll pardon me if I don't believe you."

"That's your prerogative, but it would go better for you if you were cooperative."

"As in telling you why we're going to the Antonine?"

"Precisely. Now remember, you've taken an oath not to lie."

"I don't need to lie," replied Charlaine. "The truth is I don't know why we were summoned. I suspect your superiors are already aware of that, considering they intercepted my orders."

"What makes you say that?"

"How else would you know we were heading to the Antonine?"

"Someone in Lidenbach could have alerted us."

"You mean like that Temple Knight of yours who's several days ahead of us?"

"Yes."

"Yet that still wouldn't tell you why, would it?"

The Temple Captain slammed his hands down. "Enough of these games, Commander. Why are you going to the Antonine? And this time, I want the truth."

"I've told you the truth. If you don't believe me, read the orders for yourself." She dug into her belt pouch, withdrew the letter from her grand mistress and tossed it on the table.

Guthrie picked it up and carefully unfolded it, expecting to make some great discovery, but he only knitted his brows and frowned before tossing the letter back. "This is most annoying."

"I agree," said Charlaine. "Now, may we be on our way?"

"A moment, Captain?" said Brother Roydin.

Guthrie looked up at his knight. "Yes?"

"If I may be so bold, sir, could a message be hidden within?"

"You mean some kind of code?"

"Precisely, sir."

Guthrie sat back. "Go ahead, Brother. Have a look at it. Perhaps you will see what I failed to."

Brother Roydin held the letter to the window, letting the outside light bleed through, but it made no difference. In frustration, he turned the sheet to let the sun bathe its surface and read it over. "A cipher, perhaps?"

"If there is one," replied Charlaine, "I failed to find it, and trust me, I've looked."

"It seems to me," offered Guthrie, "you are as much in the dark about this as we are."

"Are we under arrest?"

"No. Even if I wanted to arrest you, you hold the superior rank. I would need authority from someone higher up in the chain of command, and my superiors don't seem inclined to go that far. I warn you, however, to tread very carefully. The eyes of the Church are upon you."

"Aren't they always?"

"This is no laughing matter."

"I never said it was," replied Charlaine. "My life is an open book, Captain. I have nothing to hide."

"So I've been told, but I've often found such reputations result from careful cultivation. You'll slip up eventually, Commander, and when you do, we'll be there to put a halt to your heretical behaviour."

"Heretical?" said Charlaine. "What precisely do you think I've done?"

"That's not for me to say." He turned to regard Brother Roydin. "Give her the letter, for Saint's sake. There's no secret code in there."

The knight passed the note to Charlaine.

"You're free to go," said Guthrie. He opened his mouth as if about to add something, then reconsidered.

"What about the admiral?" asked Brother Roydin.

"Her as well."

"But, sir," said Roydin. "You can't just let them leave!"

"What would you have me do? Arrest them? They did nothing wrong."

"They are implicated in a plot against our order."

"There is no proof of that."

"Then why would our superiors ask us to detain them?"

Temple Captain Guthrie took a deep breath to calm himself. "Have you heard nothing here today? This is an interview to determine why they travel to the Antonine, nothing more. It's clear to me, as it should be to you, they are unaware of the reason for their summons."

Roydin stepped forward menacingly, but his captain cut him off. "That's enough. Return to your quarters before you face disciplinary action."

The Temple Knight went rigid. He nodded, his only acknowledgement of the order, then left, his footsteps heavy in the hallway outside.

"You must forgive Brother Roydin. He means well but has yet to temper his enthusiasm with experience."

"We shall be leaving as well," said Charlaine. "We can offer no more to this conversation."

He smiled sheepishly. "Please accept my apologies for the manner in which you were brought here."

"I will do no such thing!" declared Charlaine.

Guthrie took in a sharp breath at Charlaine's rebuke, but before he could speak, she continued. "I am a Temple Commander, a senior rank to your own, yet you treated me like a knight under your command. The contempt you've shown both myself and Admiral Danica is not fitting of a person of your rank."

She reached the door and paused, turning to face him. "I suggest you learn manners, Captain. You'll find it's much more effective at achieving results than threats. Come, Danica. It's time we were back on the road."

They left the office unaccompanied by guards, their steps deliberate, maintaining a steady pace as they returned to the courtyard. Charlaine said nothing save for calling for their horses. Picking up on her comrade's mood, Danica waited until they were halfway down the street before she decided to speak.

"Well, that was interesting."

"It most certainly was," replied Charlaine. "It also confirms our suspicions that someone intercepted our orders. That's a willful and definite breach of Church protocols."

"They're worried about something. I'd love to know what they're up to."

"As would I, but we'll get no answers from these Cunars. They're not high enough up in the Church hierarchy to know anything. Their superiors, however, are obviously worried."

"I agree," said Danica, "but how far up the chain of command does it go?"

"An excellent question. It appears our grand mistress discovered something about them that they don't want anybody to know."

"They suffered a defeat at the hands of Therengia. Could that be related?"

"Possibly, but I can't see how. Their loss is well-documented, and it's not as if they're trying to cover it up. No, this sounds more sinister."

"Because they aren't informing their subordinates of the details?"

"Precisely," replied Charlaine. "While I understand senior officers don't always tell those under their command everything they do, they bear a responsibility to keep them informed, particularly regarding such unusual orders. How do they expect their captain to dig into the details of our trip when he's unaware of what he's looking for?"

"That's a good indication it comes from the very top."

"Yes, but does that mean their grand master, patriarch, or representative on the Council of Peers?"

"I've never quite understood how that works," said Danica. "I know each discipline has its own patriarch or matriarch, but why don't they sit on the council?"

"Usually, they do, but they're sometimes too busy to take a direct hand in the voting, in which case they delegate someone to vote on their behalf. The Council of Peers consists of only one representative from each sect of the Church."

"That makes sense but doesn't explain the primus."

"The primus is chosen by the patriarchs and is supposed to demonstrate neutrality when running the Council of Peers. Originally, their role was to vote in the case of a tie, but in recent years, they've taken a more active hand in directing the council."

"Directing, how?"

"There are several ways, chief amongst them the ability to pick the topic of discussion, allowing him to control which matters are brought before the council."

"Or which aren't," added Danica. "He could bury a topic by refusing to bring it up!"

"A very astute observation."

"And how long does the primus serve?"

"Five years, although it's not uncommon for one to continue into a second or even a third term. The record was five, but that was close to two hundred years ago, and he came to the position at a relatively young age."

"How young?"

"Fifty-five. He was almost eighty when he died, thus ending his tenure. Of course, when I say young, I mean in comparison to his predecessors. Most are into their sixties or seventies before they're elected."

"You certainly know a lot about this."

"I do," said Charlaine. "Part of it is due to the requirements of being a Temple Commander."

"And the other part?"

"Interest, particularly after our last experience in the Antonine. I swore to myself that if I ever returned, I'd know the ins and outs of how things operated."

"Anything else you've discovered worth mentioning?"

"Are you aware that the Matriarch of Saint Agnes is a lifetime appointment?"

"Yes," replied Danica. "I remember that from my training. I am curious, however, how the position is filled."

"When a matriarch dies, the archprioresses gather to elect a new one from amongst their number. A time-consuming process, as they must travel to the Antonine to cast their vote, and even then, there's no guarantee they'll come to a consensus. The election that chose our current matriarch took four months, and that was after they'd all gathered."

"I assume the other sects do the same?"

"They do. Four centuries ago, the archpriors of Saint Mathew took two years to name a successor. Then, he only lived for seven months, requiring another to be chosen."

Danica shook her head. "It's a wonder anything gets accomplished."

"Most of the Church's work is done by those lower down in the hierarchy, typically the priors and the Holy Fathers."

"We don't hear much from them."

"Of course not," said Charlaine. "They deal with matters of faith while we, as Temple Knights, concentrate on guarding those we swore to protect."

6

ON THE ROAD
SUMMER 1106 SR

Summer was upon them by the time they reached Erlingen. They crossed the Rasfeld River at a place called Zurkirk, continuing southeast towards the capital of Torburg.

East of the river, the countryside grew more rugged, the road bending and turning to avoid steep inclines. The heat of the day forced them to occasionally seek shade in the woods to the south to get some respite from the sun.

On one such rest, they spied a mounted figure cresting the top of a hill. They realized he was not alone as he descended, for he dragged a pitiful creature by a rope secured around its neck.

Charlaine watched as the captor and captive neared. "What do you make of that?" She nodded her head towards them.

"A knight, perhaps?" offered Danica. "He has the armour for it."

"Agreed, but what's that trailing him?"

"Perhaps a prisoner he's tracked down?"

"I think this bears investigation, don't you?"

"If you insist."

Charlaine detected the hesitation. "You don't agree?"

"I have no quarrel with asking a few questions," replied Danica, "but we can't interfere in secular matters. If that person is a legal prisoner, we are honour-bound not to interfere."

"Since when is asking questions interfering?"

"I know that look."

"What look?" said Charlaine.

"That look that says you don't agree with something."

"I can't help it if I don't like witnessing injustice."

"Fair enough. Let's go and interfere, then, shall we?"

Charlaine smiled. "I knew you'd come around to my way of thinking."

They climbed back into the saddle and set their horses on a course to intercept the knight. Catching up to him wasn't difficult since his prisoner slowed him down, but as they drew within a hundred yards, he turned in the saddle, their hoofbeats alerting him to their presence.

He slowed, placing his horse between his prisoner and the Temple Knights. "Who are you that dares threaten a Knight of the Sceptre?"

"We mean you no harm. I am Temple Commander Charlaine of the Order of Saint Agnes, and this is Temple Captain Danica. We are headed to Torburg and would be grateful for the company."

"My pardon, Sisters. I am Sir Nathan of Feldmarch, and am also on my way to the capital."

"I'm sorry. Did you say, Sir Nathan?"

"Yes, of Feldmarch. Why?"

Charlaine backed up a little, her hand reaching for her scabbard. "I have it on good authority Sir Nathan died back in ninety-five, the result of wounds inflicted during a tournament."

The knight dropped the end of the rope tied to his prisoner, then spurred on his horse and tore down the road at a gallop.

"Watch that prisoner," Charlaine shouted at Danica as she urged Stormcloud to follow. The Calabrian, prized for its speed, burst into action, quickly gaining ground in pursuit of her target.

"Halt in the name of the Saints," she called out.

The fellow glanced over his shoulder and quickly realized he couldn't outpace her. Desperate to lose her, he turned south, riding directly towards the forest.

Charlaine moved Stormcloud off the road, jumping a small stream that might have given a lesser mount pause. The fellow was at the treeline when Charlaine called out again, this time almost within sword reach. He raised his hands in surrender, his horse halting without direction.

"Dismount," ordered Charlaine, "and keep your hands away from your weapon."

He did as ordered. She then dropped to the ground and drew her sword, keeping her eyes on him. "Who are you?"

"I told you earlier, my name is Sir Nathan of Feldmarch."

"Then why did you run?"

"I thought you were bandits."

"Is it the habit in these parts for bandits to wear the raiments of Temple Knights?"

His shoulders sagged. "No."

"Undo your belt and scabbard and drop it to the ground." She waited as he complied.

He remained silent until he did what she requested. "I made sure to pick an obscure knight. How in the name of the Saints did you know about him?"

"It just so happens a friend of mine was at that tournament. Years later, he wrote to me of Sir Nathan's death, and how much it affected him."

"So he and Nathan were good friends?"

"On the contrary," replied Charlaine. "They didn't know each other at all, but a death like that is a most tragic event and not one to be forgotten."

"Of all the luck, I had to run into the one person who could unmask me."

"Who was your prisoner?"

"Just an Orc. No one of any consequence. I planned on taking him to Deisenbach, where there's a bounty on their heads."

"And that requires you to impersonate a knight?"

He shrugged. "People take no notice of what a man in armour does. They assume he's working for the king."

"That's a poor excuse for assuming a fallen knight's identity. Why not invent a knightly name for yourself?"

"There was always the risk of running across someone of import, and I thought an actual knight would invite less speculation about my true motives."

She shook her head. "I cannot allow you to continue on with your prisoner."

"Why? What's it to you if he's made a slave?"

"The Church forbids slavery."

"Many kingdoms still practice it. Besides, is it slavery if the subject isn't Human?"

"Yes!" insisted Charlaine. She heard hoofbeats and risked a glance over her shoulder. Danica approached, the Orc running behind her even though its rope bindings had been removed.

"Everything all right here?" the admiral called out.

"Yes. This fellow was just about to reveal his real name." Charlaine turned to regard her prisoner.

"Ah, yes," he said. "Well, that might be a tad difficult."

"Are you suggesting you don't possess a name?"

"Oh, I have several, depending on what realm I'm in."

"This is Erlingen."

"Yes. Hmmm, let's see now…" His voice trailed off.

"We must call you something."

"Then call me Lloyd. That will suffice for the time being."

Danica dismounted and moved towards the man. "Hands behind your back, Lloyd." She waited for him to comply so she could bind his wrists together.

"I did nothing wrong," he insisted. "It's not illegal to capture a bounty."

"We're not arresting you for that," said Charlaine.

He stared back in surprise. "You're not?"

"No. You're being taken into custody for impersonating a Knight of the Sceptre."

"What do we do with his prisoner?" asked Danica.

Charlaine shifted her focus to the Orc. "Do you speak our tongue?"

He stared back, clearly not understanding.

"You may go," she said. "You are free." She pointed at him, then to the hills he presumably came from.

He gestured towards the horse.

"I think he wants Lloyd's horse," said Danica.

"No. He likely wants his belongings back. Let's see what we have here, shall we?" She approached the horse, pulling a sack from behind the saddle. Rather than sift through it, she emptied the contents onto the ground, using hand gestures to invite the Orc to come and get whatever he wanted.

He moved closer, choosing an axe and a knife. He then stood, ignoring the rest of Lloyd's possessions and nodded. Charlaine mimicked his movement, watching as he ran off, heading back into the hills.

"You have a knack for this," said Danica, "although I'm still confused about how you knew Sir Nathan was dead."

"Ludwig wrote to me about it years ago. He was young and brash when it happened, and though he wasn't responsible, it shook him terribly. I think, in a sense, it taught him we are all mortal."

"Ah, yes," said Danica. "Young men always think they're indestructible. I suppose that's why so many are eager to march to war." She picked up the discarded sword belt. "What do we do with Lloyd?"

"We'll take him to Torburg and hand him over to the duke's people."

"What do you think they'll do with him?"

"I can't say, but I don't imagine they'll be too pleased with him."

The prisoner cleared his throat. "You'd be better off to let me go. After all, it's your word against mine."

"Who do you think they'll believe: a criminal or a pair of Temple Knights?"

He nodded at the pile of belongings on the ground. "There's a purse in there with a significant number of coins. What say you take them and look the other way?"

"Are you seriously suggesting I let you bribe your way out of this?"

"Listen, you might be a Holy warrior, but deep down, you're still Human, which means you have a price."

"I don't know what's sadder," said Danica. "The fact he's so disenchanted with the Human race, or his attempt to bribe a Temple Knight."

They rode on in silence, their prisoner mounted on his horse. Danica led the beast using the very rope with which Lloyd had secured his own prisoner, but the creature proved stubborn, resisting her efforts at every opportunity.

"Where did you get this horse?" asked Danica.

"From a wealthy benefactor."

"You mean you stole it?"

Lloyd sat up straighter in the saddle. "I can neither confirm nor deny that accusation."

"But you admit it's not your horse?"

"They say possession is nine-tenths of the law. By that reckoning, it's mine now."

"That's not how the law works," insisted Charlaine.

"Oh? Are you an expert in such things?"

"Temple Knights are sworn to uphold the law of whatever kingdom we serve. It'd be foolish to expect them to carry out that task were we not familiar with the laws of the land."

"Are you from Erlingen?"

"No, but I'm well-acquainted with the common laws of the Petty Kingdoms."

"Which are?"

"After the defeat of the Old Kingdom," explained Charlaine, "most of the Successor States deemed it advantageous to codify a set of common laws which would be enforced throughout the Continent. The laws of their old nemesis may have influenced them, as it's said they have much in common, but I digress. The laws of each Petty Kingdom varies greatly now, but the core remains largely unchanged."

"Which are those?"

"Punishment for crimes, including robbery, murder, thievery, that sort of thing. They were called the common laws due to the fact they mostly affected the common folk. Nobles found this system easy to introduce and enforce because, for all practical purposes, they were already in effect in those areas formerly under Therengian rule. Indeed, they might have been called the Therengian laws had the name not been so distasteful."

Lloyd let loose with a series of grumbles and grunts.

"Something you want to say?" asked Charlaine.

"Would it matter if I did?"

"I'm not here to try you, merely take you to those who will. Speak your mind."

He pursed his lips, refusing to speak.

Danica tried a different tactic. "Why did you become a brigand?"

"It's not so much a question of why as how," replied Lloyd.

"How, then?"

"I was a mercenary, formerly a member of the Grim Defenders."

"I've heard of them. They helped repel the invasion of Erlingen back in ninety-five."

"Yes. I was there at the Battle of Chermingen."

"Another lie to add to your collection?" asked Charlaine.

"It's true. I swear."

"Then tell me who was responsible for winning the battle?"

"A knight named Sir Galrath of Paledon, who fell in service to His Grace, the Duke."

"And what part did you play?"

"The Grim Defenders occupied an old, abandoned farmhouse in front of the duke's position, which became the focus of a heavy assault."

"Tell me this, then—who commanded the Grim Defenders?"

"A fellow named Captain Ecke, but he died during the fight. Ludwig Altenburg took his place."

"You knew Ludwig?"

"I did," replied Lloyd. "Unfortunately, he and I didn't always see eye to eye on things. Of course, it didn't help that I associated with Baldric."

"Baldric? I assume he caused a lot of problems?"

"That's putting it mildly. In any case, he died trying to storm the keep at Regnitz. By the time Chermingen rolled around, I'd taken it upon myself to make better choices."

"Yet here you are, now, impersonating a knight."

"Yes. Once the battle was over, we had no place to call home. The Grim Defenders were a shadow of their former strength, and our most effective warriors had moved on to greener pastures. I was at my wit's end, and I resorted to brigandry to fill my belly."

"That was eleven years ago: plenty of time for you to find gainful employment elsewhere."

"What can I say? Mercenaries are not in demand of late."

"While it's an interesting story, it doesn't absolve you of your crimes. If I were you, I'd spend my remaining moments praying for a sympathetic judge."

Late that evening, the city of Torburg came into view as they topped a rise, the buildings illuminated by flickering lights. Charlaine halted, pausing to enjoy the view.

Danica's words interrupted her. "They say Torburg is one of the larger cities in the Petty Kingdoms."

"It doesn't look any larger than Rizela."

Danica stared down at the city before answering. "No, it doesn't. That's disappointing."

"Why would you say that?"

"I built up this image of an immense city. I was looking forward to it."

"And you still can. A city's worth is not measured by its size but by its people."

"Is that a quote from Saint Agnes?"

"No," replied Charlaine. "My father."

"You miss him, don't you?"

"I hadn't seen him since I joined the order, yet somehow, knowing he was safe and sound back in Malburg gave me a sense of comfort."

"Your mother's still there."

"She is, but we didn't have the same connection I shared with my father. It doesn't help that when we were in Calabria, it was suggested Tomas wasn't my father."

"He was a father in every way that mattered."

"True," said Charlaine, "and I've accepted that, but I don't know if I can forgive my mother for not telling me the truth."

"Perhaps she couldn't find the right time?"

"That's just it—she did try. She once told me she loved a cavalero before my father but faced ostracism. I wasn't certain she was telling the truth then, but events in the south eventually confirmed the story."

"Why would you not believe her?"

"Her timing was suspect. She was trying to convince me to stop seeing Ludwig."

"Perhaps it's time for you to mend things with your mother. After all, forgiveness is one of Saint Agnes's defining characteristics."

"I will eventually," replied Charlaine, "but that's something best done face to face, and I'm a little preoccupied presently." She glanced once more at the city and then at their prisoner. "Do you think we can make it there before midnight? Our new acquaintance is looking tired."

Danica chuckled. "He'll miss all this exercise once he's rotting in jail. I say push on. Once we hand this fellow over to the authorities, we can spend the night at the local commandery. They'll be pleased to see a Temple Commander, unless the city has a regional commander of their own?"

"Not that I'm aware of, but then again, it's not my responsibility to keep track of such things." Charlaine urged Stormcloud into a gentle canter.

"Come along, you," said Danica, her attention directed towards Lloyd. "A few more miles, and then you can sleep all you want."

A grumble erupted from their prisoner, but they both ignored it.

"I wonder how many more disappointments we'll experience on our way to the Antonine?"

"Disappointments?"

"Yes. First, we find a false knight escorting a slave, then learn Torburg isn't as large as we believed it to be."

"That last one's all on you," said Charlaine. "You're the one who built up your expectations; I prefer to take things as they are."

"Hold on. I must write that down."

"Why would you do that?"

"So future generations will know the wisdom of the great Temple Commander Charlaine."

"I never claimed to be great."

"True, but all the same, I recognize greatness when I see it, and you have it in bushels."

"Is that a northern expression?"

"No, southern," said Danica. "I heard it used by Casimo Venucci. Do you remember him?"

"The Ilean winemaker? If I recall, he had some remarkable vintages."

"You know I've still got a bottle of his red back in Temple Bay."

"You do?"

"Yes. I've been saving it for a special occasion."

"And defeating the Halvarian fleet at Lidenbach didn't qualify?"

"What can I say? I live a life of action and adventure. It'll take something much more exciting for me to pop that cork!"

7

TORBURG

SUMMER 1106 SR

Charlaine expected turning over their prisoner would be a lengthy process but was pleasantly surprised to discover that was not the case when they encountered a group of the king's men as they entered Torburg. After hearing the details, the one in charge gave Lloyd a stern look.

"Oh yes," he said. "We know this one. We've been looking for him for a while now."

"Perhaps you might reveal his true identity," said Danica. "He claimed to possess several."

"It's Quentin, and he's wanted for murder."

"Might I ask who he killed?"

"A tavern keeper, along with two of the fellow's customers. About three years ago, Quentin got drunk and then decided to carve a few people up with his knife. He's been on the run ever since. Where did you find him?"

"To the northwest, along the road to Anshlag. He wandered out of the hills as we rested our horses."

"I'm surprised he returned to the area, considering the charges against him. Mind you, he's always been a troublemaker."

"He claims to have been a member of the Grim Defenders. I understand they distinguished themselves at the Battle of Chermingen."

"That they did, but it doesn't excuse his subsequent behaviour. He'd been arrested three times before the murder, twice for brawling and once for theft, although the witness later recanted her story. Rumours were he'd left town, so we thought the matter settled."

"It appears he's taken up the trade of slavery," said Charlaine.

"Slavery, you say?"

"Yes. When we encountered him, he was leading an Orc he'd captured."

"There's no Orcs in this area," replied the guard. "Are you certain you didn't make a mistake? Perhaps it was a trick of the light, and his prisoner was a Human?"

"I stood as close to him as I am to you."

"This is dire news. I shall have to alert my superiors. If Orcs are nearby, it could spell trouble."

"Is there a history of hostility from the Orcs?"

"Not in my lifetime."

"Then I suggest you drop the matter before you make it worse."

"You just informed me there are savages nearby. How could it be any worse?"

"We saw one Orc," replied Charlaine, "not a war party, and he seemed at home in these parts, which leads me to suspect he's native to the area. As this is the first you are hearing of them, they have no desire to wage war on the fine people of Erlingen. Sending warriors after them, however, might provoke an armed response."

"Precisely why we must act."

"Wouldn't you take up arms to protect family and loved ones if threatened?"

"Of course."

"Then try to see the situation from their point of view," said Charlaine. "There is already enough conflict in Eiddenwerthe; let us not add to it unnecessarily."

"You make a good point."

"Will you need us to give you a written statement?"

"No," replied the warrior. "The word of a Temple Knight is sufficient, and in this case, we have two."

"Then we shall be on our way."

"May the Saints go with you, Sisters."

"And with you," replied Charlaine. They rode on, minus their prisoner and the extra horse.

"There you go," said Charlaine. "Some excitement for you. Perhaps it will help you overcome your disappointment at the size of Torburg."

"It definitely makes for an interesting story," replied Danica. "I thought impersonating a knight was bad enough, but he was also a murderer. The Saints have seen fit for us to do their work yet again. Sometimes, it feels like that's all we ever do."

"Are you complaining that we make the Continent a better place?"

"No, but I have to wonder why we discover problems wherever we go."

"That's easy to explain," said Charlaine.

"Please do,"

"We, as an order, seek to make Eiddenwerthe a better place. It's only natural that when we see injustice, we take steps to correct it. It's not that we find trouble everywhere; it's that it's ever-present. Without someone who seeks it out, it rots the core of our society."

"You've put it very eloquently," said Danica. "The rot is always there; someone just needs to open their eyes to see it."

"Yes, exactly. You'd best write that down in your journal and note that you said it, not me. I don't want credit for something I didn't do."

Danica mimicked writing on a parchment. "There we go. All written down, nice and proper." She chuckled.

"You find something amusing?"

"I couldn't read and write when I joined the order, and while training, I spent more time learning to read than wielding a sword."

"We all have our burdens to carry," said Charlaine. "I had trouble fitting in with the other recruits. I had nothing against them but was much older than they were."

"You'd already had a career as a smith, which makes a huge difference. Most initiates are barely adults. I was only sixteen."

"You were fifteen," Charlaine corrected her. "I know your story. The Holy Mother lied about your age to allow you entry."

"You mean to escape my tormentors." Danica shivered. "It makes me uncomfortable to even think about what I went through. Thankfully, with time, the memories have faded."

"I'm glad you had someone to tell your story to when you came to the order. As the Book of Agnes tells us, a burden shared is easier to bear."

"Isn't that the Book of Mathew?"

"I don't know. Is it? I don't suppose it matters. They're both Saints."

Like all commanderies, Saint Agnes's in Torburg was the same layout as those back in Arnsfeld. As they advanced, the two Temple Knights on duty took notice of their arrival.

"Who goes there?" came the challenge.

"Temple Commander Charlaine, Regional Commander of the Northwest Region, and this is Admiral Danica of the Temple Fleet."

True to protocol, a guard went inside to inform her superior while the other kept watch. "Welcome, Commander. We weren't expecting visitors, especially at this late hour."

"We're passing through Torburg and hoped to seek shelter here for the night."

"I doubt Temple Captain Lysela would object. I'm certain she'll come down to greet you once she's been informed of your arrival."

"Then we'll wait here for her."

"Shall I call someone to look after your horses?"

"If you would be so kind," replied Charlaine.

The Temple Captain arrived with a pair of knights to take their mounts.

"Greetings. I'm Temple Captain Lysela. I'm sorry I wasn't here to greet you upon your arrival, but I missed the missive indicating you'd be visiting."

"We're not visiting," replied Charlaine, "at least not officially. We're on our way to the Antonine and hoped we could stay here for the night if it's not an imposition?"

"Not at all. Won't you come in?"

They handed over their reins and then went inside.

"It's late," said Lysela. "Have you had anything to eat?"

"No," replied Danica, "but we don't want to be a bother."

"It's no bother as long as you don't mind cold meat and bread."

"That will do nicely. Thank you."

"Come. We'll go to the dining hall, and Sister Kiara will find you something to keep your hunger at bay." They entered the building and were soon heading down a corridor. "Any news from the west?"

"How did you know we were from the west?" asked Charlaine.

"You did say you were the regional commander of the northwest, and your name has been widely circulated amongst the order. You're the only sister knight in living history to lead an army in battle... well, you and the admiral. I don't wish to lessen her contributions."

"It's been quiet in Arnsfeld of late. How about here?"

"We received news that the duke died while campaigning in the crusade, but that was some time ago. The only other thing of note was a lay sister from the Antonine who passed through here last year on her way to Reinwick to assume her new duties."

"Had she anything to report?"

"I'm afraid it was more rumour than substance," said Lysela. "Ah, here we are—the dining hall." She opened the door, waved for them to enter, and followed them in. "Kiara," she called out. "We have guests. See what you can rustle them up to eat and bring some wine while you're at it, will you?"

"Yes, Captain."

They all took a seat.

"You mentioned you were heading to the Antonine," continued Lysela. "Might I enquire about the purpose of your visit?"

"I'm afraid I can't speak of that," replied Charlaine. "The grand mistress stressed it was of great import."

"Does it have anything to do with the rumours of dissolution?"

"What rumours are those?"

"I hesitate to give credence to them, but it's going around that the Temple Knights of Saint Cunar wish the other fighting orders placed under their direct command. If that came to pass, the orders would cease to be anything other than Cunars. I realize it's not complete dissolution in the classical sense but amounts to the same thing."

"Did you hear this from the lay sister?"

"Yes. She said all Temple Captains and above would be replaced by Cunars, but the rank of knight would still be respected."

"That sounds unlikely," replied Charlaine. "I can't imagine the Council of Peers seriously considering such a motion. Each order has its own role within the Church, and tampering with that would seriously undermine confidence. Who could be trusted to investigate matters internally if the Ansgarites had to report to Cunars instead of superiors of their own order?"

"It is vexing," replied Lysela, "but I've heard it's primarily a financial decision rather than one of ideology. It costs the Church so much to maintain senior officers for all six orders."

"True," said Danica, "but the Cunars are primarily a fighting order. We can't expect them to understand what's needed to help women or the sick and poor in the case of the Mathewites."

"I am in complete agreement, but I'm afraid there is little we can do, save hope these rumours turn out to be false."

"On another matter," said Charlaine, "how is the new duke doing?"

"He was inconsolable after the news of his father's death reached him, but he has yet to take any decisive action."

"Decisive? On what, might I ask?"

"Any number of things. I've seen Duke Alain once or twice at court, and he doesn't strike me as someone eager to shoulder the responsibility of ruling. I might even go as far as to describe him as indecisive, a characteristic of little consequence amongst the common folk, but it can prove troublesome in a leader. Still, I hold hope that in the fullness of time, he will come to grips with his present circumstance and become the ruler Erlingen needs. I'm told it's not unusual for new rulers to be hesitant when they begin their rule. Did you find it so in Arnsfeld?"

"I'm sorry?" said Charlaine.

"Well, the king died during the war, didn't he? How did his successor do?"

"King Handrik has never lacked for courage. He began issuing orders the same day he was crowned."

"Would that the rest of the Petty Kingdoms were so blessed."

"Has the new duke any military experience?"

"No," replied Lysela. "He prefers scholarly pursuits."

"Scholarly can be good," offered Danica. "Oftentimes, a thinker is better than a military man, especially when running a kingdom, or in this case, a duchy."

"Under other circumstances, I'd agree, but I'm not so certain that's what Erlingen needs, not when the threat of a Halvarian invasion hangs over the heads of the Petty Kingdoms."

"They've been a threat for centuries," said Charlaine. "There's no indication that the empire is massing anywhere."

"True, but isn't it their vowed intention to pacify the entire Continent?"

"Yes, it is, but we can't let the threat of them colour our everyday lives."

"You certainly have a way with words, Commander."

Sister Kiara appeared, bearing a tray with meat, cheese, bread, and two tankards of ale. "I trust this will be to your satisfaction?"

"Yes. Thank you," said Charlaine. "Now, Captain, I wonder if you might answer a question for me?"

"If I can, certainly."

"What is the Cunar presence like here in Erlingen?"

"Their commandery lies on the north end of the city."

"But…"

"But what?"

"The presence of a commandery tells me little about the order. However, your silence on the matter reveals much. Out with it. This may have some bearing on recent events."

"I am of the opinion they are preparing to abandon the city like they did in the western Petty Kingdoms."

"What makes you say that?"

"We purchase our supplies from local merchants, and there've been many complaints of late."

"Such as?"

"The Cunars are no longer stocking up on supplies like in the past, which indicates they are either reducing their numbers here in Torburg or leaving the city altogether."

"Curious," said Charlaine, "but not in itself definitive. Perhaps they simply went with new suppliers?"

"Only so many merchants are capable of feeding an entire commandery of Temple Knights, and I know them all."

"Has there been any talk at court on the matter?"

"None whatsoever," replied Lysela. "There's been a deafening silence on all talk of the Church. It's as if the very topic has become forbidden."

"Could that be due to His Grace, the Duke?" asked Danica. "You mentioned earlier that he was a scholar; does that include religious readings?"

"I hadn't considered that. I suppose it's not beyond the realm of possibility. Not that the Church was a regular topic under his father, you understand, but the occasional mention of the fighting orders wouldn't have been out of place."

"Do the Cunars still maintain a presence at court?"

"Their captain is always present for official ceremonies, as am I, but he's not the sort to engage in idle chit-chat. Lord Alain, the new duke, holds court far less often than his father did. I've heard he has a distaste for the fighting orders, seeing them as rivals to his own knights, but if that's true, he's never shared his opinion with me."

"You've given us much to think on," said Charlaine. "Would you be so kind as to show us to our rooms?"

"Yes, of course," replied the Temple Captain.

That night, Charlaine tossed and turned as thoughts rolled around in her head. The withdrawal of the Cunars from the western Petty Kingdoms made sense from a certain perspective, as it allowed them to mass the Holy Army in the middle of the Continent in relative safety should war come.

However, the news that they were reducing their presence here in Erlingen made no sense, as it was considered a central kingdom, ideally suited to have sufficient time to call up their army should Halvaria invade. It was beginning to look more and more like the order was deliberately undermining the security of the Petty Kingdoms to destabilize the region.

The question on her mind was where they were headed. One didn't simply vanish an entire company of Temple Knights into thin air, so what were they up to?

She tried to shake it off, half convincing herself that they were sending their men to Zowenbruch or one of Erlingen's other neighbours, but that made even less sense. The closer she got to the Antonine, the more questions arose. Would she find the answers she sought when she finally reached her destination, or would there simply be more questions?

Morning came far too early for Charlaine's liking. Danica slept well and talked non-stop through breakfast, sharing her plans for the fleet, a topic which demonstrated her enthusiasm for the role.

Charlaine tried to engage but found it challenging to give her full attention. It was as if a dark cloud gathered, one that would spread to encompass the entire Continent if left unchallenged. Neither physical nor spiritual in nature, it seemed to defy all reason yet hung over her head like a storm about to break. Every day, she felt it closing around her and knew with great certainty she and Danica were heading into the eye of it. Part of her wanted to turn away from the Antonine, to pretend none of it was real, but deep down, she knew her destiny was to face whatever was coming.

8

ULRICHEN

SUMMER 1106 SR

The change of scenery was remarkable as they crossed the bridge at Galmund. On the Erlingen side were open fields and well-travelled roads, while Ulrichen was anything but, with a road more like a goat track with the forest pressing in from both sides.

"Ah, yes," said Danica. "I'd forgotten how wild this place was. You don't suppose things have improved since then, do you?"

"In nine years? Not likely. It's always been a poor kingdom, and I doubt their king wishes to spend coins on seldom-used roads."

"It's one of the weaker Petty Kingdoms, isn't it?"

"Most certainly," replied Charlaine. "At least from a military point of view, but to my knowledge, they've never been invaded."

"Why is that?"

"For one thing, there's little of value save for harsh terrain."

"And for a second?"

"The Kings of Ulrichen have always taken pains to avoid getting embroiled in politics, at least with those outside their borders. Although it's worked for them so far, it's left them behind in many ways."

"Such as?"

"Trade comes to mind first. If you recall our last visit, we saw very few people on the road. That sort of isolation makes folks wary of travellers."

"Yes, I remember. Just as I remember there were very few cities of any size. Still, no one was rude to us or hostile, for that matter. Do the Cunars maintain a presence here?"

"I haven't the faintest idea. I don't recall a commandery in the capital, not that we spent much time there."

"You know," said Danica, "travelling through Ulrichen will put us close to Hadenfeld. We could stop off and visit if you like?"

"No. On the day I left, I promised I would never return. Besides, you need a lesson in geography. You're thinking of Ardosa, not Ulrichen."

"But we are going through Ardosa, aren't we?"

"We are," replied Charlaine, "but the eastern extents of Hadenfeld are nothing but wilderness. If you were heading to Harlingen, the capital, it's almost as far as going back to Rudor."

"I had no idea Hadenfeld was so large."

"Some say it's one of the largest Petty Kingdoms, although that doesn't account for the thick forest occupying the east. Take that away, and you've got a kingdom similar in size to Erlingen."

"Yet its reputation is that of a great power."

"Its army used to be the envy of the Petty Kingdoms, but that reputation has fallen off in recent years, the result of not one, but two civil wars."

"But now it has an accomplished military commander as king."

"It does," replied Charlaine, "but ruling a kingdom isn't the same as leading an army."

"You don't believe Ludwig is up to the challenge?"

"Oh, he'll manage well enough. Something tells me his queen will be the key to his success."

"Charlotte, isn't it?"

"You know full well it is. She's the daughter of the Baron of Blunden in Reinwick."

"I could hardly forget that. The wedding was quite the spectacle. You'll recall I sailed them part of the way home."

"Oh, yes. I'd forgotten about that. That was, what? Seven years ago?"

"Close. Six and a half, give or take a month. It's strange how you two keep crossing paths."

"Crossing paths? We've only met once since I left Hadenfeld."

"True, but you've remained in contact thanks to the smiths guild, and your warning about the Stormwinds appears to have worked to his advantage, not to mention what we learned about the Sartellians. I'm beginning to wonder if all mages should be considered suspect."

"Careful with that line of thinking," said Charlaine. "Orlina Day is a mage, as was Gwalinor."

"I concede the point. It feels like we run across a disproportionate number of spellcasters with their own agenda everywhere we go."

"You could say the same about Humans in general, especially when dealing with the courts of the Petty Kingdoms."

"So you're suggesting politics is the culprit rather than Human nature?"

"Power and influence are like the candle that draws the moth."

Danica laughed. "Now you're comparing the wealthy and powerful to insects. I don't know if I'll ever get that image out of my head! You're right, though. Power draws people to its flame."

"It does, and many have been burned by their desire for power."

"Wise words. I think one day they will make you a Saint."

"Now you're just being ridiculous."

"Am I? Others might not agree. Look at all you've accomplished."

"I could say the same for you. Perhaps one day, folks will gather to worship Saint Danica?"

"I don't think I'd like that."

"Nor would I, so let's not mention the subject again."

"I must say I admire your ability to remain humble. Others achieve promotions and let it go to their heads, but you've remained true to your beliefs."

"You're referring to Temple Commander Nina?"

"I am," replied Danica. "I wonder what she's up to these days? Last we heard, she was off to a new position in the Antonine. You don't suppose she's still there? Could she have something to do with this summons?"

"Anything's possible, but she always impressed me as someone more concerned with her own interests than those of others. She and I never got along, but I hold no ill feelings towards her."

"I wish I felt the same, but I always saw her as incompetent back in Ilea, and nothing in Arnsfeld changed my opinion."

"You should be more charitable," suggested Charlaine. "She may have her faults, but never plotted against the order like Hjordis did."

"I suppose that's true, but it doesn't necessarily make her a good commander."

"And what makes a good commander?"

"Let's see..." replied Danica. "First and foremost, a person must care about the people under their command while being disciplined enough not to show favouritism. Giselle was like that, even though she was only a Temple Captain. I've always wondered why they didn't make her a commander; she definitely had the skills for it."

"A cloud hung over her career thanks to the unfounded accusations of Sister Wilhemina."

"True, but she was cleared of that while we were still in Ilea. She must be a Temple Commander by now."

"If she is, I've had no word of it. Then again, we've been on the border with Halvaria, where news travels slowly. We must also face the possibility of someone actively working to isolate us."

"To what purpose? Ever since you arrived in Arnsfeld, we've been busy keeping the empire at bay, not involving ourselves in the affairs of the Petty Kingdoms."

"I wonder if someone learned about my letters to Ludwig?"

"Those were all sealed by a phoenix ring," said Danica, "unless you believe the smiths guild is responsible for leaking information?"

"No. I trust them," replied Charlaine, "but we don't know how many people on Ludwig's end have access to the contents of those letters. We also need to consider he's a king now and, therefore, must see to the welfare of his realm, which could mean informing others why he doesn't want the Stormwinds or Sartellians at his court."

"And you think that might have reached those in the Antonine who work against us?"

"Precisely."

"It all makes perfect sense when you look at it like that, but what can we do?"

"I'm not certain we can do anything but be prepared for trouble once we get there. We don't know who is responsible or their ultimate goal."

"Could it be a power grab?" asked Danica. "You said yourself that power was like a candle, and the Antonine would make for a very large flame."

"You may have the right of it. The problem is, we have no idea how far these people are willing to go. Take the Cunars, for example. Is every member aware of the plotting or just a few?"

"I'd have a hard time believing they're all involved."

"As would I," replied Charlaine, "but the order stresses obedience to one's superiors. It'd only take a group of senior officers to issue the right commands, and they'd possess an instant army capable of enforcing their will." She shook her head. "All this speculation is getting to me. Let's change the subject, shall we, or I'll be seeing conspiracies everywhere."

"I understand," said Danica, watching the road ahead. "If I recall, we're getting close to a roadside inn."

"How can you tell?"

Danica pointed. "I remember that from our last trip."

Charlaine turned, noticing a tree split by lightning. One side soldiered on while the other lay on the ground rotting. She was suddenly struck by the thought it was a sign. Was the tree symbolic of the Church and the rift threatening to destroy it? If so, was she destined to be on the side that flourished or died?

Stormcloud slowed suddenly, her ears picking up on something her rider didn't.

Charlaine was instantly on the alert. "Danica, something's—" Her words were cut off as a trio of horsemen burst from the woods. Charlaine barely had time to draw her sword before the attackers were amongst them, leaving the Temple Knights fighting for their lives. She parried a blow with her left gauntlet, countering with a strike that landed on her opponent's leg, but his plate armour prevented it from doing any harm.

He retaliated with a flurry of blows with a great strength behind them, and Charlaine, unable to draw her shield, was forced to spend all her time parrying to avoid damage. She wanted to check on Danica, but her foe demanded her full attention, his next attack wedging between her pauldron and gorget. The weapon ripped from the man's grip when she twisted, and then she drove her sword across the fellow's gauntlet, the tip digging into the mail beneath. It wasn't a deep cut, yet her opponent pulled back, spurring his horse up the road.

Free from the assault, she turned to see how Danica fared. Blood spattered the admiral's chest plate, but her opponent had fled, much like Charlaine's. "Where's the third?" Charlaine called out.

"He ran away as soon as the fighting started. I imagine he's halfway to Galmund by now." Danica paused to catch her breath. "I exaggerate, but he's well out of sight." She looked the other way. "Do you think those other two will trouble us anymore?"

"I nicked my opponent—you?"

"I managed to jam one of my daggers into his knee joint, which I doubt he's happy about. Who were those people? They certainly didn't dress like typical bandits."

"Let's find out, shall we?" Charlaine dismounted and bent down to retrieve the discarded sword.

"What have you there?"

"I was lucky during the fight, and this sword got caught in my armour. My attacker abandoned it when he fled."

"Will that tell us who he was?"

"No, but it'll at least give us a clue to his identity."

"How?"

Charlaine remained silent as she examined the sword, swinging it around experimentally, then turned to regard her closest friend. "This is well-balanced, yet not overly expensive."

"How does that help us?"

"I'd surmise that whoever carried it was either a mercenary or a knight."

"That fits their description," said Danica. "They wore plate armour, although they bore no surcoats."

"Yes. A curious thing, don't you think? Most knights want others to learn of their deeds. That seems to indicate they knew we were coming."

"They could have fallen on hard times. Perhaps they hoped to waylay some rich merchant?"

"We've talked about this," said Charlaine. "These roads see little traffic. If they were after a merchant, why not ride to Erlingen, where they'd have a better chance of finding someone with coins? What did you make of their fighting style?"

"Pretty basic. Their blows had a lot of strength but lacked finesse."

"Did you find their technique similar to ours?"

"Now that you mention it, yes. You don't think they're Cunars?"

"There can't be much doubt, can there? We know they fear us getting to the Antonine, and what better way to stop us than murder on a deserted road?"

"That makes sense," said Danica. "It also explains why one rode back up the road to Galmund. He needed to report our presence to someone."

"Yes, but why? To tell them we're dead or to ask for more knights to track us down."

"Look on the bright side. They're not wearing their colours, which indicates they're still trying to hide their involvement in whatever this is."

Charlaine tossed the sword aside.

The move surprised Danica. "Don't you want to keep that? The maker's mark would likely tie it to the Cunars."

"No. If we show up at the Antonine and begin making accusations, it'll tip off someone that we know Temple Knights attacked us. Better to report we were set upon by ruffians and managed to fight them off."

"But they tried to kill us!"

"Yes, they did," replied Charlaine, then exhaled loudly. "I'm sorry. You were as much a target as I; you should have a say in how we proceed. Shall I retrieve the sword?"

"No. You're right. Showing up and revealing what we believe happened would give away how much we know. We'll need to think this over carefully. No one in their right mind will believe a band of thugs wore plate armour."

"Then we'll describe it as a group of disgruntled knights trying to prove themselves."

"By attacking Temple Knights?"

"We could always say we weren't wearing our tabards."

"Or we could just not tell anybody."

"That works." Charlaine climbed back into the saddle, rubbing Stormcloud between the ears. "You've done very well today," she said. "We're lucky to have you."

. . .

They continued, soon coming across the Hopping Frog, a roadside inn that had seen better days. The faded wooden placard hung from only one chain rather than the two it was designed for, but the place still held signs of life as the sounds of folks chattering away inside spilled out.

Charlaine dismounted, tying Stormcloud off to a nearby tree. "We'll have something to eat before we continue, but keep your eyes out for those knights. I don't want to be surprised a second time."

Danica nodded, following her into a small room, barely twice the size of Charlaine's old office, yet they'd somehow crammed in dozens of individuals. Thankfully, none wore plate armour, so the two Temple Knights manoeuvred their way through to a spot at the bar.

A grey-haired woman in a dirty apron appeared on the other side. "What can I get you?"

"Two ales," replied Charlaine. "Are you serving any food?"

"Aye, but I'm afraid the pottage is done for. There's some bread and porridge if you like."

"That would be fine. Thank you."

She disappeared into a back room, presumably the kitchen.

"This place is busier than I remember," said Danica. "I wonder what's up?"

Charlaine waited for the barkeep to return, then tossed a coin on the counter. "This smells good." She looked around the room. "Is this a celebration of some kind?"

"Celebration? No, it's the news. Word doesn't travel to these parts often, but when it does, everyone gathers."

"And what, might I ask, has them so animated?"

"War. They say our southern neighbour has fallen into fighting."

"Against whom?"

The barkeep shrugged. "Can't rightly say, and I'd bet everyone in this room has a different opinion on what it means."

"Can you be a little more specific? What, precisely, was reported?"

"A merchant passed through here on his way to Erlingen last night. Said Ardosa was going to war."

"With whom?"

"He didn't rightly say, but he was in an awful hurry to get clear of the place." She stared up at the ceiling momentarily. "No. That's not quite right. He did say something… Now, what was it? Oh yes. He said everyone was worried about an invasion."

Charlaine turned to Danica. "What do you know about Ardosa's neighbours?"

"You mean aside from Ulrichen? Galoran lies southwest, Menzen to the south, and there's Hadenfeld, but you said there was nothing in the eastern reaches of that kingdom. Another lies to the northeast, but I can't recall its name."

"Parzen," offered the barkeep. "It lies to our east."

"What do you know about the place?" asked Danica.

"Not much. We tend to keep to ourselves, as do they, supposedly. I'd be astonished if they showed any interest in Ardosa."

"Why is that?"

"The same river that separates them from us continues along the eastern border of Ardosa." She halted, looking at both of them as if the answer was obvious.

"And?" prompted Danica.

"Well, it's a wide river, isn't it? Something like that would be easy to defend."

"Fair enough. That leaves only Galoran or Menzen."

"Yes," said Charlaine. "Which puts us in a difficult position. It appears to reach the Antonine, we must ride straight through a kingdom at war!"

9

A KINGDOM AT WAR

SUMMER 1106 SR

It was as if a fresh breeze had sprung up to lift their spirits as they crossed the stone bridge leading into Ardosa, but an approaching group of mounted warriors soon spoiled the effect. Charlaine was immediately wary, for they'd already been accosted by Temple Knights. Were these more assailants sent to prevent them from reaching their goal?

She relaxed as the group neared, for these men wore simple mail instead of plate armour, with surcoats bearing a coat of arms, unlikely garb for bandits who wished to remain anonymous.

"Greetings, Sisters," called out their spokesman. He slowed his mount, halting five paces away. "What brings you to Ardosa?"

"We are on our way to Regensbach," replied Charlaine, "to visit the Antonine."

"Might I trouble you to identify yourselves?"

"I could ask the same of you."

He smiled, his affectation appearing sincere. "My apologies, Sister. I am Captain Reiser of the Royal Horse. We've had some trouble on the border of late and are on the lookout for enemy activity. Not that we suspect a pair of Temple Knights as such, but my orders are to be thorough."

"I am Temple Commander Charlaine, and this is Temple Captain Danica of the Order of Saint Agnes. You say you've had troubles on the border. Can you be more specific?"

"I don't know the details, but we've been informed Galoran is preparing to invade. We fear war will soon be upon us."

"Galoran? That's unfortunate, as we need to pass through there."

"It'd be far safer for you to head south through Menzen."

"Yet we must still journey through, even if the kingdom is at war. Is there no hope for a peaceful conclusion to the situation?"

"As I said, I don't know the specifics. If you visited His Majesty's court, you might be able to intervene on behalf of the Church. I'm sure he would welcome someone of your stature."

"I wasn't aware you knew my background."

"I don't. I merely assumed that as a Temple Commander, you are a senior officer of your order."

"Have you no Temple Knights in Ardosa?"

"Not since those of Saint Cunar abandoned us, no. Some suggest their leaving led to the current situation with Galoran."

"How so?" asked Charlaine.

"Ardosa is a small kingdom with a suitably modest army to protect it. The presence of a company of Temple Knights helped act as a deterrent to those interested in claiming our lands."

"That particular order strictly adheres to the rules of non-intervention. Had you gone to war, they would have avoided getting involved."

"Perhaps," replied Captain Reiser, "but we had no such trouble while they were present. Now that they are gone, we face the prospect of invasion."

"Where would I find your king?" asked Charlaine.

"His Majesty, King Jaroslav, is currently in residence at the Royal Palace in Zeinhoffen, or at least he was, last I heard. I suppose there's always the possibility the army has already marched. Shall I dispatch a man to guide you there?"

"Is it difficult to find?"

"No," said Reiser. "This road leads straight to it."

"How far?"

"Three days, perhaps two if your horses are up to it."

"Then we shall find it ourselves. I wouldn't like to deprive you of your men when the enemy may be causing trouble."

"I need to give you a writ, however."

"A writ?" said Danica. "To what end?"

"To allow you safe passage on the road. We are in a state of war, and you'll likely run into further patrols. A note from me will save you much time and trouble."

"Thank you," said Charlaine. "That would be most appreciated."

Captain Reiser called over one of his men, who produced a scroll case. "Shall I sign one document for the two of you, or do you prefer individual writs?"

"One will do as we're travelling together."

They waited silently as he scribbled their names and handed over the document. "There you go. All neat and proper."

"Thank you, Captain. You've been most accommodating."

"It was my honour, Commander. My best wishes for a peaceful trip."

Charlaine nodded, then nudged Stormcloud onward.

Danica waited until they were well out of earshot before saying anything. "We're getting involved, aren't we?"

"Have we any choice in the matter? We both took vows to protect women, and a war would result in the deaths of hundreds. It is to be avoided at all costs."

"Do you really believe we can prevent a war?"

"We won't know till we try. The first step will be to discover the cause of this conflict. Then, we must strive to find a solution."

"Could this be the work of the empire?"

"It's hard to say," replied Charlaine. "Ardosa is not a large kingdom by any means. At first glance, it makes no sense for them to plunge it into war."

"Ah, but you're forgetting about all the alliances that permeate the Petty Kingdoms. This conflict might be small, but it could develop into a much larger conflict if it triggers their allies to march."

"That's true, which makes it all the more important that we get to the root of it as soon as possible."

"And if we find out someone is behind it?"

"Then we do whatever we can to expose the plot."

Zeinhoffen was a smaller capital than Lidenbach, yet somehow it appeared busier. They frequently had to alter course or risk running into people as they progressed through the streets. The townsfolk were a stubborn lot, refusing to move despite the presence of the temple horses. They ended up leading their mounts instead of riding them, the better to avoid injuring anyone.

Charlaine stopped to take in the view of the building now standing before them. Compared to the Ducal Palace in Reinwick, this was smaller, but what it lacked in size it more than made up for in opulence.

Two massive stone staircases twisted up on either side of the front of the white stone building, supported by half columns with some of the finest stonework Charlaine had ever seen. The green-tinged copper roof gave the place an ethereal beauty.

"Marvellous, isn't it?" said Danica. "I imagine an Elf designed it."

"I'm not so certain about that, but it is spectacular. I wonder how old it is?"

"Old enough for the roof to turn green, although that's only a couple decades at most. The workmanship, however, is extraordinary. It must have cost a bundle."

"Unfortunately," replied Charlaine. "Imagine how much good those coins could have done feeding the poor. Sometimes, I wonder if the ruling classes should be forced to live in poverty for a few years so they'd better understand their subjects."

"Ardosa is, by all accounts, a prosperous realm."

"Prosperous for merchants and nobles, but I have my doubts about the rest." Charlaine nodded towards a woman begging in the street. Shortly after a passerby dropped a coin into her hands, she looked over her shoulder and suddenly rose, scrambling down an alleyway.

"What was that all about?" asked Charlaine.

Moments later, six armed warriors entered from a side street with a gaggle of seven young men following. Townsfolk fled as they approached, and Charlaine struggled to determine why.

A second group of men edged out of another alley, forced back by more soldiers. The first six warriors moved in, and then arguments broke out.

"I've seen this before," said Danica. "They're rounding up men for service in the army. They do the same thing in Abelard from time to time. Last year, they grabbed a crew member from the *Fearless* by mistake, and I had to plead with the king's representative to let him leave."

"And how did that go?"

"We got him back, but only after paying a bribe to the local magistrate. I say bribe, but officially, it was an administrative fee."

"If they're forcing people into the army, the situation must be dire. Come on. We'd best get inside and find His Majesty."

As they approached the closed palace gates, they were met by a trio of warriors wearing mail, much as Captain Reiser had, but their surcoats were of finer material.

"Ah," said Charlaine. "This must be the king's personal guard, a common sight amongst the Petty Kingdoms."

"You there," came the challenge. "What's your business here?"

"We're Temple Knights, here to see His Majesty, the King. I bear a writ signed by one of his captains." Charlaine brandished the document.

The guard moved closer, putting his hand through the bars to retrieve the writ. Charlaine handed it over, waiting as he perused its contents.

"You've come at an auspicious time, Commander. King Jaroslav is inside, meeting with his ministers. I shall bring you to him." He called to one of his comrades to unlock the gate and then to another to take their horses. He led them up the right-hand staircase to a long, wide balcony where a group stood outside the door.

The guard paused momentarily, scanning the area before making straight for one individual. "Lord Gerrin, might I have a word?"

The gentleman turned, his hair snow-white against his dark skin. "What do we have here?" He struggled to focus, and then his eyes went wide. "Temple Knights in Zeinhoffen? How unusual."

"This is Temple Commander Charlaine, my lord, and Temple Captain Danica. They wish to speak with His Majesty. I thought they best see you first."

"You've done well, Edun. You may return to your post."

The fellow bowed. "Of course, my lord."

Lord Gerrin watched the guard descend the stairs, then turned to the newcomers. "I must say, it's not very often we get visitors here, particularly Temple Knights. I was under the impression the Church had abandoned us."

"Only the Temple Knights of Saint Cunar," replied Charlaine. "The rest of the Church values its worshippers."

"I imagine they do, considering the size of our donations, but that is another matter. Now, as to the king, he is a busy fellow these days. Might you give me some idea of what you wish to see him about?"

"We are here to help in any way we can," offered Charlaine. "We were headed to the Antonine when we ran into a king's officer who informed us that war is on your doorstep."

"It is, and from Galoran, of all places, but it's unheard of for the Church to take an interest in such things."

"Are you familiar with the recent events in Arnsfeld?"

"You mean the attempted invasion? Of course. It's the talk of the Petty Kingdoms."

"What do you know about it?"

"There was a battle where the king defeated the invaders. A great victory for the Continent, wouldn't you say?"

"Would it surprise you to learn that Temple Knights participated in the fighting?"

"It would, indeed. I was under the impression they didn't interfere in secular matters."

"We do now, providing the cause is just."

"I see," said Lord Gerrin. "Well, I must say that changes things considerably."

"Will His Majesty agree to speak with us?"

"I can find out, but I'm not certain what you're hoping to accomplish unless you've brought a company of knights with you?"

"I'm afraid it's only the two of us," replied Charlaine, "but this isn't the first time we've dealt with the possibility of war."

"Your presence will be welcomed, if only for spiritual support."

"Might I enquire about the cause of this conflict?"

"There've been numerous border incidents," replied the noble. "It all started this spring, just after the thaw."

"Are they making demands—ceding of territory, for example?"

"Not that I know of. However, our agents report that King Ingmar, their ruler, has called for their barons to assemble their forces in the capital, so it won't be long before they march for the border. Who knows, they may already be on the way."

"Yet they've made no demands?" said Charlaine. "I find that difficult to believe."

"You have my word on it, but if you don't trust me, perhaps another can convince you." He turned to the others. "Yevani. Come over here, will you? There are some people I want you to meet."

A middle-aged man broke off from the crowd and approached, his nearly clean-shaven face sporting a moustache that drooped down at the sides of his mouth. When his eyes met those of Charlaine, they burned with an intensity she found disquieting.

"Greetings," he said, his voice betraying an accent Charlaine couldn't place. "To what do we owe the pleasure?"

"We are here seeking an audience with the king."

Yevani let out a sigh. "As are all of us, but I'm afraid His Majesty is a busy man. He has much to occupy his mind, what with the border and everything."

"That's precisely why we're here."

"And you are?"

"My apologies," said Gerrin. "In my rush to invite you over, I forgot to introduce you. This is Temple Commander Charlaine and her fellow sister, Captain Danica."

"That's Temple Captain Danica," corrected Charlaine. Yevani kept his eyes glued on her. "Do I know you, my lord?"

"No," he replied, "but I know you, or rather, I know OF you. You've made a name for yourself."

"In what way?"

"I understand modesty is a trait your order values, but can you tell me you aren't proud of your achievements in Reinwick? Your order certainly was, hence your promotion to Temple Commander."

"You have the advantage of me," said Charlaine. "I know so little of you."

The fellow bowed. "What you see is precisely what you get."

"Might I ask what you do, my lord?"

"Why, I advise, like everyone else here. Of course, we're not above receiving gifts in exchange for our service to the Crown; it's how things are done in these parts. How about yourself? Have you received anything due to your service to the order?"

"The only gift I required was the knowledge that I'd protected others."

"Said like a true Saint." He held up his hands. "Sorry. I mean no disrespect to your religion."

"My religion?" replied Charlaine. "Are you a worshipper of Tauril or Akosia, perhaps?"

"The old Gods? Saints, no." He grinned. "There I go again, condemning my soul to spend an eternity in the Underworld. I hope you'll forgive me the jest, but court life can be dull on occasion."

"Except when a war is brewing?"

"Ah, yes. It has kept us busy these last few weeks." He turned back to Lord Gerrin. "What do you intend to do with them?"

"I was going to speak with His Majesty to find out if he's willing to meet with them. I was hoping you'd look after them during my absence?"

"I would be delighted."

"Good. Then it's settled." Gerrin bowed. "Now, if you will excuse me, I'll see what I can arrange." Without another word, he passed through the crowd and into the palace.

"Don't worry," said Yevani. "If anyone can arrange a visit with the king, it's Lord Gerrin."

"Know him well, do you?" asked Charlaine.

"Who, Gerrin? We've been colleagues for years."

"And what, might I ask, is his position?"

"He's the Baron of Rothay, one of our southern regions. Admittedly, it's not large compared to some of the baronies of the Petty Kingdoms, but he does well for himself."

"What precisely do you advise the king on, my lord?"

"Trade, politics, war: anything that strikes His Majesty's fancy."

"Then you must be familiar with the situation regarding Galoran?"

"Yes. Nasty business, that. It seems King Ingmar wants to conquer us."

"Why?" asked Danica.

"I beg your pardon?"

"It's a simple enough question. Galoran is, from what I understand, a prosperous realm. Why do they covet Ardosa?"

"Why does anyone want to conquer their neighbour? Greed, power, perhaps some imagined slight to his character? It isn't the 'why' that matters; it's our response."

A servant appeared bearing a silver tray holding a sealed note. "Message for you, my lord."

Yevani snatched it up, broke open the seal and perused its contents.

"Not bad news, I hope?" said Charlaine.

"No. Simply a routine matter." He looked at the servant. "Fetch us some wine, would you? Perhaps the red?" He directed this last comment at Charlaine, but she was too distracted to reply, for the letter His Lordship held had his full name written on the outside—Yevani Sartellian.

10

A MATTER OF DIPLOMACY
SUMMER 1106 SR

Lord Gerrin returned to inform them that King Jaroslav would meet with them but was presently busy with affairs of state. He conducted them to a room and asked them to wait. Charlaine sat quietly, too astounded with her discovery to speak.

"You seem pensive," said Danica. "Something on your mind?"

"As a matter of fact, there is. What did you make of Yevani?"

"He seemed knowledgeable."

"He's a Sartellian."

"Are you certain?"

"I am. I saw his name on that note he received."

"That can only mean one thing," said Danica. "He's up to no good."

"Not all the Sartellians at court across the Petty Kingdoms are plotting."

"Perhaps, but this kingdom is about to go to war. I don't see that as a coincidence. Do you?"

"No," said Charlaine, "but I'm still struggling with why."

"It's like I suggested earlier, an attempt to widen the war."

"I'm not convinced that's it. There's more going on here; I just can't figure out what it is."

"Perhaps the king will have an idea, assuming we ever meet him."

"I doubt he'd make us wait if he didn't intend to speak with us."

"How do you want to proceed?" asked Danica. "Do we reveal the possible treachery of Yevani Sartellian or pretend we don't know anything?"

"The latter. If we start by accusing one of his advisors, he'll likely turn against us."

"Then how do we convince him to stop this war?"

"I can't tell you till I learn more about what's happening. We know next to nothing about the circumstances involved, and I doubt Yevani would reveal his true motives for being at court."

"This will require a lot of digging. I'm beginning to think I would've been better off remaining at sea."

"And miss all this excitement?" replied Charlaine. "We have an opportunity to make a meaningful change here and have the advantage for once. Admittedly, it's small, but I'll take whatever I can get."

"You don't suppose Ardosa is responsible, do you? We only have the word of two of the king's advisors to support the accusation that Galoran started it."

"You raise a good point. We need some way to corroborate their story. Unfortunately, we can't do that, sitting here, waiting for the king."

"Are you suggesting we abandon the attempt to see His Majesty?"

"No. If we did, we'd likely never get another chance. We'll have to wait here until he finally summons us. After that, though, let's see what we can do about learning the truth."

"Perhaps you can get it out of the king?" suggested Danica.

"That largely depends on him. Other than his name, I know nothing about him. You?"

"Don't look at me. I spend almost all my time at sea, not exactly where you run into people from the heart of the Petty Kingdoms." She wandered over to a table with a few bottles on it. She picked one up and examined the label. "It's not all bad. They say the wine here is some of the best in the Continent. Look at this. Do you have any idea what it's worth?"

"No, I don't, but I have this feeling you're about to tell me."

"Fifty crowns."

"Is that a lot?" asked Charlaine. "I've never been one for fancy wines."

"You drank enough of it in Ilea."

"We all did. It's more common than water down there. No, these days, I prefer ale."

"You're revealing your upbringing," said Danica. "Not that there's anything wrong with that, but after spending all that time at court, I figured you would've developed a taste for finer things." She paused a moment. "What was I thinking? Of course you wouldn't. You're a woman of modest tastes."

"Except in my friends; they're my real treasure."

The door opened to a stiff-looking servant garbed in an elaborately braided surcoat. "His Majesty will see you now." He stepped to one side, allowing them to pass.

He led them to a long, narrow room that looked more like an extra-wide hallway. Its floor consisted of alternating black-and-white squares, so highly polished they were almost mirrors.

At the far end stood King Jaroslav, a tall man with thinning, mostly grey hair and a wispy beard that had seen better days. His wrinkled and ill-fitting clothes suggested he'd just woken up. Beside him were Yevani Sartellian and Lord Gerrin, their eyes boring into the approaching Temple Knights.

"Ah, there you are, Commander," said the baron. "I was curious when you might put in an appearance. I trust you haven't been waiting long?"

Charlaine wanted to tell him he knew full well how long they'd been here, for he'd left them in that room. Rather than create a scene, she suppressed the urge, putting on her best courtly behaviour and bowing deeply. "Your Majesty, I am honoured to be in your presence."

The king smiled at her compliment. "How gracious of you to say so, Commander."

Lord Gerrin seized the opportunity to control the conversation. "Commander Charlaine is here because she's worried about our troubles with Galoran, Majesty."

"Is she, indeed? Well, I can't say I'm surprised, considering the enormity of the problem. It is at the topmost of my mind as well. What are your thoughts on the subject, Commander?"

Charlaine thought through several responses before finally speaking. "It has always been my belief that war should be avoided whenever possible."

"Yes, of course," replied the king, "but as Yevani is fond of saying, when push comes to shove, you mustn't back down. Doing so would be a sign of weakness."

"Might I ask what caused this enmity between your two realms, Majesty?"

"My father's behaviour, if you can believe it. I won't get into details other than to say that my mother was supposed to marry someone else."

"And how long ago was this?"

King Jaroslav pursed his lips, thinking it over. "Half a century or so."

"That seems an awfully long time to bear a grudge," said Charlaine. "Has something more recent triggered this latest fear of war?"

"Oh yes, of course." The king glanced at Lord Gerrin before continuing. "They imposed a tribute on our merchants who enter their lands."

"He means an extra tax," added Yevani. "A common occurrence across the Petty Kingdoms but obscenely heavy-handed in this instance. Why, it's enough to drive our merchants into ruin. Trade will dry up, leaving the kingdom's coffers to suffer as a result."

"I see," said Charlaine. "Have you attempted to rectify the situation? Sending a diplomat to negotiate with their king, for example?"

"No," said Jaroslav. "According to my advisors, Ingmar is a tyrant, and such a move makes our kingdom appear weak."

"Perhaps their king is unaware of the hardship he is causing?"

"He is no fool! He knows what he's done."

"And what else do your advisors have to say?" Charlaine looked at Lord Gerrin.

"It's a deliberate incitement," replied the baron. "He's pushing us to see how far he can go. Their next step will be invasion if we don't respond with force."

"That seems a bit of a leap. Would it not make more sense to impose a tax of your own on those merchants of Galoran who bring their goods across the border?"

"We already pay too much for their goods," said Yevani. "Would you make the king's subjects even poorer by inflating prices?"

"Did I hear something about border incidents?"

"Yes," Gerrin confirmed. "There's been at least two clashes between our warriors and those of Galoran."

"And when you say clashes, I presume you mean fighting?"

"Yes, although there've been no deaths, thank the Saints."

"If I may make an observation," offered Danica. "Lord Gerrin stated there had been 'at least' two. What does that mean, precisely?"

"Ah, well," replied Yevani. "Only two were officially reported, but rumour has it there were other altercations not reported for one reason or another."

"How many more?"

"Dozens! They range from trading insults to actively attacking our men."

"And how many were wounded?"

"Only three," offered the baron, "but it could have easily been worse. We must thank our captains for keeping a close eye on their subordinates."

"While this is informative," said Charlaine, "I find it hard to believe Galoran started attacking your men for no good reason. Was there some diplomatic issue that preceded these events?"

"We did nothing to deserve this!" declared the king, his high-pitched voice revealing his frustration.

"And how long ago did they introduce this extra tax?"

"We caught wind of it a few months ago," said Yevani. "We thought at first it might be the work of guards taking it upon themselves to earn some extra coins, but it continued."

"You say you are not on good terms with Galoran and haven't been for decades. Is there a trusted third party who might intervene on your behalf? A representative from Parzen or Menzen, perhaps?"

"Have I not made myself clear?" said Jaroslav. "Much as I loathe the very idea, I must stand firm against the King of Galoran; to do otherwise makes me look weak! My advisors tell me that if Ingmar does not back down, I shall have no recourse but to assemble my army."

"Are you certain that's wise, Majesty?" asked Charlaine. "A war would kill many and might empty your coffers, particularly if it becomes a long, protracted affair."

Jaroslav's voice went even higher. "My army is more than capable of dealing with Galoran!" He turned to Lord Gerrin. "Tell them!"

"They are, indeed, Majesty," added the baron.

"That being the case," said Charlaine, "would it not be preferable to leverage the threat with some diplomacy?"

Her question appeared to catch King Jaroslav off guard. "Diplomacy? What are you suggesting?"

"Allow me to travel there on your behalf. I could use the threat of your army to force him to rescind the tax."

"I'm not certain that would be enough," said Yevani. "King Ingmar might back down for now, but what guarantee do we have he wouldn't turn around and launch an invasion?"

"Oh dear," said the king. "We can't have that." He scanned the room as if the very walls had ears, then leaned towards Charlaine and Danica. "Now that I think about it, how do I know you Temple Knights are not working for Ingmar?"

"I assure you," replied Charlaine, "that is not the case. Temple Captain Danica and I were on our way to the Antonine and happened to be passing through."

"So you would try to convince me this was nothing but a coincidence? You ask a lot."

"The Saints move in mysterious ways," said Danica. "It wouldn't be the first time we've found ourselves where we're needed most."

"Agreed," added Charlaine, "but we aren't here to take sides; we're offering our services to find a peaceful solution to this conflict."

Jaroslav knit his brows. "How do I know you won't join the other side once you're in Galoran?"

"I give you my word that we shall attempt no such thing."

"Easy to say, but how can you prove it?"

"Temple Knights take a vow to never lie. Are you accusing me of doing just that?"

"If I may say so, Majesty," interjected Lord Gerrin, "the word of a Temple Knight is considered sacred. It is impossible to believe they are telling anything other than the truth."

King Jaroslav cleared his throat. "I shall take them at their word, but I'm not happy about it. This conflict has nothing to do with the Church, and I dislike the idea of outsiders meddling in our affairs."

"If you don't trust us," said Danica, "then perhaps we can offer an alternative."

"What do you propose?"

"That Temple Commander Charlaine remain here in Zeinhoffen while I go to Galoran on your behalf."

"You would be willing to do that?"

"Yes, providing the commander agrees?"

"I have no objection," replied Charlaine, "although I still feel it would be better if I went and she stayed here."

"You're more important to the order," replied Danica. "We can't risk it."

"You're as important as I am. Without you, there is no Temple Fleet."

"There are plenty of others who can take on that burden should I meet with unfortunate circumstances."

"I don't know," said Yevani. "It sounds dangerous."

"I'm a Temple Captain of Saint Agnes," replied Danica. "Do you think King Ingmar wishes to incur the Church's wrath by killing me?"

"She's got a good point," offered Gerrin. "To kill a Temple Knight is not an insignificant act, considering the possible consequences."

"Those being?" asked Jaroslav.

"Excommunication," replied Charlaine. "The entire kingdom could be punished by them refusing to conduct services, or worse, withdrawing all their people."

"But wouldn't that affect the Church more? They'd lose a tremendous source of donations."

"That punishment is seldom handed down to an individual, let alone an entire kingdom. I can't imagine King Ingmar being so foolish as to murder a Temple Knight, but that doesn't preclude the possibility that other actors are at play here."

"Other actors?" said Jaroslav. "What in the name of the Saints are you talking about? Surely you're not suggesting another kingdom is trying to destroy us?" He looked around the room in fear, as if someone were battering at the palace gates as they spoke.

"Most borders are left unguarded except in times of war, Majesty. How is it possible your warriors are being attacked there?"

"I can answer that," said Yevani. "Our agents in Galoran warned us King

Ingmar was threatening to invade. We responded by posting men at the border to watch for their army."

"Agents?" said Charlaine. "Are you suggesting you have spies in the Galoran court?"

"Of course we employ spies," replied Yevani. "How else are we to watch our enemies?"

"Perhaps these agents of yours could be induced to provide more information?"

"That all takes time, which is the one luxury the king doesn't have. Before you came in, we were discussing mustering the army."

"That can still continue," suggested Lord Gerrin. "The Temple Captain can proceed into Galoran and attempt to convince Ingmar to abandon his thoughts of conquest. Meanwhile, Temple Commander Charlaine could assist us with the army's organization. After all, she has battle experience. Her Temple Knights were present at the empire's defeat, and we've now established her order forbids her to lie."

Jaroslav rubbed his hands together. "A marvellous idea. It will give our army a much-needed boost to our morale for a Holy warrior to be present, especially one of such high rank."

"I would urge caution, Majesty," said Yevani. "The appointment of an outsider, particularly a member of the Church, could produce unintended consequences."

"And what would those be?"

"Well, I..., er..., that is..."

"I think what he's trying to say," offered Gerrin, "is that it's dangerous for the Church to be seen taking sides. It also could invite their future interference in internal matters."

"Are you suggesting the Church would make demands of me?" said Jaroslav. "I can't be beholden to anyone. I am the king!"

"You wouldn't be," Charlaine assured him. "If Temple Captain Danica's attempts at a peaceful resolution fail, you would be no worse off than you are now." She recognized the look of concern on the king's face. "Might I ask the strength of your army?"

The king looked to Yevani for the answer. "We possess several companies of professional warriors," offered Yevani, "while the remainder of our forces are comprised of militia."

"Have you any cavalry?"

"Some, but we lack knights."

"It's not all bad news," added Gerrin. "Galoran is in a similar state. By my reckoning, our armies are roughly equal in strength."

"If invasion comes," said Charlaine, "is there a strategy in place to deal with it?"

"There is," offered Yevani. "The Royal Army marches east to the border along the only road that joins our two realms."

"You're suggesting you march your men up the road to meet the enemy?"

"We have no other choice," supplied the king. "For that matter, it's Galoran's only option as well. Does this mean you'll help us?"

"I will do what I can to prevent Galoran from invading," replied Charlaine, "and if that means helping you with your army, then so be it. I will stipulate, however, that I only agree to this if Temple Captain Danica is allowed to proceed to King Ingmar's court."

"I accept your condition." Jaroslav turned to Lord Gerrin. "This calls for a celebration, wouldn't you say?"

"Of course, Majesty. Shall I call for the servants?"

"If you would be so kind." He waited for the baron to summon someone, then shifted his gaze to his new guests. "Are Temple Knights permitted to drink?"

Danica struggled to keep a straight face. "Yes, Majesty."

"Excellent. Then you are invited as well. If you follow me, we'll head into the garden to enjoy this warm weather." With that, he left at such a brisk pace that Lord Gerrin struggled to keep up.

Charlaine waited, giving the king a chance to get out of earshot. "Is it just me, or is he acting strange?"

"Oh, he is. Did you notice how he kept looking around as if he expected someone to be listening?"

"I did, but is that him being careful, or is he convinced someone is hiding behind those walls?"

"He's in a difficult position," said Danica, "and I'm not certain his advisors have his best interests in mind. I shall have to be very careful when I go to Galoran."

11

GALORAN

SUMMER 1106 SR

Danica left Zeinhoffen early the following day, and although Ardosa was roughly half the size of Arnsfeld, it still took four days to cross the realm. The border was unmistakable, consisting of an arched stone bridge beneath which the waters of the Silver River roared. A small complement of King Jaroslav's soldiers guarded the western side, and as soon as they noticed her, they moved to block her way, their sergeant standing in front of his men.

"Halt!" he called out. "The border is closed."

"I am on a mission for King Jaroslav," replied Danica. She slowed her horse as she advanced, finally bringing her mount to a halt before the sergeant. She then pulled out the document, guaranteeing her safe passage. "This is my permission."

He took it, opening it to scan its contents. "How do I know this is real?"

"Do you doubt the word of a Temple Knight?"

"You travel in dangerous times, Sister. War will soon be upon us, and I cannot guarantee the roads will remain safe."

"I am travelling to Galoran," she replied, "and I doubt you have any say in whether the roads there are safe. Now, will you allow me to continue on the king's business, or must you waste more of my precious time?"

He handed back her document. "My apologies, Sister. I meant no ill will."

"Has there been any activity here of late?"

"We saw some movement on the other side but nothing of note."

"Movement?"

"The odd soldier or two, but none came within bow range."

"Strange," said Danica. "With the current situation, I'd have thought they'd guard their end of the bridge as you do yours."

The sergeant shrugged. "I cannot speak to their state of mind, Sister, merely relate what I've seen."

Danica was about to continue on her way, but something nagged at her. "What do you know about the recent incursions?"

"Incursions?"

"Yes. I understand there've been several incidents of violence here at the border."

"Not while I've been here. When did you say these incidents took place?"

"I didn't, but according to official reports, there's been at least two clashes."

"No man of Galoran has crossed the border under my watch."

"And how long have you been stationed here?" asked Danica.

"My men have been guarding this position for months."

"Is there another border crossing?"

"So far as I know, this is the only bridge."

"I would've thought there'd be more."

"The river is fast moving in these parts," replied the sergeant. "Were you to try swimming across, you'd soon be washed away. Are you certain you heard correctly?"

"Your men are on high alert, are they not?"

"They are. We've been warned to watch for any notable activity on the other side."

"And to what do you owe this increased vigilance?"

The sergeant took a bit to respond. "It is not my place to question the orders of a superior."

"You have a mind with which to think, do you not?"

"I do. I suppose I assumed there was some discontent at court. You know how kings are, arguing over things the rest of us don't understand."

"And you're willing to go to war over something you don't understand?"

The sergeant bristled. "I will not shirk my duty, if that's what you're implying."

"Not at all," replied Danica. "I'm merely trying to gauge the depth of your convictions. I cannot fault a man for his devotion to his duty; that's what makes the Temple Knights so effective."

"Apology accepted."

She was about to reply that it hadn't been an apology, merely an observation, but then thought better of it. "I thank you for the warning, Sergeant. I shall endeavour to keep my wits about me while travelling through Galoran."

"Saints be with you."

"And with you." She urged her horse into a canter across the bridge and continued along the road heading east, riding up a slight incline. Danica had faced battle numerous times, yet found the idea of dealing with a king by herself far more intimidating. Charlaine always had an easy way about herself when it came to others, which is what made her so effective as a Temple Commander. On the other hand, Danica felt awkward when she was alone with the nobility, something she must strive to overcome to succeed in her mission.

And what was her mission, exactly? Avert war, but how would she accomplish that? The more she mulled it over, the more she suspected the key to the entire situation was talking directly with the King of Galoran. He, alone, had the power to end this foolishness, but if he was being manipulated, an introduction might be difficult to arrange. Indeed, she herself might become a target once it became clear what her objective was.

A Sartellian was present at the court of Ardosa; would she find the same with King Ingmar, or would a Stormwind perform that role in Galoran? It suddenly struck her how little they knew about these two families of mages. Were other families involved in this grand conspiracy, or was she imagining things? Without Charlaine to talk it over with, her mind raced with all sorts of possibilities.

She topped the rise to more hills, which wasn't surprising, but the smoke trails she noticed far off to the east were. To her mind, it meant only one thing—an army. She spurred on her horse, eager to discover what lay in her future.

By the standards of the Petty Kingdoms, the Army of Galoran wasn't overly large, but seeing it spread out before her emphasized how real the threat of war was. Danica halted, estimating how many men were assembled. The vast majority were footmen, with a smattering of archers thrown in for good measure. Of cavalry, there were few, and if their armour was any indication, none appeared to be knights.

She moved closer, surprised no one took the time to challenge her. Only a few paid her any attention, and those who did nodded in respect, then continued about their business. She searched in amongst the tents, seeking anything to identify whoever was in charge.

"You there," called out a woman's voice.

Danica turned to see a young woman in an immaculate yellow dress, which was entirely out of place amongst the browns and tans of the Army of Galoran.

The woman came closer. "Who are you?"

"My name is Danica Meer, a Temple Captain of Saint Agnes."

"And what is your business here?"

She ignored the request. "In most lands, it's common to introduce oneself when meeting another."

The young woman hesitated. "My apologies. My name is Evenia. I am the aide of Elka Stormwind."

"A Stormwind, here?"

"Of course. Only the most influential courts employ members of the Stormwind line, and King Ingmar is one of our greatest patrons. Might I ask your reason for being in Galoran?"

"I am here to speak to the king on Church business." Danica caught her breath. Was it considered a lie when someone didn't tell the complete truth? She was, after all, doing the Church's bidding—trying to prevent a war, but that wasn't the whole story.

"What has the Church to do with the king?"

"I'm afraid I'm not in the habit of discussing Church matters with those I'm unfamiliar with. You say you serve Elka Stormwind?"

"I do. Shall I bring you to her?"

"If you would be so kind."

"You will have to walk." Evenia beckoned to a nearby soldier. "Oskar will take your horse."

Once Danica dismounted, the young woman led her towards the centre of the camp. "Mistress?" Evenia called out as they stopped at a tent like all the others. "A stranger has entered the encampment."

"A stranger?" came the reply, then an older woman with a touch of grey to her elaborately braided hair opened the tent flap. "Who do we have here?" she asked.

"Temple Captain Danica Meer," replied Evenia, "of the Order of Saint Agnes."

"I can see that," snapped Elka, glaring angrily at Danica. "What brings a Temple Knight here to Galoran?"

"My arrival amongst your army was purely by accident. I crossed the border intending to continue to Gessen, the capital."

"Your order has no commandery in Gessen."

"I never said it did, but Temple Knights often carry messages on behalf of the Church, and the lay sisters maintain a presence in most of the cities of the Petty Kingdoms."

"I must wonder at the import of messages when a Temple Captain carries them rather than a knight."

"None of us are too proud to carry out menial tasks."

"Where do you come from?"

"What business is that of yours?" asked Danica.

"I am here in the service of King Ingmar."

"I see no sign of a Royal Pavilion."

"His Majesty has yet to join us."

"Are you in the habit of intercepting Church couriers?"

"You wandered into the middle of an army camp," replied Elka. "I find that highly suspicious."

"Yet you chose to camp on the road to Gessen, or at least I assume you did. You certainly look as though you're in charge here."

"I assure you I am. Now, as to your presence, I must know more before I can release you."

"Release me? Am I to assume you've decided to detain a Temple Captain?"

"And if I have?"

"I applaud you. That's a brave decision, considering the possible ramifications."

"Are you threatening me?" demanded Elka. "Have you no idea who I am?"

"Oh, I know exactly who you are. You're a court mage in service to King Ingmar. How might he react to the news you've detained me?"

A red hue crept up Elka's neck, colouring her cheeks. "I am far more than a simple court mage."

"Perhaps," said Danica, "but interfering with Church business is not something to be taken lightly. Are you so confident of your relationship with His Majesty that you'd willingly put it to the test over something of this nature?"

"If I so wished, I could detain you, which would be the best course of action, yet I am obligated to carry out the king's wishes in his absence."

"Which would be?"

"To let you proceed on your way, unhindered."

"If you truly serve the king, then that is what you must do."

"Must?" said Elka. "You are in no position to make demands, Captain. For all I know, you've been sent here to spy on our numbers."

"When has a Temple Knight ever acted as a spy? We are sworn to speak the truth, hardly an oath one could keep under such circumstances."

"You make a good point. Then again, you might be posing as a Temple Captain to infiltrate King Ingmar's court."

"If that were my objective, I'd have a far easier time were I dressed as a Temple Knight instead of a captain."

"Ah, but a captain might win access to the king's ear."

"By that reasoning, why only a captain? Would I not have an even better chance dressed as a Temple Commander?"

"True, but that might attract an undo amount of interest."

"And a Temple Captain doesn't? Your very own actions suggest otherwise."

Elka smiled. "We are arguing in circles, each with our own logic. I like you, Captain. You aren't afraid to challenge me."

"Should I be?"

"We Stormwinds are a powerful family."

"I'm well aware of the influence your family wields," replied Danica, "but my order is sworn to serve the betterment of women. Not that it necessarily puts us in opposition, you understand, but you serve the king, while we try to help women, regardless of their societal status. You enjoy a life of privilege and are held in high regard by His Majesty, while others are not so fortunate."

Elka turned to her aide. "Fetch the Temple Captain's horse. She'll be leaving us."

"Thank you," said Danica.

"Do not make me regret my decision."

"I shall, in all things, honour my oath to my order. You have my word."

They waited in silence for Danica's horse. The warrior, Oskar, appeared and handed over the reins, then she climbed into the saddle.

"My apologies for the intrusion," Danica said, looking around. "I shall pray that whatever provoked the need for this assembly is resolved before it's too late." With that, she urged her mount towards the road, her course taking her through much of the camp.

She noted the warriors, along with their weapons and armour. Few were equipped with mail, suggesting they were more of a militia than professional fighters, yet by her estimation, there were almost a thousand. Was that enough to invade Ardosa, or was this part of some elaborate ruse? Were more men coming to swell their numbers? Perhaps the king was bringing his own private guards?

Elka Stormwind suggested King Ingmar was arriving soon, meaning Danica might be able to intercept him before he entered the camp. With that in mind, she picked up her pace.

Danica had been on the road for a day and a half when she spotted what could only be the King of Galoran sitting in an open-topped carriage, riders to the front and rear of the Royal Procession. He was accompanied by a bevy of presumably nobles, each with horses and their own guards. The assembly crept slowly towards her, making it easy for the footguards to keep up.

She halted on the road to let them approach her. King Ingmar appeared in good spirits, talking animatedly with a well-dressed man sitting across from him.

The king was of average build, with a neatly trimmed moustache and a clean-shaven chin, but his protruding jawline and forehead seemed far too big for the rest of his face, giving him an unusual appearance.

As they drew closer, she noticed something amiss, for the king's wrinkled face belied his age, while his hair remained a deep brown, suggesting he'd taken pains to give the appearance of youth. Two riders leading the way sped up, heading directly for her.

"Greetings," she called out. "I am Temple Captain Danica of the Order of Saint Agnes."

They slowed when they were within ten paces. "Captain," said the taller one, nodding a greeting. "King Ingmar is abroad this day. You must clear the road."

"Certainly." She trotted off to the side, but the two guards followed her. "Is there a problem?"

"We are merely doing our duty, Sister. The king has enemies who would see him slain."

"Does that include Temple Captains?"

The warrior's smile did not reach his eyes. "Not that we're aware of, but we must be vigilant."

"You take responsibilities seriously, but I assure you, I have only your king's best interests at heart."

Back on the road, the carriage drew to a halt. Danica couldn't make out any words, but she had drawn the king's attention, for he waved for his guards to come closer.

"Wait here," the tall one replied, then rode to the carriage. More words were exchanged, along with several glances in her direction.

Finally, after far too long, the guard returned. "His Majesty wishes to speak with you."

"I would be honoured."

"I must insist on taking your sword."

Danica handed it over, hilt first. She thought about surrendering her daggers, but he hadn't mentioned them, so she decided not to bring it up.

The guard escorted her to the carriage. "This is Temple Captain Danica, Majesty, of the Order of Saint Agnes."

"Good day to you—," replied the king.

"What my cousin is trying to say," interrupted the carriage's other occupant, "is welcome to Galoran. Might I enquire what brought you here?"

"Most assuredly," replied Danica. "I come here seeking His Majesty, King Ingmar."

"Then you have found him. What matters do you wish to speak with him about?"

"War," said Danica, "or rather the prevention of it."

12

JAROSLAV
SUMMER 1106 SR

Charlaine stopped in the doorway of the room when she noticed that King Jaroslav was in the midst of a discussion with a young woman.

"You must leave the governing of this realm to me, my dear." The king patted the woman's hand. "It is not something that you need concern yourself with."

"It is not the governing that concerns me, Father; it is your behaviour. You've dismissed so many of your closest confidantes, and spend your days alone in the Palace."

"Nonsense," said the king. "I am merely relying on the advice of those best suited to guide us through this crisis."

"They're only interested in furthering their own interests. Can't you see that?"

The king clenched his jaw. "I've heard quite enough from you, Carina. You may be my daughter, but that doesn't give you the right to criticize me."

"If Mother were here, she would say otherwise."

Jaroslav sighed. "Perhaps, but we'll never know. She's been gone for three years now, and it's time you realized your proper place."

Her voice rose. "Proper place, is it?" She pulled her hand away from her father's in frustration, but Charlaine noticed her fighting to regain control of her emotions. "What's happened to you, Father?" With that, Carina stood up and left the room through a door on the opposite side, taking great pains to keep her dignity.

King Jaroslav stared at her back as she departed, the look on his face heartbreaking. Charlaine waited, then knocked on the door frame.

He cleared his throat. "Sorry, Commander. I didn't see you there. What can I do for you?"

"You invited me to dine with you?"

"Oh, yes. Come, the rest are waiting for us."

"It is inevitable, Majesty." Yevani Sartellian carefully placed his goblet on the table, his meal now complete. "Had we not intercepted Ingmar's plans, we might have been caught unawares, but this information gives us the advantage."

"He is counselling war," insisted Lord Gerrin. "I understand the kingdom may be in danger of invasion, but to cross the border ourselves would be inviting calamity."

"The Army of Galoran is weak, my lord. We shall easily overcome it."

King Jaroslav turned to Charlaine, who, up until this point, had remained silent. "I don't know. What think you, Commander?"

"War should be avoided whenever possible."

"A wise sentiment, but my question to you is whether this warrants us risking an invasion of Galoran?"

"The evidence is overwhelming," insisted Yevani. "To ignore it would be unconscionable."

"I appreciate your thoughts on the matter," replied the king, "but I still wish to hear from the commander before we commit."

"You should explore all options," replied Charlaine. "Might I ask some particulars regarding the composition of your army?"

"By all means," replied Gerrin. "What would you like to know?"

"You mentioned earlier that the bulk of your forces are militia. Might I ask how many you have?"

"Enough to fill nine companies. They are, for the most part, equipped with axes or spears but lack any protection aside from shields and helmets."

"And your bowmen?"

"They number one hundred and sixty-two, although I'm afraid none bear crossbows."

"And they are unarmoured as well?"

"That is correct," replied the baron. "Not the best army to begin a campaign, I'll admit, but their hearts are in the right place."

"You forgot about the cavalry," said Yevani. "We have two full companies in mail, ready to take the fight to the enemy."

"That's right!" shouted Jaroslav with glee. "Then there's my personal retinue—close to two hundred mailed footmen who form the backbone of our army."

"According to my calculations," said Charlaine, "that gives you somewhere in the region of nine hundred men. Does that match your own estimate, Lord Gerrin?"

"Most definitely."

"It is considered practical to employ numbers at least equal to the enemy when invading another realm. Do you have any updates on their strength?"

"While we previously believed them to have an equal-size army, our latest intelligence reveals theirs to be smaller than ours," replied Yevani, "and slow to gather. If we marched immediately, we could catch them unawares."

"And what strategy would you employ?" asked Charlaine.

"Strategy?" said the baron. "There's no strategy required. From here, the only way into Galoran is over the bridge."

"Your only route of attack is a single bridge? That sounds a mite constricting to me."

"It can't be helped," replied Yevani. "The Silver River forms our border with Galoran and is otherwise impossible to cross."

"Yes," added the baron. "Naturally, we'd take pains to ensure we secured the bridge before crossing."

Charlaine took a breath to steady herself. These men had no concept of war yet were so eager to head into battle that they would rush in without proper preparation. "The bridge is key to this entire campaign, Majesty. Blindly charging in could result in a lack of success."

King Jaroslav knit his brows in consternation. "Oh dear," he said. "We can't have that. Might I ask why you think that?"

"If, as your advisors suggest, Galoran is preparing to march, would they not employ the same strategy? If the bridge is the only way to cross, then it stands to reason they will take steps to defend it."

"Yes, but my people tell me my warriors are superior!"

"With all due respect, Majesty, every ruler in the Petty Kingdoms believes their army is superior to their neighbours. Logic alone suggests they can't all be correct."

The king frowned. "What qualifies you to counter my advisors' assessment of my army?"

"I've seen my share of battles," replied Charlaine.

"Really? Where?"

"As a Temple Knight, I was at the Battle of Alantra. I was also in Reinwick when the empire tried to establish a foothold in a group of islands to the northeast."

"Impressive," said the mage, "but there's a big difference between fighting in a battle and commanding it."

Charlaine met his gaze. "As you well know, I commanded the Army of Arnsfeld when they defeated a Halvarian legion."

Yevani's mouth hung agape, unable to formulate a response.

The baron filled the silence. "I believe the Commander has proven her abilities to us, Yevani."

The king nodded enthusiastically. "Agreed. Might we prevail upon you to give us your impression of our army?"

"I believe I already have," she replied.

"In terms of numbers, yes, but I propose you inspect them yourself. Who better to judge their quality than one who's led an army to victory?"

"I am a Temple Knight. As such, I'm not supposed to become embroiled in secular matters."

"By your own words, you did in Arnsfeld."

"That was a matter of survival, Majesty."

"And this isn't? The empire may not be breathing down our necks, but a successful invasion by Galoran would tip the balance of power in the region."

The king made an excellent point. The Petty Kingdoms were a complex web of alliances and agreements; if one faction gained the advantage, it could lead to a Continent-wide war. To prevent the situation from blowing up, she must gain time for Danica to complete her mission, but how could she accomplish this task? The answer came to her as she met the king's gaze. "I shall be pleased to give my opinion," she said at last, "but it will take more than watching the men standing in the sun."

The king's eyebrow raised. "Meaning?"

"I need to see your warriors as they practice, Majesty. The better to assess their skill levels."

"That will take too long," said Yevani.

"I disagree," replied King Jaroslav. "I think it worth the delay. She may have suggestions about how to best utilize them."

"I agree," added Lord Gerrin. "Perhaps, afterwards, we can discuss strategy and tactics? I assume that still fits with your oath to avoid secular matters? After all, you wouldn't be leading them, merely giving us suggestions.

"I can agree to that," said Charlaine, "although I fear it's much too late to begin today."

"Nonsense," insisted the baron. "We have plenty of light left."

"Perhaps, but I am a Temple Commander of Saint Agnes and thus need time to pray."

"Oh yes. My apologies, Commander."

The king clapped his hands, absolutely giddy. "We'll have the men assemble first thing tomorrow morning for her inspection."

"No, Majesty," said Gerrin. "They should train tomorrow so the commander can give us an honest appraisal of their abilities."

"Yes, that's right. Sorry. In my excitement, I forgot."

Charlaine noticed the king acted confused, as though he was having trouble thinking clearly. "Are you well, Majesty?"

"Of course he's well," snapped Yevani, a little too quickly for Charlaine's liking. "What kind of question is that to ask a king? In any case, his health is not your concern."

"I am concerned for the well-being of all, Master Sartellian."

"That would be Master Yevani. Mages are not addressed by their surnames."

"Come now," said the king, with a bit of authority in his voice. "Surely we can forgive the commander her lack of etiquette. After all, she's a Temple Knight, not a courtier." At the look of disapproval from Yevani, his voice grew quieter. "L-l-let us allow the good commander some privacy so she may pray to her Saint. Shall we see you this evening at dinner?" He looked at Charlaine.

"Most definitely," she replied.

"Good. Come along, gentlemen. Wine awaits us in the parlour."

On her way back to her room, Charlaine discovered Princess Carina wringing her hands as she paced the hallway.

"Are you looking for me, Highness?"

"I am," replied the princess. "When I learned a Temple Commander of Saint Agnes was at court, it was as if my prayers had been answered. Will you help me?"

"With what?"

"I fear my father has been led astray."

"What leads you to that conclusion?"

"He has withdrawn from life and is rarely seen outside the walls of this palace."

"Was your father always this insulated?"

"Not at all. He used to host lavish dinners with all the nobles of the realm in attendance."

"When was the last such gathering?"

Carina paused, thinking through her answer. "Nearly two years ago, I think?"

"I see," said Charlaine. "Did this, by chance, coincide with the arrival of Master Yevani?"

"I'm… not certain. I shouldn't like to blame someone based on mere coincidence."

"Yet you have suspicions."

She nodded. "I'm told Master Yevani had been in Zeinhoffen for some time before he came to court."

"Might I ask who introduced him to your father?"

"I believe it was Lord Gerrin. You don't think the two of them are deliberately isolating my father, do you?"

"You have a keen mind," replied Charlaine, "but for your own sake, I suggest you abstain from mentioning your suspicions in the presence of others."

"You think them dangerous?"

"There is always an element of danger at a Royal Court, particularly when a war is brewing."

"So there's nothing I can do? My father is lost to me?"

"Have faith," said Charlaine. "Even the lost can eventually find their way home."

"Only if he can remember that's what he wants," replied Carina. "I fear he won't be able to find his way free."

"I sympathize with your plight, Princess, but there is little I can do unless you're asking for sanctuary?"

"Not yet, though it may come to that eventually. What should I do in the meantime?"

"I would have you do whatever you need to in order to remain safe."

"I won't abandon my father."

"Then watch and learn. The more we can discover about his situation, the more likely that an answer can be found."

Carina smoothed the front of her dress. "Thank you. You've been most helpful."

"I'm glad to have been of assistance. Saints be with you, Highness."

"And with you, Temple Commander."

Charlaine sat in her room, contemplating her situation. She had inspected the men of Ardosa three days ago, but she was deeply troubled. King Jaroslav had behaved almost paranoid during their first introduction, and during subsequent interactions, he'd been forgetful, which only confirmed Carina's observations. Was something else at play here? It wasn't uncommon for rulers to suffer bouts of illness, but these symptoms seemed an odd combination.

Then there was Yevani, who was definitely up to something. Was he trying to inflame a war between Ardosa and Galoran? Neither was a kingdom of much significance, yet they were both near to the Antonine. A war here could easily spill across the border into Regensbach, forcing the Church to defend itself.

On her previous trip to the Antonine, they'd uncovered a rot within their own order. Could this rot have spread? The Temple Knights were the sworn enemies of Halvaria; would it not be in the empire's best interests to see them contained? A war in the middle of the Petty Kingdoms would achieve that and give the empire a victory after their disastrous defeat in Arnsfeld. The more she mulled it over, the more it made sense.

A knock on her door interrupted her thoughts. "Who is it?" she called out.

"Lord Karstan Bach," came the reply. "You don't know me, but I'm the Baron of Mitterling."

She opened the door to a middle-aged man of average height, his eyes suggesting a keen intelligence. "What can I do for you?" she asked.

"I wondered if we might have a quick word?"

She threw the door wide open. "Come in and take a seat. I'd offer you something to drink, but I'm afraid there's not much to choose from."

"I'm fine, thank you. I heard a Temple Commander had reached our court, but I never imagined it would be one with such a distinguished record. You were at the Battle of the Brinwald, were you not?"

"I see news travels far."

He shrugged. "What can I say? We all live for court gossip, and your name garnered considerable interest."

"You said you have questions?"

"No. I asked if I might have a word with you. There is a significant difference."

"Yet, so far, you haven't said anything of consequence."

"My apologies," replied Lord Karstan. "Although I know OF you, I know nothing about your views."

"I see. What views in particular are you seeking to identify?"

"I hoped we might be of a similar opinion concerning this upcoming campaign."

"That depends entirely on your views of the matter."

Karstan smiled. "Ah, I see where this is going. Neither wishes to commit to an opinion until we know the other's mind. A clever tactic, Commander."

"It might help if you recall you sought out me, not the other way around."

"Yes. I suppose I did, didn't I?" He took a deep breath before continuing. "Several of my colleagues have expressed some misgivings about this coming war."

"As they should," said Charlaine. "If more men thought as they did, the Petty Kingdoms would be a far more peaceful land. What is it that concerns them?"

"The king's behaviour of late," replied the baron. "Several have noted his erratic conduct on those rare occasions when he holds court."

"And what about your own observations?"

"I would tend to agree. I hold the deepest respect for His Majesty, but I can't help but feel he's ill."

"Ill or mad?"

"Either, and that's my fear."

"Is there any history of illness in his family?"

"None that I am aware of. His father died after a riding accident some ten years ago but showed no signs of mental decline. I fear the same can no longer be said for our current ruler. You met the man. What was your impression?"

"Making an assessment is difficult. I've only been with His Majesty a few times, and I'll be the first to admit I'm no healer."

"Yet you sensed something?"

Charlaine nodded.

"Do you think him touched?"

"No. I believe someone may have slipped him something."

"Are you suggesting he was poisoned?"

"Poison suggests the intent to kill," said Charlaine. "I think he's being given something to make him more malleable."

"To what end?" asked Lord Karstan. "You're not proposing that someone wants a war with Galoran, are you?"

"That's precisely what I'm saying. Courts are a hotbed of gossip. Is there no one you can think of who seeks to arrange such a thing?"

"Why would someone want a war?"

"There are many reasons," replied Charlaine. "Chief amongst them the acquisition of wealth or power. We also can't rule out the possibility of outside interference."

"You think someone from Galoran might be responsible?"

"Ask yourself this—who benefits from a war between your two kingdoms?"

"The smiths, perhaps?" said Karstan. "They make all the armour and weapons and would be in demand if war came."

"You should consider the wider political ramifications. It's not the smiths you need to worry about, it's other kingdoms. What do you know of Ardosa's other neighbours?"

"I can't imagine it being Ulrichen; they're far too impoverished. There are rumours of trouble in Hadenfeld lately; perhaps they're behind this?"

"I assure you they're not," said Charlaine.

"How can you be so certain?"

"I'm from there originally, and the eastern extents of the kingdom are nothing but wilderness, which gives them plenty of room to expand without disturbing their neighbours."

"That leaves only Menzen and Parzen."

"What can you tell me about them?"

"Not much. Menzen is of similar size to us. We've had conflicts in the past, but that was largely resolved by Hadenfeld."

"Resolved, how?"

"Our three kingdoms, Ardosa, Menzen, and Kingshaven, argued over the land to our west. The matter was settled by all agreeing it belonged to Hadenfeld. In exchange, we became their allies."

"What?" said Charlaine. "Are you telling me Ardosa is allied with Hadenfeld?"

"Yes, at least it was, under King Otto. The place has been through two civil wars recently, and we've heard nothing from his successors."

"That makes things even more confusing. Galoran wouldn't consider invading if it brought Hadenfeld into the war."

"Why ever not?"

"Hadenfeld has one of the largest armies in the Petty Kingdoms, not to mention a king who is a seasoned warrior."

"Correction," said the baron. "They HAD one of the largest armies. After their recent troubles, it's unlikely there's much left. Besides, I doubt it would make a difference. The war with Galoran would be over in a fortnight, and I daresay it wouldn't be Ardosa who comes out victorious."

"You don't think you can win?"

"I have no doubt our warriors are the equal of anything Galoran can field; it's our leaders I lack faith in."

"I assumed the king would lead your army."

"Under normal circumstances, but someone convinced him to name a general."

"When did this happen?"

"Just this afternoon," replied Lord Karstan.

"And whom did he choose?"

"A fellow by the name of Garadino Boniface, who claims to be from Ilea. Apparently, he was a general of some repute who served the king there."

"I served in Ilea," said Charlaine. "How long ago did this fellow serve?"

"Ten or so years. Why?"

"I was there back in ninety-six; I don't recall hearing his name."

"Why would you?"

"I spent time with the Baroness of Rizela, and she never saw fit to mention him."

"He was a general, not a courtier."

"True, but my order was assisting in a military campaign. Surely it would have been prudent to seek out a man of such renown when dealing with strategy?"

"Are you suggesting the fellow's an imposter?"

"Not necessarily, but I think it wise to learn more about him."

"What more is there to know? He's an accomplished general."

"We have only his word for that."

"Careful, Commander. The same could be said of you."

"It could, but there is one important difference between he and I."

"Which is?"

"I am a Temple Knight of Saint Agnes. We take a vow to always tell the truth."

"Everyone lies on occasion," said Lord Karstan. "We are Humans, after all."

"You may deem it appropriate under certain circumstances, my lord, but I assure you, that is not something I aspire to."

"I accept your statement as fact, but that raises an important point: who this fellow Garadino Boniface actually is? Any ideas on that?"

"Not at present, but I spent several years in Ilea. Get me close enough to talk to him at length, and I can determine if that's where he truly came from."

13

INGMAR

SUMMER 1106 SR

Ingmar the Fifth, King of Galoran, sat in the carriage, staring back at Danica. "What business does a Temple Knight have in my lands?"

"I come from Ardosa, Your Majesty," replied Danica.

"Let me guess, you're here to plead their case?"

"I come only in the interest of peace."

"I'm afraid you're a little too late for that."

"You have yet to reach the border, sire, and no blood has been shed. The ideal time to discuss this matter is now, before both realms are engulfed by war."

"That's a touch melodramatic."

"My apologies," said the fellow sitting beside the king. "I don't think we've been properly introduced. I'm Prince Aurick, the king's better-looking cousin."

"Greetings, Highness."

"You say you came from Ardosa? I don't suppose you brought word of their surrender?"

"I'm afraid not," replied Danica. "Admittedly, I'm an outsider here, but perhaps that might be considered an advantage in this situation, for it allows me to give an unbiased opinion."

"An intriguing thought," said Aurick. He turned to King Ingmar. "Perhaps we should hear her out?"

Ingmar grumbled something under his breath, then nodded.

"Go on, then," said the prince. "I, for one, am eager to hear what you have to say."

"Might I enquire about the sequence of events that led to the current state of affairs?"

"That doesn't concern you," replied the king.

"On the contrary," replied Danica. "I am sworn to protect women, and a war endangers them all."

"She makes a good point," offered Prince Aurick. "And we've done nothing to be ashamed of."

"Then you tell her," snapped the king.

The king's cousin offered a slight bow of the head, then met eyes with Danica. "King Ingmar feels Galoran has had enough of being spurned by the other Petty Kingdoms. It's time we took our rightful place amongst the wealthy and influential."

"By going to war?" asked Danica. "Surely there are better ways of securing your legacy?"

"The conflict with Ardosa is a long-standing feud which we can no longer endure. They have refused all offers of restitution, so we are forced to take more drastic action."

"Might I ask the nature of this feud?"

"You may not!" replied the king.

"It's too late," added Aurick. "Our reports tell us that Ardosa is raising an army."

"War brings misery to many," said Danica, "including those I am sworn to protect. I cannot, in good conscience, allow this war to break out without making an attempt to prevent it."

"A noble sentiment," said Prince Aurick. "Would that my cousin's counterpart in Ardosa thought the same as you."

"This is a war neither of you can win."

"Says who?" said the king.

"I possess some battle experience, Majesty, and I've seen your army. By the standards of the Petty Kingdoms, it's small and likely similar in size to that of Ardosa. How do you propose to beat them?"

"I'll admit I'm no strategist," replied King Ingmar. "That's why I have advisors."

"And are these same advisors the ones commanding your army?"

"They are, though that's not any of your concern, Captain. I suggest in the future, you confine your efforts to religious matters as befitting one of your order."

"I'm sure she means well," said the prince. "I hope you don't mind me saying so, Sister, but you look young for a Temple Captain. I would have expected someone of your position to have grey hair and a wrinkled countenance."

"I've been a member of the order for over a dozen years."

"And in that time, you've achieved the rank of Temple Captain. You must have had quite the storied career."

The king frowned at his cousin. "That does not excuse her behaviour."

"Nor did I mean to infer that it does. Still, you must give people the benefit of the doubt, Cousin. Not everyone is trying to curry favour from your Royal Majesty."

"You would think differently were you the king."

"I daresay I would. Then again, for me to be in that position, you would have to be dead, and I much prefer your company, even if you do suffer from bouts of pigheadedness from time to time." He raised his hand to stifle any retort. "I meant that only as a jest, an attempt to lighten the mood."

"As king, many people try to sway my opinion, but in my experience, very few have anything worthwhile to contribute to a conversation. It makes it very difficult to find competent people to trust."

"You can trust me, surely? We've known each other since childhood."

The king's eyes softened. "You speak the truth, Aurick, but it is of little comfort in these trying times. Now, as to our Temple Captain here, what do you propose we do?"

"I say we take her with us," replied the prince. "If nothing else, she'll certainly liven up the conversation."

Ingmar regarded Danica. "We are on our way to join the Royal Army. I trust you have no objection?"

"None at all, Majesty."

"Then you may accompany us if you feel so inclined."

"I would be honoured."

"Good. Sergeant? Be so kind as to retrieve the good captain's horse, will you? We can't have a knight travelling on foot. What would the nobles say?"

"Splendid," said the prince. "Now a member of the Church is in our retinue. The Primus would be most pleased."

"I am a Temple Knight, not a lay sister," said Danica.

"Is there a difference?"

"I am not trained to conduct religious ceremonies."

"Truly?" replied Aurick. "How fascinating. I always thought you lot prayed all the time."

"Officers of our order lead the sister knights in prayer, but that's not the same thing."

"I'm afraid you'll need to explain that to me."

"A Temple Knight cannot conduct a marriage or lead others in prayer, save for fellow members of the order, although the latter is often waived in the case of the Mathewites."

Prince Aurick snorted. "The Mathewites? I fancy your people get into all sorts of mischief where they're concerned." He turned to the king. "Think about it, Cousin. All those women fawning over their fellow brothers-in-arms."

Danica cleared her throat. "I assure you the relationship is purely professional."

"Oh, I'm certain it is." Aurick winked at her. "On another note, I wonder what brings you to Galoran. Oh, I know you want to prevent war. You've given that much away, but surely your order didn't send you here with that specific goal in mind? Are you, perhaps, stationed in Zeinhoffen?"

"No. My most recent assignment was in the north, but I'm travelling to the Antonine."

"Ah, yes. The home of the beloved Church of which you're no doubt so proud."

"Do I detect a note of cynicism there?"

"For an organization that prides itself on remaining apart from secular matters, they take a keen interest in our king's court."

"It is Human nature to take an interest in local politics, especially when one is in a position of influence. Holy Fathers are no exception, or are you suggesting they're interfering somehow?"

"No, he's not," replied the king, "but they often poke their noses in where they're not welcome."

"With all due respect, Your Majesty, you are the king. You need only ask them to stop, and they will abide by your wishes."

Ingmar sat back in the carriage, a look of exhaustion washing over his features. "I have had enough of this conversation. Move on, driver. It's time we were on our way."

The king's retinue camped on the roadside that evening. His Majesty slept the night away, precluding any attempts by Danica to speak with him again. By morning, he was up and in his carriage before first light, eager to reach his army. Danica followed, content to play along, confident an opportunity might present itself sooner or later.

They kept up a fast pace, and by late afternoon, campfires appeared in the distance. The king, spurred on by the sight, ordered them to forego their evening meal and press on despite objections from his cousin, the prince.

The sun was near the horizon, a sign that not much daylight remained by the time they arrived. The king's entourage was greeted by Elka

Stormwind, who, accompanied by some captains, stood waiting as the carriage rolled to a stop.

"Greetings, Majesty," she called out as the officers bowed. "I trust your trip was uneventful?" A flicker of annoyance flashed across her face as she caught sight of Danica.

"Ah, splendid! The army looks magnificent; don't you think, Aurick? We'll soon have those Ardosans running for the hills."

The prince smiled. "Indeed, Majesty. I daresay it's the finest army north of the Antonine."

"Highness," said Elka. "I didn't expect to see you here?"

"I thought the king might like some company, and a nice trip across the country seemed just what I needed."

"We are going to war, Highness. It is unwise to risk both the king and his heir under such circumstances."

"Yet here I am, in all my glory." Prince Aurick hopped down from the carriage. "Come, Majesty. Let's see this army of yours, shall we? I'm eager to learn what all the fuss is about?" He paused, looking behind the carriage to where Danica waited. "Come, Sister, or should I say, Temple Captain? I'm never quite certain about the correct form of address. Won't you join us?"

The request caught her off guard. She'd been hoping to avoid a direct confrontation with Elka Stormwind until she'd formulated a plan of attack, but that now looked unlikely. "I should be happy to," said Danica, passing off the reins of her horse to a nearby warrior.

Her arrival brought a stern look from Elka. "So, it seems we meet again, Captain. I trust you have been well?"

Danica smiled, suddenly pleased she'd caused some discomfort to a Stormwind. "Quite well. Yourself?"

The mage ignored the question, turning to the king. "Majesty, if you come this way, I'll show you around the camp."

"Yes, of course," said the king.

They weaved their way through the tents, the king stopping occasionally to engage in light banter with the warriors. Danica hung back, observing everything she could. If she couldn't prevent the war, she'd at least bring back an accurate accounting of this army's composition. The thought gave her some satisfaction, but the more she pondered it, the more uneasy she became. She'd set out from Ardosa convinced Galoran was the cause of this war. She realized she'd unconsciously committed the sin of taking sides.

A Temple Knight must be neutral in all things; that's what she'd been taught when she first joined the order. In Arnsfeld, it'd been far simpler, for the empire was the Church's sworn enemy. It suddenly dawned on her that

Charlaine may have run across the same moral dilemma. The Temple Knights of her order were sworn to protect women, not go chasing off after Halvarians, yet Charlaine had shown no signs of hesitation, not in Arnsfeld, Reinwick, or even Ilea. To Danica's mind, it represented a true devotion to the faith rather than a strict and unyielding adherence to the tenets of the Church. She hoped she proved worthy enough to follow in her mentor's shoes.

That evening, they sat around a campfire, the king reclining in a comfortable chair Elka had somehow produced. The wine flowed freely, but Danica drank little. The atmosphere was amiable, perhaps even jovial, for the king laughed on several occasions.

For her part, Danica kept a close eye on Elka. If there were a plot afoot, she, as a Stormwind, would be the most likely candidate at the centre of it. The king retired for the night, leaving his cousin to entertain those of his captains still awake.

Danica saw her chance. "If I might ask you a question, Highness." He nodded, so she continued. "What brought about such great hatred between the kingdoms of Galoran and Ardosa?"

"Ah," replied the prince. "Now, that is a twisted tale of betrayal." He rubbed his hands together, then leaned forward. "It began many years ago, during the reign of King Eckhard, Ingmar's father. He was betrothed to Princess Luisa of Parzen, a marriage that would have cemented an alliance between the two realms. It was to be a great celebration. Nobles and royals from all over the region came as guests of the crown, amongst them Prince Gotfried of Ardosa, father to King Jaroslav. Everything went smoothly until the morning of the wedding when it was discovered that Princess Luisa had run off with Gotfried."

"How long ago was this, precisely?"

"I want to say fifty years, but I'm not the best at dates. In any event, it was before I was born."

"Did it result in a war?"

"It easily could have," said Aurick. "Saints know, wars have been fought over less, but I'm told we lacked sufficient numbers to do so at the time. The entire affair became a major embarrassment for us, and Galoran became the laughingstock of the Petty Kingdoms. As a result, no king wanted to marry their daughters to Eckhard, forcing him to take a Galoran noble as a wife rather than a royal."

"But that would have been Ingmar's mother, wouldn't it? I would think His Majesty would be thankful."

Aurick smiled. "My cousin could care less about Princess Luisa. Over the past few years, his obsession with reclaiming the kingdom's honour in the eyes of the Petty Kingdoms has grown to consume him. And with the Cunars' abandonment of Ardosa, he sees his chance at redemption through force of arms."

"And you don't agree with that philosophy?"

"I don't, but then again, I'm not the king."

"The drink has loosened your tongue, Highness," said Elka Stormwind. "Perhaps it would be best if you retired for the evening?"

"Nonsense," replied Aurick. "I'm feeling alive for the first time in years."

Evenia appeared, the light of the flames dancing off her face. She approached her mistress, whispering in her ear, then slipped her a note.

Danica was instantly alert. Where she sat, she couldn't distinguish what was on it, but from Elka's response, whatever it contained pleased her. The mage returned the note to her aide, then grabbed her arm and whispered something.

"It's getting late," said Danica, rising from her seat. "If you'll excuse me, Highness, I must get some sleep."

"Certainly," replied Aurick. "My apologies for keeping you up so late."

Danica left them, finding a nearby tent where she hid in the shadows. She was after the note that Evenia carried, although how she'd get her hands on it was another matter entirely.

Evenia finally passed by, heading towards her mistress's tent. Danica followed, keeping as quiet as possible while hopefully staying far enough away to avoid detection. The young woman stepped inside and lit a lantern, her shadow reflecting on the canvas. She then stood there, opening a small box and closing it before she moved to a chair to pick up a cloak lying across its back. Leaving the lantern lit, she exited the tent, heading back towards the campfire.

Danica moved quickly, sneaking into the tent and searching for the box. She found it sitting atop a small writing desk. At first glance, she would've taken it for a jewellery box, but upon opening it, she discovered letters instead of rings and bracelets. The first, written in a fine hand, was brief yet concise, the contents mundane, but there could be no mistaking the name at the bottom—Yevani Sartellian.

Danica dug through the rest, searching for clues about what all this correspondence might mean. She found a note concerning the relative strengths of the armies of both Ardosa and Galoran that ended with a chilling statement:

The two are well-matched. A conflict will result in many casualties on both sides. With a little effort, we can ensure the two principles become battle victims and install those who are more sympathetic to our cause.

Danica believed war was a costly way of replacing a king, but this wouldn't be the first time someone manipulated a ruler to accomplish a goal. Her thoughts returned to Arnsfeld, where the Halvarians had tried to manipulate King Stefan. In the end, their agent, the mage Ashan Sartellian, had killed him.

She continued looking through the letters for more information, but voices approached before she found anything else. With the evidence in hand, she snuck back to the entrance, eager to avoid being caught, and then Elka spoke from outside the tent flap. "Tell the captain I want to see him first thing in the morning."

"Yes, Mistress," replied Evenia. "Are we to march tomorrow?"

"We are, providing the king can be convinced to move."

"You think he won't?"

Danica cast about, seeking an avenue of escape. To one side lay the mage's cot, snug up against the outside wall. She moved closer, drawing a dagger in case she must cut her way out, but it proved unnecessary as there was a gap below the wall. As the tent flap opened, she dove under the bed, crawling beneath the edge of the canvas.

Mounted and ready to ride at first light, Danica originally intended to take the evidence directly to King Jaroslav, but she'd realized that only solved half the problem. Galoran readied for an invasion, and whether Yevani was behind it or not, the King of Ardosa must respond to the threat. Should she present the evidence to King Ingmar? No. She decided her best course of action was to remain with the Army of Galoran and wait for the right opportunity to reveal what she'd learned. She had no idea when that might occur but had faith she'd know it when she saw it. In the meantime, she must bide her time and hope the Water Mage didn't discover the theft.

Her mind wandered back to how the letter came into her possession. It didn't feel like theft, but she couldn't deny taking it without permission. When she was inducted into the order, she took an oath to be honest in all things and never lie. No, that wasn't entirely true. The oath was to keep her word and never lie. Technically, it was not a promise not to steal, but it felt wrong just the same.

On the other hand, she'd acted to try to prevent a war, a war that would end in the death of hundreds. Did that justify her actions? Part of her wanted to scream out in frustration. This weighed heavily on her conscience, and she promised herself that upon reaching the Antonine, she'd seek out a Holy Mother and confess her sins.

"Good morning, Captain."

The prince's words startled her out of her reverie. "Good morning, Highness. You're up early this morning."

"I could say the same of you," replied Prince Aurick. "Are all temple officers early risers?"

"I can't speak for all of them, but in my experience, it's not unusual. What about the king?"

"Ingmar? No, not this morning. I expect it'll be almost noon before he drags his sorry arse out of his bed. It's what comes of overindulgence."

"Are you suggesting he drank a lot last night?"

"Not by his standards," replied the prince, "but should he die in the coming days, his body will be well-preserved."

14

INVASION
SUMMER 1106 SR

From the safety of the riverbank, Danica observed the men of Galoran approach the bridge marking the border between the two realms. The Ardosan warriors guarding the other end called out for them to stop but fell back as soon as it became apparent the Galorans were intent on crossing.

King Ingmar's personal guard marched across, taking up positions on either side, allowing the cavalry to follow. These horsemen soon outpaced the enemy, rounding up ten prisoners as a trophy of war.

The cavalry captain returned, dismounted, and stood before his king. "Majesty, the enemy has fled. Victory is ours."

"You performed your duty well this day and are to be congratulated on your efficiency."

The man bowed, pleased by the praise, but he remained standing before the king.

"You have a question?"

"I do, Majesty. What are we to do with the prisoners?"

"That is an excellent question." Ingmar turned to his entourage. "Your thoughts, Elka?"

"We cannot afford the men to guard any prisoners, Majesty. Hard as it seems, the only logical choice is to execute them."

"You cannot!" exclaimed Danica. "These men threw down their arms and surrendered. To execute them now is tantamount to murder."

"This is war, Captain, not a social gathering. Such times call for hard decisions. Would you weaken your army by dispatching men to guard enemy warriors?"

"Hmmm," said Ingmar. "A valid point. What say you, Temple Captain?"

"This war has only just begun, Majesty. Although your army was victorious on this first encounter, there will be other skirmishes."

"What is your point."

"Imagine your own men captured by the enemy and then executed in so callous a manner?"

"Jaroslav wouldn't dare!"

Danica nodded. "If word reaches the Ardosan capital that you executed prisoners, it will inflame the enemy to fight even harder." She waved her hand to encompass the prisoners. "These men surrendered, but the next ones you encounter will fight to the death, knowing you offer them no mercy."

"Mercy," scoffed Elka. "Mercy is for the weak. If you are to govern this kingdom once it's conquered, Majesty, you must establish how ruthless you can be."

"Do that," said Danica, "and the people of Ardosa will rise up against you. Your army cannot be everywhere at once, Majesty. Such an act would force you to garrison every village and town in the region."

"Ardosa has no stomach for a fight, sire. The look of defeat on these prisoners indicates there will be no uprising."

"You must do what you believe is best, Majesty," said Danica, "but killing these men will imperil your immortal soul." At her words, the colour fled from Ingmar's face.

"More religious nonsense," said Elka.

"You've both made good points," replied the king, "but I am the ruler here, and I shall defer to the good Temple Captain's wisdom on this. Take the prisoners away and ensure they are treated with civility."

The cavalry commander bowed, then returned to his prisoners.

The king redirected his focus to his army, the remainder moving up to cross the bridge. "The Saints have blessed us this day, allowing us a bloodless victory. It is the beginning of the end for Ardosa."

"That was not the Saints doing," replied Danica.

"I'm surprised to hear you say that. I would have thought you, of all people, believed in divine providence."

"The Saints are not gods; they are guides seeking to lead us to a better life."

The king offered a nod of his head. "And for that, we are thankful. Now, let's look at that road, shall we?"

. . .

While it should have taken very little time to march the army over the bridge and into Ardosa, the company captains argued about the order they'd cross in, and then there was the nightmare of their supplies. A wagon pulled by oxen accompanied each company, and those in charge were ill-disposed to follow orders.

Finally, with the sun at its highest point, the army stood ready to resume its march on the Ardosan side of the river. Before the order to commence was given, King Ingmar decided to meet with his advisors, insisting on doing it in a tent to keep the sun off his Royal personage. This involved unpacking his pavilion from his wagons and staking it down.

It was well into the afternoon by the time they'd assembled within. Elka Stormwind was there, along with the king's cousin and the twenty captains who commanded the companies making up the army.

Danica squeezed in, eager to learn what they were planning. The tent was beyond crowded, with no space to move without stepping on someone else's feet. Only the king had space around him due to his royal status.

"It is time to plan the next stage of this campaign," Ingmar began. "With our capture of the bridge, we have secured our way home. Now, we must take the fight to the enemy. I propose we march straight for Zeinhoffen and finish this as quickly as possible. Your thoughts?" He looked around the pavilion.

"I suggest an alternate strategy," offered Elka. "Marching on the Ardosan capital will only result in the enemy withdrawing."

"But that's a good thing, surely?"

"Is it? If we wait here, they have no option but to come and meet us, whereas if we force them from their capital, they could go in any number of directions."

"I agree," said Prince Aurick. "By forcing them to attack us, we gain the advantage of selecting where this battle is fought. That's how the Army of Arnsfeld defeated the Halvarians." This last remark caught Danica off guard.

"Is this true?" asked the king, his gaze turning to the Temple Captain.

"Yes," Danica replied, "but the situation was more complicated there. The terrain was prepared with defensive works, and a nearby keep diverted a portion of the enemy."

"Still," said the prince, "the Halvarians were defeated."

"They were."

"Then that is what we'll do," declared Ingmar. "Should we form up for battle now and wait for the Ardosans to arrive?"

"No," replied Elka. "We should place sentries on the roads and take up positions once they're sighted."

"Good. Excellent, in fact."

"If I may make a suggestion," offered Prince Aurick. "It would be advantageous to determine our dispositions for the coming battle so the men can get into their assigned places quickly."

"Yes, of course," agreed King Ingmar. "Elka, as a battle mage, you're the expert. What would you recommend?"

"Our strength lies in our footmen, Majesty. I therefore propose we form them into a line with archers on either flank."

"And the cavalry?"

"They shall form a reserve, ready to take the fight to the enemy should a break appear in their formation."

The captains spoke all at once, each demanding to know where their company would be located. As far as Danica could tell, the right flank was considered the place of honour, as it was the most sought-after position. The arguing overwhelmed all conversation, leading her to exit the tent to find somewhere quiet to think. The strategy was rudimentary at best, yet Elka Stormwind was reputed to be a battle mage. With three types of footmen at her disposal: the king's personal guard, axemen, and poorly trained spearmen, she hadn't even bothered to arrange them in any particular order. The more Danica thought about it, the more it appeared the court mage was setting Galoran up for defeat.

She shook her head, trying to clear it, yet questions swirled within. What was the true purpose of this war? She knew the two mages were involved in orchestrating it, but to what end? Was this a ruse to give Ardosa a victory, or was something more nefarious at work?

Danica tried to apply some logic to the situation. If Ardosa proved victorious, it could cause Galoran to become a vassal state. The reverse was true should Galoran win, yet how did that benefit these two mages? She knew the Sartellians and the Stormwinds were in league with Halvaria, meaning their ultimate plan would have to benefit the empire. A protracted war between the two kingdoms could result in allies crossing the border, and if left unchecked, the conflict might spread to the other Petty Kingdoms. If that was their ultimate goal, it indicated the empire was readying for another invasion, one aimed not at seizing a border realm but conquering the entire Continent.

That thought brought her a sense of completeness as if all the pieces had suddenly fallen into place. "Saints be with us," she said aloud.

"Saints be with us all," replied a nearby guard.

. . .

Charlaine shifted in her seat. Word had arrived that Galoran had crossed the border, spreading panic throughout Ardosa's nobles. Everyone was convinced the enemy would soon be entering the city, yet there was no sign of their scouts or warriors. She'd done her part, inspecting King Jaroslav's army and offering words of encouragement, but it appeared little more than a hastily assembled militia.

"Where are they?" asked Lord Gerrin. "You'd think they'd at least be within marching distance by now."

"They are likely still at the bridge," replied Yevani.

"But why?"

"To draw you out. They need a decisive victory to win this war, and they can't do that unless they force a battle."

"The same is true for us," urged the baron. "This is unwelcome news, Majesty, but there is no choice other than to meet them on the field of battle."

Lord Karstan shook his head. "Don't listen to them, Majesty. This strategy plays right into Ingmar's plans."

Jaroslav sat quietly, his hands steepled together, not revealing any sign of his mood. Was he contemplative or scared? Perhaps a little of both, Charlaine thought. General Boniface, who now commanded the army, was the only one who appeared calm.

"Your Majesty?" prompted Lord Karstan.

"I think we should hear from the Temple Commander," said King Jaroslav. "What think you, Sister?"

"Me?" replied Charlaine. "Would your general not be more qualified to comment on strategy?"

"She has you there," said Gerrin. He turned to regard the fellow. "Well, General? Care to comment?"

General Boniface stood and straightened his tunic, which had bunched around his ample belly. "Master Yevani made a good point, sire. With the Army of Galoran in our territory, we have only one option—march east and send them back across the river. To that end, I ask that you give Royal Consent to allow me to do just that."

"And when would you march?" asked Jaroslav.

"Immediately. Any delay could cost us dearly. It's not as if Galoran would willingly give up and return home, and the longer they remain in our territory, the weaker we appear."

"You seem eager for war," said Charlaine, "but caution would serve you better than haste."

The general turned on her, his stare intense. "Who are you to lecture me?"

"One who values the lives of others. Soldiers are not the playthings of nobles, my lord, their lives to be thrown away on a whim."

"Every soldier knows that if the situation demands it, they must sacrifice their lives for the good of the realm."

"Sacrifice for a greater good is to be lauded," replied Charlaine, "but throwing away lives from incompetence is criminal, or at least it should be."

"I am the general here!" said Boniface. "I'll thank you to remember that."

"Tell me, General. How many victories do you have?"

"More than you."

"I'm not the one whose credentials are under scrutiny."

"I agree," said Karstan. "Humour us, General. Tell us of your victories."

"I don't like to brag, but my greatest triumph was at the Battle of Alantra, where I defeated the Halvarians."

"Did you, indeed?" said Charlaine. "Tell me, if you would be so kind, what tactic you employed?"

"We deployed our foot in line, the more experienced warriors in the centre, while our archers took up a position behind."

"And your cavalry?"

"On the right flank, ready to exploit any break in the enemy line."

"See?" said King Jaroslav, though he spoke to no one in particular. "I knew he was a master strategist."

"A master, indeed," said Charlaine. "I do wonder, though, how the horses managed to breathe."

Everyone gave her a confused look.

"Would you care to explain that statement?" asked Karstan.

"It would be my pleasure. The Battle of Alantra was a sea battle in which the Holy Fleet, under the command of Father Commander Marius of the Temple Knights of Saint Cunar, defeated the Halvarian Fleet."

"Alantra is a city," snapped Boniface.

"Yes, and the battle was fought a few miles east, out on the Shimmering Sea."

"And you know this, how?" asked Jaroslav.

"I was there, as was Temple Captain Danica."

"She lies," said Boniface. "She's trying to discredit me. If you want proof of my capabilities, I refer you to my letters of recommendation. What have you to say to that, Commander? You are a commander, aren't you? We only have your word on that, after all."

"The details of the Battle of Alantra are well-documented by the Church. If you don't believe me, I suggest you send word to the Antonine, seeking clarity."

"That would take weeks, and there's an army breathing down our necks!"

"This argument is getting us nowhere," interrupted Yevani. "We must march our army from the capital and push Galoran back across the border."

"True," said Lord Gerrin, "but the question has now arisen whether we can trust General Boniface to command it."

"I agree," said Karstan. "Might I ask who secured the services of the general?"

"I did," replied the king. "His name came to my notice after the troubles began."

"Ah, yes," said Charlaine. "The troubles. When you say he 'came to my notice,' what does that mean, precisely?"

"Someone at court mentioned he was in Zeinhoffen."

"And would that someone happen to be Master Yevani?"

"I… don't rightly remember. I suppose it could have been. My memory isn't what it used to be. Does it truly matter?"

"No," replied Gerrin. "Not really, but it still begs the question of who is to command the army."

"I shall do so myself," declared Jaroslav.

"Majesty, are you certain that's wise?" asked the baron.

"Why wouldn't it be?"

"You are a capable king, Majesty, but you are not trained in the disposition of troops."

"Neither is the general, if the commander's accusations prove true."

"Perhaps the good sister would consider commanding the army herself?" suggested Lord Karstan.

"No," replied Charlaine. "I cannot, in good conscience, take sides in this conflict, particularly when I'm not familiar with the region's politics."

"Wait a moment," said Gerrin. "Master Yevani, you're a trained battle mage, aren't you?"

"I am."

"Then would you consider taking command?"

"That is up to His Majesty."

All eyes turned to King Jaroslav.

"Very well," he replied. "Command of the army shall revert to Yevani Sartellian. I suppose that means we'll march first thing tomorrow morning?"

"Indeed, Majesty."

"What about me?" asked General Boniface. "I possess a Royal Contract."

"You shall be paid in full," the king assured him. "Let it not be said that King Jaroslav is not a generous ruler."

The general sat back, smirking at his good fortune. Charlaine ignored him, trying to piece together who was working with whom. She knew Yevani served the empire's interests, but was someone else helping him? It certainly seemed like it. And what was all that about the Battle of Alantra? Did Boniface honestly believe he could lie about that and get away with it? Then again, he very nearly had.

She had to admit, it was a clever ploy. Alantra was a long way from Ardosa, and matters in the south were seldom of interest to the rulers of the Northern Petty Kingdoms. Had she not been here, his lie would never have been exposed. Was this a sign the Saints were at work? She smiled, suddenly realizing she was right where she needed to be.

15

CONFRONTATION

SUMMER 1106 SR

The Army of Galoran stood waiting as the Ardosan warriors formed up opposite them. There was no finesse to their positions, merely two long lines of footmen facing one another. Both armies kept their cavalry in reserve with their archers on either flank, an unimaginative arrangement offering nothing in the way of a tactical advantage.

Charlaine knew Danica was over there somewhere, but her attempts to halt the invasion had failed. Not that she herself had been any more successful: far from it. Both kings wanted this conflict, and no reasonable arguments had dissuaded either side.

"We have them," called out King Jaroslav as he rode up beside her, gazing over the flat terrain. "I must admit it's a magnificent sight!"

"Not the word I'd choose to describe a battle where men are about to die," she replied.

"Sacrifices must be made in the name of honour!"

One of the king's escorts turned in the saddle, his attention caught by movement behind them.

Charlaine followed his gaze to see Princess Carina galloping towards them, her hair streaming out behind her. "It appears we have company, Majesty."

"What's this, now?" Jaroslav turned to look, then his cheeks flushed with anger. "I told you to remain in the capital!" he yelled.

Carina ignored his protestations, slowing her horse to come to a halt beside him. "I'm happy to see you alive and well, Father." Her eyes drifted to the distant Galoran army. "Have I missed anything?"

Charlaine took it upon herself to talk before the king continued his shouting. "The armies are lined up, ready for battle."

"What are they waiting for?"

"The order to attack." She looked at King Jaroslav, who was sweating profusely. "Might I make a suggestion, Majesty?"

"But of course."

"Let us meet with our opponents under a flag of truce. Perhaps they can be persuaded to halt this invasion and return home?"

"I don't know," replied the king, looking over his shoulder. "That might make me look weak."

"On the contrary. Your people would view you as benevolent, an important characteristic in a king. Wouldn't you agree?"

He hemmed and hawed a bit before answering. "Yes. I suppose there is some truth in that. Let us see if the King of Galoran will come to his senses and withdraw from our territory." He stood in his stirrups, giving him a slight height advantage to spy out his advisors. "You there, Yevani. Come here. I would have you at my side."

The mage rode over, a scowl etched upon his face. "Yes, Majesty?"

"I've decided to parley with the enemy."

"I wouldn't advise it, sire. King Ingmar is rumoured to be a treacherous soul."

Jaroslav hesitated, looking at Charlaine for reassurance. She simply nodded. He sat up straighter in his saddle. "I must insist. Send a rider to see if my counterpart will meet between our two armies."

"Yes, Majesty." Yevani jerked back on his horse's reins and rode off at the gallop.

Noting the action, Lord Gerrin rode over to them. "Trouble, sire?"

"Not at all," replied Jaroslav. "I decided to give the enemy an opportunity to withdraw."

"Doing so only delays their plans."

"Come now," said Charlaine. "You're not suggesting they'd return to their own side of the border only to launch another invasion?"

"That's precisely what I'm saying. You can't trust Ingmar, sire. The man's wanted your lands for years."

"I can't imagine Galoran launching another invasion with your army here. Can you, Majesty?"

"The Temple Commander makes a valid point," said the king. "I've made up my mind. We shall offer the enemy the chance to save their army."

The baron took a deep breath before answering. "As you wish, sire."

Yevani returned, along with three mounted warriors, their escort for the parley. Behind him, a fourth began riding towards the Army of Galoran.

· · ·

"What in the name of the Saints are they doing?" asked King Ingmar, his gaze locked on the lone Ardosan warrior riding towards his line of battle.

"He's mad," replied Elka Stormwind.

"No," said Danica. "He comes bearing a flag of truce. I suspect King Jaroslav wants to talk."

"Refuse him," insisted the mage. "He's trying to delay the inevitable."

"The inevitable? Guess again. Look with your own eyes, Majesty. The Army of Ardosa is the same size as that of Galoran. If you fight here today, both sides will suffer heavy casualties."

Elka answered for the king. "It is the lot of the common folk to spill their blood in service to their king."

"Easy to say for you. You won't be in the thick of the fighting."

"I am no coward!" replied Elka.

"I never meant to infer you were, but you hold a privileged position at the king's court, one shielding you from the need to wield a weapon your-self." Danica turned to King Ingmar. "I've experienced too much fighting, Majesty. It is not something to embrace when there are alternatives."

"Alternatives?" replied the king. "What are you suggesting?"

"That you hear out King Jaroslav."

"Both sides are poised for battle," insisted Elka. "You're not saying he might reconsider and withdraw?"

"We shall never know if we don't listen to what they propose," replied Danica.

The mage shook her head. "The very idea is most preposterous. It could be a ruse to lure you into a trap, Majesty."

"Then you shall accompany the king, as will I. If a Temple Knight and a battle mage can't keep His Majesty safe, what good are we?"

Ingmar turned to his cousin. "What think you?"

"I think it worth investigating further," replied Aurick.

"Then I shall accept," said Ingmar, his eyes once more focusing on the approaching messenger, "providing that it is the reason for this fellow's arrival." He waited as one of his horsemen intercepted the rider. After a brief exchange, they both rode towards the King of Galoran.

The warrior from Ardosa halted some ten paces away while his Galoran counterpart handed the king a note.

"Ha!" proclaimed Ingmar. "The Temple Captain was correct. Jaroslav wishes to parley!" He turned to address the Ardosan messenger. "You may inform your king that I agree to meet with him." He looked skyward, judging the time. "Shall we say at noon?"

The rider half bowed. "Most assuredly, Majesty." With that, he turned around and rode away, his counterpart escorting him.

"Are you certain that was wise, sire?" asked Elka. "This meeting will delay the start of the battle."

"I'm still the king," declared Ingmar. "The decision is mine."

"You must at least take some guards."

"I will, along with you and the Temple Captain, providing she agrees?"

Danica smiled. "Of course, sire. I would be delighted."

"Don't forget me," said Prince Aurick. "I wouldn't miss this for anything!"

"Very well. Now, let's find some men to keep me safe, shall we?" Ingmar rode towards his cavalry, who'd massed at the rear of his line.

Elka's gaze turned to Danica. "I shall not forget this, Captain."

"Nor will I."

Usually, in a situation like this, Danica would've been nervous, but a feeling of comfort spread over her as if Saint Agnes was looking down on her.

Three of Jaroslav's horsemen rode ahead of the king while Charlaine, Yevani, and Lord Gerrin followed His Majesty by a horse length. Just behind them rode Princess Carina, determined to be a part of the meeting. King Ingmar's group appeared, matching their numbers. They met between the two armies, the guards stopping ten paces from each other.

Jaroslav rode forward, coming to a halt alongside his guards. "Greetings," he called out.

Ingmar moved up between his own warriors to get a better view. "And to you, Majesty. I couldn't help but note you oppose me with an army."

"But you were the one who invaded my territory. What else was I to do? Let you have it?"

"If I may," offered Charlaine. "We are here to parley, not fight." She urged Stormcloud forward, nudging one of Jaroslav's guards aside. She glanced at Danica, who gave a slight nod in response. "Perhaps it might be best to begin by airing your grievances, then the negotiations can commence. I suggest King Jaroslav go first."

Elka protested. "This is foolish. I—"

"Silence," said Charlaine. "The king is about to speak."

Jaroslav cleared his throat. "Your men have been harassing trade. Several even crossed the border and attacked our farmers."

"According to who?" said Danica, suddenly finding her voice. She moved up, just as Charlaine had done. "Your pardon, Majesties, but you've each been the victim of an elaborate deception, and I can prove it."

"Don't listen to her!" shouted Elka. "This is all a fabrication."

"How do you know that?" asked Charlaine. "She hasn't revealed her proof."

"She is an outsider, Majesty. It's obvious she and the Temple Commander conspire against you. Next, they'll try to convince you this has been one big misunderstanding."

Ingmar frowned. "This is all highly irregular. I thought you wanted to discuss surrender, Jaroslav, not make strange accusations."

"Give him a chance," said Aurick, "before blood is spilled."

The King of Ardosa cleared his throat. "I assure you this has nothing to do with me. I came here to ask you to withdraw and avoid a senseless slaughter, not surrender."

"Perhaps we should see this proof," suggested Lord Gerrin, "then Their Majesties can decide for themselves if the accusations have merit."

Danica withdrew a document from her belt and handed it to King Ingmar. "Here, sire. The proof I spoke of."

"What lie is this?" said Elka. "It's a forgery."

The King of Galoran unfolded the note, perusing it. "I'm surprised to hear you say that, considering you don't even know its contents. Or do you?" He turned to regard his mage. "Something to hide, have you, Elka?"

"What's going on here?" asked Gerrin.

"It appears a plot is afoot," replied Charlaine, "and I suspect Elka is not the only one involved."

"A plot?" said Jaroslav. "What in the name of the Saints are you talking about?"

King Ingmar held out the note. "Here, see for yourself."

Charlaine moved closer, taking the note and passing it to King Jaroslav, but the paper burst into flames before he could read it.

He dropped the flaming missive and quickly looked at Yevani. "What is the meaning of this?"

"I can tell you," said Danica. "Yevani Sartellian plotted with Elka Stormwind to bring your two realms to war. The proof was in that letter."

"Lies!" shouted Yevani. "You no longer possess any proof; the evidence is destroyed."

"Are you so foolish as to doubt the word of a king?"

"The Temple Captain lies, sire. She fears the Army of Ardosa will be victorious in this conflict."

"No," said Charlaine. "She wants the same thing I do—a peaceful resolution."

A shard of ice struck Charlaine's chest plate. Her armour saved her from injury, but the impact forced her backwards, almost toppling her from the saddle. Danica reacted quickly, drawing her sword and rushing at the Water Mage.

Yevani called on his Fire Magic, and her sword glowed bright red. Danica dropped the weapon as she closed in on Elka, drawing a dagger in its stead.

Charlaine reacted quickly, unsheathing her weapon and charging towards the Fire Mage. Another streak shot out, this time aimed at Charlaine, but she twisted in the saddle, and the flames flew past her. A moment later, she sank the tip of her sword into the Sartellian's bicep.

Danica moved in with her dagger, but Elka countered with a touch that sent frost up the Temple Knight's gauntlet, forcing her to drop the blade to the ground. The mage hadn't counted on Danica's free hand, and her second dagger sliced the Water Mage open from one side of her neck to the other. Elka's eyes rolled into her head, and she slumped forward, toppling from the saddle.

It started and ended so quickly, the guards had no time to react. They reached for their weapons, a natural reaction to the attack, but both kings yelled for them to stop.

Charlaine held her sword at Yevani's neck. "I do not know for certain what motivated them to urge war," she said, "but I suspect it has to do with the other Petty Kingdoms. A protracted war here would result in your allies joining the fray, causing a much larger conflict."

"But how?" asked King Ingmar. "We were about to resolve this with a battle."

"A battle where both sides would have endured heavy losses, resulting in a stalemate, which would lead to a lengthy and prolonged war, allowing the time needed for allies to march to your aid."

"This plot changes nothing," said Ingmar. "Galoran still needs a victory to regain its standing in the Petty Kingdoms."

"I don't understand," said Charlaine.

"I do," said Danica. "The sins of the parents have come back to haunt the children. Years ago, the betrothed of King Ingmar's father ran off with King Jaroslav's father."

"But without that event, neither king would be here today."

"That's not the point," said Ingmar, his voice rising. "Galoran suffered an indignity in front of foreign royalty and fell from grace, a grace which I now seek to restore. Return to your lines, Jaroslav, and prepare to do battle!"

"No, wait," said Carina. "There must be a better way to resolve this issue?"

Prince Aurick moved up, greeting her with a smile. He bowed his head. "My apologies, madam. I don't think we've been introduced. My name is Prince Aurick, heir to the Crown of Galoran. Who might you be?"

"Princess Carina, daughter of King Jaroslav."

Aurick turned to his cousin. "I have an idea, sire, one which would, I think, satisfy your desire to regain standing amongst the Petty Kingdoms."

Ingmar stared back. "Out with it, then. Don't leave me hanging!"

"I propose a union of our two houses. With your blessing, sire, I would ask for the hand of Princess Carina, a daughter of Royal Blood. Would that be sufficient to wipe away the shame of your father's disgrace?"

"It would certainly be a good start."

Jaroslav stared back, mouth agape. "Are you serious? What makes you think I would accept such a proposal? Why, if I—"

"I accept," said Carina, cutting him off.

"It appears," said Charlaine, "that you both have a solution before your eyes. Will you now show wisdom in forgiving the acts of your parents and begin working towards a future united in peace and prosperity?"

The two kings stared at each other, a test of wills that threatened to overwhelm them.

Jaroslav glanced at his daughter. "Are you certain this is what you want?"

Aurick stepped forward. "I promise that I shall always treat her with grace and respect."

"He's a good man," said Ingmar. "You have my word on it as king."

"Then I agree," said Jaroslav. He rode forward, moving close enough to extend his hand in friendship.

Ingmar looked down at the proffered hand, then grasped it firmly. "It appears we shall soon be related."

Charlaine felt her muscles relax. "I think you'll find that your two kingdoms have much in common."

"Tell me, Commander," said the King of Ardosa, "have any of these conflicts been real, or were they all contrived to support this plot?"

"I suspect the latter," replied Charlaine. "In Ardosa, Yevani convinced you that Galoran warriors had crossed the border and attacked the locals."

"Sounds familiar," added Danica. "I believe Elka has been stoking the flames of revenge in Galoran."

"We've been fools," said Jaroslav.

"There may be more," added Charlaine. "There is reason to believe your food was tampered with, Majesty. Many around you have noted your erratic behaviour of late, which indicates you were under the influence of something. Have you experienced trouble sleeping?"

"I have. Thankfully, Lord Gerrin supplied me with a sleeping draught." As soon as the words left his mouth, the king turned to face the baron. "How could you?"

"I know nothing of which you speak," the fellow replied.

"Ha!" called out Yevani. "At least I know when I've lost. You should come clean, my lord, and beg your king for forgiveness."

"Take Lord Gerrin into custody," ordered Jaroslav. "I shall deal with him later."

"We are both victims here," said Ingmar. "The question on my mind is what do we do about it? Have you any ideas on that, Temple Captain?"

"The first step," replied Danica, "would be to march the Army of Galoran back home."

"Yes," added Jaroslav. "I'll take my men back to Zeinhoffen once you're gone. May we trust in these two Temple Knights to supervise?"

"Most certainly," said Charlaine, "but can I offer a suggestion?"

"By all means."

"You are to be united by a Royal Marriage, but misunderstandings can still occur. To avoid trouble in the future, I would suggest you two meet regularly, say twice a year? You could alternate who hosts."

"A brilliant idea," replied King Ingmar. "We must thank you. I could even send a permanent representative to the court of Ardosa, and they could do the same in return."

"I should like that," said Jaroslav. He surveyed his army. "It appears I need to find some new advisors. Commander, would you have any recommendations?"

"Sorry, no. My only advice is to never again allow Sartellians at your court, or Stormwinds, for that matter."

"We were lucky you uncovered their plot. How did you come to suspect them?"

"We've encountered them in the past. A Stormwind was responsible for trouble in Reinwick, while a Sartellian murdered the King of Angvil."

"But couldn't they have been individual acts?"

"Perhaps, but in both cases, it furthered the cause of the Halvarian Empire. I also have it on good authority that they tried to influence events in Hadenfeld. Thankfully, their plotting was uncovered, but had it not been, you might have found a hostile realm on your western border."

"But we're allied with Hadenfeld," insisted Jaroslav.

"I suppose you are, in theory, but tell me this—when was that treaty signed?"

"Years ago."

"When King Otto ruled Hadenfeld?"

"Yes. Why?"

"Two kings have ruled since Otto's death, and there have been two civil wars. Events of that nature tend to drain even the largest of treasuries. Even if they did honour your alliance, and I'm not saying they wouldn't, I doubt they'd have the funds to raise much of an army."

"You are remarkably well-informed, Commander," said King Jaroslav, shaking his head. "More so than me, it seems."

"I was born and raised in Hadenfeld, Majesty, and I take a keen interest in their affairs."

"I shall heed your counsel. From this day forth, no Stormwind or Sartellian will be permitted at my court."

"The same goes for me," added Ingmar.

"And what of you two Temple Knights?" asked Jaroslav. "Will you stay to witness the fruits of your labours?"

"No," replied Charlaine. "Much as I'd like to, we have urgent business in the Antonine."

"I'm sorry to have delayed you. You'd be there by now if it wasn't for our mistakes."

"Do not apologize, Majesty. You were being manipulated by people trained in subterfuge. There's a reason these two families have been able to spread their power across the Petty Kingdoms. What matters is your willingness to listen when the time came."

"Yes," agreed Danica. "It could have gone far worse."

King Jaroslav bowed. "Well, I thank you, nonetheless."

"As do I," added Ingmar. "The both of you will always be welcome at the court of Galoran."

"Thank you, Majesty," replied Charlaine. "Now, before we leave, let's get this army of yours back across the border, shall we? It's getting late, and you don't want to set up camp in the dark."

"Yes, of course." King Ingmar wheeled around, riding off towards his army.

Jaroslav did the same, along with his guards and prisoners, leaving Charlaine and Danica between the armies of Ardosa and Galoran.

"Well," said Danica. "That gives us something to report to the grand mistress."

"Agreed," replied Charlaine, "but I fear it will go higher than that."

"Whatever do you mean?"

"We just averted a war close to the Antonine. We may be ordered to report directly to the Council of Peers."

16

ARRIVAL

SUMMER 1106 SR

The gates of the Antonine stood before them, while behind lay the streets of Reichendorf, the massive city that completely surrounded the Church grounds.

"We're finally here," said Danica. She urged her mount forward, and a trio of Cunars moved to block her.

"Not so fast," came the challenge. "We need to determine if you have just cause for entering the Antonine."

"Since when has that been necessary?" asked Charlaine. "Aren't all members of the Church granted equal access?"

"We're only doing our duty, Commander."

"Then ask your questions and be done with it."

"Please state your names."

"I am Temple Commander Charlaine, and this is Temple Captain Danica. We've come from Arnsfeld at the behest of the Grand Mistress of Saint Agnes."

"Have you orders to that effect?"

"What kind of question is that?" demanded Danica. "Are you suggesting we travelled more than a thousand miles on a whim?"

The guard maintained his calm demeanour. "I must see your orders to permit you entry."

Charlaine produced the letter from her grand mistress, and handed it over for inspection. The fellow perused it before passing it back. "All appears to be in good order, Commander. You may enter and visit your grand mistress, not that any of you will be wearing the scarlet of your order much longer."

"Why?" said Charlaine. "What have you heard?"

"Just that you might soon be wearing grey."

One of his companions shook his head. "Don't be ridiculous. That's true of the others, but we don't want those women in our order."

"Your order?" said Danica. "Are you proposing that all the orders would become Cunars?"

"That's the general consensus. No one knows the full story except those in charge, but everything's heading in that direction." He stood to one side, motioning for his comrade to do likewise. "Are you familiar with the route to the Agnesite commandery?"

"We are," replied Charlaine. "This is not our first time in the Antonine."

"Saints be with you."

"And with you, Brother." She urged Stormcloud forward, and they passed through the gates.

Danica waited until they were well out of hearing before making a comment. "What do you suppose that was all about?"

"The same thing it was about back in Torburg. The Cunars want everyone under their command."

"There's a big difference between being under their command and becoming full-fledged members of their order."

"There's no need to worry," said Charlaine. "You heard the other brother's comment; the Cunars don't want women in their order."

"True, but where does that leave us? Are they to disband our entire order?"

"THEY can't do anything. The Council of Peers rules over the Church, and there's no way they'd vote to disband the orders, let alone amalgamate them into the Temple Knights of Saint Cunar."

"Those guards appear to think otherwise," replied Danica.

"True, but they likely don't understand how the Antonine works." She brought Stormcloud to a sudden stop, catching her companion by surprise.

"Don't tell me you've forgotten the way?" said Danica.

"No. I just didn't expect this." She nodded in the direction they were heading.

The Antonine was mostly a wide-open space, with the Grand Sanctum at the north end and the building housing the Council of Peers to the south. In between, stood the great commanderies of each order, with open spaces where Temple Knights practiced their riding and martial skills. All were busy today, but most disturbing was the preponderance of grey-clad knights at work, honing their skills.

Charlaine frowned. "We've discovered where all the Cunars went when they pulled out of Arnsfeld."

"There must be a thousand of them here! What do you suppose they're up to?"

"We won't find out by standing here and gawking. Let's press on. Hopefully, the grand mistress can shed some light on this."

They increased their pace, turning right, eager to reach the commandery of Saint Agnes.

"I have an idea," said Charlaine.

"Let's hear it."

"This road takes us past the Mathewite commandery. What do you say we pay them a visit?"

"Won't the grand mistress be waiting for us?"

"We've spent months traversing the Petty Kingdoms, Danica. Do you think another couple of hours will make a difference?"

"Likely not, but it's been nine years since we were last here. Who do we know there that could be of assistance?"

"Temple Commander Jamarian?"

"Wasn't he an adjudicator at our trial?"

"Yes, and he was new to the Antonine then."

"Wouldn't he have moved on by now?"

"To where?" asked Charlaine. "There are only so many openings for regional commanders, and the Temple Knights of Saint Mathew are not a large order."

"Not large? They have a presence in almost every city in the Petty Kingdoms."

"True, but most locations only warrant a few knights, not the sort of place to send a Temple Commander."

"Meaning what? That he's become a glorified administrator?"

"It takes a great bureaucracy to run an order of Temple Knights. It's also common for our senior officers to be given responsibilities outside of the order."

"You mean like running the rest of the Church?"

Charlaine laughed. "No. The Council of Peers does that, but administrators still need to look after the day-to-day operations. You have a modest fleet and find it difficult to keep up. Imagine having a ship in every city in the Petty Kingdoms."

"Just thinking about it makes my head spin, but I concede the point."

The commandery of the Temple Knights of Saint Mathew was no different from the other orders, save for the brown banner hanging outside its doors. Across the Petty Kingdoms, one sentry normally halted visitors while the other went inside to report the presence of outsiders. Here in the Antonine, visitors from other orders were commonplace, leading to a simple nod in recognition of their rank and the offer to take their horses, which was gratefully accepted.

"I don't believe I've ever been inside a Mathewite commandery," said Danica. "I'm not certain what to expect."

"A lot of brothers milling around in their cassocks, I expect. Their knights don't generally don armour unless needed."

"I can see why; chain isn't the most comfortable attire."

They proceeded indoors, heading upstairs, seeking the offices of the senior officers. The commanderies in the Antonine, though similar in layout to those across the Continent, were different in one significant way —they were at least threefold larger. They knew they'd reached their destination because of the guards standing at attention at the entrance to the hallway.

"Is Temple Commander Jamarian still here in the Antonine?"

"Yes, Commander. His office is three doors down."

"Thank you, Brother."

They walked down the hallway to the correct room and knocked on the door frame. Inside, Temple Commander Jamarian sat behind a large desk littered with papers. Even though his hair had greyed considerably in the last few years, his eyes still held the same penetrating gaze when he looked up at them.

"Commander Charlaine, good to see you again. You, too, Captain Danica. I hear you've both been busy of late."

"We live to serve," replied Charlaine.

"I'm surprised to see you back here in the Antonine. I would've thought people with your skills better utilized on the border with the empire."

"Our grand mistress summoned us."

Jamarian nodded. "Yes. I suppose that makes sense, considering recent events. I assume she has something particular in mind for you?"

"I wouldn't know," replied Charlaine. "We've yet to report to her."

His eyebrows raised. "You decided to come see me first? I can only assume you wanted to get caught up on local events before seeing her?"

"That was the intent, yes."

"Many things are happening in the Antonine. Perhaps you could narrow down what you're interested in?"

"How about we start with the rumours of dissolution?"

"Ahh. That requires a lengthy explanation. I'm not certain how up to date you are concerning the politics of the Church, but last year, a new Primus was elected, a Temple General of Saint Cunar, who took the name of Wilmar upon his elevation to the position. Adopting a new name is commonplace, while the fact he was a Temple General rather than an archprior was most extraordinary. Of course, it's always assumed that a new Primus will leave their old order behind once elected, assuming a mantle of neutrality."

"I assume he failed in that regard?"

"Since his elevation to that office, he's been replacing key administrators with men of his former order."

"Excuse me?" said Danica. "Are you suggesting he's filling the Church bureaucracy with Temple Knights? Wouldn't lay brothers be more appropriate?"

"Admittedly, there are a few exceptions, but by and large, they've all been Temple Knights he previously served with."

"Has the Council of Peers not objected?"

"Most vehemently, but he was elected in a perfectly legal manner, and, unfortunately, there's no rule that disallows such action."

"That may be," offered Charlaine, "but there's an obvious issue of favouritism."

"The subject has been brought up on multiple occasions. However, there's no mechanism in place to punish a Primus who oversteps his authority. This has led to a fractious Council of Peers, so much so, little gets accomplished."

"Is it true he's been pushing for the orders to be disbanded?"

"That's a complicated mess. Originally, he announced he intended to make the Cunars the senior military order, allowing them to assume command of the other Temple Knights in times of conflict, but he's becoming even more demanding of late."

"Interesting," said Danica. "We heard a rumour he wants to fold the other orders into the Cunars."

"Yes. I've heard that, too, but to do that, a majority of the Council of Peers would have to support him, which appears unlikely at present."

"People can be persuaded," said Danica.

"Perhaps, but not, I think, in this. You need to remember, the Council of Peers numbers no Temple Knights amongst its members, only lay members."

"The Primus must have some support," said Charlaine, "else he wouldn't press the matter. Have we any idea who's on his side?"

"I know our patriarch has taken exception to the suggestion, and I can't imagine your matriarch agreeing, but as for the rest, I couldn't say."

"We must endeavour to find out. The Council of Peers only holds six votes, one for each order, with the Primus breaking any ties, which means he only needs three to support him, and you can be certain the Cunar will be on his side. If he passes this motion, he'll disband us all. I'm beginning to understand why the grand mistress called us to the Antonine."

"It is a most troubling development," noted Jamarian, "yet I fail to see how your presence here would help her. The grand masters of every order can be removed at their patriarch's discretion. There's not much you or I could do about that."

"I understand the political situation," replied Charlaine, "but I can't just sit idle while my order falls into obscurity."

"I agree with the sentiment; something needs to be done, but what does that look like? We can't force the Primus to resign. There's no precedent for that, and I doubt you could get enough of the patriarchs to agree to remove a sitting Primus. No. I'm afraid the only solution is to wait until his term ends, and they elect someone to take his place. Until then, we must hope his efforts concerning our orders go unrewarded."

"Thank you for your help, Commander. You've provided some key insights into this situation."

"I am but a humble servant of Saint Mathew. Are you expecting to remain in the Antonine for long?"

"We don't know," replied Charlaine. "We might be sent elsewhere, and this current situation is merely an unpleasant coincidence."

"I sense you don't believe that."

Charlaine shook her head. "I don't. It's strange that after withdrawing all their Temple Knights from the western Petty Kingdoms, the Cunars mass them here, in the Antonine, particularly having learned the new Primus is a former member of that very order."

"Are you suggesting this might be an attempt to seize power?"

"It's more likely a move to weaken the Petty Kingdoms."

"The Petty Kingdoms? I'm afraid you'll have to explain that leap of logic to me."

"Most assuredly," replied Charlaine. "For decades, the threat of the Holy Army held the Empire of Halvaria at bay."

"But that's not their way, surely? They always absorb one kingdom at a time."

"Have you ever asked yourself why? I believe they've done that to prevent the Church from mobilizing. They sweep into a single kingdom, and the invasion is over in a month or two, leaving little time for the Holy Army to assemble a defensive force. With the Cunars no longer stationed near the border, what's to hold them back?"

"The Petty Kingdoms, surely?"

"I admire your faith," said Charlaine, "but I've fought the Halvarians. It'll take more than a regional army to defeat them."

"You did so in Arnsfeld."

"I did, and I'll be the first to admit it was difficult. It took a concerted effort by many people, including members of your order."

"Are you seriously suggesting the Primus is serving the Halvarian Empire?"

"Perhaps not directly, but you must admit if this directive passes, it aligns with the empire's interests."

"You make a compelling argument, Commander, but I pray you are mistaken. If there's anything I can do to assist you in your endeavours, whatever they may be, please don't hesitate to seek me out."

"Thank you," replied Charlaine. "It's good to know we have someone on our side."

"What will you do next?"

"We'll report to our commandery to meet with our grand mistress."

"Then I bid you a good day, Commander. May the Saints be with you."

"Saints be with us all," replied Danica.

They retrieved their horses and continued on their way, their route taking them through the famed gardens and towards the fountain that marked their next turn. They halted momentarily to take in the view of the water splashing high in the air.

Danica moved closer, examining a bronze plaque at the pool's edge. "This says the fountain commemorates the fall of Herani. Strange to think we celebrate a failure."

"It's not a celebration," replied Charlaine. "It's a reminder of what can happen when we aren't vigilant."

"It wasn't all bad," said Danica. "Due to that debacle, they reorganized the fighting orders, not to mention creating a Holy Fleet. I remember Cordelia talking about it at some length."

"Yes. She was always interested in history."

"I wonder where she is now?"

"The last I heard, she was posted in the east, in Caerhaven."

"I would assume she's a Temple Captain by now," said Danica.

"No. She's still a knight but fulfilled her ambition of becoming an equerry. I wrote to her last year, but she never replied."

"She may have moved on to another posting."

"That's what I thought. I intended to follow up with further enquiries, but then we were summoned here."

"Well, there's no better place to discover the whereabouts of a fellow knight. I wonder where everyone else from Ilea is now?"

"I imagine they're scattered all over the Continent, except for Teresa, assuming she survived."

"You did the right thing," said Danica. "You either let the Sea Elves take her or let her die."

"We've lost a lot of sisters over the years."

"They all knew the risks. It's what comes of taking vows in a fighting order."

"That doesn't make it any easier."

"I know it doesn't," said Danica, "but in each case, they died serving their Saint. A Temple Knight can ask for little else."

"I would like to believe their sacrifices weren't in vain."

"They weren't. In the south, we broke the Halvarian Fleet, bringing safety to the people of Ilea. The entire north might have descended into conflict without their sacrifice at Temple Bay. I shouldn't have to remind you of what was at risk in Arnsfeld."

"Thank you, my friend."

"For what?"

"Restoring my faith."

17

THE GRAND MISTRESS
SUMMER 1106 SR

Temple Captain Nicola looked up from her desk as Charlaine and Danica entered. "I was beginning to think we'd never see you two again."

"Sorry," replied Charlaine. "We were delayed by circumstances in Ardosa."

"It would seem you were delayed by more than that."

"What do you mean?"

"The grand mistress will doubtlessly explain. Wait here, and I'll see if she's available." Nicola disappeared through a doorway, returning a moment later. "Come inside, both of you. There's much to discuss."

They entered the room to see the grand mistress, Kaylene Gantzmann, sitting behind her desk. "Have a seat," she said. "There's a lot to go over. You can wait outside, Nicola. I'll need you to inform me when our guest arrives."

"Yes, Your Grace."

"We came as soon as your summons reached us," said Charlaine. "I must apologize for the delay, but events in Ardosa commanded our attention."

The grand mistress went still. "What events are you referring to?"

"The kingdoms of Ardosa and Galoran were on the brink of war. An old grudge resurfaced, and both armies were prepared to march to battle."

"I'm guessing you managed to talk sense into them?"

"We did," replied Charlaine. "We uncovered a plot to destabilize the region and draw others into the war."

"Have you any idea who was behind this?"

"Yes, the Stormwinds and Sartellians. I believe I've mentioned their interference in previous reports?"

"If I recall correctly, a Sartellian murdered the King of Arnsfeld."

"Yes, Your Grace. And without their presence in Ardosa and Galoran, the entire affair would never have arisen in the first place."

"Did you resolve the situation without bloodshed?"

"The only death was the Stormwind."

"I cannot fault you for doing your duty. Having said that, it is not that delay which concerns me. I sent my original orders summoning you here almost three years ago after you reported your success at the Battle of the Brinwald."

"We never received them."

"That became painfully obvious when you failed to reply. Now, I know it's not uncommon for the Church's couriers to take their sweet time delivering messages, but after six months, I began to worry, so I dispatched another letter ordering you here. That, too, it seems, was intercepted. I had Nicola conduct a discreet investigation, but whoever was responsible took great pains to cover their tracks. In the end, I sent correspondence through the Mathewite Prior in Reinwick. I presume those were the orders you received?"

"They were," replied Danica. "Although even those weren't safe from the prying eyes of others."

"Meaning?"

"A Temple Captain of Saint Cunar accosted us on our way here, insisting on learning why we were journeying to the Antonine, which indicates he was privy to your attempts at contacting us. Did any of that correspondence reveal your reason for summoning us?"

"No," replied the grand mistress, "but someone must have been worried enough to prevent the first messages from reaching Arnsfeld."

"And the reason you sent for us?"

"Three years ago, the Cunar Patriarch pushed to disband the other fighting orders. The Primus at that time held no interest in it, but our new Primus has resurrected the idea."

"Yes," said Charlaine. "We've heard about him. Wasn't he a Temple Knight?"

"That he was, and he's a very persuasive fellow. In the last few months alone, he's convinced the Patriarch of the Augustines to support this ridiculous notion. He obviously has the Cunar Patriarch's support, so he only needs to sway one more vote for the motion to pass. I shouldn't have to explain the ramifications of that to you."

"What can we do?"

"I'm not entirely sure. The last time you were here, you helped uncover a rot within our order. I fear it's now spread across the entire Church."

"Could this be another example of outside interference?" asked Danica.

"It's certainly a possibility. It's odd to be facing this crisis right when the fighting orders are needed most."

"I agree," said Charlaine. "Have we any proof that the empire is behind this?"

"None at the moment, I'm afraid, although your recent experience in Ardosa suggests they have an interest in the region. That's where you two come in."

"You want us to investigate?"

"Precisely. Of course, that would've been easier had you received my original summons. With our new Primus, you may find it difficult to get to the heart of the matter without drawing attention. I must stress this is a dire situation. If you fail, it could mean the dissolution of our order."

"We understand," replied Charlaine. "What can you tell us about the current political situation? Where do the other orders stand?"

"The Patriarch of the Mathews stands firmly with our matriarch, but there is a growing feeling within the lay brothers of Saint Ansgar that this change in doctrine might be the sensible approach to managing the Church's finances."

"Are you suggesting this is a purely financial matter?"

"It's being framed as such. Maintaining a large force of Temple Knights is an expensive proposition. Many outside our respective orders prefer the funds be spent on other things. Primus Wilmar made the case that placing all the fighting orders under a single command structure would reduce costs significantly."

"With those command positions filled exclusively by Cunars?"

The grand mistress nodded. "He hasn't specifically stated that, but why else would he do it? There's also the intimidation factor. As you undoubtedly noticed on your way here, a large contingent of Cunar Temple Knights resides within the Antonine, far more than what was traditionally housed here."

"How much time do you think we have?"

"I can't say," replied the grand mistress. "The matter has yet to be officially raised in the Council of Peers, but that's only because the Primus knows he hasn't the votes. He'll force the issue if he somehow swings another patriarch over to his way of thinking."

"Is that likely to happen?"

"I wish I could say no, but even now, the council is discussing funding several new Cathedrals, including some for the Mathewites. It's an obvious attempt at a bribe, but I'm not the one in charge, and may soon be replaced."

"Replaced?" said Charlaine. "Why?"

"I've had several disagreements with the matriarch over funding our Temple Knights. In case you haven't noticed, we've been increasing our numbers of late. Your success brought recruits flocking to our academies. Unfortunately, we only have a limited number of instructors, so I decided to close the smaller academy in Carlingen and move the students to larger facilities here in the Antonine. This increased enrollment, however, means we need more weapons, armour, and mounts, putting a dreadful strain on our finances. The truth is, we've had to make do with less to achieve our aims."

"Which are?"

"To resist the expansion of the empire. We are at a critical point in time. The Cunars might seize control of the other orders, but they made it abundantly clear they have no stomach for women in the Holy Army. It would mark the end of us as an order."

The door opened to Temple Captain Nicola. "Sorry, Your Grace, but the grand master is here."

"Thank you, Nicola. I'll be with him shortly." She stood, indicating the meeting was over. "Settle yourselves into your rooms and report back to me tomorrow. Hopefully, by then, I'll have somewhere for you to begin your investigation."

"Yes, Mistress," they both echoed.

"Nicola will show you out."

They followed the captain into the outer office, coming face to face with the wrinkled countenance of a man in brown robes, the Grand Master of the Temple Knights of Saint Mathew.

Charlaine bowed. "Your Grace."

"Temple Commander Charlaine, isn't it?" he replied. "I read all about your exploits in Arnsfeld. You are to be congratulated on a job well done." He turned to Danica. "And you must be Admiral Danica. I've heard you've done wonderful work in the north. Keep it up."

"I will, Your Grace. Thank you."

"Now, you must excuse me. I have business with your grand mistress." He disappeared through the door.

"Wait here," said Nicola. "I need to give you your billeting orders." She went to her desk and produced a blank parchment.

As the captain put quill to paper, Charlaine moved to the window. Like all commanderies, the senior member of the order's office faced west, a tradition dating back to the reorganization of the fighting orders in the mid-740s. Her present position gave her an excellent view of the Ragnarite commandery and the Grand Avenue that ran between it and her current location.

The Temple Knights of Saint Ragnar, sometimes called witch-hunters, were dedicated to finding and eradicating the foul practice of Necromancy and, to a lesser extent, that of Hex Magic. The members of their order often travelled in the guise of commoners to conceal their presence, although they wore a green tabard for official ceremonies. Charlaine noted six of them coming around the north end of their building, having presumably just spent time on their practice field.

The sight made her think of Brother Aiden, the Ragnarite she met in Ilea. She'd last seen him in Alantra, along with the Kurathian Life Mage, Jarak. Was he still acting as a spy for the Church or fulfilling his vows as a seeker of Death Mages?

"Here," Nicola said, holding up the completed document. "This will see you safely billeted. I hope you don't mind sharing a room; the commandery is overfull. It's what comes from bringing all our initiates here from Carlingen." She glanced at Danica. "That's where you trained, wasn't it?"

"No. I went to Corassus. Why?"

"I thought you might run across some of your old instructors."

"Even if I had trained there, it's been over ten years since I joined. Most of my instructors would've moved on by now."

"Oh no. When we find a talented instructor, we try to keep them in place."

"I wonder," said Charlaine, "did we abandon Carlingen completely?"

"No. The commandery still exists, just not the training facility. The current garrison consists of a full company under the command of a Temple Captain who reports directly to us here in the Antonine."

"That's a little unusual, isn't it? Is there no regional commander?"

"The countries to the west comprise the central region, while to the east lies nothing but wilderness."

"And south?"

"That's Ostrova, where we lack a presence."

"And the north?"

"I can answer that," said Danica. "My ships have sailed those waters enough to know the coast. It's Zaran."

"Which is?"

"A wilderness where the brave or foolish, depending on your point of view, enter and disappear, never to be seen again. North of that lies Ruzhina, where the Stormwinds call home. Needless to say, we have no presence there either."

"Danica is correct," added Nicola, "which is why Carlingen only warrants a Temple Captain."

"Have we no plans for expansion in the area?" asked Danica.

"At the moment, the grand mistress has her hands full worrying about our continued existence. Let's hope she doesn't become the last person to hold her position. Much as I'd like to continue chatting, other duties demand my attention."

"Sorry to have kept you so long," said Charlaine. "When would you like us back here tomorrow?"

"Let me check." Nicola consulted a list. "Her Grace has nothing scheduled for mid-morning. Does that work for you?"

"Most definitely."

"Good. I'll see you then. Oh, and don't worry about wearing your armour; cassocks will do."

Charlaine and Danica returned to the entrance of the commandery to report to the duty officer, a dour-faced Temple Captain named Elliana, who took the billeting orders Nicola had so carefully prepared and made a note in her logbook.

"These state you're to share a room."

"That's correct," replied Charlaine. "We were told the commandery was stuffed to the gills. Is there a problem?"

"You're a senior officer, Commander, whereas Sister Danica is only a Temple Captain. It's highly irregular for sisters of two different ranks to share accommodations."

"Are you doubting Temple Captain Nicola's orders?"

Elliana frowned. "No. I'm not that stupid."

"Captain, are you new here?"

"I arrived from Draybourne last week. I'm going through training for my new rank."

"Draybourne? Where is that?"

"It's in the Duchy of Holstead, one of the easternmost realms of the Petty Kingdoms. Do you know it?"

"Is that somewhere near Krieghoff?"

"Krieghoff lies on its western border."

"I know the equerry in Caerhaven, its capital. Sister Cordelia?"

"Can't say I recognize the name," replied Elliana. "Then again, I didn't leave the city very often. I'd offer to pass on your good wishes if I see her, but the chances of me getting sent back there are slim. I'm hoping to go south to the Shimmering Sea."

"Are you from that area?" asked Danica.

"No. I'm just tired of living where it's always cold. I hear Ilea is nice."

"It is," said Charlaine, "providing you can tolerate being on the border with Halvaria."

"I'll keep that in mind. Now, as to your accommodations, you'll be on the third floor, with all the instructors. Room 317."

"Thank you, and good luck with your training."

Like that of the Mathewites, their commandery in the Antonine was a larger version of those found throughout the Petty Kingdoms. The top floor usually housed the Temple Commanders and grand mistress. Now, with the training academy here, someone thought it best to keep the instructor's living quarters separate from their students.

The small room had barely enough space for two beds, although at least the window was south-facing.

Danica sat on a bed. "This is quite comfortable," she said, bouncing on the mattress. "Do all senior officers get such soft beds?"

"Don't look at me. My bed back in Arnsfeld was about as soft as a tree trunk." Charlaine moved to the window, scanning the environs. "I can see the Augustine commandery."

"They're a smaller order, aren't they?"

"I don't know the exact details, but I read somewhere it's the smallest."

"It stands to reason," replied Danica. "After all, their only job is to guard the Holy Relics." She sat up suddenly. "Where do they keep those?"

"I beg your pardon?"

"The Holy Relics? They must have them somewhere secure."

"I imagine they're in the Council of Peers or the Grand Sanctum, which reminds me: if you're ever out late at night and need something to eat, that's the place to go."

"And you know this how, exactly?"

"I had reason to visit it the last time we were here. Why the curiosity about relics? Looking to steal one, are you?" Charlaine said with a grin.

"Not at all, although I might look up Brother Leamund while I'm here."

"He's the ship expert, isn't he?"

"He prefers the term naval architect, though it amounts to the same thing. I'm eager to exchange ideas with him. I've learned so much since we last met."

"I imagine you'll have ample opportunity to do just that," replied Charlaine, still staring out the window. "It's not as if we're going to be leaving any time—" She suddenly went quiet.

"Something wrong?"

"I'm not certain. What do you know about the Augustines?"

"Likely not as much as you do."

"Do they employ women?"

"Not that I've heard of. Why? Did you see one?"

"You tell me." She waved over her comrade.

Danica spotted a person dressed in all white, cutting across the practice field north of the Augustine commandery.

"Could it be a man with long hair?"

"In a braid? That seems unusual."

"Perhaps he's a foreigner? Kurathians have been known to serve as Temple Knights. Anyway, what difference does it make? It's not as if it's any of our business?"

"No," said Charlaine. "I suppose it isn't. It just wasn't something I expected."

"And I didn't expect to see so many Cunars in the Antonine, but there you go."

"Was it busy when you trained in Corassus?"

"Depends on your definition of busy. I was one of thirty recruits, but they kept us active all day long. You undertook your training in Eidenburg, didn't you?"

"Yes, in Talstadt. We called it the Forge." Charlaine paused. "We wore white surcoats in training. I wonder if that's who we saw down there?" She nodded out the window.

"I doubt it. I saw some recruits downstairs, and they wore light green."

"That's unusual, isn't it?"

"Is it?" replied Danica. "Back in Corassus, we wore pale blue. I think each academy has its own traditions. Perhaps Carlingen was always green?"

"Why does the order allow that? We're training initiates to become part of something bigger, so I'd think uniformity would be preferred."

"I imagine it has more to do with dye availability than any desire to carry on with traditions. I'm afraid it means our unknown visitor down there will remain a mystery, not that she's our visitor unless an Augustine has smuggled a woman into their commandery?"

Charlaine chuckled. "In the middle of the Antonine? I find that highly unlikely, don't you?"

"I do, but it would certainly give everyone something to talk about!"

18

RUMOURS

SUMMER 1106 SR

Danica stared down at her bowl, frowning. "I've had better-smelling food after three weeks at sea. Do they not know how to make stew here?" The packed dining hall held mostly new trainees, forcing her and Charlaine to share a table.

"You've been to sea?" asked a blonde initiate sitting beside her.

"You might say that."

"What does that mean?"

"It means," replied Charlaine, "Temple Captain Danica is the Admiral of the Temple Fleet."

The recruit looked at her with renewed interest. "Is that true?"

"Of course it's true," said Danica. "Do you suppose a Temple Commander would break her vow of honesty?"

"No," replied the blonde, "but then again, there's a big difference between breaking a vow and exaggerating."

"What do you think, Charlaine?"

"Charlaine?" said the initiate. "As in Temple Commander Charlaine?"

"Yes. Have you heard of me?"

"Of course. You're the victor of Arnsfeld."

"Hardly that," said Charlaine. "The Arnsfeld Army did most of the fighting."

A short-haired brunette leaned forward. "Is it true that Elves helped you at the Battle of the Brinwald?"

"Yes, but if we are to continue this discussion, don't you think it would be proper for you to introduce yourselves?"

"Sorry," said the blonde. "I'm Sister Magda."

"And you are?" asked Charlaine, looking at the brunette.

"Anthea, Commander. And this is Mariele, Genevieve, Lucille, and Iris."

"Did you all come from Carlingen?"

"No," replied Magda. "Lucille and Iris joined us here in the Antonine."

"And has your training already started?"

"It has, although we're only three weeks in. Most of us joined over a year ago, but moving from the north took the bulk of that time. I'm not complaining, but there were a lot of crates to pack up. What was it like when you were there?"

"I didn't train in Carlingen," replied Charlaine, "and Captain Danica trained in Corassus."

They all stared expectantly at the admiral.

"I was young," replied Danica, "and don't remember much."

"Except how to fight," added Charlaine.

"Have you done a lot of that?" asked Anthea.

"We both have."

"They say the order is a place where you find your family. Did you make a lot of friends at the academy, Commander?"

"No," said Charlaine, "but I was one of the older recruits. Thankfully, that changed once I became a Temple Knight."

"How did you two meet?"

"My, you're full of questions. Why don't you tackle that one, Danica."

"We met in Ilea," her comrade replied. "It was the first assignment for both of us."

"I heard there was some trouble down there a few years ago," said Lucille.

"There was, but the Holy Fleet was there to set things right."

"That's the Cunars for you," said Anthea. "Always doing the hard fighting."

Charlaine was about to correct the initiate but changed her mind. These were young, impressionable minds, and she didn't want to upset their instructor's lessons. She looked at Danica. "Are recruits getting younger, or are we just getting old?"

"Perhaps a little of both," replied Danica, "but I doubt any are as young as I was."

"I joined as soon as I could," offered up Magda. "For me, it was the stories coming out of Arnsfeld. Your exploits convinced me women can make a difference."

"Me too," added Anthea. "And I'd do almost anything to escape my parents' farm. Not that I have anything against them, but I was growing tired of smelling like the pigs."

"I wanted to be like my brother," said Lucille. "He's a Temple Knight of Saint Mathew. I also have an older sister who ran away to serve the Saints, although she's only a lay sister. You might say serving the Church runs in our family."

"I wanted to see the Continent," offered Mariele.

"Good luck with that," said Magda. "You don't have any choice about where you'll be assigned; we go where the order needs us."

"True," replied Danica, "but we've been to Ilea, Reinwick, and Arnsfeld."

"Yes," said Charlaine, "and Danica's sailed all along the coast of the Great Northern Sea."

"That's most interesting," offered Iris. "Did you come here from Arnsfeld?"

"We did."

"That must be almost as far as the lady in white."

"Lady in white?" said Charlaine.

"Yes. We see her in the dining hall from time to time."

"Is she a member of the order?"

"She was at one time, but no longer wears our colours. She dresses all in white now."

"Why?"

Iris shrugged. "Nobody knows, but—" She was about to say more when someone rang a bell, calling the initiates to classes. They hurried from the table, their conversation forgotten.

"Who do you suppose this lady in white is?" said Danica.

"I have no idea," replied Charlaine. "More importantly, though, if she's no longer a member of the order, why is she eating here at the commandery?"

"She must be the same woman we saw earlier. Do you think this relates to what's happening with the Council of Peers?"

"Are you suggesting she might be a Stormwind?"

"Either that or a Sartellian," replied Danica. "I can't imagine any other woman who'd be interested in this place unless she's a former lay sister."

"There are dormitories for lay sisters; the commandery is only for Temple Knights. Besides which, you heard Iris: she said this lady in white claimed to have been a member of the order. That's a term generally used to describe Temple Knights, not lay sisters."

"Temple Knights of Saint Agnes can leave at any time. Could this be someone who now wants to return?"

Charlaine shook her head. "She could have reported to any commandery in the Petty Kingdoms to do that. No, she came here for a purpose, and we need to find out what that is."

"And if it's nothing to do with the current situation?"

"Then we've only wasted a little of our time."

Danica pushed away the bowl. "I'll pass on this meal; I wasn't hungry anyway." With the initiates having left, the dining hall was getting quieter. She lowered her voice. "What's our next step?"

"We can't do much until we see the grand mistress again. What do you say we take a stroll around the commandery?"

"Let me guess. You're eager to get a look at this 'lady in white'?"

"Why, Danica. You've learned how to read my mind! Either that, or I'm too obvious."

"The latter, I'm afraid. You have a singular focus at times—not that there's anything wrong with that. Where shall we begin?"

"Let's visit the practice field."

"You believe that's the best place to find an ex-Temple Knight?"

"No, but the initiates knew about this woman. Who knows what else we might uncover?"

"You're suggesting we look for gossip?"

"I am. It may require some effort to separate facts from speculation, but it gives us somewhere to start without upsetting the hierarchy of the Church. Who knows? Perhaps we'll learn something worthwhile."

The initiates rode forward in a line, their formation loose and ill-disciplined.

"They've got a lot of practice ahead of them," noted Danica.

"Oh, I don't know," replied Charlaine. "Anthea over there appears to have some skill."

"She was from a farm, remember? Probably been riding a horse since she was a child. Iris, on the other hand, looks very uncomfortable in the saddle."

The riding instructor brought them to a halt and then chided them on their performance.

"That takes me back a few years," said Danica. "I took forever to learn how to ride, and I'm still not much good at it. I suppose that's why I feel so at home on the deck of a ship."

"We all have our weaknesses," noted Charlaine. "Mine was socializing."

"I find that difficult to believe."

"No, it's true. I grew up working in a smithy, not a trade that encourages being around others. Add to that the long hours required to forge swords, and there was no time left for friends."

"Had you no friends, growing up?"

"I didn't make any until I reached Ilea."

"Except for Ludwig."

"Well, yes," said Charlaine. "I suppose that's true."

"I was the same way. That is one thing those initiates got right; the order becomes your family."

"Let's hope that continues to be the case. If the new Primus has his way, all this training may be for naught."

The instructor called on the next group of trainees to take up the reins, freeing the first to have a break.

"Commander, Captain," said Magda. "You honour us with your presence. I hope we're not disappointing you?"

"It's always like this in the beginning," replied Charlaine. "Riding is one thing, but maintaining a mounted formation is far more complicated. You'll all master it in time; you just need to be patient."

"Any tips?"

"Heed the advice of your instructors. They know what they're doing."

"I have my doubts," said Iris. "All they do is yell at us."

"It seems like it now, but that won't always be the case. You'll find it easier once you're acclimatized to this place."

"Yes," agreed Danica. "The key to training is to act as a group rather than individuals. It's what makes us so effective on the battlefield."

"That would be easier with a little encouragement," said Anthea. "Commander Nina threatened to throw me in the dungeons if I didn't stop asking so many questions."

"Did you say Nina?" asked Charlaine.

"Yes. She came with us from Carlingen. Do you know her?"

"I served with her briefly, down in Ilea."

"Lucky you."

"You shouldn't speak ill of others," chided Charlaine. "It may come back to haunt you someday."

"How did Nina end up in Carlingen?" asked Danica.

"I imagine they sent her there after I took over in Arnsfeld."

"I thought she was ordered back here, to the Antonine."

"She was. My guess is they briefed her on what was needed to bring the academy here and then sent her north to organize everything."

"And now she's here?" replied Danica.

"She is the headmistress of the academy," offered Iris. "She deals personally with every rule infraction, no matter how minor."

"Yes," added Anthea. "Poor Magda was called to her office three times in the last week alone." She paused, her face betraying her sudden embarrassment. "Sorry. I know it's not right to criticize, but it seems excessive, considering we're just beginning our training."

"I'll withhold judgement on that for now," replied Charlaine. "Anything else you'd care to share?"

"Such as?"

"Rumours, perhaps?"

"None that I know of," replied Anthea.

"What about that knight?" asked Lucille.

"Knight?" said Charlaine. "What knight?"

"They say the Ansgarites are holding a knight."

"That's their job," said Danica. "They investigate all the Temple Orders."

"Yes, but he's not a member of the Church. He's a Knight of the Sceptre, whatever that is."

"Knight of the Sceptre? Are you certain?"

Lucille nodded. "That's what I heard. Why? Who are they?"

"An order of chivalry from Erlingen," replied Charlaine. "I can't figure out what one of them is doing here, let alone why he's rotting in a dungeon."

"It is only a rumour," Danica reminded her. "As such, the details often get muddled."

"We'll ask the grand mistress about it tomorrow, along with our questions concerning the woman robed in white."

A Temple Captain leading a horse exited the stables. "Do my eyes deceive me or is that Sister Danica?" she said as she drew closer. "My pardon, it's Temple Captain Danica now." She then caught sight of Charlaine. "And Charlaine, a Temple Commander! What are the odds?"

"Erika?" said Danica. "What are you doing here?"

"Temple Captain Giselle sent me here for training after recommending me for promotion."

"How long have you been here?"

"Almost two months now. I hear Charlaine has been busy. Were you with her at the Battle of the Brinwald?"

"No," replied Charlaine. "She commanded the fleet at the Battle of Lidenbach."

"My apologies for the slight," said Erika. "I had no idea you were in charge. We heard about the victory, but Danica's name was never mentioned. You two have been busy since Ilea."

"That we have. How have things been since we left?"

"Pretty quiet. The only thing of note was when the Cunars withdrew, leaving us the daunting task of protecting the area."

"That must've proven difficult."

"Oh, it did, but it also allowed us to call in more knights. The garrison was up to half a company when I left."

"And Giselle?"

"She was still a Temple Captain. A pity, really, considering they cleared her name. As for the rest from back in the day, most moved on."

"Miranda was with us in Arnsfeld," said Charlaine, "but unfortunately, she didn't survive the battle. Florence is still around, though, and commanding a full company."

"That's good to hear."

"What brings you out here to the training ground? Considering doing a little riding?"

"Temple Commander Nina informed me I was to practice with the recruits. They need someone to order them around, which is something I lack experience in. It appears some things never change." She looked over at the trainees. "Who are these women?"

"Initiates," replied Danica.

Charlaine turned to the students. "This is Temple Captain Erika. We served together in Ilea."

"Another lifelong friend?" asked Anthea.

Erika shook her head while a grin spread across her face. "We didn't get along initially but learned to put aside our differences."

"Yes," added Charlaine, "and I'd be proud indeed to serve alongside her again, should the need arise."

"You must excuse me," said Erika. "I must inform the instructor I'm here and ready to do my part."

"Find us later, and we'll catch up."

"I most certainly will." With that, Erika left them.

"That was a nice surprise," said Danica. "Who else might we know here?"

"We should have a peek at the order's records and see what we can discover. At the very least, it might help us track down the others from Ilea."

Danica grew sombre. "I wish Aurelia were here, not to mention Helena. She was the first of us to go to the Afterlife."

"She died doing what she loved. We can ask for little else when our time comes."

"I, for one, am not in a hurry to die."

"I'm glad to hear you say that because we've got a lot of work ahead of us." Charlaine smiled. "Come to think of it, our task might've become much easier."

"How so?"

"A burden shared is a load lightened," said Charlaine, "and I've got a sense this investigation is about to get more complicated."

"So you're going to pull in Erika?"

"We could help," offered Magda.

"You're still initiates," replied Danica. "You'll be too busy with your studies."

"I beg to differ," offered Charlaine. "Some training in problem-solving might prove useful to their careers."

"So you are now suggesting we get help from trainees?"

"Not right away, no, but once they're past the first months, they'll have some free time."

"Free time?" said Mariele. "What's that?"

"I know it doesn't seem like it," continued Charlaine, "but once you've settled into your training regime, you'll find it's not so bad."

"What was your training like?"

"I was lucky. I already knew how to ride a horse."

"I suppose," said Mariele, "you could fight as well."

"I had some rudimentary training before joining, but I'd hardly call myself trained."

"She was a smith, though," added Danica. "So, in a sense, her muscles were ready to be trained."

Mariele knitted her brows. "How does that help?"

"You'll understand when you're properly trained."

"What she means," offered Charlaine, "is that your muscles eventually learn how to wield weapons, allowing you to concentrate on other things."

"Like what? Shouldn't you always be alert in battle?"

"There's more to it than swinging a sword. There's battle awareness, which is a simple way of saying you need to pay attention to the ebb and flow of the melee. Fighting isn't just about slaying the enemy; it's knowing when to swing your sword and when it's wiser to withdraw."

"But wouldn't that be considered cowardly?"

"To fight when there's no chance of victory is throwing away your lives. Sometimes that's necessary, so long as it serves a higher purpose, but more often than not, it's better to safeguard your numbers in hopes of employing them when you can make more of a difference."

"That's very interesting," said Magda. "Why don't our instructors teach us such things?"

"That's an excellent question," replied Danica.

19

THE MEETING

SUMMER 1106 SR

Kaylene Gantzmann, the Grand Mistress of Saint Agnes, set down her quill, her gaze wandering around her office. "I shall miss this place."

"You talk as though you've already left," said Charlaine. "Have you heard something we haven't?"

"Not yet, but I fear it's only a matter of time."

"How much time?"

"Things have calmed down, and I've been assured the Council of Peers won't convene again until next spring."

"Is that typical of how they do things in the Antonine?" asked Danica.

"It is now. Our new Primus prefers to winter in Corassus, and the Cunar Patriarch invited him to examine the Holy Fleet while he's there."

"And the others?"

"The council does not meet without the Primus."

"But wouldn't that happen when a new Primus has to be elected?"

"Only when the previous title holder dies in office. Otherwise, the outgoing Primus oversees the process. Even if the council did pass an edict, it couldn't be enforced until it bears his seal."

"That's interesting," said Danica. "Speaking hypothetically, what would happen if the Primus refused to sign an edict?"

"It would be unenforceable," replied the grand mistress. "Admittedly, that situation has never happened before, but it reveals a potential weakness in the running of the Church."

"Getting back to your previous comment," said Charlaine. "What leads you to presume your position is in jeopardy?"

"Late last night, the Matriarch of Saint Agnes summoned me to give me a good talking-to. Your resistance to the Halvarian expansion was recently a hot topic of conversation amongst the highest-ranking levels of the Church."

"In what way?"

"For centuries, the Church insisted on not intervening in secular matters. Some feel your actions crossed that line. Don't worry, I'm not one of them, but this situation illustrates the fracturing of Church doctrine. If you recall, the Grand Master of the Mathewites came here yesterday."

"Yes," said Charlaine. "That's right. You cut our visit short so you could meet with him."

"His order is also drawing the ire of certain members of the Church hierarchy."

"For their part in Arnsfeld?"

"No," replied the grand mistress. "For their interference in Hadenfeld. In Arnsfeld, we held the moral high ground when we faced off against the Halvarian Empire, but Hadenfeld was a clear case of favouring one claim to the Throne over another."

"How does the grand master feel about that?"

"As I do, that the interference was for the greater good. The council, however, is uncomfortable with a fighting order taking sides in what they consider a regional conflict. Some are even using it as an excuse to isolate us—politically, that is. The Ansgarites were already sympathetic to the concept that combining the orders would be more cost-effective. This latest argument only pushed them further into the Primus's corner."

"But we only increased our presence in Arnsfeld because the Cunars withdrew."

"Which is why I sent you there in the first place. This situation in Hadenfeld, however, is much more difficult to justify."

"Did the Mathewite Grand Master order their involvement?"

"No. The regional commander made that decision, and I understand why. If he'd sent word to the Antonine, the conflict would've been over long before he received permission to act."

"There's something you should know," said Charlaine, "that may have some bearing on these events."

"Go on."

"There is evidence the empire was interfering in Hadenfeld."

"Interfering how, exactly?"

"As you know, the Stormwinds and Sartellians have been employing their influence to disrupt realms across the Petty Kingdoms, and a Sartellian killed the king in Arnsfeld."

"Yes," replied the grand mistress. "I remember reading your account. Are you suggesting they were doing the same thing in Hadenfeld?"

"I know it for a fact."

Kaylene Gantzmann leaned forward, resting her arms on her desk. "How?"

"I've been in correspondence with His Majesty, King Ludwig."

"Since when?"

"Some years," replied Charlaine. "I knew him before I joined the order."

"And you chose to keep in touch? That's highly irregular, Commander."

"It's not what you think, Your Grace. He was married in Reinwick while I served there. I thought it best to warn him about the Stormwinds' role at the duke's court. Later, when we uncovered the Sartellians' duplicity, I also passed that information on to him."

"So his seizing the Throne was a direct consequence of a Halvarian plot?"

"I'm certain it's much more complicated than that," said Charlaine, "but he obviously felt King Morgan was under their influence. Ludwig is not the type of man to seek power for its own sake. If he felt he had no choice but to seize the Throne, we must consider how dire his circumstances had become."

"That explains a great deal," said the grand mistress. "It's obvious the Mathewite Regional Commander understood the risk. I'm surprised the presence of a Sartellian at Hadenfeld's court wasn't brought up in the council."

"Perhaps someone suspects the empire has ears there."

"Here? In the Antonine? I think you overestimate their influence."

"Do I? We thought we were dealing with sea raiders in Ilea, but it proved to be Halvaria. In Reinwick, we ran across the empire once again, attempting to influence matters. Even after that, they could've blamed things on an overzealous leader, but then the invasion of Arnsfeld happened."

"Yes," added Danica. "Though they tried to blame the legion commander for that. The Halvarians are a plague on the Petty Kingdoms, and those mages, the Stormwinds and Sartellians, are just as bad... Well, perhaps not all of them."

"What are you saying?" asked Kaylene.

"Some renegade Stormwinds are out there, fighting to reduce the family's influence."

"It began as rumours," continued Danica, "but as the Temple Fleet expanded, we reached more ports, and the stories built. Just last year, we received word the Kingdom of Therengia was reborn in the east, and it's rumoured a Stormwind leads their army."

The grand mistress shook her head. "None of that would've come about had it not been for that ill-fated crusade in the east."

"Yes," said Charlaine, "but if true, it shows the family is fractious, which is a good sign."

"Perhaps, but it's of little concern to us now. I need you two to determine where the other orders stand regarding amalgamating the Temple Knights."

"Couldn't you ask them?" replied Danica.

"Not without raising the matriarch's ire."

"And if we find that any are likely to agree with the Primus?"

"All we can do at this point is gather information. Acting on it may prove viable when not so many eyes are upon me."

"We understand completely," replied Charlaine. "We shall endeavour to be as discreet as possible."

"Good," said the grand mistress. "Have you any further questions?"

"A couple, if you can answer them. We've heard reports that a secular knight is being held in the Antonine. Do you know anything about that?"

"I'm afraid I don't. Are you certain it's not just a rumour? It's unlikely an outsider would be kept under lock and key."

"Would you be opposed to us finding out more?"

"Not at all. I assume you'd start with the Ansgarites?"

"That is the most logical place," replied Charlaine.

"Let Temple Captain Nicola know what you discover."

"I will. There's also the matter of the woman in white."

"Who is?"

"Apparently, an ex-Temple Knight seeking readmittance to the order."

"Nothing has crossed my desk regarding anything of that nature. Are you certain this person used to be one of our knights?"

"We've only heard rumours," replied Charlaine, "but we'll certainly make efforts to discover her story."

"It's a strange situation, to be sure. Typically, those who leave the order need only seek out whoever's in charge of the local commandery and press their case."

"Yet she came all the way to the Antonine."

"I can think of only one reason why she'd come here," said the grand mistress. "To seek forgiveness for something."

"So she might've been expelled from the order?"

"That'd be my guess unless you're suggesting someone came back from the dead?"

"Why would that be a problem?" asked Danica. "I'm not suggesting it's even remotely possible, but clerical errors can happen."

"The names of sister knights who die in service to the order are placed in the hall of heroes. If one re-emerged alive and well, it would be difficult to remove her name."

"If someone sought readmission," asked Charlaine, "who in our order would be responsible for allowing or disallowing it? Would that be you?"

"No. I'm far too busy as the grand mistress. The senior Temple Commander would deal with that, which is Nina, but she's in charge of the training academy. You'd have to ask Nicola who's next in seniority."

"But you're in charge of the order?"

"Do you have any idea how many Temple Commanders we have spread across the Petty Kingdoms?"

"I assume one for each region."

"That would be a start," said the grand mistress, "but we tend to be a top-heavy organization here at the Antonine. Your arrival here puts the number at thirteen."

"Does that include those in training?"

"It does not. You have to realize we need someone to oversee new constructions, look after administrative details, see to the financing of the order, and so on. These tasks are unsuitable for a Temple Captain because they carry considerable responsibility. You remember Hjordis?"

"I could hardly forget her," replied Charlaine.

"She maintained discipline within the order, yet another position requiring a Temple Commander. We often think of Temple Captain as the primary working rank amongst officers, but when orders are handed down from the Antonine, the person issuing them must have a rank higher than the officer receiving them, or no one would be compelled to follow. Seniority can play havoc with that, but at least our rules are easy to understand. If you want to be confused, try reading how the Cunars run things."

"I thought they worked with ranks, the same as us?"

"Oh, they do, but then they add a complication—ordination. Some of their Temple Commanders are ordained as Holy Fathers, allowing them to conduct ceremonies outside their order—that's where the term Father General comes from. To make it worse, they also have Temple Generals, some of whom are ordained and use the same name."

"Is there no way to determine which actual rank a Father General holds?"

"Not unless you see them in person. Temple Captains' surcoats have silver embroidering, while Temple Commanders' have gold. We use sashes to distinguish our officers, particularly when marching with the armies of the Petty Kingdoms, not that it happens very often outside the Crusades."

"Do we have Temple Generals?" asked Danica.

"In theory, we do. That is to say, we have the rank, but in the entire history of the order, no woman has ever held it." The grand mistress stopped talking, her gaze drifting to a bookcase on her right.

Charlaine leaned forward. "Is something wrong, Your Grace?"

Kaylene's gaze snapped back to her visitors. "No. Everything's fine. You reminded me of something, that's all. Now, unless you have more questions, you'd best be on your way. Remember, this is not an official investigation, as that would draw too much scrutiny. I'm counting on you to be discreet—fail in that, and you may hasten my dismissal, and I can't guarantee my successor would be so understanding."

Danica appeared in the doorway, bearing two tankards and a platter heaped with food. "I thought I'd save us the trouble of going down for dinner." She noted Charlaine sat on the edge of her bed, perusing an old tome. "What have you got there?"

"A book detailing the rules and procedures used by the Council of Peers."

"Anything interesting?"

"That depends on your definition. Are you aware that members of the fighting orders are specifically banned from holding a seat on the council?"

"I suppose it makes sense. The highest-ranking member of the order is a grand mistress, and she's appointed by the matriarch, who is a senior arch-prioress."

"I understand that," said Charlaine, "but the new Primus is a Temple General, or rather, was."

"The Cunars are more than just a fighting order. Like us and the Mathewites, their lay members conduct services in their temples for regular folk. I've heard they're popular in some Petty Kingdoms."

"The more warlike ones."

"Is there any other kind?"

Charlaine set the book down. "It's not the most exciting thing to read, but I want you to at least put in the effort."

"You believe we'll need it?"

"I don't want to go into this blind, and we'll be dealing with Church bureaucracy. Something in here could help us."

"Such as?"

"For a start, we'd know what we're empowered to do and what we're not. Too many people were asserting their authority the last time we were here."

"Don't remind me," said Danica. "I spent a lot of time in the dungeon beneath the commandery, remember?"

"Precisely, and we don't want a repeat of that."

A Temple Captain knocked hesitantly on the door frame behind Danica. "Commander Charlaine?" she asked.

"That's me. What can I do for you?"

"I'm Temple Captain Mila, the duty officer for today. I'm here to inform you that, as the most senior Temple Commander in the commandery, you've been assigned as its commanding officer."

"I understood Temple Commander Nina was senior to me."

"That's true, but she's far too busy as the commandant of the training academy to oversee the efficient running of the commandery."

"But isn't the school part of the commandery?"

"It is," replied the captain, "which would, on paper, make you her superior."

"Do I detect some hesitation on your behalf?" asked Charlaine.

"I'm only the duty officer, Commander. By this time tomorrow, someone else will be carrying out these duties. All I know is Temple Commander Gianna departed this morning for her next assignment, leaving the position open. I consulted the duty officer's book to see what was to be done and discovered I needed to check the roll of Temple Commanders and determine who was next in line."

"I was under the impression there were at least ten others in the Antonine."

"Oh, there are, but they're all spoken for. I'm afraid you're it for now, although there's always the possibility another one more senior will come along."

"I see. And am I allowed to name my aide?"

"I assume so."

"Good. Then you may record in the log that Temple Captain Danica is officially filling that position."

"I shall note that, Commander." The captain let loose a sigh of relief, then paused. "But I suppose you'll see that when I hand it over at the end of my shift."

"I imagine I will. Where do I find my new office?"

"It's on this floor, Commander."

"Wait. I know. Facing west?"

"Yes. At the south end of the same corridor as the grand mistress's office."

"It looks like my days are about to get a lot busier. Thank you, Captain. You may return to your duties."

"Yes, Commander."

They waited until she was well out of earshot before continuing their discussion.

"What do you make of that?" asked Charlaine.

"I find it strange the grand mistress asks us to investigate the Church only for you to be assigned as the person responsible for running the commandery."

"As do I. Something strange is going on around here."

"Could someone else have arranged this?"

"Like who? I can't see Nicola doing this, can you?"

"No, but you'd think the grand mistress would say something about losing a Temple Commander, wouldn't you?"

"My guess is there's another player in here somewhere. The grand mistress told us twelve other Temple Commanders of our order are here in the Antonine; perhaps one of them engineered this?"

"Who'd have the authority to do that?"

"I intend to find out."

"And in the meantime?"

Charlaine shrugged. "I was a regional commander back in Arnsfeld. I can't imagine the commandery here being any more difficult, can you? And look on the bright side."

"Which is?"

"We have an office to work out of now."

20

THE WOMAN IN WHITE
SUMMER 1106 SR

Temple Commander Gianna had left a note on the desk and an assortment of ledgers for whoever replaced her as head of the commandery.

"Not much in the way of furniture," noted Danica. "Did she never entertain guests?"

"I imagine whoever reported to her remained standing. I've heard that's a common practice."

"Will you continue with that tradition?"

"No. I think chairs are preferable." Charlaine moved to take her seat, reading over the note.

"Anything of interest?" asked Danica.

"Just the usual. It lays out the basic duties of the office, then refers to these ledgers."

"Which are?"

"One is the roster, recording everyone here at present. The other is the master logbook. I'll let you know if I find anything interesting in it."

"What's your first order?"

"I need to set the duty officer roster. Every Temple Captain, including those in training, is expected to take her turn."

"Allow me to take the next assignment. It'll give me a chance to meet people, not to mention access to the duty officer's log."

"Are you certain?" said Charlaine. "Everything in that book is transcribed into the master log. There's also the point you're officially my aide."

"I wouldn't want to be seen as someone who curries favour. I'll take on the responsibility for one shift, like everyone else. Better now than later, when it's not so convenient."

"Then the job's yours, although you technically don't begin until the logbook is turned over."

"And when does that occur?"

"When the bell sounds for dinner."

A bell tolled outside, soon taken up by the other commanderies.

"Well-timed," said Danica. "Did you arrange that?"

Temple Captain Mila appeared in the doorway. "Reporting as ordered, Temple Commander. I trust I'm not late?"

"Come in, come in," replied Charlaine. "You're right on time."

Mila placed the duty officer's log on the table and a small box containing ink and a quill. "Everything is in order, Your Grace."

"I'm a Temple Commander, not the grand mistress. As such, you refer to me as Temple Commander or simply Commander. Understood?"

"Yes, Commander."

"Anything noteworthy to report?"

"The woman in white showed up again."

"Did you get her name?"

"I did," said Mila. "I made an entry in the logbook."

Charlaine opened the tome, scanned through the entries, and then sat back in her chair, a smile breaking out. "That will be all. Thank you. You are relieved of your duty."

The Temple Captain bowed her head slightly before she turned and left the room.

"I assume the mystery is solved?"

"Yes, although I must admit it's somewhat of a shock."

"Why? Who is it?"

"Teresa."

"Didn't she leave with the Sea Elves?"

"She did."

"But Gwalinor said she could never return to the Continent."

"Something must've changed," replied Charlaine.

"Then why didn't she rejoin the order?"

"I think I know. We reported her as lost, not dead, but I suspect whoever is responsible for maintaining the order's records listed her as dead, making it impossible for her to resume her life as a Temple Knight. Ordinarily, it wouldn't make much of a difference since she wasn't supposed to return, but now we find ourselves in a predicament."

"What do we do?"

"You're officially the duty officer," said Charlaine. "Find her and bring her here so I can speak with her."

"The bell has rung, calling everyone to the evening meal, which means she's likely in the dining hall." Danica turned to leave.

"Aren't you forgetting something?" Charlaine held up the duty officer's log and the box of ink and quills. "You'll need this to record anything of note."

Danica smiled, then scooped up the two items and raced off. Charlaine pondered this development. Sister Teresa had served in Ilea with them and been critically wounded at the Battle of Alantra. The Elven healer, Gwalinor, could not mend her wounds, so in desperation, he'd placed her in a state of perpetual sleep, hoping someone in the Elven Isles might be able to save her. It had been a heavy price to pay, for once there, she'd been banned from returning to the Continent, but it was either that or let her die, and Charlaine had seen enough death that day.

Teresa had surprisingly survived the ordeal and now, almost ten years later, was here in the Antonine, ready to assume her previous calling. Or was she? Was that her objective, or was she here for an entirely different reason?

Darkness had fallen by the time Danica returned with a guest in tow. Teresa entered the room, her long black hair tied back in an elaborate braid rather than hanging loose. Her blue eyes appeared to hide a world of secrets behind her intense stare.

Charlaine immediately stood, then moved around her desk to embrace the woman, tears welling up in her eyes. She found it difficult to speak.

"See?" said Danica. "I told you she'd be happy to see you." She looked around the room. "Ah. You found some chairs. Let's sit, shall we?"

"Good idea," said Charlaine, finally finding her voice. "I must say this comes as a bit of a shock. What brings you to the Antonine?"

"I could ask you the same question," replied Teresa.

"The grand mistress summoned us."

"To what end?"

Charlaine nodded at the door. Danica stood and closed it, then returned to her seat. Charlaine rested her chin on her steepled fingers. "We're here because the order is in danger."

"In danger, how?"

"How up to date are you on Church politics?"

"Not very, I'm afraid."

"A new Primus was elected last year, an ex-Cunar who seems to think the Church is better served by having all the Temple Knights under his old order's command."

"Are you suggesting everyone would become Cunars or that the Cunars would be put in charge of everything?"

"That has yet to be determined," replied Charlaine.

"And the Council of Peers supports this?"

"Some do, but not enough for the motion to pass."

"What does the grand mistress think you can do about this?"

"Danica and I faced something similar on our last trip here, back in ninety-seven."

Teresa muttered under her breath.

"Sorry," said Charlaine. "I missed that."

"My apologies. It's an Elven curse. That's what comes of spending so much time amongst the Sea Elves."

"Can you tell us what happened to you?"

"The last thing I remember was being tied to the mast of that Halvarian ship. Did Cordelia survive?"

"She did. I heard she was in Krieghoff, one of the easternmost Petty Kingdoms, and doing well for herself."

"I'm relieved," said Teresa. "I asked Gwalinor about her, but he didn't recognize her name."

"You were saying?"

"Yes. I must've passed out while hanging from the mast. When I awoke, I was in a house of healing in Lithandor."

"Which is?"

"One of their port cities. They healed me, but their laws do not allow outsiders to leave once they set foot in Eloria."

"I assume that's the name of their lands?"

"It is."

"Then how are you back in the Antonine?"

"I learned to speak their language while there and mastered the healing arts under the guidance of Gwalinor. He spoke to the High Lord of Eloria in my name, eventually convincing him to permit me to leave, but required me to take a sacred oath not to reveal the location of Eloria."

"I understand completely," said Charlaine. "You may rest assured I shall not press the matter. I am curious why you came here rather than return to Ilea, where Captain Giselle could've sworn you back in as a Temple Knight?"

"As I told Temple Commander Gianna when I arrived, I'm not here to resume my duties with the order," said Teresa. "At least not in the traditional sense."

"Then why are you here?"

"I've been given the gift of healing and wish to share my knowledge with others."

"In what way?"

"I would like to establish a sect within the order dedicated to the pursuit of healing magic, but that requires restructuring our vows."

"I'm not certain I follow."

"When I became a healer, I vowed never to kill. I would expect the same of any others who took up the calling."

"You can't expect Temple Knights to do that," said Danica. "We're a fighting order."

"And I wouldn't. Only those becoming healers would be required to swear such."

"A noble sentiment," said Charlaine. "Would these sisters be allowed to protect themselves in battle?"

Teresa smiled. "I'm not suggesting they stand meekly by while an enemy attacks, merely that they refrain from seeking out battle."

"And try not to kill their attackers?"

"Yes. Of course, accidents do happen, but learning the art of Life Magic is a heavy investment. I shouldn't like to see my apprentices risk being slain."

"Speaking of apprentices, have you any way of identifying them? My understanding is that it's difficult to tell when a person is capable of using magic."

"Do you recall when we first met Gwalinor?"

"Yes. It was right after I was wounded. If I recall correctly, he sensed your magic potential."

"He did, and then he confirmed it by passing into the spirit realm and examining my aura."

"That's right," said Charlaine. "I'd forgotten about that. Are you saying you can do the same?"

"Yes, although it took me longer than expected to master that spell, for I needed to learn to read a subtle canvas."

"I'm not sure I understand."

"Everyone gives off an aura, but while I'm in the spirit realm, the type of magic residing within them shades their aura. Were I to examine an Earth Mage, for example, I would see an aura tinged by brown, while a Life Mage would have a predominantly white one. The colour of those untrained are subdued, making it more difficult to ascertain. Elves find it easier than I, but I suspect it has more to do with Elven eyesight than any innate magical ability, for they can see much farther than us."

"Is it true they see better at night?"

"No. To my knowledge, only the Orcs are so gifted."

"Were there Orcs in Eloria?"

"If there ever were, they were slain long ago. There is great enmity between the two races from a war long past, which led to the split in the Elven lands."

"The split?"

"Yes. Those who opposed the war fled the Continent in a fleet of ships to seek a new land, becoming what we now know as the Sea Elves."

"So they didn't fight the Orcs?"

"No. Although they loathed them, as did their brethren, they refused to dedicate their lives to eradicating an entire race."

"So much hate," said Danica. "How long ago was this war?"

"At least two thousand years have passed, although I don't claim to be an expert on dates."

"Two thousand years, and they still hold a grudge?"

"Elves are immortal, and don't age like us Humans. As a result, they recall events from long ago as if it were yesterday."

"But surely all Elves aren't two thousand years old?"

"No, but they reproduce slowly. It's one of the reasons they want to keep their island home a secret: they fear invasion and lack the numbers to oppose one."

"I understand their reasoning," said Charlaine, "but the Petty Kingdoms are expanding. I'm afraid it's only a matter of time before seafarers enter their waters."

"A dense fog protects them," replied Teresa. "Any ship entering it becomes disoriented and finds itself turned around; either that, or they succumb to the reefs and perish. It takes a skilled navigator to penetrate that type of defence."

"You're being refreshingly open with us."

"Like you, I took an oath to tell the truth. I am, at heart, still a Temple Knight."

"And you will always be welcome at the commandery so long as I command."

"Would you be willing to assist me with persuading the grand mistress to adopt my proposal?"

"Under normal circumstances, I'd be delighted, but I'm afraid you've caught us at a bad time. It's highly probable our order could be disbanded entirely within the next year."

"Is it truly that bad?" asked Teresa.

"I'm afraid it is."

"Then let me help you in whatever way I can."

"I appreciate the offer," said Charlaine, "although I'm not aware how you might be of assistance."

"As an outsider, I have the advantage of not being affiliated with any single faction."

"Except you were once a member of our order."

"That is something known to only a few."

"I'll have to think about your offer carefully. As Danica would say, 'We're in uncharted waters here; we need to tread carefully.' I shouldn't wish to put you in any danger."

"I've faced ill-treatment at the hands of the Halvarians," replied Teresa. "If that didn't break me, nothing will."

"It's not breaking I'm worried about—it's murder."

"You really believe whoever's behind this would go to that extreme?"

"I think they'll do whatever they need to achieve their objectives."

"We could assign her a bodyguard," suggested Danica. "Saints know we have enough Temple Knights here."

"No," said Teresa. "That might draw too much attention to my comings and goings. If I'm to be of use to you, it's better that I act alone."

"Let me think it over," said Charlaine. "In the meantime, I ask you to be careful out there. There's far too many Cunars crawling around the Antonine for my taste."

"Yes. I noticed that, although I'm surprised to hear you hold them in so little regard. Aren't they the fighting arm of the Church?"

"They are, but in the north, they actively interfered with our defence of Arnsfeld."

"I've heard nothing of this."

"Nor would I expect you to. The Church won't acknowledge their bad behaviour, and it's not as if the senior officers of our order want to emphasize the rift between two orders of Temple Knights."

"This is a sad state of affairs."

Charlaine held up her finger. "Actually, you can help us with something. We recently heard rumours the Ansgarites are holding a secular knight."

Teresa stood. "Say no more, Commander. I know someone who might be able to shed some light on that."

"Thank you, and let's forgo the 'commander', shall we? I'd prefer you call me Charlaine. Remember, you're technically an outsider."

The woman smiled. "I've missed you, both of you. I'm thankful to the Elves for saving me, but they're an aloof folk. It's made for a very lonely existence."

"You're back with your family now," said Danica, "just as you should be, even if we can't openly acknowledge it yet."

"Where are you staying?" asked Charlaine.

"Temple Commander Gianna put me down on the first floor," replied Teresa. "Alongside the students."

"Let's move you to the third, away from too many prying eyes. You'll find it a lot quieter."

"Thank you. That is greatly appreciated. As to the other matter, I shall seek out my connection with the Ansgarites first thing tomorrow. I'll hopefully have some news for you before midday." She smiled. "A fitting time, don't you think?"

"I'm not sure I follow?"

"Tomorrow is the first official day of autumn." She waited for their response but only received blank stares. "Sorry. I've been amongst the Elves so long I grew accustomed to their ways. They view autumn as a time of reflection, where one clears their mind of conflict and uses reason to find what they're looking for."

"I'll bear that in mind," replied Charlaine. "Will we see you at breakfast?"

"Most definitely. We've got a lot of catching up to do." Teresa left, her footsteps light.

"It's good seeing her again," said Charlaine. "It gives me hope for a brighter future."

"Do you believe she can help us?" asked Danica.

"She's been here long enough to make a contact amongst the Ansgarites. Then again, she was always personable. Thankfully, that doesn't appear to have changed after her time amongst the Elves." She chuckled. "I can still remember the first time she laid eyes on Gwalinor. She feared Elves practiced strange rituals, and now here she is, a student of the very race she feared."

"Having Life Mages around could prove helpful to the order."

"I agree," said Charlaine, "but there's no sense in organizing anything with our future in doubt."

"Let's hope tomorrow brings some good news. I'm getting tired of all this doom and gloom. Speaking of which, what do we do if the rumours about that knight prove true?"

"That largely depends on circumstances. His imprisonment might be politically motivated but could just as easily be related to crimes against the Church."

"But wouldn't that be the local ruler's responsibility to adjudicate?"

"Not if it occurred within the Antonine's walls. Honestly, Danica, you really should read ALL those books the order supplies to its senior officers."

"I'm still a Temple Captain, remember? That reminds me, I'd best get back to my responsibilities as the duty officer. I'll see you in the morning." She left, closing the door quietly behind her and leaving Charlaine to ponder her next move.

Teresa's arrival added an extra complication, but she'd yet to determine if that was good or bad. It offered an opportunity to gain information that would otherwise be unavailable to her, yet the poor woman had suffered terribly, and the last thing Charlaine wanted to do was add to her woes.

21

THE PRISONER

AUTUMN 1106 SR

"Are you certain this isn't some trick meant to distract us?" asked Charlaine.

Teresa stared back. "It's true. I swear. My contact amongst the Ansgarites is a distant cousin of mine."

"How distant?"

"Not so distant we didn't live in the same village."

"And you trust him?"

"I have no reason not to. I've always looked up to Casimiro; you might say he inspired me to join the order."

"And where does he sit in the Ansgarite hierarchy?"

"He's a Temple Knight but spends most of his time in the kitchen, where he puts his skill to use."

"His skill?" asked Charlaine.

"He taught me everything I know about herbs and spices. He's an amazing cook, so they keep him busy, which is how he knew about the prisoner. After all, even a captive must eat."

"I'll take your word on his trustworthiness. What can you tell us about this prisoner?"

"He's from Erlingen, wherever that is."

"We rode through it on the way here. Go on."

"He's a member of the Knights of the Sceptre who serve their duke."

"Any idea why he's here in the Antonine?"

"He came of his own free will, but that's all I could get out of my cousin. There are limits to what he knows. Should I ask him to make further enquiries?"

"No," replied Charlaine. "I shouldn't like him to get in trouble. From what you've said, they're holding him in their commandery?"

"Yes. In the dungeons beneath it. He said they're more like guest rooms than cells yet are still under lock and key."

"Thank you. This information may prove useful."

"You believe this knight has something to do with the order's problems?"

"Not directly," replied Charlaine, "yet I can't help feeling he's been locked up to hide something. The question is, what is this something, and does he know how important it is?"

"Where do we go from here?"

"Danica and I will visit the Ansgarites. I'm hoping if we explain the situation, they'll allow us to question this knight."

"Have you a contact amongst the order?"

"I do, or rather, I did. The last time we visited the Antonine, I worked with a Temple Captain named Zander."

"And you trust him?"

"He helped me thwart the efforts of Hjordis, so, yes."

"And Hjordis is?"

"A disgraced member of our order. She tried to have Danica and I imprisoned."

"I see. When do you think you'd go?"

"I'd like to head over there as soon as possible, but my predecessor was a tad behind in her duties, leaving me with a lot of catching up to do."

"Perhaps Danica and I could go in your stead?"

"Let me make an official request first," replied Charlaine. "I don't want to tread on any toes unless it's absolutely necessary."

"How long before you expect an answer?"

"My guess is a week. Why? Is the prisoner in danger of being moved?"

"I doubt it. If my cousin is to be believed, the fellow's been here for many months. If someone were going to move him, they'd already have done so."

"Then I shall wait for a reply before I follow up with a visit. I'll let you know if I need you to take my place."

Charlaine dutifully sent off an official request through the office of the grand mistress. Merely a formality with communications between the orders, yet it still posed a potential risk, for it indicated to those concerned there was an interest in visiting the prisoner in question.

She waited for a week, only to discover her request had been denied without a reason given. A most unusual development, but it bore the Ansgarite seal, leaving her confident of its authenticity. However, Charlaine wondered who else now knew of her request.

She took a couple of days to write another request, citing Church law. This in itself proved most difficult, for it required an extensive search of the order's library to find the legal precedents. Ultimately, it proved unnecessary, for Danica opened the door as she put her name on it. "Temple Captain Zander is here to see you. Shall I show him in?"

"By all means," said Charlaine. "Please join us. I might need to rely on your memory later."

Temple Captain Zander was of moderate height, his dark brown hair greying at his temples. "Temple Commander Charlaine," he said by way of introduction. "You've prospered since our last encounter."

"I serve where I'm needed," she replied. "Please, take a seat. Can I offer you some refreshment?"

"No, thank you. I'm not thirsty."

"What can I do for you?"

"I think the question should be, what I can do for you. I understand you requested to speak to one of our prisoners?"

"I did, but that hardly warrants a visit from you, or is there something I'm missing?"

"The prisoner in question is of great interest to us, as are those who ask to speak with him. Not that you're under investigation, you understand. This is merely a formality."

"Are you at liberty to discuss his situation?"

"I may reveal details at my discretion. Why? Who is this fellow to you?"

"To be honest, he may be only a coincidence. Our grand mistress summoned Temple Captain Danica and I to investigate... let's call them rumours."

"What type of rumours?" asked Zander.

"There's a possibility our order faces extinction."

"You're referencing the amalgamation of the orders, which is on everyone's mind of late. I don't see what that has to do with this prisoner."

"Nor do I, but the fact that he's here during this crisis is too coincidental to be ignored."

"Very well," said Zander. "What would you like to know?"

"Could you start with his name?"

"His name is Sir Raynald. He served under Lord Deiter Heinrich, the former Duke of Erlingen. He accompanied his master on the crusade that sought to clear the area around Ebenstadt."

"Would that be the same one that resulted in the Cunar loss?"

"It would."

"And how is it he ended up here in the Antonine?"

"He came here of his own volition, claiming to have knowledge that would shake the foundation of the Church."

"Are you aware of the nature of these claims?" asked Charlaine.

"I'm afraid not. We received orders to isolate him before we could arrange an interview."

"From whom?"

"The Primus himself, or at least his office. The order for imprisonment bore his seal."

"Did this order indicate why?"

"They claimed he was a foreign agent here to destabilize the Church."

"A foreign agent of who—the empire?"

"No, the Easterlings. The kingdom we now know as Therengia."

"Is there any proof of these accusations?"

"He admits to having spent time amongst them," replied Zander, "thus placing doubt on any information given."

"Did he admit to being a spy?"

"No."

"And the information he claims to possess?"

"We are under strict orders to keep him in isolation. As such, we've not yet conducted an interrogation."

"That's unusual, isn't it?" said Charlaine.

"It most certainly is, but we cannot defy the orders of the Primus."

"Have you ever encountered anything like this before?"

"No, which is why I came to see you. Your interest in the matter is the first we've had since we detained him."

"If I may be so bold," said Danica, "might I ask a question?"

"Of course," replied Zander.

"Did the Primus's command state that only your order should leave him in isolation, or everyone?"

"His orders were, I understand, directed specifically towards our interrogators. Why?"

"It occurs to me there's a way to circumvent that order."

Zander leaned forward in his chair. "I'm listening."

"If Temple Commander Charlaine talked to him, it wouldn't violate your orders."

"That's stretching it a bit thin, don't you think? Still, it would help to have a better understanding of the situation."

"Could you get me in to see him?" asked Charlaine.

"I will do what I can to arrange it, but you must be discreet."

"Meaning?"

"I'll need to adjust the schedule for those on watch to ensure no one speaks of your presence there. Can you give me a week?"

"If it allows me to talk to him."

"Good. I shall send word once I have things in place. Oh, and it would be easier if you came alone. Numbers tend to draw more attention."

"I look forward to hearing from you."

After waiting over a week, Charlaine started to worry nothing would happen, and then Danica appeared at her door bearing a letter.

"An Ansgarite dropped this off. It's got your name on it." She handed it over.

Charlaine broke it open and perused its contents.

"Good news?" asked Danica.

"Depends on what you consider good. Temple Captain Zander arranged for me to visit the prisoner."

"About time. When do we get to see him?"

"I'm afraid I'll be doing this alone; it was one of his conditions, remember?"

"But it could be a trap."

"You've told me several times I'm a good judge of character, and I detected no deceit on behalf of Temple Captain Zander."

"What can I do to help?"

"I'll need you and Teresa up here, in my office."

"To what end?"

"To act like I'm too busy to see anyone."

"I can't lie like that."

"You won't be lying. I will be too busy to see anyone because I'll be talking to this mysterious prisoner. I just won't be in my office."

"And if the grand mistress arrived in your absence?"

"I very much doubt that, but if she does, you'll have to reveal what I'm up to."

"Why the both of us?"

"One to stop anyone who comes to the door, the other to walk around the office, giving the impression someone is inside."

"Very clever. When are you to undertake this?"

"Tonight, after the sun sets."

"Are you wearing your armour?"

"No. That would draw too much attention, but I'll take my sword."

"Be careful, Charlaine. We can't afford to lose you."

"I'm talking to a prisoner, not fighting my way through a commandery."

"Still, we don't know how deep the Cunar's influence goes."

Charlaine nodded solemnly. "True. I shall heed your advice and take care."

Walking to the Temple Knights of Saint Ansgar's commandery was easy enough. However, approaching it without drawing notice was much more difficult.

Charlaine stood beneath a tree, watching the door near the stables, where a guard walked back and forth, intent on his duty. Another Temple Knight opened the door after she'd been there for a while and spoke to the first knight, who then stepped inside.

This was the pre-arranged signal for her to approach. She moved cautiously, alert for passers-by, but if anyone watched, the darkness of the night hid them well.

"Sister Charlaine?" called out the new guard.

"That's me," she replied.

"Follow me. I shall take you to the prisoner."

They entered the commandery and proceeded down an empty hallway, halting at a set of stairs leading up. Instead of ascending, her guide led her behind, where another set led downwards.

"The dungeons are down here," he said. "Let me go first to ensure the way is safe."

"Safe?" replied Charlaine. "Are you expecting trouble?"

"Sorry to give the wrong impression, Sister. I meant that I would ensure only trusted individuals were on duty. It's not uncommon to have unexpected changes to the guard roster. Wait here while I take a look."

Down he went, leaving Charlaine alone with her thoughts. Coming here was a gamble, for she'd no idea if this man had anything to do with the movement to disband the orders. She struggled to understand why he, a secular knight, was even here. The more she thought, the more she worried she'd wasted her time.

The guard reappeared holding a lantern, the light playing across his face. "This way, Sister."

She descended the steps, her hand on the hilt of her sword. A door stood at the bottom, opening into a long stone corridor.

"These are the cells," he explained. "The prisoner you want is over there." He led her down the hallway, past several doors with small barred windows. They'd just passed the third when a face appeared, screaming in a high-pitched voice, "They're coming! They're coming! We can't stop them!"

"Ignore him," said the guard. "He's lost his mind."

"What happened to him?"

"We're not certain. He was pulled from the wreckage of a ship down near Corassus."

"And they sent him here?"

"He was a member of the Holy Fleet. They saw to his physical injuries, but his mind never recovered."

"Are you now a house of healing?"

The guard stopped, turning to regard her. "The cells of this commandery serve many purposes, Sister. Some here broke Church law, while others are here for their own protection. This poor soul, however, has nowhere else to go. Leave him alone; he'll settle down soon enough."

The screams continued as they proceeded, stopping at a robust wooden door with a lock, like the other cells, but no window. A gap at the bottom of the door revealed light flickering within.

The guard knocked three times before pulling forth his ring of keys and inserting one into the lock. "You have company," he announced, swinging open the door to a room similar in size to Charlaine's lodgings back in her old commandery. A bed stood on one side while the prisoner sat at a small table, book in hand, reading by the light of a flickering candle.

"Ah, who do we have here?" the fellow said, standing.

"I am Temple Commander Charlaine. I've come here to speak with you, providing you have no objection."

"If you're hoping for a confession, you'll be sorely disappointed."

"I am no confessor. However, I am greatly interested in your story."

"Are you, now? I find that most perplexing. I've been here for months, and no one has seen fit to listen to my tale."

"You are a Knight of the Sceptre, are you not?"

He bowed, a courtly display out of place in the confines of the cell. "Allow me to introduce myself. I am Sir Raynald, a knight formerly in the employ of the Duke of Erlingen."

"Formerly?"

"Unfortunately, he died in the Eastern Crusade. I have not returned home since."

"Is that why you're here—to talk about the crusade?"

"In a manner of speaking." He glanced at the guard. "Would you mind stepping outside?"

The Ansgarite appeared uncertain.

"I'll be fine," insisted Charlaine.

With that assurance, the fellow stepped into the hallway, closing the door behind him.

"Where would you like me to start?" said Raynald.

"I'd appreciate you getting to the heart of the matter as quickly as possible. However, since I don't know what you will tell me, I must rely on your judgement."

"You've heard of the Eastern Crusades?"

"Of course," replied Charlaine. "Though I can't say I approve of them. I assume you refer to the last one, back in oh four?"

"I do. Like many of my order, I went east with our duke, determined to do our part in the name of the Holy Church and drive out the barbarian heathens, establishing a cultured society in their place."

"Yet the army was defeated."

"It was," replied Raynald. "I came to the realization the entire endeavour was… How shall I put this?"

"A farce?"

"No. I was going to say a deliberate mismanagement."

"Deliberate?

"Yes. As you are no doubt aware, the grand master of an order must give permission for its knights to declare a crusade, and only after receiving the Council of Peers' blessing."

"Are you suggesting this wasn't the case in this instance?"

"I witnessed the last of the Cunars fall at the Battle of the Wilderness." His voice choked up. "It was a brutal affair, with the Temple Knights of Saint Cunar refusing to surrender despite being given every opportunity. I found Father General Hargild's orders after his demise, and they seemed to indicate that the grand master had given his blessing to the crusade."

"But…?"

"The orders were dated only three weeks prior, not nearly enough time to travel from Corassus to Ebenstadt. I suspect they're forged."

"So you came here to report a forged document?"

"No," replied Raynald. "There's more, much more. While in Ebenstadt, I chanced upon a pair of… Well, I suppose I'd have to call them adventurers, for lack of any better description. One was named Natalia Stormwind."

"I know that name," said Charlaine. "The Stormwinds can't be trusted. They're working in league with the empire."

"Not these two, I assure you. She and her husband came from where the crusade was set to invade."

"That still doesn't explain why you're here."

"Ah, I'm getting to that. It all has to do with the Cunar regional commander, a fellow named Talivardas. Do you recognize the name?"

"I can't say I do. Was he a Temple Commander?"

"He was, but we discovered he was also a Stormwind."

"Are you certain?"

"Absolutely. Natalia informed me that members of that family wear jewellery which changes colour based on the strength of their magic, and his clearly showed he was of considerable power. I returned to Ebenstadt after the Holy Army's defeat, but Talivardas had fled by then. That's when I decided to bring word of all this to the Antonine."

"A most logical decision," said Charlaine. "I applaud your bravery. That couldn't have been an easy choice."

"I'm a devout follower of Saint Mathew and wanted the truth to be known," replied Raynald. "I never imagined I'd be imprisoned when I arrived. Perhaps I should've written a letter instead?"

"It would likely have been intercepted."

"Has this anything to do with why you're here?"

"I fear it does, although I've yet to see precisely how. This Talivardas may not be acting alone, which explains many things."

"I'm afraid I don't follow."

"In the last few years," explained Charlaine, "I've discovered the Stormwinds are working on behalf of the Empire of Halvaria. That this Talivardas infiltrated a fighting order is of great concern, particularly in light of recent events."

"Which are?"

"You haven't heard?"

"No," said Raynald. "They've kept me isolated since my arrival. The only ones I've seen, aside from the guards, are you and the Cunar."

"A Cunar visited you?"

"Yes, some time ago. I said nothing to him. I'm not a fool."

"Have you told anyone else of your claims?"

"No one in the Antonine."

"So others know?"

"A few of my companions from the order, but Erlingen is halfway across the Continent from here."

"Not quite," said Charlaine, "though it's a bit of a trip."

"You believe a fellow knight revealed my purpose?"

"Your order accompanied the crusade. Some might see your actions as traitorous."

"Yes, I suppose," He lowered his head in defeat. "I was a fool to believe I could make a difference."

"Not a fool," said Charlaine, "merely not cautious enough. You presumed that all members of the Church were to be trusted. My experience says otherwise."

"Whatever do you mean?"

"I commanded a detachment of Temple Knights in a place called Arnsfeld."

"Yes. I've heard of it."

"When our grand mistress sent reinforcements, a company of Cunars tried to block their way, almost leading to bloodshed."

Raynald's breath caught in his throat. "Saints alive! Do you realize what that means?"

"Yes," replied Charlaine. "The Church can no longer be trusted to serve the best interests of the Petty Kingdoms."

22

THE MESSAGE
AUTUMN 1106 SR

Charlaine stared out her office window, deep in thought. Sir Raynald had been adamant a Temple Commander was a Stormwind. Was he the only one, or were others poised to make their move?

A knock on her door drew her attention, and Danica poked her head in. "Busy?"

"For once, no. I'm caught up on all my reports, and I've created the schedule for the duty officer for the next month. Why? You don't have more work for me, do you?"

"I couldn't say precisely."

"What in the name of the Saints does that mean?"

"You've got a visitor," replied Danica. "A Dwarf of our acquaintance."

"Rurlan is here?"

"Indeed. Shall I show him in?"

"Of course, and fetch some cups, will you? Then join us for something to drink."

"Are we celebrating?"

"That depends on what news he brings."

Danica left, reappearing with the Dwarf.

"I hope I'm not disturbing you," he said.

"I'm surprised to see you here in the Antonine."

"As am I, if truth be told. I went to Arnsfeld with correspondence for you, only to discover you'd come here. Not that I mind travelling, you understand, but I could've saved myself considerable time had I come straight here." He reached into his sling bag and extracted a sealed envelope. "Let me unseal the outer wrapping, then it's all yours." He placed his phoenix ring over the seal and broke it open, withdrawing the letter within. "Here you go."

"It's from Cordelia," said Charlaine. She read it over twice before sitting back and handing it to Danica. "These are serious allegations. How much do you know, Rurlan?"

"The guild's agents in Therengia confirm the story."

"So you've known about this for some time?"

"I was only informed after I picked up this letter for delivery."

"You read all our correspondence?"

"Of course we do. We commit it to memory in case the letter gets destroyed. I thought you understood that?"

"I suspected as much," said Charlaine, "but I assumed you kept such things to yourself."

"I typically do, but I thought it best to ask some questions of the guild on your behalf."

"The guild's expanded into Therengia?"

"Indeed, in the form of a couple of Dwarven smiths. The events in that letter didn't happen in Therengia; they occurred in Krieghoff, but some of those involved later moved on to what's now called Therengia."

"Would one of those be named Natalia Stormwind?"

"I'm surprised you know that name. If you've heard of her, you need to know she works to discredit the rest of the family—the Stormwinds, that is."

"Am I reading this correctly?" said Danica. "Cordelia says she arrested a Father General?"

"Yes, Father General Gilbert," replied Rurlan.

"This letter was sent months ago. Where is this fellow now?"

"Nobody knows."

"This is not good news," said Danica.

"That's putting it mildly," replied Charlaine. "First, we discover the treachery of Talivardas and now Father General Gilbert. This indicates the Cunars are far more corrupt than we ever imagined."

"Now, now," said the Dwarf. "There's no indication this was anything more than greed on Gilbert's part."

"It's not his motivation I'm concerned about, it's his whereabouts. If Cordelia arrested him, he'd have been put in irons and shipped to the Antonine."

"Perhaps he's here even as we speak, rotting away in a cell somewhere."

"I suppose that's possible, but where?"

"The Cunar commandery?" suggested Danica. "Seems like the logical place to hold him."

"He interfered in secular politics without the approval of his superiors, a most serious crime."

Danica laughed. "Isn't that exactly what we did in Arnsfeld?"

"We were holding back an invasion, not trying to steal godstone from someone else's lands."

"How much is godstone worth?" They both turned to Rurlan.

"That depends on the amount," replied the Dwarf, "but enough to craft even a single weapon would be worth a king's ransom. Mind you, the stuff's notoriously difficult to work. The guild has forges capable of generating the intense heat required, but I know of no others with that capability."

"Could mages do it?" asked Charlaine.

"Aye. I suppose a Fire Mage could if they were powerful enough."

"Like the Sartellians?"

Rurlan nodded. "They ARE said to be amongst the strongest casters on the Continent."

"Would the guild know if any of its members worked godstone?"

"Most definitely, but in this case, it remained in the possession of the Orcs in that region, who later moved on to Therengia."

"Do you think Gilbert knew about the godstone?"

"Why?" said Danica. "What are you suggesting?"

"What if he passed on the knowledge to his superiors? It might explain why Talivardas called for a crusade."

"All that fighting to retrieve some mythical stones?"

"They're not stones," replied Rurlan. "It's a metal that falls from the sky. Some even call it skymetal, and it's the most valuable metal in all of Eidden-werthe. I'd say that's a strong incentive to invade. Wars have been fought over less."

Charlaine shook her head. "I hear what you're saying, but there's more to it. Halvaria is already a wealthy empire. What need have they for godstone? No. I think they used it as an excuse to carry out their real plan."

"Which was?"

"To weaken the Temple Knights of Saint Cunar, the greatest threat to the empire's dominance."

"Are you suggesting the entire crusade was an attempt to wipe out the Cunars?"

"What better way to reduce their influence?"

"There's a lot to digest," said Danica, "but if you look back on recent events, it all makes sense. They've withdrawn their forces from the borders of Halvaria, which is tantamount to an open invitation for the empire to invade. We stepped in to stop them, and now our order faces extinction, which is too convenient for Halvaria to be considered a coincidence."

"I agree," said Charlaine, "yet we have no proof with which to act."

"There's Cordelia's letter."

"Which amounts to little more than hearsay. I'm certain the arrest of Gilbert would be investigated, but he's likely long gone, as is this fellow Talivardas."

"Whoever is behind this must still hold influence over the Church, hence this motion to amalgamate the orders."

"You've tied it all together nicely," said Charlaine. "Now, what do we do about it?"

"The grand mistress tasked us with finding out how other orders feel about the proposal."

"At least now we're armed with the what and the why. We just need to confirm the who."

"It's definitely the Cunars," insisted Danica.

"Agreed, but we need to find out how far up the hierarchy it goes. Is the Primus part of this? He used to be a Cunar after all."

"He did, and he's the one who reintroduced the idea of combining all the orders under the command of the Cunars."

"This is bad news," said Rurlan. "What can I do to help?"

"This isn't your fight," replied Charlaine.

"Nonsense. You're still a guild member, and in good standing, I might add. Besides, our business would suffer greatly if the empire got the upper hand. They're not keen on us mountain folk."

"What makes you say that?"

"Ever hear of Dun-Galdrim?"

"No. What is it?"

"A Dwarf kingdom that stood for over a thousand years before Halvaria destroyed it. So you see, the guild has good reason to want this situation remedied."

"I'm not certain there's much we can do," said Charlaine, "particularly yourself, who'd be seen as an outsider here. I do thank you for the offer, though."

"I'll leave you to it, then. I've been instructed to remain in the area until needed, whether that's a week or a year. The guild is very interested in what's happening, so I'll be outside those walls whenever my services are needed. I trust you know how to find me?"

"I do. Thank you, Rurlan. You've been most helpful."

"Will you stay for some ale?" asked Danica.

"Much as I'd like to, it's getting late. Don't hesitate to seek me out if things slip off the anvil."

"Slip off the anvil?"

"An old smiths' expression," replied Charlaine. "It refers to an occasion where things don't go as planned, resulting in unexpected circumstances."

"And here I thought us sailors had unusual expressions."

Rurlan chuckled. "Perhaps, when this is all over, we'll sit down and share our experiences. For now, I must be off. I've other people to see while I'm here."

"In the Antonine?"

"No, in Reichendorf, the city outside the Antonine's walls."

"Good luck to you."

"And to you," he replied. "I've got a feeling you need it more than me."

Charlaine waited for the door to close, the Dwarf's footsteps echoing down the hall. "How do you feel about visiting your old friend Brother Thorley at the archives?"

"Let me guess," replied Danica. "You want me to look into Talivardas and this other fellow, Gilbert?"

"That was my hope."

"You realize their records are probably stored at the Cunar commandery?"

"I do, but there are all sorts of mundane reports that might hint at what they've both been up to."

"Am I looking for anything in particular?"

"I'm hoping you'll find some sort of connection between them. Otherwise, this may prove to be a complete waste of time."

"I'd best get straight to it first thing in the morning. This might take a while."

"Let me know if you discover anything useful."

Inside the Council of Peers, the main chamber housed the meeting area used by the senior Church members, with a gallery in the form of a balcony where the affairs of the Church could be viewed. Danica's interest, however, lay below, in the cellars, where they archived old records.

Each order took its turn guarding the entrance, with Temple Knights of Saint Ragnar standing guard this day. Since the council wasn't currently in session, Danica approached them, seeking entry.

"Greetings, Sister," called out the senior of the two green-clad knights. "What brings you here today?"

"I am seeking the archives," she replied. "My order is interested in some documents of a historical nature."

"You'll be wanting to see Brother Thorley, then. You may proceed."

"Thank you," said Danica, continuing on her way.

She entered the building to find another Ragnarite sitting at a desk off to the left, an open ledger before him.

He looked up at her approach. "Name?"

"This is new," replied Danica. "When did we begin recording visits?"

"It's a new directive implemented after the ascension of Primus Wilmar. Could I have your name, please?"

"I'm Temple Captain Danica. I've come seeking Brother Thorley?"

"I'll send for him." He rang a small bell, sitting off to one side, then waited patiently. After a short time, a young initiate arrived, his robes marking him as a Mathewite in training.

"Find Brother Thorley," said the knight. "He should be down in the archives." The young student rushed off through the hallway behind the desk.

"They're all so eager when they first join," remarked the Ragnarite.

"Weren't we all?"

He nodded in reply. "What brings a celebrated Temple Captain to the archives today?"

"Celebrated?"

"You identified yourself as Temple Captain Danica, although you omitted you're the Admiral of the Temple Fleet."

"That is a position, not a rank."

"Still, it's an impressive achievement."

She looked down at the ledger, which now bore her name. "Who has access to that book?" she asked.

"Aside from the patriarchs, only those on the next shift."

"And that would be?"

"Our shift ends at first light tomorrow morning. The Mathewites are scheduled next, and then, I believe, your own order. I'm surprised you didn't know that. Then again, you haven't been here long, else I would've heard of your presence."

"I was under the impression my name was not well-known."

"Perhaps it's not to others, but we Ragnarites travel the length and breadth of the Continent in the performance of our duties. The presence of the Temple Fleet makes that much easier. Keep up the good work, Admiral."

Brother Thorley entered the room. "I recognize you," he called out. "Sister... Let me think now."

"Danica," she supplied.

"Ah, yes. I remember now. I assume you've come seeking more answers?"

"Indeed I have."

"Then follow me." He turned, leading her along the hallway he'd just come from. "What brings you this time?"

"I'm looking for records concerning two individuals."

"I'm afraid you must be much more specific than that. The archives house thousands of documents. Finding two names in all that would prove very difficult."

"They both belong to the Temple Knights of Saint Cunar. Does that help?"

"A little. Are we talking about something recent or decades ago?"

"Recent, I think. No more than a year or two."

"That helps immensely, at least to a certain extent."

"Meaning?"

Thorley paused before offering an explanation. "The Church does not employ many archivists, leaving us behind in filing documents. The information you seek is likely in the sorting room, where such things go before long-term storage. Do you know where these documents may have come from?"

"In a manner of speaking, yes. The first name is Father General Gilbert; his reports would be from a place called Caerhaven."

"Ah, yes. In Krieghoff. I know it well."

"You've been to the Duchy of Krieghoff?"

"Not in person, but I feel I know it in great detail. The Temple Captain there writes the most eloquent reports. I admire her prose." He turned around suddenly, returning the way they'd come.

"We're not going into the archives?" asked Danica, trying to catch up.

"My apologies. I should have done better at explaining. The sorting room is on this floor." He leaned in conspiratorially. "Natural light makes it much easier to read everything, making the sorting process quicker. Now, off we go to the rear of the east wing."

"You said these reports came from Caerhaven," he continued, "yet you mentioned another individual. Are they both from the same area?"

"No. The other would've been in Ebenstadt."

"Ah, let me think. Ebenstadt was an independent city in the northeast region. I'm told it now falls under the domain of Therengia, although strangely enough, the Temple Knights of Saint Mathew still maintain a presence there." He knit his brows. "You don't reckon they converted the Therengians, do you? That would make life so much easier."

"I'm interested in past events, not current politics."

"I do beg your pardon." He halted at the door. "Ah, here we are." He dug into his robes, extracting a ring of keys, then began fumbling through them, mumbling accompanying his search until he held up a key in triumph. "I knew it was here somewhere." There was an audible click as he twisted the key in the lock. "Let's go inside, shall we?"

"I'm surprised you lock this door," said Danica.

"Correspondence is considered the private property of the Church. We can't let just anyone in here."

"You're allowing me."

"That's different," said Thorley. "You're a Temple Knight. If we can't trust a member of your order, whom can we?"

Danica followed him into the room, where a large table stood in the centre while shelves containing boxes lined the walls.

"When correspondence comes to us," he explained, "we sort it by region, hence the boxes. Krieghoff should be over here." He wandered over to a box near the floor. "Yes, this is it." He hauled it out, then placed it on the table, and removed the top. Inside, dozens of papers were rolled up into scrolls, while others were neatly folded.

"If you can tell me exactly what you're searching for," said Brother Thorley, "I can help you look."

"A connection between the two Cunars I spoke of earlier."

"And by connection, you mean…"

"We're not certain. Maybe a common posting or a presence in the same region. We have reason to believe they might be working together, but we've been unable to ascertain when this occurred."

"Can you give me their names?"

"As I mentioned, the first is Father General Gilbert, who was reportedly in Caerhaven two years ago."

"And the other?"

"A regional commander named Talivardas."

The colour drained from Brother Thorley's face. "C-c-could you be mistaken?"

"No. Why? Is something wrong?"

"Talivardas was the original name of our new Primus!"

23

A MATTER OF DISCIPLINE
AUTUMN 1106 SR

"Are you certain of this?" asked Danica.

"Absolutely," replied Thorley. "We've only just finished removing all his records. That's why we fell behind in sorting this lot."

"Removing? I don't understand."

"When a new Primus is named, it's customary to seal their records, so someone can't use their past against them."

"If something here incriminated a Primus, shouldn't the Council of Peers be advised of it?"

"We must acknowledge Human nature. Everyone makes mistakes, and we don't want the Primus subject to be controlled by others."

"Are you suggesting someone might try to blackmail the Primus?"

"That is not as far-fetched as you'd think," said Thorley. "It's happened several times in the Church's history."

"So where do these records go?"

"They are handed into the care of the Primus himself. Once he's completed his term of office, the documents will be returned unless he's chosen to serve a second term. I can say with absolute certainty you won't be able to learn any more about his background."

"But there must be general information somewhere?"

"Only from second-hand accounts."

"Meaning?"

"Let's look at your grand mistress as an example. If we were to take her records as we do those of the Primus, we would gather every document she has written. However, that would not include your account of meeting her, should you choose to write such a document."

"Ahh, I see. Where do we begin looking?"

Charlaine glanced up to see Teresa standing in front of her. "Yes?"

"Sorry to intrude, but I was wondering if you've heard anything from Danica? She's been gone all day."

"I imagine she's deep in the bowels of the archives by now. We likely won't hear from her until well after dark, and even then, she may have nothing to report. It might be days before she learns anything useful. Having said that, if there's something to find, she'll locate it."

Teresa opened her mouth to speak, but a familiar face appeared in the doorway before she could say anything.

"Temple Commander Nina," said Charlaine. "To what do I owe the pleasure of your company?"

"I don't appreciate your interference with my students," Nina replied through gritted teeth.

"Interference?"

"Yes. Initiates are not to be used as couriers for delivering personal messages."

"I was unaware they were."

"Then how do you explain this?" Nina produced a folded-up letter and tossed it on the desk. Charlaine picked it up and carefully unfolded it. She recognized Danica's hand, but the message was gibberish.

"What's this all about?" asked Nina.

"Did you read this?"

"I did, or rather I attempted to. Whoever wrote it had atrocious handwriting."

"So I see. What do you expect me to do about this?"

"You can start by staying away from my students."

"They are not your students," replied Charlaine. "They belong to the order. If they belonged to anyone, it would be the grand mistress."

"Yes. The woman who appointed me to oversee their training."

"Yet I'm in charge of the commandery, which makes me your direct superior." Charlaine waited for a response, but Nina stared back, open-mouthed.

"I'm not here to argue with you," continued Charlaine. "I promise to address this at the first opportunity. Might I enquire which of your students was approached?"

"Initiate Anthea."

"Did you ask her who she received this note from?"

"Of course," said Nina. "What do you take me for, a fool?"

Charlaine kept her voice calm. "And what was her answer?"

"She refused to tell me, said her conscience wouldn't permit it. Now I ask you, what kind of response is that? Why, I've got a good mind to put her on sentry duty for the next month."

"Before you do that, might I make a suggestion?"

Nina seemed to be trying to calm herself, yet her hands shook. Charlaine wondered if she was truly upset over the antics of a student or if something else was happening. Nina finally closed her eyes and let out a deep breath. "I would welcome any suggestions you might offer."

"Have her report to my office," said Charlaine. "I'll explain to her how important truth is to a Temple Knight."

Temple Commander Nina finally noticed Teresa's presence. "Do I know you? You look familiar."

"I would hope so," replied the knight. "I served with you in Ilea."

"That is no way to speak to a superior."

"You are not my superior, as I am no longer a member of this order."

"Then you shouldn't be here."

"That," said Charlaine, "is not your decision. I invited her to remain with us while we examine her application for readmission."

"Application?" said Nina. "Are you proposing we allow her back into the order?"

"Do you truly not recognize her? She was one of only twelve knights under your command."

"I've had a long career in service to the order. I can't be expected to remember everyone I served with."

Charlaine noticed the fear in the woman's eyes, and it dawned on her that perhaps Nina's mind was slipping. Suffering from memory loss was not uncommon for those of advanced years, yet Nina was far from old. "Let's not worry about the past. Let us instead deal with the present. Have Anthea report to me immediately, and I'll speak with her."

"Thank you, Commander. I didn't expect you to be so accommodating."

"We are all here to serve the order."

Nina turned around and departed without another word, leaving the door open behind her.

Teresa waited until the footsteps receded. "Have I changed that much?"

"Danica and I recognized you, so it's strange she didn't. Would your magic help with memory loss?"

"That largely depends on what's causing it."

"I'm not certain I follow."

"If she's forgetting things due to a physical ailment, I can cure it, but if it's the ravages of time, I doubt Life Magic could do much for her."

"Would you be willing to try?"

"If Nina agrees to it."

"You were already in Ilea when I arrived. How long had you been under Nina's command?"

"I reported there roughly two years before you did, right after she assumed command of the detachment."

"Would you say she was forgetful then?"

"I would've described her as solitary, but I don't recall her being forgetful." She paused. "Now that you mention it, she sometimes confused our names. Do you believe that might be related?"

"You tell me—you're the healer."

"Considering your shared past, I'm surprised you'd want to help her."

"I might not have liked how Nina commanded the detachment, but I never wished her ill."

"And now you outrank her."

"Only because I was put in charge of this commandery. Were that not the case, she'd have seniority over me."

"I hold no love for Nina," replied Teresa. "I found her selfish, hardly the sort of personality one expects in an order like ours that stresses the importance of sacrifice and service. Having said that, I will do all I can to help her, not because she deserves it, but because no person should suffer when there's a way to cure an affliction."

"Thank you," said Charlaine. "I know that couldn't have been easy for you."

"You've always been the forgiving type. I suppose that's what gives you your strength of character. Were you always this way?"

"I suppose I was, and it's all due to my father. He tried to see the best in people."

"I'm sure he's very proud of you."

"He was," replied Charlaine. "He died two years ago."

"I'm sorry for your loss. He was a smith, wasn't he?"

"Yes. In Malburg, one of the cities of Hadenfeld."

"Hadenfeld? I've heard mention of that recently. Wasn't there a war there? Is that how your father died?"

"Yes. He fell during the Battle of Erhard's Folly, fighting on the side of Ludwig."

"Isn't that the baron who became their new king?"

Charlaine nodded. "I've since learned he had little choice. The previous king, Morgan, had become a tyrant, so much so that the Temple Knights of Saint Mathew supported Ludwig's claim to the Throne."

"Truly? I thought the Church wasn't supposed to interfere in secular matters?"

"That's what I thought when I first joined the order, but my entire career thus far indicates otherwise."

A knock on the door frame drew their attention.

"Sorry, Temple Commander," said Anthea. "The door was open, and I didn't know what else to do."

"Come in," said Charlaine. "Temple Commander Nina sent you?"

"She did." The initiate's eyes flicked to Teresa. "I see you found the woman in white."

"She did," replied Teresa. "I'll leave you to look after this matter, Charlaine. I'll drop by later to find out if you've heard anything new."

"I'll see you at dinner?"

"Of course." Teresa left, closing the door behind her.

"Now, where was I?" Charlaine picked up the note. "What was this all about?"

"It's from Temple Captain Danica."

Charlaine flattened out the letter. "This is nothing but gibberish."

"She said it was in code, whatever that means."

"Did she say anything else?"

"Yes. She wanted me to tell you it's her ship."

"Her ship? Are you certain?"

"Absolutely. She made me repeat it back to her. Why? Is it important?"

"It's best if you don't know any more about this. You're dismissed. Please return to your studies."

"That's it? Temple Commander Nina told me you were going to discipline me."

"I can't do that when you've relayed such important information to me."

"But what do I tell Temple Commander Nina?"

"Tell her I lectured you on the morals of being a Temple Knight, and if anyone asks you about this letter, it never existed. Understand?"

"Yes, Temple Commander."

"Oh, before you go, when did you see Temple Captain Danica?"

"We'd finished our midday meal and were heading to the practice field. I suggested she take it directly to you, but she said she was eager to get back to it. I'm afraid she didn't offer any further explanation."

"Did anyone else see this exchange?"

"No."

"Then how did Nina discover you were carrying it?"

"I'm afraid it slipped out of my sleeve during a lecture. Just my luck that the Temple Commander was the one giving it."

"Out of curiosity, what was the lecture about?"

"Discipline and the importance of maintaining it."

Charlaine couldn't help but smile. "Off with you. I have work to do."

"Yes, Temple Commander." Anthea fled the room, eager to return to her classmates.

"Danica," said Charlaine, "you clever woman." She stared down at the gibberish, nothing more than a simple cipher. All that was needed was a key, and in this case, that key was *Valiant*, the first ship of what would become the Temple Fleet. She wrote the name out. Seven letters, the key. She began picking out every seventh letter on the note, and the mysterious message came to life.

"Are you absolutely certain of this?" asked Temple Captain Nicola.

"Yes," replied Charlaine. "I'd hardly bring it to the grand mistress otherwise."

"This is dire news. Wait here, and I'll see if she's available." She disappeared through the door, then reappeared, along with Temple Captain Nina.

"The grand mistress thanks you for bringing this to her attention," said Nicola. "If you'd care to return at the same time tomorrow, we'll see what we can do about it."

"Thank you," replied Nina. She was about to say more when she spotted who was waiting. A splash of red coloured her cheeks, and then she swallowed, offering a slight nod as she left.

Charlaine returned the motion before following Nicola into the grand mistress's office. Behind the desk, Kaylene Gantzmann, the head of her order, looked as if she hadn't slept much lately.

"I'm told you've learned something important?"

"I have, Your Grace, although I'm afraid it's not good news."

"Then best we get it over with. What is it?"

"I have reason to believe the Primus is in league with the Halvarian Empire."

"It appears Nicola wasn't exaggerating when she said this was important. Sit down and tell me the entire story."

Charlaine took a seat. "These past few weeks, Danica and I've been looking into the arrest and imprisonment of a secular knight, a fellow who we learned was named Sir Raynald. He revealed a Father General of Saint Cunar was secretly working for the empire, conspiring to launch the Eastern Crusade without the permission of his grand master, possibly to weaken the military might of that order."

"Interesting. The backlash from the failure of the Crusade led to the replacement of the Cunar Grand Master. Is this prisoner the only witness to these accusations?"

"I have no reason to doubt him, Your Grace. He claims to have seen forged documents from the grand master authorizing the crusade, but the orders were said to have come from Corassus, and it would've taken months for the message to arrive. The only logical deduction was that they were forged, and the Father General knew it."

"I've never liked that expression."

"Which one, Your Grace?"

"Father General. It confers an air of respect that hasn't been earned. Most who carry it are, in fact, Temple Commanders. The Cunars have only two Temple Generals. One commands the Holy Fleet, while the other is here, in the Antonine, overseeing the deployment of their order."

"Be that as it may," said Charlaine, "there's more to report. Sir Raynald spent time amongst those who defeated the Holy Army and learned the regional commander of the order was a Stormwind."

"That's a grave accusation. Have you any proof?"

"I'm afraid not, Your Grace, but it explains many things."

"Please continue," said the grand mistress. "I'm interested to hear where this is going."

"The Eastern Crusade resulted in the loss of over seven hundred Temple Knights, forcing the Cunars to abandon Ebenstadt. It also served to weaken the very order that stood to resist Halvarian aggression should war come."

"And what became of this individual?"

"That's where things get very interesting," replied Charlaine. "He returned to the Antonine to continue his work. His name was Talivardas."

"You must be mistaken. That was Primus Wilmar's name."

"Precisely, Your Grace. It also explains why he wants to amalgamate the orders since they'd all be under his ultimate control."

"But they are already under his control, at least in theory."

"We both know that's not entirely true. The Mathewites interfered in the civil war in Hadenfeld, while our order fought in both Reinwick and Arnsfeld. None of that would've happened had we been placed under the command of the Cunars."

"I cannot argue your reasoning, Charlaine, but if this is true, there's little we can do about it."

"Surely we could take this to the Council of Peers?"

"Without proof? The only evidence we have is the word of a prisoner, and the Primus is no fool. He'll claim the fellow was coerced."

"We cannot sit by and do nothing!"

"You are correct, but your part in this is done, at least for the present. I shall take this news to the Matriarch of Saint Agnes, but I doubt she'll be inclined to act on it."

"Why ever not?"

"Mother Julianne has never liked the idea of Temple Knights. She would much rather the order's coins be spent on further places of worship. In addition to that, she and I have butted heads on many occasions. She may see this as another example of us overstepping our authority."

"Temple Captain Danica is still searching for information, Your Grace. If you allowed us the time, she might discover more compelling evidence."

"How much time?"

"I'm afraid I can't say."

The grand mistress dug through the papers on her desk, holding up one in particular. "The matriarch is leaving us at the end of the week and won't return until the Midwinter Feast. You have until then to find something to support these claims."

"That's months away," said Charlaine.

"Yes. It appears the Saints have seen fit to let things fall in our favour. Don't waste the opportunity, Commander, or else we'll all suffer for it."

"We shall do all we can, Your Grace. I promise."

The grand mistress stared at her.

"Is there anything else, Your Grace?" asked Charlaine.

"I must admit to some trepidation. There is every probability that if I press the matter with the matriarch, she may see fit to remove me from the position of grand mistress."

"Surely not?"

"As I said, we've butted heads on more than one occasion. Should that occur, I shall look to you to secure the future of the order."

"I am in no position to do much of anything, Your Grace."

"Perhaps not at this precise time, but sometimes fate takes unexpected turns."

24

AN UNTIMELY DEATH
WINTER 1106 SR

The blanket of white covering the grounds of the Antonine gave it an ethereal appearance, as though it resided in the Afterlife.

"This is driving me mad," said Danica as she stared out the window. "We've been sitting here for months doing nothing."

"Not nothing," replied Charlaine. "Running this commandery is challenging. Back in Arnsfeld, six companies scattered over four kingdoms were under my command. Now I'm here with even more, all packed into one building. Admittedly, most are initiates, but it results in endless paperwork."

"Paperwork," repeated Teresa. "The polite way of describing the stagnant bureaucracy of the Church."

"Do the Elves not have records?"

"They do, but only in the broadest of terms, whereas we seem to record every minute detail of daily life. I can't help but feel that, as an order, we'd get more accomplished if we eliminated the need to write everything down."

"Reports make us accountable," said Charlaine. "Without them, regional commanders might take things into their own hands, and then where would we be?"

"Perhaps in a better world?" replied Teresa. "I understand the need for it, but if we had trusted people in positions of authority, we wouldn't need to insist on all these letters. Do you know how many serve as couriers for the Church to keep the reports flowing?"

"Out of interest," said Danica, "who looks after that?"

"It comes under the direct authority of the Council of Peers."

"You seem knowledgeable for someone who's been away for over a decade."

"What can I say?" Teresa shrugged her shoulders. "My cousin is a fount of knowledge, and I have far too much time on my hands these days."

"How does the Antonine compare with the Elves?"

"I'm in no hurry to return to Lithandor, if that's what you're asking."

"I was more interested in how they run things," said Danica, "particularly their fleet."

"They have no fleet, at least not in the traditional sense. Every ship is independently owned, and they take turns patrolling their waters."

"There's no one overseeing their ships?"

"No," replied Teresa. "At least not that I'm aware of."

"How many ships do they possess?"

"The port was full, although the vast majority were small craft, more akin to the fishing boats in Ilea. They have larger vessels, but I suspect most remained out at sea for extended periods. Either that, or they sheltered in a different port."

"Do the Sea Elves have more than one city?"

"They do, although Lithandor was the only one I saw. I read about others, which leads me to believe their lands are similar in size to that of a smaller Petty Kingdom."

Danica went quiet, her attention elsewhere.

"See something interesting?" said Charlaine.

"Temple Commander Nina has the initiates out marching."

"You mean riding, don't you?"

"No, they're on foot. I wouldn't want to be marching around in this weather. It's freezing out there, and she's got them in full armour."

Charlaine moved to stand beside her, then knitted her brows.

"Can you say something to Nina?" asked Danica.

"No. She has full authority regarding the initiates' training."

"Could you bring it to the grand mistress's attention?"

"That would only make things worse. I can't say I agree with her methods, but it's not my place to interfere."

"And if you could?" asked Teresa.

"I have no problem with knights being out in this weather, but they should be dressed appropriately. Some will likely be suffering from frostbite by the time they're done."

"Am I interrupting?"

They all turned to see Temple Captain Nicola standing in the doorway.

"Not at all," replied Charlaine. "We were just chatting about training methods."

Nicola moved into the room. "Let me guess. Nina's got them marching out in the snow again?"

"You've been keeping an eye on them?"

"It's hard not to. She has a habit of forming them up right below the grand mistress's chambers."

"Nina does this herself?" said Charlaine. "She hardly seems the type to take them on a march."

"Oh, she doesn't. She orders them to form up, then sends them off under the tutelage of her captains in training. After that, she goes inside for breakfast."

Charlaine shook her head. "Some people never change."

"Much as I'd like to stay and chat, I'm here on business."

"Go on."

"There are two things. The grand mistress wanted me to pass on the news before you heard it elsewhere. The Patriarch of the Augustines died last night after a lengthy illness. Their order will be convening a convocation of archpriors to select his replacement."

"Any idea when?"

"Not at present, but it's still early days. When it does occur, the other orders are expected to take on the duties of guarding the Council of Peers, as their Temple Knights will be too busy with other matters."

"And the second thing you mentioned?"

"The grand mistress wants to see Danica immediately."

"That sounds serious."

"It is, but I assure you she's not in trouble."

"Hello," said Danica, waving her hands. "You're talking about me as if I'm not standing right here."

"Sorry," said Nicola, with a grin. "I couldn't resist."

"You said she wanted to see me right now?"

"I did, so we'd best get moving. I've found it's always better to deal with such things when she's in a good mood."

"What things?" asked Danica.

"You'll see."

"Reporting as ordered, Your Grace," said Nicola.

Kaylene looked up from her desk, her lips pursed together in a frown. "You took your time getting here."

"I'm sorry, Your Grace," replied Danica. "I only just learned you wanted to see me."

"Have you any idea why you're here?"

"None at all."

The grand mistress stood and moved to a small table behind her, where she picked something up, although Danica couldn't see what it was.

When she turned around, she held a tabard. "You're not wearing the correct colours. Temple Captain Nicola, would you do the honours?"

Her aide moved to stand before Danica. "Temple Captain Danica, kneel."

As she did so, the grand mistress and Nicola draped a new surcoat over her shoulders, one with the gold thread of a Temple Commander.

"Arise, Temple Commander," said Kaylene.

Danica stood, not quite sure what to say.

"Congratulations," offered Nicola. "You deserve it."

"Yes," added the grand mistress. "Your achievements in the north prove you're more than worthy. There will be an official ceremony at some point, but your new rank takes effect immediately." She handed over a scroll. "This is the formal announcement, signed by me and bearing the seal of the matriarch. She and I may disagree on many things, but we were in complete agreement on this."

"Thank you," said Danica. "I wasn't expecting this."

"This is not an act of charity, Danica. Your building of the Temple Fleet will go down in history as one of our greatest achievements." Kaylene took a breath. "I should warn you, however, that some might take offence at your promotion, not because you don't deserve it, but because they see your relative youth as a detriment. That, I suspect, will only be a problem while you're here at the Antonine."

"How long am I to remain here?"

"I brought you and Charlaine here originally to help get to the bottom of these rumours of amalgamation. It's now apparent Talivardas, or rather, Primus Wilmar, is determined to see an end to this order. Sending you back north with that threat looming over us would be a misuse of your skills."

"That doesn't answer my question."

"No," replied the grand mistress. "I don't suppose it does, but I'm afraid I have no better answer for you. Nicola has no doubt informed you of the death of a patriarch?"

"Yes," said Danica. "The Augustine. Where does that leave us concerning defeating the vote of amalgamation?"

"It makes little difference. The old patriarch leaned towards unification, while his successor could just as easily be against it, but things get more dangerous during the selection process."

"Why is that?"

"Under circumstances like this, the Council of Peers could continue without representation from the Augustines, leaving the council with only five votes, six including the Primus. Theoretically, motions can be passed with less support, although a majority is still needed."

"Making a majority three votes instead of four."

"It would indeed," replied the grand mistress, "and while we know our matriarch is against it, only the Mathewite Patriarch has made his stance known. It's possible the Patriarch of Ragnar, or even Ansgar, could turn on us. The moment that happens, the Primus will call for his vote."

"Surely there's some safeguard against such a thing?"

"You're under the illusion that all the patriarchs favour the Temple Orders continuing as they have been. Nothing could be further from the truth. With the threat of a Halvarian invasion growing more likely, coins are in short supply these days. The Petty Kingdoms are withholding funds for their own needs instead of donating them to the Church."

"I thought we operated with funds we gather at our temples?"

"Your fleet operates through the northern rulers' generosity, does it not?"

"It does," replied Danica, "but we guard the sea lanes in exchange—a financial arrangement that benefits everyone."

"Which makes perfect sense when there's a fleet patrolling offshore. However, when a realm in the middle of the Continent does not see the benefit of the Church so directly, the ruler tires of the expense."

"Are the Church's finances that badly off?"

"I haven't seen them myself, but I've been told as much by those who know."

"What can we do about it?"

"At the moment, nothing but wait and hope the new Patriarch of Saint Augustine can put an end to such foolish thoughts once and for all."

"And if he doesn't?"

"Then we are no worse off than when you and Charlaine first arrived. Now, go celebrate your promotion. You've earned it."

Teresa lifted her cup, with Charlaine loudly joining in. "Here's to Temple Commander Danica. Long may she serve!"

The shout carried across the dining hall, echoing back as the majority there repeated it. This wasn't an official event, merely a typical dinner, yet everyone was in a celebratory mood. All except for Nina, who glared from where she sat on the other side of the room.

A stream of initiates, captains, and even commanders came to offer their congratulations, leaving Danica beaming.

"Well done," said Charlaine. "I always knew you'd get there, eventually."

"Your recommendation is what got me here."

"Nonsense. Your own accomplishments did that. You commanded the ships at Temple Bay and the fleet at Lidenbach. The glory is all yours."

"How does it feel?" asked Teresa. "Has it sunk in yet?"

"No. I still feel like the same old Danica."

"That's to be expected, except for the old part. What are you now, twenty-seven?"

"Twenty-eight."

"You must be the youngest Temple Commander in the history of the order."

"Yes," added Charlaine, "and also one of the most experienced, at least in terms of actual fighting."

"So what happens now?" asked Teresa. "Do they send you back to Temple Bay?"

"I asked the grand mistress that same question. She wants to keep us both in the Antonine, although she failed to mention any other assignment."

"I suppose I'll need a new aide," said Charlaine. "I can't have a Temple Commander serving as one."

"I could act as your aide," offered Teresa.

"You're not officially a member of the order at present."

"You could grant me provisional status; either of you could. A Temple Commander can take a prospective initiate under their wing for up to a year."

"But you're not a prospective initiate," said Danica. "You're a trained Temple Knight."

"Yes, but one that theoretically no longer belongs to the order."

"I'll begin the paperwork," said Charlaine. "That way, you'll receive official recognition, which will at least give you some standing here in the Antonine."

"Thank you. I appreciate that."

"Not to change the subject," said Danica, "but whatever happened to that knight, Sir Raynald? Are the Ansgarites still holding him?"

"They are," replied Teresa. "And he's still not allowed visitors other than his guards."

A hand fell on Danica's shoulder. "Congratulations."

"Thank you, Erika."

The Temple Captain sat. "The old crew from Ilea is doing well for themselves." Her gaze met Teresa's. "I hear you're now a Life Mage."

"I prefer the term healer, but yes."

"I would've thought the order would embrace your return to the fold."

"They would, had I not been listed as deceased. Apparently, there's no place in the bureaucracy for someone who's missing."

"We'll straighten that all out eventually," added Charlaine. "Unfortunately, things move at a snail's pace in the Antonine."

"I don't understand," said Erika. "Can't the grand mistress reinstate her?"

"In a word, no. Our charter defines the grand mistress's power, and this situation is not covered by that, which means it can only be changed by an amendment, and that requires the Council of Peers, who won't reconvene until the spring. Even then, I doubt they'd have the time to consider the plight of a lonely sister. They'll be far too busy arguing over the changes the Primus proposed."

"You mean the amalgamation of the orders?"

"I'm afraid it's much more than that. Rumours are circulating that he wants the Temple Fleet turned over to the Cunars."

"I understand why," said Erika. "They command the Holy Fleet down south, so it only makes sense that they should want to do so in the north."

"Then you don't know our history," said Charlaine. "The Temple Knights of Saint Agnes used to command the Holy Fleet."

"Yes, but our role is defending women, not sailing around looking for pirates."

Danica knit her brows. "Is that what you think we do? The Temple Fleet does much more than that; it keeps the sea lanes free of Halvarian interference. And as a direct result of our efforts, trade has increased significantly."

"But at what cost?"

"Surprisingly, it's cost the Church very little."

"Then where do the funds come from?" asked Erika.

"The northern Petty Kingdoms. They donate money to the cause, and we patrol their waters for them, keeping them safe."

"How many ships have you?"

Danica smiled. "More than enough to do the job, thanks to the empire."

"How does the empire figure into all of this?"

Charlaine chuckled. "What she's not telling you is the vast majority of her ships were captured from Halvaria."

"We're building our own ships now," added Danica. "Come spring, almost a quarter of the fleet will be comprised of our designs."

"Will they be galleys," asked Erika, "like the Holy Fleet?"

"No. The Great Northern Sea is far too rough for such craft. Instead, we designed vessels more akin to cogs. Do you remember the *Constance?*"

"Wasn't that the ship dropping raiders off along the coast of Rizela?"

"It was, and like that, the Temple Fleet's ships are longer, with a narrower beam."

"Beam?"

"Sorry," said Danica. "I sometimes forget I'm talking to people not familiar with the language of the sea. The beam is the width of a ship."

"Wouldn't it be better for it to be wider rather than thinner?"

"That's a common misconception, but history tells us otherwise. We've also recruited the finest shipbuilders the northern kingdoms have to offer, and their collective knowledge has been instrumental in developing our new designs."

"You've certainly been busy," said Erika. "I don't suppose you've got room for a recently promoted Temple Captain?"

"I'm always looking, but you'd have to serve an apprenticeship under an experienced ship captain."

"I'd be willing to do that."

"Hang on a moment," said Charlaine with a grin. "You've only just made Temple Commander yourself. Are you already suggesting your ship captains be promoted to Temple Captain?"

Danica chuckled. "As I've said on several occasions, it would certainly help matters. It's too bad that only the grand mistress chooses who to promote."

"That's not quite true. Temple Commander is the only rank that's the sole prerogative of the grand mistress."

"Ha!" said Erika. "I finally know something you don't."

"That being?"

"Someone else can approve promotions to Temple Commander, that being a Temple General."

"Only the Cunars have those, and just two the last time I checked."

"I realize it's a technicality, but it helped me pass my last written test."

"And who gave you that question? Let me guess, Temple Commander Nina?"

"Yes," replied Erika. "Unlike you two, she remembers me with great affection."

"Speaking of Nina," said Charlaine. "Did you ever get a chance to heal her, Teresa?"

"No. I tried broaching the subject, but you know how stubborn she can be. She also exhibits a sense of repulsion at the idea of magic."

"That's ridiculous. She knows Gwalinor healed me back in Rizela."

"It's one thing for magic to heal another, quite another to have a spell cast on yourself. In the end, we must respect the decision of others, so I gave up trying."

25

MIDWINTER

WINTER 1106 SR

"Busy?" asked Danica, poking her head into Charlaine's office.

"Always, but never too busy to see you. Come in and take a seat. I need a break from all this..." She spread her arms wide, indicating the papers on her desk.

"What's all that?"

"Reports from the kitchen explaining why they need more funds to purchase food, requisitions from the stables for replacement mounts, yet more requests for additional blankets for the initiates—the list goes on and on. Sometimes, I wonder if I wasn't summoned here solely to look after the paperwork."

"I spoke with the grand mistress today."

"Oh yes? How did that go?"

"The Council of Peers wants me to make a report concerning the Temple Fleet."

"And when is this report due?"

"I'm to present it in person when it reconvenes in the spring."

"Is that sufficient time for you to get the information you need? It's a long way to Temple Bay."

"I doubt that'll be necessary," replied Danica. "I can give them all the information they need from up here." She tapped her temple. "My fear is they will use this against me somehow."

"You're worried about the Cunars taking control of the fleet?"

"Yes. Especially after that stunt they pulled back in Arnsfeld."

"They tried to block our reinforcements," said Charlaine, "not commandeer our ships."

"True. Now, imagine the damage they could do if they gained control of the entire fleet. The Great Northern Sea would become a Halvarian lake."

"I agree with your assessment, but I doubt that would hold much sway over the Council of Peers."

"Care to offer any advice?"

"You will be addressing the patriarchs of all the orders, not people familiar with sea warfare. I suggest you keep it as simple as possible."

"How, exactly, do I do that and still explain the importance of the fleet remaining in our hands?"

"By stressing you already have experienced captains in place. Any new command would gut the Temple Fleet of its captains, although I suppose they could phase in the changes over a few years."

"I won't hand over the fleet, not to the Cunars, especially considering what we've learned about the Primus."

"You may have no choice. You can't defy a direct order."

"Which makes it all the more important that I convince them the Temple Fleet should remain as it is."

"You worked with that naval architect the last time we were here. What was his name again?"

"Temple Captain Leamund, a Cunar."

"You should visit him and ask if he might write a letter of recommendation. Having such an important individual on your side would help make a favourable impression."

"That's an excellent idea. I shall see to it at once."

"You'd best hurry, then. We have the Midwinter Feast this evening, and it wouldn't be advisable to be late, particularly when we're celebrating your promotion."

Danica stepped into the snow, her breath frosting in the crisp afternoon air. Leamund's office was housed within the Cunar commandery, its dark grey stone imposing compared to the other orders, even though they were identical layouts.

She walked along Saints Way, the road directly south of the Agnesite commandery. The route took her directly past the Ragnarites, an order whose entire presence had been questioned in recent years. It wasn't that they weren't valued, for they'd rooted out many Necromancers, but they'd done their job so well there were none left to find, resulting in their funding dropping, along with their numbers.

She glanced up at the building, her gaze lingering on the upper-floor windows. Was the place as empty as it appeared, or were hundreds of Temple Knights inside, learning how to deal with Death Mages?

Eventually, she reached Herani Avenue and turned south, the Cunar commandery coming into sight. To the west stood a clutch of trees, while to the east, a row of maples lined the road, marking the edge of the Ansgarite training field.

A stiff breeze whipped up a swirl of snow, temporarily blocking her view, and threatened to pluck the hood from her head. She clutched at the neck of her cloak, pulling it closer to ward off the sudden chill.

The wind calmed almost as suddenly as it started, and then she heard snow crunching behind her. She turned, expecting a fellow traveller, only to find a trio of men covered in furs, bare knives held ready to attack. The first came at her in a rush, slashing with wild abandon. Danica, used to the close confines of shipboard fighting, blocked with her forearm, letting her hand slide up to grab his. A quick twist snapped his wrist, and he went down screaming, clutching his broken arm.

The second assailant approached more cautiously, jabbing the point of his knife at her to keep her on the defensive. She backed up, making space to manoeuvre, but the third individual went wide, attempting to sneak behind her. She quickly shifted, turning around to attack the one trying to surprise her.

His knife slashed out, cutting into her forearm as she moved in close and grabbed his furs. Already moving in for the attack, his momentum kept him coming at her. Danica stepped aside, extending her right leg to trip the fellow, which caused him to lose his balance and fall.

She wheeled around to face the last attacker as he rushed towards her, thrusting his knife into her right side just below her ribs. Danica stumbled backwards, blood dripping down her tabard, and he followed with another attack, slicing her thigh open. The agony of the wound brought her to her knees, the crimson-spattered snow breaking her fall. Her head spun as she clutched her hand to her side, attempting to stem the flow of blood. White dots flashed before her, and then she fell backwards, now staring at the sky.

Her attacker was kneeling over her, his knife ready to slit her throat, when someone gave a distant yell. The fellow looked away from her momentarily, then rose and fled, along with his companions.

The next thing she knew, a Temple Knight stared down at her. "Sister, can you hear me?" he asked.

She grimaced with the pain. "Yes, but I'm bleeding badly."

"I shall get you inside the commandery where we can better examine your wounds."

"Send someone to the Agnesites to find Sister Teresa. She can help."

He nodded before turning and talking to somebody out of her eyesight. Danica tried to understand what he was saying, but everything went black.

"How are you feeling?"

Danica opened her eyes to Teresa's familiar face. "I see they found you," she said, her voice thin and reedy.

Charlaine's face soon appeared. "You had us worried there." She clutched Danica's hand. "You're in the Ragnarite commandery."

"A trio of men tried to kill me. I would've been dead had someone not borne witness to the attack."

"That was Brother Julius. You're lucky he happened to be nearby."

"I was headed to the Cunar commandery," came the knight's voice.

Danica turned and saw a weather-beaten face with a long, brown beard liberally sprinkled with grey. "Do I know you?" she asked.

"No. Our meeting was purely by chance. As I said, I was on my way to the Cunar commandery. You?"

"I, too, was on my way there."

"An odd place for a sister knight, if you don't mind me saying so."

"I went to visit Temple Captain Leamund, the naval architect."

"I'm afraid I'm not familiar with him."

"What can you tell us of your attackers?" asked Charlaine.

"They were thugs," noted Julius. "I have no idea how they got inside the Antonine?"

"They weren't thugs!" declared Danica. "They were Cunars."

"Are you certain?"

"I can't prove it, but it's the only thing that makes sense."

"I'm sorry," said Charlaine. "I should've realized they'd want you out of the way and insisted you take an escort."

"Escort?" asked Julius. "Here in the Antonine? I'm afraid you'll have to explain that one to me."

"This is Temple Commander Danica."

"Yes, so you explained when you arrived here with Sister Teresa to see to her injuries."

"What I didn't tell you is she's the Admiral of the Temple Fleet."

"And you think someone wants her dead because of that?"

"It's not as far-fetched as you might believe. There's a notion being bandied about that the Temple Fleet should be placed under the Cunars' purview. Danica was to present a report to the Council of Peers concerning the ships under her command. We'd appreciate it if you kept this to yourself, at least for now."

The Ragnarite nodded. "Am I to assume the presence of a Life Mage amongst your order is also a secret?"

"Yes."

"Probably a wise move. How do you wish to proceed? You're welcome to leave the admiral here for now; at least we can ensure she remains safe."

"Thank you," said Charlaine. "That's most appreciated."

"I shall remain here," added Teresa, "so I can keep an eye on her. Her physical injuries are healed, but she's lost a lot of blood."

"Remarkable," said Julius. "I know my own order employs Life Mages occasionally, but I've never seen one perform their magic. I assume she'll make a full recovery?"

"Yes. You made that possible by sending someone to us as soon as you did. Had you delayed, she would've perished."

"How long until she's back to normal?"

"She'll be weak for a week or so. It varies considerably with the patient's overall health."

"Danica's not the sort to sit idly by," said Charlaine. "Can you shed any more light on the attack, Brother?"

"I'm afraid not," replied Julius. "I didn't see their faces."

"Did anyone attempt to pursue them?"

Julius shook his head. "I stayed with Sister Danica and sent my companion Brother Torlin for help. Once my fellow knights appeared, the admiral had already fallen unconscious. We carried her here and immediately sent for Sister Teresa. I'm afraid the wind would've obliterated any tracks of her attackers by the time we finished."

"I should've worn my armour," said Danica.

Teresa placed her hand on Danica's shoulder. "No one could possibly expect to be attacked in broad daylight. For that matter, who even knew you'd be out there? Did you send word ahead that you'd be going?"

"No."

"Then there's only one answer," said Charlaine. "Someone's been watching the commandery, waiting for the right opportunity."

Danica tried to sit up, but her head spun.

"Easy now," said Teresa, her hand still on her shoulder. "You're supposed to be resting."

"How long have I been here?"

"You were attacked this very afternoon."

"What time is it now?"

"Past dinner-time."

"The Midwinter Feast!"

"Don't worry," said Charlaine. "I sent word to the grand mistress explaining the circumstances."

"We have our feast this evening as well," said Julius. "No doubt it's not as festive as your order, but I think you'll find the food decent enough. I shall arrange for some to be sent to you and Sister Teresa. You, too, Temple Commander, assuming you're staying?"

"Much as I'd like to," replied Charlaine, "I must report to the grand mistress."

"I shall arrange for two of our knights to escort you. I'd hate for these same men to attack you as well."

"Thank you. That is most appreciated."

"What about this fellow the admiral was going to visit?"

"He wasn't aware I was coming," Danica reminded him.

"I understand this. What I meant to ask is whether you still wanted to speak with him. If so, I could arrange for him to meet you here, with guards present, if you wish. It wouldn't be this evening, for he'll have his own banquet to attend, but he'd likely be amenable to the idea if we explained the circumstances." He raised his hand to hold off any objections. "I promise, we won't reveal who we believe responsible for this attack, only that you'd been injured."

"That would be most agreeable."

"Excellent," said Brother Julius. "I shall make the arrangements first thing tomorrow. Now, if you'll excuse me, I have a feast to attend. You know the way out?"

"I do," replied Charlaine.

"Then I shall leave you to it." He exited the room, leaving them in peace.

Charlaine sat on the side of the bed. "If you wanted time to relax, you could've just asked."

"That's me," said Danica. "Always doing things the hard way."

Temple Captain Leamund arrived to visit Danica two days later, escorted by a Ragnarite who assumed a position by the door.

"I heard about the attack," Leamund said by way of greeting. "I trust you are doing well?"

"I am," she replied. "Thanks mostly to Sister Teresa."

"I'm told you were headed to visit me when you were accosted."

"Accosted? That's a polite way of putting it; they tried to murder me."

"Any idea who was behind it?"

"I have my suspicions," said Danica, "but nothing I can prove."

"Those responsible will be punished for their crime, if not in this life, then in the Underworld." He paused, running two fingers from chin to navel, the traditional blessing of Saint Cunar. "As for yourself, I can only assume you were coming to see me regarding shipbuilding?"

"While I'm certain that would've come up, I was hoping you might help me persuade the Council of Peers of the effectiveness of the Temple Fleet."

"You would be much more persuasive than I," replied Leamund. "I only build the ships—you command them."

"Still, your words illustrate that others recognize its value."

"I would love to, I really would, but I'm afraid I've been specifically instructed not to help you with this report. I cannot go against the wishes of my grand master."

"Are you suggesting the head of your order is speaking out against me?"

"I'm not suggesting, I'm telling you that's exactly what he commanded, and in person, no less, which came as a great shock. I've been an architect for decades, yet this is the first time a grand master has ever come to my office!"

"Then I'm afraid you've wasted your time coming here."

He glanced at the Ragnarite standing by the door before lowering his voice. "Not entirely. I was instructed not to help you with this report, but that doesn't mean I can't offer advice."

"Go on."

"Something strange is occurring in my order. I first noticed it five years ago when Admiral Marius was removed from his position as Admiral of the Holy Fleet."

"But isn't he a Temple General?"

Leamund shook his head. "No longer, I'm afraid. He's been reduced to Temple Commander, more suited to his new position."

"Which is?"

"Fleet provisioner, overseeing the supply of all the order's ships."

"He was a seasoned admiral," said Danica, "and commanded the Holy Fleet at the Battle of Alantra."

"I am well aware of the man's accomplishments. He is also responsible for building the fleet into what it is today."

"Who commands the fleet now?"

"A new Temple General named Gilbert."

"Gilbert? Are you certain?"

"Absolutely. He ordered the cancellation of the expansion plans for the Holy Fleet. I'd developed a new design that promised faster galleys, but it now sits on the shelf collecting dust. He's also ordered a third of the fleet beached, claiming they're decrepit and rotting, a notion I find insulting, considering many are less than ten years old. Either this new admiral is incompetent, or he is deliberately attempting to weaken us."

"And this has the support of the Council of Peers?"

"The Council? Why would you think that?"

"Doesn't the Holy Fleet come under their jurisdiction?"

"Not since our new Primus was elected. He placed every ship of the Church under my order's command, which is why your actions in the north have come under such scrutiny of late. This Gilbert fellow wants control of your ships."

"Is this admiral here, in the Antonine?"

"Not that I've heard. Admittedly, though, I wouldn't know him if he stood right in front of me."

"Really?" said Danica. "Doesn't a Temple General wear some indication of his rank?"

"I suppose he does, now that you mention it, but what that looks like is beyond me."

"But you worked with Admiral Marius, didn't you?"

"Only through correspondence." Leamund paused to let out a sigh. "I sense my time as a member of the Cunars may be coming to an end."

"Temple Knights of Saint Cunar don't have the option of leaving the order, do they?"

"No, they don't. Which is what worries me."

26

REPORT

SPRING 1107 SR

Danica stared up at the formidable Council of Peers, awestruck at the staggering size of the structure. It dwarfed all other buildings in the Antonine, and, based on the places she'd visited in her career, perhaps even anything in the Continent.

"Nervous?" asked Charlaine, who'd come with Teresa to sit in the balcony and watch the proceedings.

"You must admit, it's intimidating," replied Danica.

"That's by design. It's meant to project the power of the Church."

"I'd be much happier if I could stand before the patriarchs in private and get this over with."

"Keep your focus. There are only five people you need to convince—the patriarchs. Everyone else is there to advise their respective orders."

"Five?"

"Yes. The Augustines still haven't chosen their new patriarch, although they've narrowed down the list. You need to concentrate on the facts; that's what will save the fleet."

"It's not the patriarchs I'm worried about," said Danica. "It's the Primus. How do I convince someone who's determined to ruin our order?"

"The Primus gets a vote if there's a tie," replied Charlaine. "You only need to convince three patriarchs to keep the Temple Fleet intact. Remember, with no Augustines, three out of five votes gives you a clear majority. The Primus won't be able to decide the matter under such circumstances."

"Supposing I do convince them? Wouldn't that all be for naught if our order is disbanded?"

"All we can do is deal with the present. State your case, Danica, and we have to hope they'll see reason."

A guard wearing Saint Ragnar livery approached. "Temple Commander Danica?" he asked.

"Yes?"

"I've been instructed to escort you into the chamber. I'm afraid your companions won't be permitted to join you. They'll have to observe from the gallery."

"Good luck, Danica," said Charlaine. "We'll be cheering you on."

"Agnes be with you," added Teresa before the two departed and entered the building.

"This way," said the guard, nodding at the Ragnarite manning the desk she'd previously been stopped at. He set off at a leisurely pace, allowing Danica to walk beside him. "Have you spoken in here before?"

"No," she replied. "I can't say I have."

"It's a circular chamber. We'll enter from the north end, and then you'll take up a position in the centre. Sound carries well, so you needn't be concerned about being heard. Each patriarch will be robed in their appropriate colours, except for the Augustine, as their seat remains empty. As for the Primus, he'll be in the balcony over the entrance to the chamber. You'll face him if you turn around once you're in the centre."

"Temple Commander Charlaine indicated there may be advisors present."

"Yes. There's a big crowd today."

"And by big, you mean…"

"I haven't counted them, Commander, but twenty per patriarch wouldn't be too far off the mark." He chuckled. "Don't worry. It's not as intimidating as you might think, as the council chamber can hold many more. From your standpoint, it'll be as if the room is half empty."

"And the observers?"

"The gallery is nothing more than a large balcony overlooking the chamber. I'm told we expect it to be filled today."

"Why?"

He grinned. "It's not very often we get a person of your renown here in the council chambers. Everyone wants to hear about how you defeated the Halvarian Fleet."

They passed through a pair of doors guarded by two more Ragnarites, then entered a waiting area.

"If you'll stay here, Commander, I'll see if they're ready for you."

"I'm sorry," said Danica. "I didn't get your name."

"My apologies. I'm Brother Carodoc." He bowed. "I was present at the commandery this last winter when they brought you in. I trust you've fully recovered?"

"I have. Thank you."

He nodded. "Then please excuse me. I shall return as quickly as I can." He left through the other set of double doors.

Danica paced, her mind going over what she planned to say. She could recite the names of every ship and crew member in the Temple Fleet in addition to all the Temple Knights under her command, but the patriarchs would not likely see that as a strength. Instead, she must concentrate on the strategy that freed the Great Northern Sea of Halvarian interference.

Brother Carodoc soon reappeared. "They're almost ready, Commander." He held one door open. "You'll be announced once they're all seated."

Danica took a breath, trying to steady her nerves. She'd faced death at sea, charging headlong onto a deck full of enemy warriors, yet here, the prospect of explaining her actions filled her with anxiety.

"That's it," said her guide. "If you'll follow me, I'll escort you to the podium."

Danica wanted to laugh, for it wasn't as if she had any choice. She'd been summoned here to defend her command. To leave now would only result in its absorption into the Holy Fleet. She took a deep breath and stepped out into the Council of Peers.

Charlaine and Teresa watched from the gallery, packed in amongst members of all orders. In addition to Temple Knights, there were lay brothers and sisters, along with Holy Fathers and even a few priors and archpriors in white, who'd made the long pilgrimage to the Antonine to oversee the election of their new Augustine Patriarch.

All conversation ceased as Danica entered the room, her back stiff with resolve as she walked to the raised platform in the centre. Her Ragnarite escort moved to stand just off the platform, facing her.

All eyes turned to the Primus as he stood. "This council recognizes Temple Commander Danica of Saint Agnes." His gaze swept across the chamber before continuing. "She is here today to give us an accounting of the affairs of the so-called Temple Fleet and its illegal founding some ten years past."

With a start, Charlaine realized this would be no ordinary report. It was an attempt to discredit her entire order; all she could do was watch and pray Danica survived the encounter.

Not content to give up his hold on the room, the Primus launched directly into his enquiry. "Commander. For the record, state your age."

"I am twenty-eight," replied Danica, "although I see no reason why that is relevant."

"Twenty-eight is very young for a Temple Commander."

"I did not seek promotion. My grand mistress awarded me with it."

"The same grand mistress who authorized you to build a fleet in the order's name?"

"Yes."

"So, in other words, you received a promotion for furthering her personal aims."

"The establishment of the Temple Fleet was designed to bring peace to the shipping lanes of the north and deter the Halvarian Empire's aggression."

The Primus smiled, making him look even more menacing. "Commander, why do you think you were chosen for this task, considering at that time, you'd only been a Temple Knight for a few years."

"I distinguished myself in Ilea, Eminence, and I already had a passing knowledge of ships and the sea."

"Yet you were barely old enough to become a knight." He glanced down at something in his hand. "Is it true you were only fifteen when you were admitted to the order?"

Charlaine died a little inside. The woman who'd recommended Danica for the order had lied to save her from a life of misery.

"It's true," replied Danica. "I'll not deny it, but my record stands for itself."

"Your record is not the issue here, Commander. Rather, it is the very existence of this northern fleet. By all rights, it should have been placed under the Admiral of the Holy Fleet's command."

"With all due respect, Eminence, it is unreasonable to expect an admiral based in Corassus to command ships in the Great Northern Sea."

"That is not your decision to make," replied the Primus. "The Temple Knights of Saint Cunar have always dealt with naval matters."

Danica straightened her back. "That is not true, Eminence. Just over fifty years ago, the Temple Knights of Saint Agnes managed the Holy Fleet."

"She's right," called out the Patriarch of Saint Mathew. "It is a documented fact."

"Then I shall amend my statement," said the Primus. "When the Temple Knights of Saint Cunar took over responsibility for the fleet, they were given command over all ships in service to the Church. By that statement alone, your Temple Fleet would be illegal."

"Not so," replied Danica. "I read that edict myself when I was sent north.

It gave command of all the ships currently in Church service to the Brothers of Saint Cunar but made no mention of future vessels."

"That is certainly one interpretation, but let us move on to other matters, those being the lack of authority on the part of your grand mistress concerning raising a fleet."

"That is not a matter I'm qualified to comment on, Eminence. I assure you, however, the Temple Fleet has been instrumental in halting Halvarian aggression in the north."

Those in attendance began stomping their feet, an act which signified agreement with her statement. They quickly quieted when the Primus stared them down.

He turned back to Danica. "Commander, did your grand mistress order you to do something illegal?"

"To answer that, Eminence, you must first define illegal."

"You dare to mock me?"

"No. I seek clarification. The term illegal can describe both secular and religious law, to which do you refer?"

"Religious, clearly."

"Then the answer must be no, as no edict of the Antonine was broken in any way with the formation of the Temple Fleet."

"Your fellow sisters crew the navy of the north, which is in direct violation of our laws!"

"You are mistaken in your assumptions, Eminence. The Temple Knights do not form the crew, only the fighting complement, which you'll find is permitted under the charter that established the fighting orders in the first place."

"But your order owns those ships, does it not?"

"The vessels that comprise the Temple Fleet belong to the community of Temple Bay, Eminence, not the Temple Knights of Saint Agnes. If you placed the ships under the command of our brothers, the Cunars, without their permission, it would be tantamount to theft. Surely you're not suggesting such an act?"

The Primus cleared his throat and clasped his hands tightly, his knuckles turning white from the pressure. "Let us return to your original visit to the Antonine. When were you informed you would go north to raise a fleet?"

"The summer of 1097."

"And at that time, what were your specific orders?"

"To travel north, to Reinwick, and purchase a ship on behalf of the order."

"So you defied orders by placing this ship under the jurisdiction of Temple Bay?"

"That happened later when it became clear the fleet required more substantive support in terms of ports and repairs. There were no funds to build such facilities, so the ships under our command became collateral to entice skilled workmen to build what we needed."

"Am I to understand you sold the Church's property?"

"No coins changed hands, Eminence. That would violate Church doctrine. The ships were offered as a safeguard against non-payment should the need arise. It is commonly done with our commanderies, as with all the orders. Logically, a ship is merely a seaborne version of one of our buildings."

"Who rules Temple Bay?"

"It is an independent town, ruled by a governing council selected from amongst the people living there."

"So you have no say in its running?"

"I am far too busy looking after the fleet."

"But earlier, you claimed your ships are the equivalent of commanderies. How can you hand them over to this entity?"

"The original fleet consisted of only one ship, Eminence: the *Valiant*. All other vessels were either constructed in Temple Bay or captured from the Halvarians, and, as you know, Temple Knights are not allowed to profit from our actions."

"By your own admission, you did."

"I said no such thing," replied Danica. "Captured Halvarian warships were handed over to the ruling council of Temple Bay, who, in turn, placed them under my command and allowed us to assign fighting complements aboard them."

"Ah, but you said *Valiant* belonged to the order."

"It does, Eminence, and I would be more than willing to turn it over to our brothers, the Temple Knights of Saint Cunar, should this august council desire."

"How many ships does your order actually own?"

"We had two, but *Valiant's* sister ship, *Vanguard*, was sunk by the empire during the Arnsfeld campaign."

"What of *Vigilant*? Was that not another similar vessel?"

"That vessel is owned by Temple Bay, as are the others forming the Temple Fleet."

"You are pushing the boundaries of my patience," said the Primus, "and I might remind you of your vow to tell the truth."

"I speak only the truth," replied Danica. "I was ordered to form a fleet, but the manner of its creation, composition, and the ownership of those vessels was of secondary importance as long as our order maintained control of them. I knew there would be a push to take these ships away from us sooner or later, as they did in Corassus, so I took steps to eliminate that possibility."

"Your actions are contrary to the benefit of the Church."

"Not at all, Eminence. My actions saved the Antonine from a major expense. Had I not taken these steps, the presence of the Temple Fleet would've emptied our coffers."

"Now, now," said the Primus. "Are you expecting us to believe this Temple Bay is capable of sustaining the entire fleet?"

"Not at all, Eminence. Most of the realms on the northern coast of Eiddenwerthe contribute to the coffers of Temple Bay to help defray the cost."

There it was, thought Charlaine, Danica's masterpiece.

"Is that true?" whispered Teresa.

"Yes. Danica would never lie; it's not in her. I must admit to some surprise, though. This is the first I've heard the full story."

Their conversation was cut short as a patriarch stood.

"This body recognizes the Patriarch of Saint Ansgar," said the Primus, who then sat.

"I would like to hear Temple Commander Danica's version of the events leading up to the Battle of Lidenbach, as I'm certain my colleagues would."

Danica began her tale.

The hour had grown late, and darkness was upon them by the time everyone left the Council of Peers. It had been a victory for Danica, for the motion to place the Temple Fleet under the command of the Cunars was defeated, but the Grand Mistress of Saint Agnes would be called before the matriarch to explain her actions.

Danica finally appeared, making her way towards her waiting colleagues. "Well?" she called out. "How did I do?"

Charlaine smiled. "I've never been prouder."

"Nor I," added Teresa. "You've saved the Temple Fleet, but it may have cost us our grand mistress."

Danica came to a halt before them. "That certainly wasn't my intention."

"It's not your fault," said Charlaine. "The Primus was looking for someone to blame, and she was the logical choice, especially considering her contentious relationship with the matriarch."

"There must be a way we can save her. Perhaps I should go back and take all the blame?"

"No. You're too valuable. We need you up north, keeping the fleet in fighting shape. Speaking of which, it was very clever of you to set up Temple Bay that way. Wherever did you come up with that?"

"If you recall, the first time we learned of the idea, the grand mistress stressed the Cunars might try to take command, so I took it upon myself to ensure that couldn't happen."

"And the council who rules Temple Bay?"

"They represent the shipwrights and other trades who took up residence there. I thought it best to give them self-determination. It's not as though I'm interested in the financial aspects of running a fleet, merely its military employment, and this arrangement allowed me to do just that."

"I'm curious," said Teresa. "How much do they get from the northern Petty Kingdoms?"

"Enough to equip a substantial fleet, with coins left over, allowing them to build additional dockyard space for constructing merchant vessels."

"You've done a thorough job of being admiral," said Charlaine, "but we'd best not linger here. The grand mistress needs our support, and unless I miss my guess, she'll need it sooner rather than later. We should return to the commandery before she's summoned before the matriarch."

"We have time," said Danica. "When I left the council chambers, the matriarch was in a heated discussion with the Primus. I daresay there's no love lost between those two."

"I wonder why?" said Teresa. "Could it possibly have something to do with the Primus being a former Temple Knight? She certainly has no love for our order?"

"Or it could be that the Primus is trying to force his will on everyone," suggested Charlaine. "He wants all the Temple Knights in one command structure that falls under the control of his old order, the Cunars, and we all know how that would end."

"With the empire in control," supplied Danica.

"Precisely."

27

THE GATHERING
SPRING 1107 SR

Word had spread quickly concerning Danica's report to the council, and when they arrived at the commandery, everyone was rushing around, trying to put their house in order.

It was common courtesy to report to Temple Captain Nicola's office before visiting the grand mistress, so the trio set off for the top floor. Upon arriving, they discovered the hall full of people clamouring for the attention of the head of the order.

Nicola, spotting them amongst the throng, waved them through, then closed her door, blocking the others out.

"Your timing couldn't be better," she began. "I was about to send someone to fetch you and Danica. The grand mistress has called a meeting of the Temple Commanders."

"All of them?" asked Charlaine.

"All of those within easy reach. We have a couple serving in the council chambers, with more at the Grand Sanctum, but we don't want to raise undue attention."

"How many are here?"

"With you two, the total comes to eight. Sorry, Teresa, but you'll have to wait out here."

"I understand," replied the healer.

"Let's get you inside, shall we?" said Nicola. "Ordinarily, I'd take you through the hall, but given the crowd out there, I think we'd be better off using an alternate route."

"Alternate?" said Danica. "Are you suggesting there's a secret door here somewhere?"

"Not secret, merely hidden." She moved and pressed in the middle of a brick. A section of wall sprang out a finger's breadth, and she pulled it open, revealing the room next door. "Charlaine and Danica are here," Nicola announced.

"Good," replied the grand mistress. "Send them in."

They entered the room to find Nina and five others they'd seen around the commandery.

The grand mistress didn't waste any time. "I'm sure most of you are familiar with Temple Commander Charlaine and Admiral Danica. I'll let the rest introduce themselves."

"I am Temple Commander Nina. I oversee the training here in the Antonine. I also commanded in Ilea, where Charlaine had her first assignment." She turned to the woman next to her, a tall knight with sandy-coloured hair.

The woman nodded. "I am Temple Commander Verushka, Head of Discipline for the order."

"And I'm Katinka," added a short, dark-haired woman. "The order's treasurer."

"And I'm Amalia," replied a well-muscled blonde. "I'm here in the Antonine for my training as a Temple Commander."

Charlaine turned her gaze to the last members of the group. "And you are?"

"Gerda," replied the short, dark-skinned individual, "and this is Ursula. We're both in training, like Amalia."

"Good," said Kaylene. "Now that we've all been introduced, let's get to the matter at hand." She cleared her throat and looked around the room, gathering her thoughts while everyone watched her like a hawk.

"There is no easy way to say this," she finally began. "Our order is in grave danger. If the Primus has his way, he'll amalgamate the orders, leaving only the Cunars, and I shouldn't have to tell you their opinion of Agnesites. Let there be no doubt, if this proposal passes, we will be disbanded, and that, I cannot allow."

She swallowed. To Charlaine, the woman looked as though she was stretched to the breaking point, yet somehow, she maintained her composure.

"I have no doubt I shall be removed from my position as grand mistress shortly."

A flurry of objections arose, but she held out her hand to stop them.

"I've served this order for decades. I will not stand by and let it be lost to the annals of history. Now, I imagine you're all wondering what I'm about to propose, and I'll get to that in a moment, but first, I must raise an important point. Our order plays a crucial role in the Petty Kingdoms, yet there's every likelihood we will no longer be welcome in various parts of the Continent come summer. I am the grand mistress, not the Matriarch of Saint Agnes, so I hold no power to appoint my successor, and though I can make suggestions, whoever I choose would likely be painted with the same brush as me. I can, however, take actions to ensure the survival of this order, and for it to succeed, it requires the cooperation of each and every one of you."

"How can we help?" asked Charlaine.

The grand mistress smiled warmly. "I knew you'd be the one to ask; that's why I've decided to promote you to Temple General."

A collective gasp escaped into the room.

"Are you certain, Your Grace?" said Nina. "I understand Sister Charlaine has had a remarkable military career, but this order needs stability, not some upstart who breaks the rules."

The other commanders glared at her, their looks of disapproval enough to make Nina try to walk back her words. "That is not to say such a skill is not valued. I merely question her ability to administer the order."

The grand mistress ignored her. "Charlaine, I am placing a great burden on your shoulders, one which I know you will bear to the best of your abilities. As Temple General, you wield the power to promote, assign, and dismiss members of the order. For all intents and purposes, you will be the head of this order, subject only to the rule of the grand mistress. I should also point out that the rank is permanent. Once given, it cannot be revoked by my successor or anyone else who tries to tell you otherwise."

Charlaine's heart pounded, and her legs weakened beneath her. Only Danica's hand on her shoulder calmed her. "It's all right," Danica whispered. "You were born for this."

"I know this is a shock," continued the grand mistress, "but we are running out of time."

"What, specifically, do you want me to do?" asked Charlaine.

"Your responsibility will be the order's survival; everything else becomes secondary. If that means you must fight your way out of the Antonine, then so be it."

"Even if it requires taking up arms against another order?"

"I leave that decision to you, but I will say this: if you don't get out of the Antonine, the entire order is lost."

"This is madness!" declared Nina. "You're calling on all of us to disobey our vows."

"Is she?" said Verushka. "Or is she giving us a future?"

"The Church is our future."

"Not if they disband us. Our order is dedicated to helping women. What will happen to all those poor souls if we're not there to protect them?"

"That doesn't give us the right to break our vows."

"We wouldn't be," said Amalia, surprising everyone. She closed her eyes and recited the oath from memory. "Do you swear, by all that is holy, to uphold the tenants of Saint Agnes? To protect all women, regardless of age, infirmity, or religion? And do you promise to put the needs of the order above your own, keep your word, and never lie?"

"Impressive," said Danica.

"We were going over the very topic in class yesterday. As you can see, there's no mention of serving the Church, only the order."

"Yes," said Nina, "but there is no order without the Church. The fighting orders were formed through its charter."

"Agreed," replied the grand mistress, "but nowhere in that charter was there any method to legally disband the order."

"And that's your excuse? That it was never mentioned?"

"We are fighting for our very existence, Nina. Have you no compassion for your fellow sisters?"

"Excuse me," said Ursula. "I have a question, if I may?"

The grand mistress nodded.

"Temple Captains have silver thread on their surcoats to denote rank, and commanders have gold, but how does one distinguish a Temple General?"

"Excellent question. Nicola? Come in here, will you? I know you're listening at the door."

The hidden door opened, revealing her abashed aide.

Kaylene held out her hand towards Nicola. "How do we identify a Temple General?"

"With a shoulder sash, Your Grace, although it's only supposed to be worn on ceremonial occasions."

"Scarlet, like our surcoats?"

"It's not specified, Your Grace. I suppose that means it's entirely up to you."

"I won't be around much longer," replied the grand mistress, "so I'll leave that at your discretion, Charlaine." She scanned the room, her eyes filling with sadness. "This is the last time we shall all be assembled in this office, but you need to pass on what has happened here today. Everyone, from the newest recruit to the most seasoned veteran, must be made aware that Sister Charlaine is our Temple General. You are to obey her in all things as you would normally obey me. Is that understood?"

They all nodded, save for Nina.

"Come now," said Kaylene. "Can you not put aside your differences and accept Charlaine as your superior?"

Nina finally relented. "I'm not happy about it, but I shall abide by your wishes, Your Grace."

"Good. It pleases me to know you can all see reason. Now, you are dismissed, save for Sister Charlaine."

The two of them waited as the rest filed out into Nicola's office.

"You'll need an aide," said the grand mistress. "There's a lot to accomplish."

"Teresa is in the next room."

"Then bring her in. Danica, too, for that matter. I suspect you'll want her counsel."

"Why? What do you need us to do?"

"Simplify the record-keeping of this order. If we're about to lose this commandery, I'll not have all our paperwork handed over to the Cunars. Any records you don't need will be burned; the rest you'll take with you."

"Where am I to go?"

"It's best I don't know," replied the grand mistress. "That way, I won't need to lie to protect you. I would recommend, however, that you be ready to move on a moment's notice. If things fall apart, as I suspect they will, you'll have little warning to mobilize."

"I will not abandon my fellow sisters."

"That is your decision to make." Kaylene stared back before finally nodding. "If anyone can get them out of the Antonine, it's you. Tell me none of the details, Charlaine, but take whatever actions you deem necessary to get everyone to safety."

"I will. I promise."

"Good. Fetch Teresa and Danica. There's work to be done."

Charlaine rested her back against the wall. They were sitting on the floor of her office with piles of papers scattered everywhere, trying to decide which documents they should keep.

"Instead of wading through this page by page," suggested Danica, "we should list what documents we want for the future."

"A good idea," said Teresa. "First and foremost, you'll need the full register of all active knights and officers."

"Agreed, along with the list of who's assigned where and the regional breakdown of the command structure. We need to identify where all the Temple Commanders are stationed."

"Speaking of regions, how do we notify the knights spread throughout the Petty Kingdoms about what has happened? It's not as if we can use Church couriers anymore."

"The smiths guild," replied Charlaine. "I'll have to make a trip into Reichendorf, but before I do, I need to decide where I'll take everyone."

"You mean where WE'RE taking everyone," corrected Danica.

"I'm afraid you're not coming with us. I need you to return to Temple Bay and maintain control over the fleet."

"I can't leave you here all alone!"

"She's not alone," replied Teresa. "She'll have four hundred and some-odd knights with her."

"It's closer to five hundred," said Charlaine, "although admittedly, some of those are captains and commanders." She stared silently at her dearest friend before continuing. "I know this is difficult for everyone, but for the order to survive, we must each play our part, and yours, Danica, is commanding those ships. Don't worry. I'll contact you once we've found a safe haven."

"That's hardly reassuring. You need to choose a sanctuary, and soon. You can't ride out of the Antonine and randomly pick a destination. That would be madness."

"I agree, but we're a little limited in choices, and it'll only get worse once it becomes known we've broken with the Church. For once, I'm thankful the bureaucracy of the Antonine is slow. It's given us time to prepare. Of course, the other side of that is we don't know precisely what we're preparing for."

"Escape," said Teresa. "And whatever actions might be necessary to allow that to happen."

"Yes, but what actions will those be? Do we fight everyone who opposes us? We'd quickly find ourselves overwhelmed."

"What we need is an escape plan. Think of this as a prison with the other orders as the guards."

"Through the gates is the only route," said Danica, "particularly if we want to take the horses. The problem is, we'd have to ride directly past the other commanderies."

"Not entirely true," replied Charlaine. "We could leave by the same route we took when we arrived, past the Mathewite commandery."

"That's still a commandery."

"Yes, but only one, and one that might, with a little persuasion, allow us to pass unopposed."

"Why would they do that?" asked Teresa.

"Because, like us, they interfered in a regional affair, taking sides with Ludwig when he captured the Throne of Hadenfeld." Charlaine suddenly shifted her gaze to the window, but instead of focusing on the view, her mind wandered elsewhere. They waited, and then, just as quickly, she was back in the room, her thoughts focused. "How close are the initiates to graduating?"

"You know as well as I; it varies by individual. Why?"

"It's not uncommon for graduates to ride through the city after taking their vows."

"That's true," replied Danica. "We did that very thing in Corassus."

"I remember doing it for my promotion to full Temple Knight," said Teresa, "but there's a huge difference between having a graduating class ride around the Antonine versus the entire order."

"Perhaps you're right," said Charlaine. "I'll need to give it more thought."

"You have a reputation amongst some of the other orders. Could you use that to our advantage?"

"I hope you're not suggesting I ask the gate guards to abandon their posts?"

"Not at all. However, you might have luck convincing some orders to remain in their commanderies on the night in question."

"That's difficult when we don't know when all this will happen. There's also the danger that they might take steps to actively stop us. The last thing we need is to be besieged in our own commandery."

"Let's not get ahead of ourselves," replied Danica. "The Primus still requires a majority to carry out this mad scheme of his. We can hope that reason prevails."

"The time of reason has passed," said Charlaine. "I would welcome it should it return, but I won't rely on it. Instead, we'll prepare for the worst, and if all that planning proves unnecessary, then we celebrate."

Teresa held up a scrap of paper. "What do we do about Carlingen?"

"What do you mean? We moved the academy to the Antonine, but the commandery still stands along with its complement of Temple Knights."

"Yes, but according to this note, it's short a captain as the previous one left the order."

"Does it say why?"

"All it says is personal reasons."

"That usually means they've either returned home to look after a loved one or fallen in love and wanted to get married."

"It does say she's left the city."

"Likely not a marriage, then."

"You're missing the point," said Teresa. "Things like this need to be taken care of before they cause a problem."

"Send Cordelia," suggested Danica. "She's in Caerhaven, remember?"

"She'd need training for the position."

"We don't have that luxury," said Charlaine. "I'll send word that she's been promoted to Temple Captain and include all the required reading materials. She can study in Caerhaven, then head north once she's ready."

"And who decides when she's ready?"

"We'll put the onus on her current commanding officer. Speaking of which, I hear Giselle is still in Ilea. Let's return her to the rank of Temple Commander and bring her farther north. Do we have any available positions?"

"There's always Deisenbach. It's a regional command, but if you recall, there was some animosity towards her because of her past."

"We'll let her select her own aide from her current command. That way, she'll have an ally when she reaches Agran."

"Agran?" said Teresa.

"Yes, the capital of Deisenbach. Sorry. I forgot you're not familiar with that region."

"I'm surprised you are."

"I was born and raised in Hadenfeld. It lies southeast of there."

"Oh yes. You mentioned that earlier. Wasn't that where the Mathewites supported the king? You don't know him, do you?"

"I do, as does Danica. She met him when he travelled to Reinwick to get married."

"Look at you, hobnobbing with the wealthy and powerful."

"Oh, you have no idea."

28

NEWS

SPRING 1107 SR

"Something's happening."

Charlaine looked up as Danica stood waiting in the doorway. "And by something, you mean…"

"News arrived that someone saw fit to refuse the Cunars a presence in their kingdom, and they're about to debate it in the Council of Peers today. I thought we might head over there and see what all the fuss is about."

Charlaine looked at the assorted papers lying in front of her. "Might as well. It's not as if this can't wait until tomorrow." She stood, gripping the edges of her desk. "I've a sense this may prove important in the grand scheme of things. Before we go, have Teresa alert everyone to be ready to move."

"You think this is the end?"

"Not the end, but I can't help feeling this is an important step, a beginning of the end, if you will. No matter what, it tells us if the order is ready to move at a moment's notice."

"Do we let everyone else know that?"

"No," said Charlaine. "We'll tell Teresa, but let the rest think it's real."

"I'll let Teresa know, but you'd best get dressed in your finery. We're off to the Council of Peers, so you should look the part of a Temple General. That reminds me, did you settle on a colour for your sash?"

"I thought blue might offer a strong contrast." She opened a small chest sitting beneath the window and retrieved a sash. "What do you think?"

Danica nodded. "Royal blue. Nice, and more importantly, it should stand out on the battlefield. I was led to believe blue dye was hard to come by?"

"Teresa convinced her cousin, the Ansgarite, to part with some of their cloth. Perhaps you should get some, too, to mark you as an admiral?"

"The last thing I want is to stand out in a sea battle. I'll stick with what I've got, thank you. Now, I'd best be off to find Teresa."

Charlaine's new display of rank drew considerable attention at the Council of Peers, yet none sought to engage her in conversation, no doubt a result of the even greater interest in the affairs of the Church this day.

They were packed in like rats up in the gallery, amongst a crowd whose attention was glued to the debate raging below.

"This is unconscionable," the Patriarch of Saint Cunar was saying. "We cannot stand by and let a Petty Kingdom treat the order, nay the Church itself, with such disrespect!" The audience lapped it up, stomping their feet against the floor with such enthusiasm that Charlaine's feet bounced with the vibrations.

The Cunar waited until the crowd quieted before continuing. "Does my esteemed colleague have something to say?" He held out his hand as an invitation for the Patriarch of Saint Mathew to speak.

The fellow struggled to his feet, his pale face a stark contrast with the brown of his cassock. He was the oldest patriarch and seldom spoke in the chambers other than to vote, underscoring the importance of this moment.

"This matter has been blown out of proportion," he began in a voice strained by age. "The Kingdom of Hadenfeld has not rejected the Church, only the billeting of additional Temple Knights within its lands."

Charlaine sat forward in her seat, straining to hear his words.

"That's all right for you," noted the Cunar Patriarch. "Your order already has knights in their cities."

"Precisely why another order's presence is not needed. It's not as if this new king dislikes the Church. He was married in the Temple of Saint Mathew for Saints sake, and he has his own Royal confessor."

"Yes, a Mathewite! Or was that by design? Is your order seeking to advance their own interests by excluding others?"

"Not at all."

The Cunar shook his head. "I wish I could believe you, Brother, but we all know you supported this upstart in his rebellion. What's next? Are you going to back any usurper who is a devotee of Saint Mathew? That would lead to utter chaos amongst the Petty Kingdoms!"

Once more, the observer's gallery broke into stomps, the accepted method of showing support. Charlaine knew she was responsible for this, for she'd written to Ludwig about the treachery in Arnsfeld. He must've taken the warning to heart and rebuffed the Cunar's advances. She had to wonder if that response would prove best in the long run.

The Primus rose, causing everyone to fall silent. "This action on behalf of the King of Hadenfeld is indicative of his attitude towards the Church in general. I call upon all patriarchs to condemn this response. Furthermore, I propose any kingdom refusing to cooperate with us be considered heathen and susceptible to the same treatment handed down to unbelievers in the east."

"I second the motion," said the Cunar Patriarch.

"The motion has been proposed. Let us now debate its merits before the vote is taken."

"I must protest," said the Mathewite Patriarch. He tried to say more, but observers from the gallery drowned him out with their stomping.

To Charlaine's mind, this appeared overly dramatic, perhaps even pre-arranged. She looked around at those in the gallery, and the preponder-ance of grey, the mark of Saint Cunar, made her think the Primus might've planned this all along. Down below, scores of advisors surrounded each patriarch in deep discussion about the details of the vote, but the noise emanating from the balcony made it impossible for her to hear what was being said. The Primus, meanwhile, sat with his arms crossed, his gaze sweeping the room, looking like a fox who'd just caught its prey.

The noise finally subsided, and the Mathewite stood once more to have his say. "I must protest," he repeated. "Ludwig Altenburg was a legitimate claimant to the Throne, not a usurper. His actions in seizing the Crown resulted from the madness of his predecessor, not any desire for power. If not for that, the Temple Knights of Saint Mathew would never have supported him."

"And by whose assessment was King Morgan proclaimed mad?" asked the Primus. "We are forbidden to take sides in secular matters. This has been the foundation of the Church since its inception more than one thou-sand years ago. The fighting orders must adhere to the Church's edicts, regardless of what they think is best. Are you suggesting we permit our Temple Knights to interfere wherever they deem fit? That, my friends, is tantamount to chaos!" Again, the thunderous foot stomps and cheers from the gallery.

The Matriarch of Saint Agnes stood, patiently waiting for the noise to die down before speaking. "I must protest, Your Eminence. It is not the place of this august body to cajole or coerce other council members. This is an open forum where we debate the merits of proposed legislation. I call for all assembled here to respect each other and act in a civilized manner. I put forth the motion that this body be adjourned for a few days to allow us to investigate this matter more thoroughly."

The Primus stood up once more. "Let the record show this session of the Council of Peers has been adjourned for the day. We shall resume three days hence, at noon, to discuss the matter at greater length."

Everyone stood, waiting as the Primus made his way from the chamber. Once he'd left, the patriarchs headed for the exits, most in deep discussion with their advisors. The noise level remained high even as the gallery rapidly cleared out, for everybody wanted to express their opinions.

"Well," said Danica. "That was interesting."

"It most certainly was," agreed Charlaine, "although I don't believe it went in our favour."

"Our favour? They were discussing Hadenfeld, not our order."

"You know what I mean. Ludwig now commands one of the largest armies in the Petty Kingdoms, making him a target. Mark my words, Danica; if the Primus gets his way, he'll declare a Holy War."

"Surely that will fail. As you said, Ludwig has one of the largest armies in the Petty Kingdoms."

"How better to eliminate that advantage than declare him a heathen and command the fighting orders to wage a Holy War? And it won't only be Temple Knights. We both know calling for a crusade brings warriors from all over the Petty Kingdoms."

"It won't come to that," said Danica. "The Primus hasn't the votes, remember? Other than the Patriarch of Saint Cunar, I saw no sign of support."

"At least we know what he's up to."

"That being?"

"He's manufacturing a crisis to sway people to his viewpoint. I suspect he adjourned the meeting to learn where the other patriarchs stand before proceeding."

"What do we do about that?"

"There's little we can do," replied Charlaine. "Except return to the commandery to see how they made out raising the alarm."

"Mistakes happened," said Teresa. She sat in front of Charlaine while Danica stood by the window, listening. "Preparing the horses took far too long, and almost half our people assembled without their armour."

"We need to do a better job of communicating," replied Charlaine.

"I would agree. Some had doubts about what to do, while quite a few only gathered because they saw others doing so. Changes must be made if we want to see any improvement."

"We'll start with a chain of command to ensure every sister, from the most senior commander to the newest recruit, knows what's expected of them when the call comes."

"I have a suggestion," said Danica. "There's a technique we use in the fleet that places a senior sister in charge of every six knights. They act as sergeants, taking command should the senior officer be rendered a casualty. We can extend that same organization to include the initiates. All officers will be given a list of which senior knights to notify in the event of an emergency, thus ensuring everyone is informed in a timely manner."

"I like that," said Charlaine. "Can you organize it?"

"Certainly."

"What about the stables?" asked Teresa. "We can't have everyone descending on them in one mad rush. It caused too many problems."

"That requires a little more effort," replied Charlaine. "We'll break down the entire commandery into companies and then assign waiting areas. Only when the first company is fully mounted will the next enter the stables. That puts an extra workload onto the stable hands, so we'll need to increase their numbers substantially."

"The stable hands will be coming with us; they're sisters too."

"True. Leave them to the last to mount up. As for their weapons and armour, let's find somewhere closer to the stables to store them."

"We have another problem," said Teresa. "Though I hesitate to mention it."

"Speak your mind. We don't have time for bruised egos."

"Temple Commander Nina insisted on the initiates remaining in the classroom to complete their lessons despite orders to the contrary. Should I bring this up with the grand mistress?"

"No," replied Charlaine. "I'll deal with that myself. As for the grand mistress, she explicitly told me to leave her in the dark so she doesn't have to lie to protect us."

A bell tolled in the distance, quickly taken up by all the commanderies.

"What's that?" asked Teresa.

"I suspect the Augustines have chosen their new patriarch."

"Any idea who they might have picked?"

"No, but I doubt it will take long to learn his stance on the new directives favoured by the Primus."

"When will they swear him in?"

"The bell means that's already happened," replied Charlaine, "although there still has to be a public ceremony. Not that the Augustines are known for such things, but choosing the patriarch of any order is a cause for celebration."

"Didn't he die this past winter? They certainly replaced him quickly."

"Perhaps a little too quick."

"What are you suggesting?" said Teresa.

"It takes months to gather the archpriors of an order. It's peculiar they were able to travel here and choose a successor so fast, don't you think?"

"Perhaps there was only one obvious candidate?"

"That's always possible," replied Charlaine, "but I suspect outside forces may be at work here. Unless I miss my guess, we'll soon discover the new Augustine Patriarch is firmly on the side of the Primus."

"Which gives him two votes," said Danica. "Still not enough to push through his agenda."

"That's assuming no other patriarchs support his policies. Consider what we know of Primus Wilmar. According to Sir Raynald, he masterminded a crusade with the express purpose of reducing the strength of the Holy Army. He's already talking about amalgamating the orders, and now he wants to declare a Holy War on any Petty Kingdom that doesn't fall into line. It's not much of a stretch to believe he's replaced the patriarch of another sect with someone on his side, and I doubt that's all he's up to."

"That's assuming you're correct about the new Augustine. Perhaps he's more moderate?"

"I pray he is," said Charlaine, "but I must trust my instincts."

"If that's true," replied Teresa, "then who else do we suspect will support him? It can't be the Patriarch of Saint Mathew."

"No, nor that of our order, which leaves the Ragnarite and Ansgarite Patriarchs. If he sways only one of those, he'll have the three votes he needs to stalemate the council."

Danica nodded. "In which case, he'll cast the deciding vote, making things very dangerous for us."

"Agreed. It's now more important than ever to get our house in order."

The moon hung high in the night sky, but Charlaine wasn't tired. She'd remained in her office, staring out the window, her thoughts elsewhere. In her heart, she knew time was running out. Within days, the Primus would make his move, rendering her order extinct as if it were little more than an insect waiting to be swatted away.

She and Danica had uncovered corruption in the Church almost ten years ago; could she have done something then to prevent this disaster? Charlaine closed her eyes, trying to calm her nerves, but all she could think about was the dissolution of her order. Panic threatened to overwhelm her, and then she remembered the writings of Saint Agnes. *Keep calm in the face of adversity, and you shall persevere.*

A sense of peacefulness descended upon her as if the Saint herself were in the room. In that instant, Charlaine knew without a doubt her plan was the right thing to do. The Temple Knights of Saint Agnes would survive, perhaps even thrive, but they must distance themselves from the Church that had become a corrupt mockery of the teachings of the Saints.

Nothing illustrated that corruption more than the Primus, for as an agent for the Halvarians, he'd actively worked to weaken the Temple Knights of Saint Cunar, and now, as the head of the Church, he sought to gain control over the other orders—all save her own.

The plan was to flee, taking as many with her as she could manage. What she hadn't figured out yet was where. The commandery currently housed close to five hundred individuals. Marching them out of the Antonine was one thing, keeping them fed, quite another. They were, in essence, an army requiring supplies while on the march.

Even if they were successful in their escape, the entire order would be labelled as heretical by the Church, which would result in the remaining Temple Knights being ordered to track them down and either arrest or kill them.

The more she mulled it over, the clearer her choice became. She must seek a kingdom that would welcome them, one ruled by a king willing to defy the Church.

She briefly considered fleeing east to the nascent Kingdom of Therengia, for the Church held no presence there, but then reason took hold. That would require her to lead her people through four different kingdoms that likely had Cunar contingents.

No, there was only one logical destination. She must lead them to Hadenfeld, the only kingdom ever to refuse the Cunars' presence. She considered sending Ludwig advance warning, but events were moving far too rapidly here. Charlaine would have to trust in her faith, and her faith in Ludwig that all would end well.

29

TROUBLE

SPRING 1107 SR

Three days had passed since the Primus called for Hadenfeld to be declared heretical. Charlaine hoped it was enough time to let tempers cool, but a nagging feeling told her that would not happen.

She and Danica ascended the steps of the Council of Peers to see the grey surcoats that marked the Temple Knights of Saint Cunar guarding the building. The fighting orders took turns, but it appeared the Cunars had that duty today, a bad omen if one believed in such.

Charlaine shook off the sense of doom, concentrating instead on her companion. "I must say you've settled into the rank of Temple Commander."

"Thank you," replied Danica. "Though I don't feel any different. How's it being the sole Temple General of the order?"

"As if the fate of the entire order rests on my shoulders."

"I feel the same about the Temple Fleet. It's sometimes nerve-wracking, knowing your decisions impact so many lives."

"Any advice?"

Danica chuckled. "You don't need advice from me; you've plenty of experience commanding." She was about to say more when she noticed a familiar face approaching. "Admiral Marius?"

"That's Temple Commander now," the fellow replied. "I'm no longer the Admiral of the Holy Fleet. You both look well, much more so than the last time we met. Congratulations, General. You've made quite a name for yourself. And you, too, Commander. I've heard great things about your accomplishments in the north."

"Thank you," said Danica. "I'm surprised at seeing you here in the Antonine. I thought you oversaw provisioning down in Corassus?"

Marius knitted his brows. "It appears the new admiral took exception to my presence there, so I've been sent here instead."

"As an advisor on naval matters?"

He lowered his voice. "No, to seek a release from my vows. I fear I can no longer blindly follow the incompetence of my superiors."

"Incompetence?" said Charlaine. "Can you be more specific?"

"My replacement has seen fit to reduce the number of available warships in the fleet and cut the fighting complement of each ship to the bare bones. He's either the worst admiral to have ever lived or actively trying to sabotage us."

"You and I should talk. There are things you should be made aware of."

"You've piqued my interest," replied Marius. "Could we arrange a meeting with less likelihood of being overheard? Say the Ragnarite commandery?"

"I'll make the arrangements and have them contact you."

Marius nodded, then made a show of backing up a step and bowing. "Again, my congratulations to you both." He turned and entered the building ahead of them.

"What do you make of that?" asked Danica.

"We already knew about the ships, but reducing the fighting complements is a surprise. He was right about one thing: their new admiral isn't working to make the fleet any stronger."

"More proof that he's furthering the empire's interests. You're more knowledgeable about such things: can Marius leave the Cunars? I know it's possible in our order, but I thought the others made a lifetime commitment?"

"I believe it would be necessary for him to prove an ailment that prevents him from continuing his service."

"An ailment?"

"Yes, either a physical injury or a reduced capacity for reasoning. The latter is typically employed to remove a fighting order's aged and infirm members."

"And then they dismiss them? That seems harsh."

"I think most become lay brothers or even Holy Fathers if they were of sufficient rank. With his record, Marius would have no trouble becoming a Holy Father, or even a prior if he wished."

"What if we could offer him something better?"

"What are you thinking?" said Charlaine.

"The Temple Fleet is getting larger. I could use a seasoned aide to help run it."

"He's a Cunar."

"Not if he leaves the order."

"He wouldn't even be a Temple Knight, then."

"He wouldn't need to be," replied Danica. "He could be a civilian advisor to the fleet."

"I suggest we wait until we've talked with him at length to make that decision. Now, let's get inside, shall we? I don't want to miss any of today's proceedings."

As before, the gallery was packed with Cunar guards positioned by the exits. The introduction of the new Patriarch of Saint Augustine began the session. Charlaine expected a man of advanced years, with a long, flowing beard, typical of the position, but his age surprised her, for he was no more than thirty-five and beardless, with hair cut close to the skin, giving him a look more typical of a Temple Knight. As he stood, those in attendance quieted, eager to hear his first words.

"My fellow patriarchs," he began. "I come to you today in all humility, chosen by my fellow lay brothers to lead the Augustines in their sworn duty of protecting the Holy Relics so valued by this esteemed organization." He paused, looking at each patriarch in turn. "This is a time of unfathomable strife, for forces are at work to undermine the very tenets of this Church. My hope is that together, we can rebuild faith in those who serve this august body and punish those who would attack the character of this great institution."

Polite applause came from the other patriarchs, though it appeared reserved to Charlaine. They were undoubtedly waiting for the newest council member to reveal whose side he served.

"As my first official act," he continued, "I call upon this body to pass a motion declaring any kingdom not sanctified by the Church be considered heathen. I would then call upon all Temple Knights to take steps to reclaim these kingdoms and re-establish the primacy of the Church of the Saints."

A thunderous thumping of feet erupted from the gallery. The Primus, enjoying the response, let it continue until he finally raised his hands, signalling for them to quiet. "My esteemed colleague, the Patriarch of Saint Augustine has introduced a motion that any kingdom not sanctified by the Church should be considered heathen. The patriarchs shall now debate this matter before the vote. Who will speak first?"

The Patriarch of Saint Ragnar raised his hand, then, at a nod from the

Primus, stood. "You ask us to declare a kingdom heathen if they are not sanctified, but what does that entail? We have no formal procedure for sanctifying a Petty Kingdom, nor is there any record of ever recognizing the official existence of a duchy or principality. As an entity, are we now required to list every Petty Kingdom and decide on a case-by-case basis which ones are considered legitimate? If so, this council will find itself busy for years to come!"

This remark brought chuckles from many of the advisors, though the patriarchs refrained from showing emotion.

"A good question," replied the Augustine. "I suggest to my learned colleague that every Petty Kingdom on the Continent is already recognized by this esteemed organization and sanctified by default."

"Then to whom would this edict apply?"

"Those who this body determines have acted against the best interests of the Church."

"I assume you mean Hadenfeld," said the Ragnarite. "That being the case, why couch the edict in such terms? Would it not be better to propose declaring that particular realm as heathen or heretical? Or have you a list of other Petty Kingdoms you wish to punish?"

The Augustine Patriarch remained silent. Charlaine couldn't decide if it was to consider his response or if he was drawing it out for dramatic effect.

When he finally spoke, it was in a clear and controlled voice. "For centuries, the Church of the Saints looked after the spiritual well-being of the Petty Kingdoms. We are the beating heart of the Continent, and as such, it is only appropriate that we are shown the proper trust and respect. Our power, the very reason for our existence, is, in a word, the Saints. It is high time the kingdoms of this land listen to us."

"And if they don't?"

"Then we declare them heathen and, if necessary, force them to obey."

The Ragnarite's mouth hung open in surprise, but he quickly recovered. "Are you suggesting we place ourselves above secular law?"

"I am, and why not? Are we not morally superior? Our very teachings hold the Petty Kingdoms together; should we not then reap the benefits of that responsibility?"

The Ragnarite shook his head. "I have no further questions." He sat, his advisors leaning in close for conversation.

"Has anyone else something to contribute?" asked the Primus.

"I do." The Patriarch of Saint Mathew unsteadily got to his feet. "You talk as if it were the Saints' will that they be placed above the common man. Nothing could be further from the truth. Have you so easily forgotten their teachings? This Church was meant to be the servant of the people, not their rulers, yet now you would place us above kings!"

"It is the only way to ensure our continued existence," replied the Augustine. "This Church faces a financial crisis. To survive, we must ensure that each Petty Kingdom pays its dues."

"What are you suggesting? Withhold spiritual guidance until they've provided suitable donations? We are a Church, not a merchant house!" The Mathewite broke into a coughing spasm, and the kerchief he'd raised to his mouth came away with red spots. "I have said my piece." He sat back down, looking even paler.

The Patriarch of Saint Cunar stood. "This topic has caused some consternation amongst my learned colleagues, whom, it appears, fear putting ourselves above the rulers of the Petty Kingdoms. The Saints teach us that order is preferred over chaos. Indeed, this Church was formed to fill the need for someone to lead after the death of our beloved Saints. Leadership has always been one of our greatest strengths, and the Petty Kingdoms have never needed us more. We live in a time of great strife, with the threat of invasion foremost in the minds of the common folk. We should follow the Temple Knights of Saint Agnes' example and support the Continent's efforts to resist the expansion of Halvaria!"

Charlaine leaned forward, finding it difficult to believe. A Cunar calling on the Church to take a stand! Everybody collectively held their breath, wondering what would come next.

"Make no mistake," continued the Cunar Patriarch. "War is coming, and if we are to survive, we must do all we can to remain strong and ready."

The sudden stomping of feet made Charlaine wonder if this had all been pre-arranged, for it seemed too timely to be spontaneous.

Once the stomping died down, the Cunar cleared his throat. "Let us put aside this motion. I move that we strike the topic from the docket. Will someone second the motion?"

The Matriarch of Saint Agnes raised her hand.

"Seconded," said the Primus. "A show of hands. All in favour of striking the topic?" All but the Augustine Patriarch raised their hands. "The motion is carried. Have you anything to add?" He looked at the Cunar once more.

"Yes, Eminence. I move that the Kingdom of Hadenfeld be sanctioned for its treatment of the Temple Knights of Saint Cunar."

"Sanctioned?" said the Ragnarite. "What does that mean, precisely?"

"Spiritual guidance is to be withheld until this esteemed council lifts such sanctions."

"That will hardly endear us to the population at large."

"True, but they will put pressure on their new king to make amends."

"I beg to differ," replied the Ragnarite. "It will serve to dry up what contributions we collect in Hadenfeld, leaving the population under-served and our houses of worship destitute."

"That is hardly of concern to your order."

"While it's true we Ragnarites do not worship in public, we still rely on the goodwill of the people to aid us in our sworn duty."

"Your sworn duty? You haven't found a Necromancer in decades!"

"Without our constant vigilance, the worship of death could resurface and spread across the Continent like a plague."

"So you claim, but I've seen no evidence to support that statement. Perhaps, if you provided us documentation?"

"Our records are sealed, as you know full well. Such information would be dangerous in the wrong hands."

"I shall not debate the matter any further," said the Cunar, "but let me reassure you, this Church can easily weather the financial burden of losing Hadenfeld for a limited time."

"Limited time?"

"Surely you don't believe we would cut them off forever? A temporary sanction would bring the other Petty Kingdoms into line. I'm confident we will soon see increased contributions to support our cause."

"Enough of this foolishness," said the Ragnarite. "I call for a vote."

The Cunar Patriarch smiled. "I second the motion."

Charlaine sensed a trap, but she could do little about it.

"The motion before us," announced the Primus, "is that we declare the Kingdom of Hadenfeld sanctioned. Having been duly seconded, it is time to vote. All those in favour?"

The Cunar raised his hand, as did the Augustine. Charlaine was ready to relax, but then the Patriarch of Saint Ansgar surprised everyone by raising his hand.

"All those opposed?" Charlaine watched as the patriarchs of Saint Mathew and Ragnar raised their hands, joined by her own matriarch.

"The vote is three apiece," said the Primus, "leaving me to make the final decision." The tension in the room built as he paused. "I support the resolution. From this day forth, the Kingdom of Hadenfeld is under sanction. All religious ceremonies conducted by this Church will cease within its lands, and our members are prohibited from offering solace or guidance in any form until this council deems otherwise."

The room went completely quiet, everyone waiting for the Primus's next words.

"I call upon all fighting orders to prepare for a crusade to restore the glory of the Church in Hadenfeld. Should this campaign prove necessary, it will be under the direction of the Grand Master of the Temple Knights of Saint Cunar."

The stomping began anew, accompanied by hoots and hollers from those in the gallery.

"By the Saints," said Danica, though hearing her above the noise was difficult. "I can't believe this is happening. We must do something!"

"Come," said Charlaine. "I've seen enough of this. I need time to think. Let us return to the commandery."

Later that afternoon, they stood before the haggard countenance of their grand mistress, the result, no doubt, of the pressures of her office, but she refused to avoid the subject, instead diving right in.

"You've heard the news?" Kaylene asked.

"Yes," replied Charlaine. "We were present when the motion passed."

"Your thoughts?"

"It was cleverly orchestrated. We had no idea the Patriarch of the Ansgarites would support the motion."

"Nor did I, but now that it's passed, we must deal with the consequences. I've ordered Nina to accelerate the initiates' martial training, spending more time on the practice field than in the classroom. Under normal circumstances, I would order you, as Temple General, to provide strategic and tactical advice to prepare for a crusade. As a native of Hadenfeld, you're more conversant with the area than any of our other members. However, given the current political situation, I suspect you are far too busy for such nonsense."

Kaylene paused, sipping a drink. If Charlaine were in the same position, she, too, would need time to think of her next words.

"My time as grand mistress is coming to an end. I received notice to appear before the Matriarch of Saint Agnes, which we all know does not bode well."

"Might I ask when?"

"Tomorrow morning. In preparation, I have this for you." Kaylene handed over a scroll. "Sorry. You might find it a bit long-winded. In simple terms, it grants you extraordinary powers for the duration of the crisis."

"Crisis?" said Charlaine.

The grand mistress's smile did not reach her eyes. "I wrote it as ambiguously as possible, making it easier for you to interpret the intent. There is every possibility there may never be another grand mistress, which leaves it up to you, as Temple General, to lead the order. Do you accept this responsibility?"

"I do."

"Good," replied the grand mistress. "Now, as to your other duties, have you a plan?"

"Yes, although I still need to address some issues."

"It soothes my heart to know you have things well in hand. Return to your office and ensure you've gathered everything you need. The time to act will soon be upon you."

30

COLLAPSE

SPRING 1107 SR

"Are you certain we're prepared?"

Charlaine looked up from where she sat behind her desk. "You tell me, Teresa. You've done most of the organizing. Are you now suggesting the sisters won't ride?"

"Oh, they'll ride, but they're nervous. It would comfort them to know where we're going."

"And I'd love to tell them, but if word leaked out, we could find ourselves blocked at every turn. Better to keep that to myself for now. Once we're free of the Antonine, I'll let everyone in on the plan."

"Does Danica know?"

"Danica won't be joining us."

"Does she know that?"

"She knows her place is in the north," replied Charlaine, "commanding the Temple Fleet. Once we're clear of the Antonine, she and a small escort will head north, their ultimate destination being Temple Bay, while our journey will be a little more problematic."

"In what sense?"

"Once we put my plan into action, we become hunted. Every Temple Knight on the Continent will have orders to arrest us for defying the decree from the Council of Peers. Against that backdrop, I must determine how to move five hundred sisters without being followed."

"The odds don't look favourable," said Teresa.

"Admittedly, they don't, so we'll have to devise a way to even them out."

"Surely you're not suggesting we fight?"

"Only if necessary. I prefer we outmanoeuvre them."

"And how do we do that?"

"That's the very question I've been asking myself these last few days. Unfortunately, I've failed to come up with a solution."

"You still intend to go through with this? Some might see that as madness."

"My faith tells me there is a way to escape. I just need to wait until the opportunity presents itself. Until then, we must prepare for a long and difficult journey. Have you solved our supply problem?"

"Only partially," replied Teresa. "The kitchen's been preparing travel rations, but dried beef can only take us so far. Each sister will carry three days' worth, which should see us well clear of the Antonine, but beyond that, we run into problems."

"We can't manage more?"

"Not without raising suspicions. Were we to suddenly order more food, someone might notice."

"Then we'll make do with that, although that could mean halving the rations for a few days once we start riding."

"And then?"

"I can't answer that question until we're at that point, as much of it depends on the reaction of outsiders. If they see us as heretics, they'll stay away, but I'm hoping we have enough goodwill to purchase supplies from nearby farms or shops."

"We'll need a significant amount of food to feed five hundred souls."

"I'm well aware of that; it's been topmost in my mind of late."

"In preparation, I used my magic to ensure every member of the order is in good health, so we won't have to worry about carrying the sick or wounded."

"Wounded?"

"Yes. Initiates sometimes get a little carried away at weapon practice. Oh, I also used your suggestions to reorganize how we prepare to march, breaking them into companies and ensuring everyone knows who commands each, making it easier to manage."

"Any more trouble with Temple Commander Nina?"

"Surprisingly, no," replied Teresa. "The council's recent edict has her worried like the rest of us. Speaking of which, where's Danica?"

"At the Council of Peers. I thought it best someone keep an eye on things in case of any new developments, and she volunteered."

Charlaine rose, walking over to the window, letting her gaze wander the street while considering their predicament. "By now, the grand mistress will be before the matriarch. I can't say I envy her."

"Do you think she'll be forced to resign?"

"Given recent events, it's inevitable. The only question to my mind is whether she'll be replaced."

"Why wouldn't she be? You need a grand mistress to run an order, don't you?"

"That's the general consensus," replied Charlaine, "but given the current political landscape, the matriarch may wish to be free of the burden."

"Why?"

"Sister Kaylene had the foresight to order the establishment of the Temple Fleet and sent me to Arnsfeld because she knew I'd intervene, but both those decisions caused significant friction with the matriarch."

"She called you here to save the order, didn't she? She must have known what was coming."

"Only in a general sense. I doubt she saw the Augustines siding with the new Primus or that the Primus himself was working in league with the Halvarians." Charlaine went silent as something caught her eye. "What's this, now?"

Teresa moved up beside her. "Are those Cunars marching towards the Ragnarite commandery? Perhaps they're practicing their manoeuvres?"

"Possibly," replied Charlaine. "The council did call on all the orders to prepare for a crusade." She watched as the grey-clad Temple Knights surrounded the building. "No. It looks like they're taking up position for an attack."

"What do we do?"

"Send word down the chain of command. All knights are to prepare for battle."

"You think it'll come to that?"

"I'm hoping not, but it doesn't hurt to be prepared."

"I'll see to it at once." Teresa left without another word.

Charlaine kept her eyes locked on the distant display. "Come on, Danica," she said. "Get your arse back here before it's too late!"

Danica raced down the steps of the Council of Peers. Like everyone else who'd witnessed the exchange, she was in a hurry to carry word back to her commandery, but she soon faced a pair of grey-clad Temple Knights.

"What's the hurry, Admiral?" said the first, his face masked by his helmet.

"Stand aside, Brother. That's an order."

"You're out of place," the Cunar replied. "You heard the Primus. All Temple Knights are now under the command of the Grand Master of the Cunars."

"I'm still a Temple Commander, and you're only a knight."

"A Temple Commander without a command. You're no more than a knight yourself, now, and we have seniority."

"What makes you think that?"

"We are the senior fighting order."

Danica's hands went to the hilts of her daggers. Thankfully, a voice interrupted her exchange.

"What's going on here?"

They all turned to see a knight wearing the green tabard of the Ragnarites.

"Ah, Brother Julius," said Danica. "Your arrival is most fortuitous. These two brother knights are determined to block my way."

The Ragnarite moved to stand before the two Cunars. "Is there a reason for your discourtesy, or are you just being pigheaded?"

"Unlike your type, who skulks in the shadows, we follow orders."

"And what orders might those be?"

Danica suddenly had great clarity. "They're trying to stop me from bringing the news back to the commandery. That can only mean one thing —they're planning something." She looked around, noticing other Cunars blocking the progress of some Temple Knights of Saint Mathew. "I don't have time for this. Step aside, or I shall be forced to act."

The Cunars both laughed. "You wouldn't stand a chance."

"Go!" said Brother Julius. "I'll take care of these two."

"I can deal with them myself. I don't need you to get involved."

"I mean no insult, Commander, but it's more important that you warn your fellow sisters of what's happening."

She nodded, then stepped aside, determined to go around the two knights.

The one who'd been talking drew his sword, but Julius moved before he could swing, grabbing the Cunar's wrist and twisting it, forcing the weapon to fall to the ground. The other one backed up, placing his hand on the hilt of his sword.

"You are under arr—" Julius moved in, the palm of his hand hitting the fellow in the throat, stopping his next words. The man's gorget protected him from any real damage, but the blow forced him to lose his balance, and he fell down the steps of the council hall.

"Go!" Julius yelled, pulling forth a sword and dagger from his belt. Six Temple Knights of Saint Cunar rushed towards him, drawing weapons as they advanced.

Danica fled down the steps, continuing her flight up Grand Avenue, the road that led directly to the Grand Sanctum but, more importantly, ran right past the Agnesite commandery.

She'd only gone a few dozen steps when she noticed a sea of grey before her. Cunar Temple Knights had taken up positions around the other commanderies and were advancing to the front doors, their weapons drawn. She pushed on, determined to reach her fellow sisters before all was lost.

Charlaine stood at the main door to the commandery, awaiting the inevitable knock. When it came, she nodded towards the sister knights to open it.

A bare-headed Cunar captain was there, holding an unrolled scroll in both hands, but the unexpected appearance of a Temple General must have taken him by surprise, for he stood there, his mouth gaping open.

"What is it, Captain?" snapped Charlaine.

The Cunar appeared to regain his composure while his voice betrayed his nervousness. "By order of the Council of Peers, this commandery is now under the direct command of the Temple Knights of Saint Cunar. Your entire order is hereby instructed to surrender your armour and weapons immediately." He tensed, perhaps sensing she might offer resistance. Behind him stood an entire company of Temple Knights, shifting their feet, eager to begin their work.

"That will take time," replied Charlaine. "We have hundreds within this building, with many still initiates. Do you honestly expect them all to file out in good order?"

"N-n-no," the fellow stammered. "Of course not, Sister."

"Tell your Temple Commander we intend to vacate the building by nightfall. I trust that will satisfy your superiors?"

He appeared unsure, turning towards his company as if trying to find an answer. Charlaine decided to try intimidation.

"I promised to vacate the premises, Captain. Do you doubt the word of a Temple General?"

"No, Your Grace."

"That's general to you."

"Sorry, General."

"Now be a good fellow and return to your men. I can't organize anything if I'm spending all my time standing here talking to you."

"Yes, General."

Charlaine nodded at her knights, who closed the door. "Bar it," she ordered, "and prepare to repel attackers." Every commandery followed the same design, including internal doors that, once closed and barred, prevented intruders from gaining control of the entire building. An inconvenience to her plans but a major obstacle to those trying to occupy the place.

Temple Commander Nina arrived with six knights. "General," she said. "Allow us the honour. I promise you no Cunar shall enter this commandery while we can still fight."

Charlaine stared back, trying to judge Nina's intent. They'd been at odds before, and Saints knew they'd not seen eye to eye on many things, but looking at her now, she saw only determination.

"I know I have wronged you in the past," Nina continued, "but the grand mistress chose you to lead us, and I'll not have anyone accuse me of not following orders."

"This puts you in grave danger."

"I am fully aware of that." Nina's features softened. "Please, Charlaine. You have your path to greatness. Allow me mine."

"You will very likely die, as will those accompanying you."

"They are aware, as am I," said Nina. "Now, go. You have much to do to save the rest. Saints be with you, Charlaine."

A great sorrow welled up inside Charlaine. She wanted to say something, anything, that would give meaning to the sacrifice these brave souls were willing to make, but words escaped her. She could only nod before making her way towards the stables.

Danica slowed as she approached the commandery. A large group of Cunars stood out front, waiting for Saints knew what, while their officer, a Temple Captain, wandered back and forth in front of them.

She avoided them, keeping to Grand Avenue, heading north, hoping to get around behind the building and somehow gain entrance. It required a minor miracle, for the entrances to the commandery and the stables faced south where the Cunars waited. She prayed to Saint Agnes, then spotted her chance; sentries were posted on the roof of the commandery to report any sign of enemy movement. A wave indicated she'd been seen, and they ushered her towards the back of the building.

A nearby Cunar called out a challenge, for they'd placed sentries around the Agnesite's commandery. Two knights hustled towards her, and she worried she might be in for a fight, but then a knotted rope dropped down from the roof.

Danica grabbed it and began climbing, quickly giving up as she realized those above were hauling her to safety. Anthea, Magda, and Mariele stood there, pulling on the rope as she reached the top.

Danica let out a breath of relief. "What brings you lot up here?"

"It's not only us," replied Anthea, moving aside to sweep her arms. Initiates across the rooftop erupted in a cheer. "The general called for volunteers."

"Thank the Saints she did," said Danica, "else I'd be rotting away in a Cunar dungeon. Where's the Temple General?"

"She said for you to meet her in the stables."

"Then lead on. We don't have a moment to waste."

Charlaine embraced Danica, then held her at arm's length. "Thank goodness you're safe. You had me worried."

"Me too."

"I assume the Primus passed his resolution."

"He did. All non-Cunar officers are to surrender their rank and become Temple Knights, except for us. We've been ordered to disband."

"I thought as much. We had a visit from a Cunar Temple Captain who wanted us to turn over our weapons and armour."

"I assume you told him no?"

"Not precisely. I said we'd vacate the building by nightfall, which is precisely what I aim to do, just not in the manner he's expecting. Did you get a good look at their numbers?"

"There's an entire company out front and likely another twenty stretched around the building, far enough apart I could get to the wall, but I doubt it's something repeatable."

"Not the best news, but I can't say I'm surprised."

"Is everyone accounted for?"

"Yes," said Charlaine. "You were the only one outside our walls today besides the grand mistress, and I suspect she won't be returning."

"Is she under arrest?"

"I doubt it, but knowing her, she left the order when she was removed as grand mistress. We have yet to hear of a replacement, but considering our present circumstances, we can assume the worst."

"One way or another, we have to fight."

"We will," replied Charlaine, "but only at a place and time of our choosing. We can't match the Cunars one-on-one, but for the moment, we have the numerical advantage."

"I saw similar-sized groups of Cunars in front of the other commanderies."

"Good. That means they're not concentrating on us alone."

"Do you think the other orders will fight?" asked Danica.

"You tell me. How did everyone vote?"

"The Augustines and Ansgarites sided with the Primus, along with the Cunars, although there's no surprise there."

"So that leaves the Ragnarites, the Mathews, and us."

"I can't imagine the Mathews fighting back, can you?"

"They surprised me by backing Ludwig," replied Charlaine, "so anything's possible."

"And the Ragnarites?"

"They're more likely to disappear without a trace. After all, they've been doing that for their entire existence."

"Even with their commandery surrounded?"

"I don't know this for a fact, but I suspect their building is filled with secret doors and passages. If you think about it, their Temple Knights have to learn their trade somewhere."

"So where does that leave us?"

Charlaine laughed. "Isn't that obvious? We're completely surrounded by the premiere fighting order of the Church. Man for man, or rather man for woman, they're far better warriors than us, so we need to hit them when they're weakest."

"You mean now? Before they seize the other commanderies?"

"Precisely. You know, you're quick to pick up on things."

"Thanks," said Danica. "I learned that from you, but what does this plan of yours actually consist of?"

"Why, getting away from the Antonine. To do that, though, we must come up with a way to deal with these pesky Cunars."

31

TRAPPED!

SPRING 1107 SR

"We're trapped!" said Gerda.

Everyone turned towards the Temple Commander-in-training as she voiced what they all feared. The commandery was surrounded by a company of Cunars outside its front door, and it didn't appear that would change anytime soon.

Charlaine had called all her commanders to the stables, and they now stood there, staring at her, expecting her to produce a miracle. Not knowing what to say, Charlaine closed her eyes in an attempt to steady her nerves. "Let us pray," she said, and everyone bowed their heads.

"Blessed Saint Agnes, give us the strength this day to overcome adversity, the courage to find a way forward, and the wisdom to choose the path of prosperity." She silently counted to five, feeling a calmness flowing through her. "Saints be with us."

"Saints be with us all," replied the Temple Commanders.

Charlaine opened her eyes. The commanders still stared at her, but now she saw them as a band of sisters, each dedicated to seeing the order through this ordeal.

"We are in a difficult situation," she began, "but we are all the stronger for being in this together." She pointed south towards the Council of Peers. "The Antonine is not our future." She placed her hand over her heart. "This is. Be true to it, and we shall see ourselves clear of these troubles."

"We can't even escape our commandery," said Ursula, "let alone pass through the gates of the Antonine."

"Don't allow our present circumstances to overwhelm you. The key to surviving this is to take each problem one at a time." Charlaine paused, giving time for her words to sink in. "Our first objective is to get clear of the commandery. Danica, would you be so kind as to summarize our situation?"

"Most certainly," she replied. "As Gerda so adeptly put it, we are trapped, but it's not as bad as it sounds. There is a full company of Temple Knights outside our front door, with another twenty or so scattered around the perimeter, but they came on foot, not mounted, giving us an advantage. On my way here, I saw similar-sized groups surrounding the other commanderies, so there's every likelihood they won't be able to send more men until those situations are resolved. In short, we have a small window of opportunity."

"Which means," added Charlaine, "we must leave here as soon as possible, but to do so, there is every probability we'll have to battle our way out. The Temple Knights of Saint Cunar are the premiere fighting order of the Church, each member a knight who's trained his whole life to fight. We cannot hope to match them one-on-one, so we'll use our strengths against them."

"Those being?" said Gerda.

"Discipline and superior numbers, at least until they send more men. Stick to your formations and assist your fellow sisters whenever possible. Remember, we'll be mounted, so don't be afraid of using your horses to break through their defences. Keep in mind our main objective is to escape; sowing confusion amongst the Cunars will be as effective as wounding them."

Katinka cleared her throat. "It's all well and good to speak of discipline, General, but what if they receive reinforcements?"

"We cannot predict what the future may hold, nor should we attempt to try. The objective here is to strike quickly, then withdraw to the southeast, towards the main gates of the Antonine. Our horses can easily outpace any foot pursuit, but that advantage will only hold for so long."

"And what of the gate?" asked Ursula. "It'll be guarded."

"The gates of the Antonine are designed to prevent outsiders from getting in, not from us from leaving. We'll need volunteers to dismount and open the gates once we arrive."

Temple Commander Scyllia raised her hand. She was the tallest of those assembled, easily a head above the rest, yet she had a reputation for being soft-spoken. "Allow my company the honour."

"Are you certain?"

"I may have spent the last six months documenting the edicts of the Church, but I assure you, I never skipped a day of weapons practice."

"Then the job is yours," replied Charlaine. "Now, let's return to the commandery. Once we throw open those courtyard doors, it'll be obvious what we're up to. We'll need the lead riders to quickly clear the doorway and tie down the Cunars before they move to block us in."

Verushka stepped forward. "Before being put in charge of discipline, I taught mounted combat in Eidenburg."

"That's where I was trained."

"I'm well aware, General, although I didn't arrive there until some months after you'd completed your training. Commander Raphaela spoke highly of you."

Charlaine smiled at the compliment. "You shall lead us out of the commandery, but I must stress your objective isn't to destroy them; it is to cause as much chaos and confusion as possible. If we get bogged down in a fight, we'll never be free of this place."

"Understood, General."

"Does anyone have any experience with quickly exiting a commandery?"

"I do," replied Amalia. "When I was still a Temple Captain back in Salovia, our regional commander ordered us to be ready to march to the aid of our sisters in Parzen should it prove necessary. Unfortunately, in my inexperience, I assumed it meant we should practice riding out of the building as quickly as possible rather than marching great distances. I had us going in and out for weeks."

"And what did you learn?"

"We typically assemble in the central courtyard and then exit in pairs, but I found it just as easy to ride four abreast, thus cutting the time required in half." She blushed slightly. "We tried a line of five, but the column was too wide to fit through the doors."

"Then we shall ride four wide."

"Do we have an ultimate destination?" asked Katinka. "Or are we trusting to luck?"

"I have a destination in mind," replied Charlaine, "but I'll keep that to myself until we're clear of this place. I can't risk it being disclosed should any of us be captured."

"And if you don't make it?"

"Teresa knows the destination, as does Temple Commander Danica. Don't worry. If I fall, the rest of you will still have a chance to make it to safety."

"We won't leave without you."

"I appreciate the sentiment, but the order's survival takes precedence. If we don't escape to find a home elsewhere, our part in the history of the Petty Kingdoms will end, and I'll not allow that to happen."

A breathless Anthea appeared, clutching a rolled-up parchment.

"Trouble?" said Charlaine.

"This note was just delivered, General." She passed over the parchment.

"The Cunars?" asked Amalia.

Charlaine read it over. "No, the Ragnarites." She looked at Anthea. "How did this arrive?"

"It was attached to an arrow shot onto our roof."

"It seems our friends, the Ragnarites, are preparing to abandon their commandery. They give no indication how they'll do that with Cunars surrounding them, but I shall take them at their word. Of greater interest is the last line, indicating they'll seize the gate just after nightfall. He invites us to take advantage of the opportunity that presents."

"He, being?" asked Danica.

"Brother Julius."

"Could it be a trap?" said Gerda. "Their commandery is surrounded just like ours; surely you're not suggesting they managed to send an arrow all this distance from atop their own building?"

"The Ragnarites are masters of stealth," replied Charlaine. "I imagine they have all manner of secret tunnels and doors in that commandery of theirs. And as for a trap, I find that highly unlikely. I've had dealings with Ragnarites before and found no reason to doubt their word."

"It could still be a ruse. Someone impersonating this Brother Julius, for example."

"The Ragnarites revealed nothing of the service they rendered Sister Danica, so how would the Cunars even know of our involvement with Brother Julius? These are difficult times, Gerda, but we still have friends outside these walls. Let's not abandon our faith in all our brother orders because of the recent activities of the Cunars."

Charlaine looked at her fellow sisters, but they'd all fallen silent, waiting for her next words.

"Prepare for battle," ordered Charlaine.

The Temple Commanders dispersed, each ready to assume command of their assigned knights, except for Nina, who made her way forward.

"General," she said. "I wonder if I might have a word?"

"By all means," replied Charlaine.

"I know you plan to fight our way out, but what if I could offer you a better way to accomplish that goal?"

"I'm listening."

"Like all commanderies, this building has doors in every hallway that can be closed to halt intruders."

"I'm well aware. What are you proposing?"

"That we allow the Cunars to enter."

"I assume you mean to trap them?"

"Indeed," replied Nina. "We should be able to get at least half of them inside before they realize what we're up to."

"But you'd have to open the door for them to enter, leaving no way for you to escape."

"We knew that when we took the responsibility of guarding the entrance."

Charlaine stared back, not quite believing her ears. "You would sacrifice yourself to save the rest?"

"The choice is yours, but if we guard only the front door, we'll only keep a few occupied before we fall. This plan will draw a far greater number into the trap. We knew we'd be sacrificing ourselves when we took up the burden; let us at least make that sacrifice more meaningful."

Charlaine stepped forward, placing her hand on the Temple Commander's shoulder. "I honour your sacrifice. We've had our differences, Nina, but you and the others will be forever remembered as heroes of the order." To Charlaine, her words sounded hollow, yet the Temple Commander stood up straighter, a look of pride on her face.

"Thank you for having faith in me," said Nina. "Now, we must coordinate this properly if we are to have any chance of success."

"You get your people into place, and we'll secure the hallways, all save for the one route, so we can alert you when to commence."

"Just make sure all those doors are closed before we invite the Cunars inside, or else the entire plan may go awry."

The courtyard sat in the centre of the commandery, allowing Temple Knights to mount their horses before exiting through the large double doors that offered egress to the outside world. Verushka looked over her knights with a critical eye while her captain fidgeted. A Temple Captain typically commanded a company of Temple Knights, but Charlaine had opted to let the more experienced Temple Commanders take over that duty, freeing up the captains to act as their aides.

Making things even more unusual was the number of higher ranks. Charlaine had twelve Temple Commanders for only ten companies. Then there were the Temple Captains, who'd been sent to the Antonine for training in their new capacity.

She spotted Erika, one of the extra Temple Captains, and waved her over. "I've decided to make you responsible for getting Danica to Temple Bay."

"I'll need twelve knights."

"I already picked them out for you. Once we're clear of the city, you head directly north into Galoran. From there, take any route the admiral deems best."

"Yes, General."

"I can't stress this enough, Erika. Danica must make it back to the fleet."

"I shall do whatever it takes."

"I knew you would," replied Charlaine.

"What do we do once we're there?"

"That's up to Danica. She'll handle the fleet, but I imagine she'll need help with the landward side of things."

"Meaning?"

"You're a Temple Captain now. With what's unfolding here, plenty of Temple Knights will be seeking refuge in the north. Someone needs to look after them, and Danica's going to be far too busy."

"Are you suggesting I be responsible for looking after a commandery?"

"I'm not suggesting anything. I'm telling you it's inevitable. I'd trust you with my life, Erika, but more importantly, I'm trusting you with Danica's."

"What about you?"

"I wish I could say I've been through worse, but I swore to tell the truth. If the rest of us survive this, you'll eventually hear of it, but that could be months or even years from now."

"How will you get word to us?"

Teresa, who'd been standing off to one side, moved up and placed a satchel in Charlaine's hands.

Charlaine held it up. "This contains several letters, each sealed with a name. You are to deliver these to the smiths guild in Regensbach if you can. If not, seek them out in any major city of the Continent. Danica will know who you can trust."

"I don't understand."

"I haven't the time to explain other than to say they can be trusted." Charlaine nodded towards a group of knights bringing their horses into the courtyard. "That's your new command, Temple Captain. See that they're looked after."

Erika made her way over to them.

"She's nervous," noted Teresa.

"Just as the rest of us are," replied Charlaine. "It's to be expected under the present circumstances."

"You don't see it, do you?"

"See what?"

"The effect you have on people—it's quite pronounced."

"What do you mean?"

"You have a gift for making people believe in you, Charlaine. You embody the spirit of Saint Agnes herself."

"I shall take that as a compliment."

"As you should. Now, things are about to get busy. I suggest you seek out Danica and say your goodbyes while you have the chance."

Danica tightened the girth on her horse.

"All set?"

She wheeled around to see Charlaine. "She's not Spirit, but she'll do. I trust Stormcloud is ready?"

"As ready as she's ever been." She stepped closer, rubbing the horse's nose. "Listen, Danica. I may not have another chance to say this, but you've been by my side through thick and thin."

Danica's voice choked. "I know what you're thinking… D-d-don't say it."

"I need to, and it's important you hear what I have to say." Charlaine paused, taking a deep breath. "We've faced a lot over the years, and we always knew the other had our back, but this time, there's no other option. You're needed in Temple Bay, while my path lies elsewhere."

"In Hadenfeld?"

Charlaine nodded. "It's the only place I can think of that might give us a chance of survival, although it means breaking my word."

"Whatever do you mean?"

"When I joined the order, I agreed to never return to Hadenfeld."

"But Ludwig is king now. Surely he wouldn't enforce that?"

"It is precisely for that reason he must uphold his father's wishes."

"Nonsense," said Danica. "What good would it do him?"

"A king who goes back on a promise can't be trusted."

"Then deliver the order to Hadenfeld, and then join me in Temple Bay."

"As tempting as that offer is, I can't. I've been entrusted with the sacred duty of securing the future of the order. I can't very well abandon them in their time of need."

"I'm not certain I understand what you're suggesting. Either you lead the sisters to Hadenfeld and break your promise or abandon them at the border. Which is it to be?"

"That's what has me so vexed. We took an oath to tell the truth, which includes honouring agreements made in good faith."

"Your agreement was with a baron who is now dead. I hardly think that qualifies. Besides, we also promised to put the needs of the order above our own. Wouldn't that take precedence?"

"I suppose it does," replied Charlaine, "yet I still feel the burden."

"What you need to do is get the order to Hadenfeld, and then seek the guidance of a Holy Mother."

"Our order has been disbanded. As a result, no member of the Church will offer aid of any sort."

"They'll find that rule difficult to enforce. You are Charlaine deShandria, Temple General of the Order of Saint Agnes. Any Holy Mother would be honoured to count you amongst her flock." Danica stepped forward, embracing her closest friend. "You'll get through this, and then you'll write to me up in Temple Bay. I can't promise I can visit, but at least we'll stay in touch."

"Thank you," said Charlaine. "I needed to hear that." She hugged her one final time, then stood back. "Erika and her knights will see you safely to Temple Bay. Don't be too hard on them. And whatever you do, stay well clear of any members of the Church."

"You don't have to tell me twice. I've been considering several routes—"

"Don't tell me," interrupted Charlaine. "It's better I don't know." She wanted to say so much more. How does one say goodbye to a family member, knowing they may never meet again? Leaving her parents had been difficult enough; this was next to impossible.

Teresa interrupted her inner struggle. "The Temple Knights are ready, General. It's time for it to begin."

32

BREAKOUT

SPRING 1107 SR

As the sun set on the horizon, Charlaine nodded to Anthea, who disappeared inside the commandery to inform Nina that everyone was ready. Once done, she would close the door behind her, sealing their fate.

Charlaine's breath caught in her throat at the thought of their sacrifice, and she struggled to control herself. It would do the order no good for their general to lose herself in mourning when she should be leading. The time for tears would come later, once they were away from this place, assuming this mad scheme of hers didn't lead them all to disaster.

She focused on the great doors leading from the courtyard to in front of the commandery, trying to imagine what the Cunars outside were up to. Part of her feared they'd anticipated her resistance and had prepared a trap.

Logic took hold. Even if they had, there was nothing they could do to hold off five hundred Temple Knights from riding forth. Charlaine forced herself to stop and observe her fellow sisters. Some were filled with anticipation, while others were nervous, but all looked prepared for what was to come. How many more names would join the Hall of Heroes this day?

She shook her head. There would be no more Hall of Heroes for them. Instead of being revered for their devotion, they'd be scorned, dismissed to history as a pack of ne'er-do-wells who had broken their oath to serve the Church. A smile crept over her face as she realized they were her ne'er-do-wells now, a small army of Temple Knights dedicated to doing what the Church failed to do: protecting the Petty Kingdoms from the threat of invasion by the Halvarian Empire. She didn't know if they'd be welcome in

Hadenfeld, but she'd do her utmost to find them a place to call their own, even if she had to lead them halfway across the Continent to do it.

Anthea reappeared in the courtyard, giving her the thumbs-up. The doors were sealed. Now, they could only wait as Nina tried to lure the enemy in. Charlaine took a cleansing breath, trying to overcome her trepidation.

Teresa appeared at her side, her mount shifting nervously. "It's been years since I rode a horse."

"How did you get to the Antonine?"

"By wagon, if you can believe it. Took me close to half a year."

"Did you land near Ilea?"

"No," she replied. "On the eastern edge of the Wildlands, at a place called Clearwater. Are you familiar with it?"

"Can't say I am."

"It's a town on the frontier, with timber buildings and a wooden palisade. It was shocking after spending so much time in an Elven city, but thankfully, a small group of Temple Knights there welcomed my return."

"I didn't realize we had sisters out east."

"We don't. They were Mathewites, and they arranged my passage to Corassus. From there, I meandered my way north, travelling with whichever merchants were willing to provide me room on their wagons."

"And now you're here to witness the end of our order. That must be disappointing."

"This is not the end," said Teresa. "I prefer to believe we're about to enter a new golden age of prosperity, and you're the one who'll guide us to it. It won't come easily, and Saints know we've got struggles ahead of us, but I have faith we'll find ourselves much better off in the long run."

"I admire your optimism, but feeding five hundred Temple Knights would be difficult at the best of times; doing so while hunted by the Church will be nearly impossible. Perhaps you'd be better served to place your hopes on someone else's shoulders."

"Do you remember when Gwalinor healed you?"

"Of course," replied Charlaine. "That's when he examined your aura and learned you had the potential to cast."

"Yes, but if you recall, he mentioned yours was unique. To be precise, he said you glowed with a bright white aura."

"I remember. He also said he didn't know what that meant, so I gave it no further thought."

"Ah," said Teresa, "but he did say he would endeavour to find out."

"And?"

"He searched through all the records the Elves had concerning magic when he returned home, but they held no additional information, so he widened his search. Five years later, he came across an account of an Elven Life Mage who'd treated another individual with a similar aura. It was an ancient tome, to be sure, and the mage in question is no longer amongst us, so verifying his story was impossible, but it contained a startling revelation."

"Which was?"

"The individual being treated was none other than Saint Agnes, though she wasn't considered a saint at the time."

"I don't recall reading anything about Saint Agnes being injured."

"I never said she was."

"But you said she was treated?"

"She was," replied Teresa. "It was a difficult birth."

"Birth? Are you suggesting she had a child?"

"The account was quite clear on that point."

"Who was the father?"

"It didn't say, although someone present noted it bore a remarkable similarity to our depictions of Saint Mathew."

"This is a lot to digest," said Charlaine.

"You're forgetting the aura. I believe it indicates you are a true descendant of that child, though Gwalinor disagrees."

"What does he think?"

"He is of the opinion your aura marks you as a rare individual, one of pure spirit, to use the Elven term, and I must say, he makes a compelling argument."

"An interesting observation," noted Charlaine, "but it makes no difference to our present circumstances. In any case, the argument is meaningless without more information. Hundreds of individuals could possess an aura like mine."

"A valid point, but whether you choose to believe in it or not, I still think you're the one who will lead us into a new age."

A horn sounded, echoing through the halls of the commandery and out into the courtyard.

"That's Nina's signal," said Charlaine. "It's time to put aside such thoughts and prepare for battle." She raised her voice. "Open the gate. Verushka, you may give the order to advance at your discretion."

Anthea lifted the drop bar, and the doors swung inward to reveal the road out front. Ten Cunars stood there while the rest had entered the building through the other door. Verushka gave the command, and her knights rode forth, four abreast, their hoofbeats drawing the attention of their attackers. One of them issued a shout of alarm, calling in his brothers from where they surrounded the building.

"For Saint Agnes!" shouted Verushka, the cry taken up by her Temple Knights.

Charlaine watched them ride out of the courtyard, then turned to where Katinka waited. "Move your company up and prepare to advance on my command. You remember your objective?"

"Yes, General. We're to turn left and circle the commandery, driving off the remaining Cunars."

"Don't get bogged down in a fight. If they don't flee, avoid them. You must return by the time the rest of the companies leave the courtyard."

"Yes, General."

Charlaine waited until the last of Verushka's company cleared the doors before counting to five. "You may begin." She turned, seeking out the next commander, but Temple Captain Nicola had already seen to it. The third company's horses were now being walked into the courtyard, their knights ready to ride out as the sounds of distant fighting drifted towards them.

Anthea, who still stood by the doors, waved. "The front road is cleared, General."

"Temple Captain Nicola, have the remaining companies ride out as soon as they can assemble. We'll mass on the road, facing east."

"Shouldn't the first companies ride on ahead, General?"

"No. I won't be spread over a large area—it makes us too vulnerable. If we're going to get out of here, we'll do so together. Is that understood?"

"Yes, General."

Charlaine sighed, an action noted by Teresa. "Does it bother you that much to be called general?"

"It sounds so stiff and formal."

"It's a sign of respect, nothing more. Under the present circumstances, it reminds everyone that we are a military fighting order."

"Where's Danica?"

"She's standing by, along with Erika and her escorts. They'll ride out between the fifth and sixth companies. What of yourself?"

"I'll bring up the rear."

"Are you certain that's wise? They need you to set an example."

"I won't leave anyone behind."

"I'm not suggesting you do, merely that you'd be better able to organize this army from the road."

"You make a good point," said Charlaine. "We'll follow the third company."

"Then we'd best get moving; they're already heading out the gate."

. . .

They rode out to find half of Verushka's command on foot, their swords drawn, blocking the entrance directly into the commandery. Having entered the building, the Cunars had apparently made short work of Nina's knights, for they were now trying to exit, a task made all the more difficult by the waiting Agnesites.

Charlaine sought out Katinka. "Commander, have your knights form up on the road west of the entrance, ready for a charge. You'll know when it's time."

"Yes, General."

She urged Stormcloud into a gallop, closing in on the fight at the front door. "Verushka, prepare to withdraw. When I give the command, you must pull back as quickly as possible."

The Temple Commander stared back, not quite understanding, until Charlaine pointed towards Katinka's command, which, even now, was falling into place. Charlaine withdrew, the better to observe.

Verushka took one last look in the direction of Katinka's knights before giving the order. Her own group fell back, fleeing the conflict and allowing the Cunars trapped within to flood out of the building.

Charlaine didn't have to give the command, for Katinka knew her business. Her company advanced in a charge, their timing perfect, crushing the hapless Cunars beneath sword and hoof. They soon broke, the grey-clad survivors fleeing in every direction.

The next two companies rode out of the commandery, falling into their designated positions on the roadway.

"Losses?" asked Charlaine as Verushka appeared at her side, still afoot.

"Seventeen wounded, General, three severely, but Sister Teresa is looking after them. The rest can still ride, but I shouldn't like them to fight again unless absolutely necessary."

"Agreed. Find Temple Commander Scyllia and tell her to form her company up in front. She'll lead us to the gates of the Antonine." She spotted Danica riding out of the gate. "It's about time you showed up."

"Don't blame me. There are a lot of horses waiting to get out that door." She halted her mount beside Charlaine. "How are things going out here?"

"We drove off the Cunars, but getting everyone out of the courtyard is taking too long."

"That's to be expected. It's not easy marching five hundred sisters through a doorway four at a time."

"Five hundred and seventeen, if we're looking at an exact count, although I suppose with the grand mistress no longer amongst us, that would make it five hundred and sixteen."

"Ten full companies," said Danica. "That's likely the largest concentration of sister knights in the history of the order. What was it you had at the Brinwald? Six?"

"Seven, if you include the Mathewites," replied Charlaine, "and that was a lot of mouths to feed. Each of our knights carries rations, but that won't see us beyond a few days at best."

"At least there's plenty of rivers around, so water won't be a problem."

"Providing we get that far."

"You think we won't?"

"We still need to escape the Antonine," said Charlaine. "The longer we remain here, the more time the Cunars have to react. Their stragglers will soon be back at their commandery, reporting to their superiors what's happened. I'm hoping they'll be spread too thin to send more after us just yet."

"Will we have enough time to reach the gate?"

"That depends on the other orders. If they resisted the amalgamation order, it would tie down more of the Cunars."

"And if not?"

"Then we can expect to meet them before we reach the gates of the Antonine."

"Let's hope it doesn't come to that."

The last of the Agnesite Temple Knights fell into position on the road. Charlaine gave the command, and the column proceeded eastward towards the fountain that immortalized the fall of Herani. Would this day be remembered by some sort of monument? Somehow, she doubted it. A feeling of gloom threatened to overwhelm her, then Danica was there, full of hope.

"This darkness works to our advantage," Danica said. "Our scarlet tabards look grey in this light. Perhaps we'll be mistaken for Cunars?" She chuckled. "I can see it now, the Primus in a tirade because his own people let us pass through the gates unscathed."

"I doubt it will be that easy," said Charlaine, "but thank you."

"For what?"

"Keeping my mind focused on what matters. Now, let's get to the head of the column. I'd like to see what's happening up there."

They both urged on their mounts, though Stormcloud was the swifter of the two. Charlaine slowed, allowing her comrade to catch up, then they rode around the column to avoid interfering with the march.

Temple Commander Scyllia led, flanked by three of her knights. Her company followed in silence, the only sound the jangling of their armour and hoofbeats of their mounts.

Charlaine rode to the head of the column, which had already passed the fountain and now headed south, directly for the Mathewite commandery, marking the second point of danger for them.

She'd considered avoiding the road altogether, but that would've put them closer to the Augustine commandery, a far more dangerous move, considering their patriarch's support for the amalgamation. At the sight of Cunars surrounding the Mathewite building, she had reason to regret her decision.

Charlaine slowed, trying to determine what was happening. From her vantage point, she could only see a thin line of knights stretched around the back of the building, there to prevent anyone from fleeing. The darkness obscured their identities, but to her mind, they must be Cunars, for who else would take up such a position?

She turned to Danica. "Fall back to Commander Scyllia. Tell her to follow me. I have an idea."

"Care to share what that might be?"

"I'm hoping we can ride directly between the Commanderies of Mathew and Augustine without getting close enough to either."

"That's a bit of a gamble, don't you think?"

"As you said earlier, we look like Cunars in the dark. Any knights posted near those buildings will carry torches, ruining their ability to see far. It's a gamble, but what other choice is there?"

"I'll let her know," said Danica. She slowed her pace, allowing those behind to catch up to her.

Charlaine veered west off the road, still heading south but now riding parallel to it. She kept her eye on the Mathewite commandery, knowing that it, too, would be surrounded.

The front of the building came into view as she advanced, revealing a group of Cunars lit by torchlight, overseeing the evacuation of the Temple Knights of Saint Mathew. The brown-clad knights were leaving in ones and twos, handing over their axes to those Cunars waiting nearby.

Concerned about her brother order, she veered towards the road, then heard yelling. The Cunars out front drew their weapons as the doors to the courtyard opened, and a group of knights rode out, axes at the ready. Charlaine urged Stormcloud into a faster gait, hoping her sisters would do the same. She glanced behind to see Danica waving back, her horse speeding up, while beside her came Temple Commander Scyllia, sword in hand.

Charlaine was already halfway to the gates of the Antonine, yet her column of sister knights stretched back to the gardens. Part of her wanted to help those Mathewites attempting to flee, but she was a Temple General now, responsible for the survival of more than five hundred souls. She gritted her teeth and kept riding south into the darkness.

33

THE GATES OF THE ANTONINE
SPRING 1107 SR

A yell from her left drew Charlaine's attention. The riders who'd escaped the Mathewite commandery headed south in a mad dash, hoping to reach the gate. She altered course, bringing her column closer and calling out, "Saint Agnes!"

The lead rider looked right at her, his face lit by the torch he held aloft, a beacon to guide his knights. "Saint Mathew!" he replied. The Mathewite then raised the torch and lowered it, repeating the gesture to indicate his men should follow. He exchanged words with someone beside him, then handed the torch to the fellow and headed towards Charlaine.

She waited until he neared before calling out. "Welcome, Brother. We ride for the gate. You?"

"The same. I'm Temple Captain Walda, and you are?"

"Temple General Charlaine."

He glanced behind her. "How many sisters have you?"

"Just over five hundred. Your own numbers?"

"Eighty-two, providing none fell coming out of the commandery. I'm afraid I've had little time to count. I saw Cunars heading there earlier to reinforce the Antonine's gates. We'll have to fight our way out."

"Perhaps not," said Charlaine. "I have it on good authority the gates may be open. I will assign a company of my sister knights to secure the gates while the rest of us file through."

He drew his axe, then held it before his face in a salute. "I shall be happy for my men to bring up the rear, if you've no objection?"

"By all means."

He slowed, letting her column take the lead. The sounds of battle drifted towards her, evidence of a struggle up ahead. She cut across a field in her rush to reach the gate in time. Sensing her anxiety, Stormcloud put on a burst of speed, racing across the grass. The torchlights on the walls ahead revealed a mass of men fighting for control of the now-open gates, the safety of Reichendorf lying just beyond.

A group of grey-clad knights attacked opponents dressed in dark clothing, but rather than fighting in ranks, it had devolved into a series of individual contests. Charlaine drew her sword and held it high.

"Charge!" she yelled at the top of her lungs.

Stormcloud exploded into a full gallop, her hoofbeats echoing in the cool night air. Charlaine swept into the gateway, her sword careening off the helmet of a Cunar, distracting him from the foe he was already engaged with. Quick to take advantage, his opponent swung his hammer, smashing into a shin and buckling the Cunar's greave. The knight fell, his part in the battle no longer of any consequence.

Stormcloud reared up, striking out with a hoof, a loud ringing noise erupting as it struck a back plate. Charlaine readied another blow, but then her sister knights poured into the gateway, pushing all before them.

A man adorned in black and armed with two swords held one up in a salute before running through the gate into the city beyond.

"Scyllia," shouted Charlaine. "Take half your knights and secure the gatehouse. Everyone else, get through and form up at the crossroads one block east." She watched the Temple Knights respond to her commands, moving aside so as not to impede their progress. Teresa found her there, watching as her command fled the confines of the Antonine.

"We did it," the healer said. "I knew your plan would succeed."

"I didn't seize the gates," replied Charlaine. "The Ragnarites did all the work."

The Agnesite companies passed, saluting her as they rode to safety.

Teresa brought three fingers across her chest. "The Saints have looked kindly upon us this night."

"So they have, but we mustn't grow complacent. We still have many miles to go before we reach any semblance of safety."

Back in the Antonine, horns sounded, the unmistakable call to arms. "They're coming," announced Charlaine. "And likely in much greater numbers."

Her Temple Knights continued filing through the gates, a process slowed by the necessity of now riding two abreast. This was by design, as it hampered the ability of an invader to enter the Antonine in time of war, yet no one had ever attacked the place, leading Charlaine to wonder who these defences were designed to keep out.

Even more confusing was the fact there was only one entrance to the Antonine, with the rest of it guarded by walls so long they'd be challenging to man should it come under siege. And the small towers supporting the thick walls looked more decorative than functional. With a start, she realized she was mentally planning how she would assault the place.

Charlaine shook her head. This was not the time to drift off into such thoughts. She should be focusing on the task at hand, that of getting her command out of the Antonine and into the streets of Reichendorf. "We need to somehow block any pursuit," she said, more to herself than anyone else.

"We could jam the portcullis," came a voice. She looked down to see a dismounted Sister Magda standing beside her. "Where is your horse?"

"Outside the gate," the woman replied. "I came back to take a look at the gatehouse."

"Why? Do you have experience with such things?"

"My father used to guard the gates of Zienholtz back in Andover. As a young girl, I'd take him his dinner."

"And so you learned to guard a gate?"

"Oh, I learned much more than that. I learned all about the winches that operate the portcullis. I reckon that if we drop the portcullis and damage the winch, they'll be unable to operate it, giving us plenty of time to escape."

"A good idea," replied Charlaine, "but you're forgetting one important detail."

"That being?"

"You'd have to be within the gatehouse to accomplish that. How would you escape?"

"I could lower myself over the battlements. There's bound to be some rope lying around here."

"How long would it take you to carry this out?"

"Give me three knights, and I'll get on it immediately."

"That doesn't answer my question, Magda. It will do no good to lower the portcullis after the Cunars pass through the gatehouse."

"Damaging the winch won't take long, General, especially if a mallet or hammer is nearby. If not, I'll have to resort to fire." She grinned. "The drum is usually made of wood and greased, so it would burn nicely."

"Choose your knights and see to it at once, but don't drop that portcullis till the Mathewites are through, understood?"

"Yes, General." Magda ran off, calling out names as she went.

"She's eager, that one," said Teresa. "Were we like that once? It's been so long, I don't remember."

"Not until Captain Giselle showed up. She had a way of inspiring all of us."

"As do you. You just haven't realized it yet."

"Get yourself into Reichendorf," said Charlaine. "And take Stormcloud with you. I'll meet you there shortly."

"Where are you going?"

"I have some business to attend to." Charlaine dismounted, passing the reins to Teresa before she entered the gatehouse, which was essentially a tower built over the gates. The upper floor contained the winch mechanism that controlled the portcullis, and above it sat the top of the tower, allowing archers to play havoc with anyone assaulting the gate.

Charlaine ascended the stairs quickly to find Magda and Anthea trying to pull a lever back, but it appeared to be resisting their efforts, for they'd resorted to striking the thing with a hammer to try dislodging it. Lucille and Iris stood to one side, their weapons drawn lest someone try to stop them.

"The mechanism's stuck," explained Magda.

"I'm not surprised," replied Charlaine. "This winch probably hasn't been used in decades." She moved closer, examining the lever. The design consisted of a chain wrapped around a drum, which, in turn, ran through two pulleys attached to the top of the portcullis. The handle on the drum turned it, raising the portcullis, but releasing it required pulling back the lever to allow the heavy iron bars to unwind the chains. Unfortunately, the new knights lacked the strength to accomplish the feat.

The horns grew closer, announcing the Cunars were gaining on them. They'd have to abandon the attempt if they didn't get that lever unstuck. Charlaine moved to the window for a view of the Antonine. By craning her neck, she could just make out those beneath them. "Our brothers, the Mathewites, are riding through."

Lucille and Iris ran to the doorway, each carrying a bundle of rope.

"Get above," shouted Charlaine. "Tie those ropes together and then create a loop on one end. Once you've done that, drop the loop over a merlon—that's our escape." She moved closer to the lever and placed her hands upon it, waiting. "We must give the brothers time to clear the gatehouse."

Lucille and Iris ran up the steps, disappearing from view. Charlaine closed her eyes, concentrating on the sounds around her. Beneath them came hoofbeats, hardly surprising, considering the Mathewites' presence, but there was something else, a palpable sense of urgency as if the very air were alive with the buzzing of magic. Then, more horses, this time, from the direction of the Antonine. The Cunars had arrived!

"Now!" she yelled, pulling with all her might on the lever. She knew that if she could only release that, the weight of the portcullis would do the rest, but the cursed thing wouldn't budge.

"Again," she cried, and all three put their backs into it. The sudden release sent them sprawling to the floor. The drum groaned and then spun, releasing the chain that lowered the portcullis. A voice from the doorway interrupted Charlaine as she scrambled to her feet.

"Traitors!"

She turned to see a Cunar Temple Knight, sword in hand. With no time to draw her own weapon, she rushed him, using the bulk of her body to push him back. The unexpected manoeuvre worked, for he lost his balance and fell, tumbling down the steps straight into two of his companions.

"Get up to the roof," she shouted, then drew her sword. "I'll hold off these Cunars."

Anthea and Magda rushed past her, taking the steps two at a time while Charlaine blocked the stairs heading down. The Temple Knights below had recovered from their fall, but the gatehouse was built to make an attack difficult, thus forcing them to come at her in single file.

Charlaine unslung her shield and then braced for the first one, waiting until he was two steps away to jab her sword into his face. The fellow's helmet prevented her from causing any damage, but his instincts worked against him, for he yanked his head away. Seeing his reaction, she deftly kicked out to unbalance him further, and he stepped back, trying to regain his footing on the edge of the stairs. Doubling down on her attack, she moved closer, thrusting at his face again.

Distracted by his predicament, the Cunar didn't withdraw, resulting in her sword smashing into his face guard. Charlaine maintained contact, putting all her strength behind the weapon, forcing his neck back until he lost his balance.

The knight behind pressed himself to one side as his comrade tumbled past, but before he could move to attack, Charlaine sprang into action, ramming her shield into him, knocking him from his feet. With her attack complete, she turned and raced up the stairs, heading for the roof, where only Magda stood by the battlements, the others having already evacuated the building.

"Go!" shouted Charlaine.

"I can't," replied the knight. "Anthea is still on the rope!"

"Then it shall have to bear the weight of both of you."

The young woman climbed into the embrasure, tightly gripping the rope. Charlaine peered over the wall, spotting the others at the bottom, some twenty feet down, steadying the rope. From the gatehouse came a cascade of stomping feet, evidence more Cunars had joined the assault and had entered the winch room.

It suddenly occurred to her that although they'd lowered the portcullis, they'd done nothing to prevent it from being raised again. She considered rushing downstairs to do just that, but it was too late, for the footsteps grew closer, and then a Temple Captain burst onto the roof, his sword drawn.

"What have we got here?" he said. "Surrender your sword, General. There's no escape."

Charlaine searched the rooftop, desperately seeking a means of escape, but found nothing but a broken piece of wood. It could not help her in her predicament, but she recognized it as the handle to the cranking mechanism used to raise the portcullis. It appeared Magda and Anthea succeeded after all!

Charlaine sheathed her sword. "You have me at a disadvantage, Captain." She inched closer to the outer wall, keeping her arms away from her scabbard as she slung her shield. She needed to buy time, so she must keep this Temple Captain talking. A Temple Knight joined his officer but stood back, watching the exchange.

"What's to happen to me?" asked Charlaine.

"You shall be tried as a traitor," replied the captain. "You've taken up arms against the Church. There's no forgiving that."

"Your knights surrounded our commandery."

"They did so under the directive of the Council of Peers, who voted to amalgamate the orders. Had you done as you promised and surrendered peacefully, you wouldn't find yourself in such an untenable position now."

Out of the corner of her eye, she noticed that the rope tied around the merlon had gone slack, indicating Magda had finished her descent. "I did not promise to surrender," she replied. "I said we'd be out of the commandery by dark, and we were."

"And that deception cost the lives of several of your sisters. Have you no shame?"

"They gave their lives so the rest would survive. Would you do any less for your own brethren?" She spotted a moment of indecision on the captain's face. Had she struck a nerve?

"I admire you, General. By all accounts, you've had a most glorious career, but I'm afraid all good things must eventually come to an end. For you, that day is today."

"Do you consider yourself a religious man, Captain?"

"I'd hardly be a Temple Knight if I was not."

"Then you understand the power of faith."

"It is not faith that brought us to this point," he replied. "It is your stubbornness in disobeying the lawful commands of the Council of Peers."

"A council that is corrupt. The Primus is an agent of Halvaria."

"Now you're just trying to waste my time. It won't work, General. I am incorruptible."

"I wish the same were true of Talivardas."

"That's Primus Wilmar to you."

Charlaine closed her eyes and took a deep breath, seeking inner peace. A warmth spread over her as if Agnes herself embraced her. She turned and jumped from the parapet, a twenty-foot drop that would undoubtedly result in serious injury if not death, yet she knew she'd survive, not because of her Saint, but because of the one thing the Cunars didn't have—Teresa.

Charlaine opened her eyes to discover herself being carried on a litter.

"It's about time you woke up," said Danica.

"Where are we?"

"On the streets of Reichendorf."

"What happened?"

"You don't remember? You jumped from atop the gatehouse. Had Teresa not been with us, you surely would've perished."

"It was her very presence that convinced me to jump. If I hadn't, I would've had to surrender to the Temple Knights of Saint Cunar."

"I'll let it go this time," replied Danica with a grin. "But in future, let's try to avoid any brushes with imminent death, shall we?"

"Says the admiral who fought hand to hand against the Halvarian fleet."

"We're Temple Knights; fighting is part of our training. Jumping off buildings, however, is not."

"It all worked out for the best," said Charlaine. "We're free of the Antonine, aren't we?"

"True, but it won't take them long to open that gate. I only hope it gives us enough time to get to safety."

34

OUTSKIRTS OF THE CITY
SPRING 1107 SR

After a busy night with Charlaine insisting on riding Stormcloud despite her weakened condition, daylight saw them resting on the outskirts of Reichendorf. According to Teresa, she'd broken both legs and possibly her collarbone. Were it not for magic, Charlaine might've succumbed to her wounds. As it was, she had suffered a substantial loss of blood, which weakened her, resulting in her sitting unsteadily on her horse.

Temple Captain Walda wandered over, pulling off his riding gloves. "I must congratulate you, General. You did what none of us believed possible."

"We succeeded because we all worked together."

"Indeed. I only hope that the future will offer us opportunities to do so again."

"I assume this is a goodbye?"

"It is," the captain replied. "My men and I are heading north into Galoran, then we hope to make our way east to the city of Ebenstadt, but we must clear the Grey Spire Mountains first."

"I'm not familiar with them," said Charlaine.

"They run roughly east-west, dividing Krieghoff and Holstead in the south from Novarsk in the north."

"And you think Ebenstadt will give you refuge?"

"Indeed. We have a detachment in the new Kingdom of Therengia. The chance of the Church having any influence in those lands is slim these days, especially after the debacle of the last Holy Crusade."

"I wish you well, Captain."

"What of you, General? Would you consider riding with us?"

"I'm afraid our numbers preclude me from travelling that far. It thus falls to me to choose a destination a little closer."

"If you don't mind me asking, where would that be?"

"Hadenfeld."

He shook his head. "I would advise against it, General. The Church has declared them heretical. It's only a matter of time before they organize a crusade to bring them back into the fold."

"All the more reason for us to go there. I know their king, and he won't bend a knee to the Church."

Walda nodded. "Meaning he'll welcome the addition of ten companies of Temple Knights."

"Well," said Charlaine, "perhaps ex-Temple Knights might be a more appropriate term."

"Nonsense. We still serve the Saints. In some ways, we are more devout than those in the Church we used to serve. Unfortunately, my order split on the idea of amalgamation, but yours appears intact."

"For now, but it won't be long before the Cunars try to ban us from all the Petty Kingdoms."

"They may try, but I doubt they'll succeed."

"What makes you say that?"

"War is coming," said Walda, "and I don't refer to the never-ending squabbles of the Petty Kingdoms. The empire will soon resume its expansion, and when it does, rulers will welcome all the help they can get. I hope we might meet again, General, but with me going to Ebenstadt and you to Hadenfeld, I doubt that will come to pass. Still, I would welcome a letter one day, if only to learn of your success."

"I promise you this, Captain," said Charlaine. "If we do indeed make it to Hadenfeld, I shall send word to all the commanderies of the Continent, Ebenstadt included."

"That will prove difficult, given the Church's control over their couriers."

"I have my ways." She extended her hand. "I'm glad to have met you, Temple Captain Walda. May Saint Mathew guide you to your destiny."

"And Saint Agnes to yours, General." He turned, making his way back to his command.

Charlaine sought out Danica, who was busy discussing strategy with Erika. They both grew silent at the sight of her approach. Danica wiped away a tear as she embraced Charlaine, holding her tight, knowing this was the moment she'd dreaded all night.

"I shall miss you," Danica managed to choke out.

"And I, you." They hugged for what seemed like an eternity, and then

Charlaine held her at arm's-length, viewing her one last time through teary eyes. "You go and look after that fleet of yours. I won't have the Halvarians believing they can have free rein on the Great Northern Sea."

Danica nodded. "I will. You have my word. And you make certain King Ludwig gives the order sanctuary."

"I will. I promise. Now, off with you, Admiral, while we still have the determination to see this through."

"I'll take care of her," said Erika. "I promise you."

"I'll hold you to that," replied Charlaine. "And remember, Danica's a Temple Commander now. That gives her seniority. I'll not have you try to boss her around."

"Understood, General."

"Come," said Danica. "We should put as much distance as possible between us and Reichendorf."

Erika nodded, and together, they walked over to their horses, climbing into their saddles. Their escort, already astride their mounts, moved into position to follow them, the entire group threading their way through the makeshift camp back towards the road.

"Parting is always difficult with loved ones. It's like losing a member of the family."

Charlaine turned at the sound of Teresa's voice to see her, too, watching their departure. "Danica's been part of my life for more than ten years."

"And unless I miss my guess, she'll remain so, but for now, we have more important things to consider."

"Yes. You're right. I have hundreds of sisters to take care of. I can hardly spare time for personal matters."

"It was not a critique," said Teresa, "merely an observation. What you share with Danica is to be lauded, but she wouldn't want you distracted at a time like this."

"You know her all too well."

"It's strange when you think about it."

"Why would you say that?" asked Charlaine.

"I haven't seen either of you for nigh on ten years."

"And yet you understand us better than anyone else I know."

Teresa smiled. "What can I say? I'm a genius at understanding relation-ships. It must have something to do with spending a decade in the company of Elves."

"Do they value friends as we do?"

"That's difficult to say. They were so reserved whenever they were around me, it drove me to distraction. It's not that they were impolite, mind you, but the very thought of showing signs of affection seemed so repulsive to them."

"Are you suggesting they have no emotions?"

"Not in the least, only that they don't reveal them to outsiders, which is all I ever was to them."

"You're back with family now." Charlaine paused. "That reminds me; I've got an important announcement." She raised her voice. "Gather round, Sisters. I've something to say."

Charlaine waited as everyone pressed in close, eager to hear. She noticed their expectant looks and took a breath. "We have gone through much this day," she began. "I don't want you to think of this as an ending but as a beginning. The Temple Knights of Saint Agnes will continue to exist, even prosper, but we can't begin that journey until we secure our freedom. I intend to march us to Hadenfeld." She paused, letting the news sink in.

"I know what you're thinking," she continued. "Hadenfeld has been sanctioned and thus has become an enemy of the Church, but so, too, have we. There is an old proverb that says those with common enemies should unite, and I can think of no better example than our current circumstances."

Their nods of approval encouraged her to continue.

"The Antonine is behind us, yet we still have a long way to go, one that is certain to be fraught with difficulties and dangers, and we must stand united if we are to win through to our new home. Follow the orders of your commanders, and remember the oath that binds you as sisters. Now, let us pray."

Charlaine paused to gather her thoughts. "Oh, Blessed Saint Agnes, watch over us in our time of need and help guide us to our new home. Give us the strength to endure hardship in your name and the will to overcome all obstacles. And if we should fall in your service, guide us to the Afterlife and welcome us with your embrace." She paused, counting to five. "Saints be with us."

"Saints be with us all," came the reply.

"Temple Knights, form up by company, under the supervision of your captains. Commanders will remain here to receive further instructions."

Charlaine waited as they returned to their mounts. Only the Temple Commanders remained, along with Teresa, looking uncomfortable around so many senior officers.

"I have one more announcement," said Charlaine. "I am exercising my right as Temple General to induct Sister Teresa back into the Temple Knights of Saint Agnes, ranked as a Temple Captain. She will be the founding member of the Sisters of Mercy, a dedicated group trained to utilize the power of Life Magic. As such, they will be exempt from taking up arms except in self-defence."

"It's a wonderful idea," said Verushka. "Who is she to train?"

Charlaine turned to Teresa. "Care to comment?"

Teresa moved closer to ensure all the commanders could hear her. "I was taught the healing arts by Gwalinor, Life Mage to Lady Francesca Gratuli, Baroness of Rizela. That training included learning how to discern the magical capabilities of others."

"Truly?" said Ursula. "Does that mean we can all become healers?"

"No. The gift of Life Magic is rare."

"How rare?"

"Some believe less than one in ten thousand, while others are of the opinion it's more common, perhaps as high as one in a hundred."

"Then why aren't the Petty Kingdoms flooded with Life Mages?"

"Several reasons," replied Teresa. "Many are unaware of their gifts, and even if they did suspect such power lay within them, who would teach them?"

"This is all very interesting," added Scyllia, "but how is this of any use if none of us have that gift?"

"I intend to check all our sister knights to determine if any possess the gift. If that proves unsuccessful, then I shall seek those beyond the confines of our order."

"This is a long-term plan," added Charlaine, "not something we need to worry about for the immediate future. It does mean, however, that we should avoid putting Teresa in danger, or these plans could be ruined, so I want some volunteers from your companies to act as a temporary bodyguard." She paused as the commanders discussed this.

Thinking about the long road ahead, she grew concerned with possible pursuit. Were she to take the most direct route to Hadenfeld, the Primus would soon guess where they were headed and send the Holy Army after her. No, she needed to somehow lead them away from her final destination.

Charlaine raised her hand, interrupting their conversations. "We are likely being pursued even as we stand here. I intend to take advantage of that. We shall travel north, like our Mathewite brothers, giving the impression that we flee to Galoran. Verushka, your company will perform the duties of rearguard. You'll watch for any signs of pursuit but not engage the enemy unless absolutely necessary."

"Yes, General."

"Katinka, are you familiar with the road to Galoran?"

"I am."

"Good. Your company will take the lead, with the rest proceeding in the same order as we left the Antonine. Once we reach the border, we'll take stock of our situation and begin the next leg of our journey. Discipline is to be maintained at all times. I will not have anyone falling behind; is that clear?"

They all nodded.

"Return to your companies and prepare to march."

They dispersed, each to their own command.

"Temple Captain?" said Teresa. "Surely I'm not qualified for such a rank?"

"You'll be in charge of the healers."

"We don't have any at present."

"That will change in due course. As to your training, I'll have to give that some thought. I'm not certain whether reading the accounts of Aeldred would be useful to someone in your position. I must also admit we neglected to collect that particular book in our rush to depart the Antonine."

"I should still learn military tactics," said Teresa. "After all, I'll be a Temple Knight."

"Agreed, but I'm afraid we'll have to wait until we've reached our new home to work out the details."

"What's Hadenfeld like?"

"I seldom set foot outside Malburg, but I think you'll find the king a reasonable fellow."

"What's he like?"

"Fair, with a strong sense of morals. He heeded my warning concerning the Stormwinds and Sartellians, averting a disaster in the making."

"While creating another," supplied Teresa. "His kingdom is now on the outs with the Church."

"Given the Halvarian's infiltration of the Church, it was inevitable. I'm afraid that also means we'll face more fighting in the future. The Primus won't stand back and let Hadenfeld continue as it is; he'll want to punish them."

"I still don't understand why?"

"It boils down to the fact that Hadenfeld has one of the larger armies of the Petty Kingdoms, and the Empire of Halvaria wants to weaken them."

"But surely they're already weakened? They've had two civil wars, for Saint's sake."

"Yes, but a crusade there would also tie up the Holy Army, making it unavailable against a Halvarian invasion."

"From what I've been told, the empire only expands one kingdom at a time. What makes you think they would take on the entire Continent?"

"My experiences in the north," replied Charlaine. "They failed in Arnsfeld because the Church interfered. With the Temple Knights under the ultimate command of their agents, they'll be virtually unopposed."

"But the Petty Kingdoms have their own armies?"

"They do. Most are small, and there's a history of animosity between the various kingdoms, duchies, and principalities that make up the Continent. Aside from the Holy Army, the biggest threat to a Halvarian invasion is the armies of Hadenfeld and Erlingen unless someone convinces the other kingdoms to work together for a change."

"You could be the one to do that," said Teresa. "You united Arnsfeld against them."

"It's too late for that now. My actions here brand me a traitor to the Church. And there's the chance King Ludwig will seek to make amends to the Church to avoid being a victim of a Holy Crusade, in which case, we won't be welcome in his lands."

"I don't think that will happen. You're an excellent judge of character, Charlaine. You always have been. If you say this King Ludwig is a good man, then I have faith he'll do the right thing."

"You're right. I should trust my instincts. It's always worked for me in the past."

"What do your instincts tell you about the next few days?"

"I have no doubt we'll be pursued. The question is whether the Church sees fit to inform the King of Regensbach about our defiance. If they do, we may be cut off by Royal Troops."

"And if not?"

"Then we need only worry about the other orders, although I can't imagine the Ragnarites or Mathewites hunting us down, can you?"

"No," agreed Teresa, "nor the Ansgarites, which means the Cunars will be doing all the dirty work. After all, the Augustines are meant to guard Holy relics, not go off cavorting amongst the Petty Kingdoms."

Charlaine chuckled. "Cavorting? You make it sound like a celebration. These are people whose best interest lies in hunting us down. They're not interested in having an actual discussion with us."

"I think it far worse than that. I suspect we won't be given the option of surrendering. They'll attack with the intent of killing us."

"A chilling scenario, but you've sized them up correctly. I might remind you, however, that we still have hundreds of miles to travel through potentially hostile lands to get to Hadenfeld. A particularly difficult thing to do, considering our lack of knowledge of the area. There's also the matter of feeding ten companies of Temple Knights. Even the most devout member of our order can't survive on an empty stomach."

35

ENCOUNTER

SPRING 1107 SR

Two days after their escape, Charlaine's lead riders returned with a report of a tributary of the Silver River that marked the border between Regensbach and Galoran. Unlike its larger cousin, this river was slow and relatively shallow, allowing a ford to be used instead of a bridge.

With her small army massed to the south, she had to choose where to march next. Their ultimate destination remained the same, but she must decide whether to reach Hadenfeld by travelling through Galoran and Ardosa or take the more direct route through Menzen.

"I say we go north," suggested Verushka. "Galoran has minimal Church presence."

"True," replied Charlaine, "but there's only one crossing into Ardosa. We'd be trapped if the Cunars got there before us."

"We could always head east and follow the Mathewites."

"Theirs is a relatively small party, whereas we would raise far too much attention from the local rulers. No, we must head west on this side of the border and hope to find an unguarded bridge leading into Menzen."

"You think that likely?" asked Verushka.

"Unfortunately, no. I suspect the Cunar Father General would've taken great pains to secure those, which will likely result in us having to march farther south to the border with Kingshaven."

"The longer we remain in Regensbach, the greater the likelihood they'll find us."

"We have little choice in the matter. Take the lead, Commander, and ensure you have riders out front. We're in hostile territory. The last thing I want is for our column to be surprised."

"Understood, General." Verushka rode off.

Charlaine urged Stormcloud onward, taking her past her Temple Knights resting on the road. She continued to the end of the line, finding Anthea and Magda formed up with the tenth company, which consisted of the newest Temple Knights. They'd all completed their training, but Charlaine knew from her own experience that most knights needed a first assignment to be seasoned, something these young women had been thrust into unexpectedly.

Anthea, the first to spot her, sat up in her saddle and greeted her with a nod.

"Good afternoon," said Charlaine. "I haven't had much of an opportunity to speak with you two since the gatehouse. How are you holding up?"

"As well as can be expected," replied Magda.

"What she means," added Anthea, "is our butts are sore from being in the saddle for two days straight."

"Give it some time," said Charlaine. "You'll get to the point where you don't even notice it anymore."

"Was it like this on your first assignment?"

"No. I was sent to a small outpost in the middle of nowhere. It was frantic at times, but I soon got used to it."

"Do you think we'll have to fight?" asked Magda.

"There's every likelihood, but the more experienced knights will look after things."

"We can fight," declared Anthea.

"I have no doubt you can," replied Charlaine, "but this isn't about going to battle; it's about building a future. To that end, you must follow the orders of your superiors and maintain your discipline."

"Is there a problem here, General?" Temple Captain Elliana rode over.

"Not at all, Captain. How are the new knights doing?"

"They are doing well, considering the circumstances, although I daresay there are a few who need to work on their horse-riding skills." She cast a glance at Magda, who suddenly began fiddling with her reins.

"They'll get there in time," Charlaine assured her. "I imagine many had never ridden before joining."

"That's true," said Elliana. "How did you know?"

"Most women who join the order are from families that can ill-afford the expense of a horse."

"Was that you?"

"No. I've been riding since before I could walk. It's a Calabrian tradition."

"Calabria?" said Anthea. "That fell to the empire, didn't it?"

"It did, and if you had any doubt about what it's like to live under Halvarian rule, let me reassure you, it's brutal."

"You've gone back?"

"Both Sister Danica and I visited, although we had to hide our status as Temple Knights while there. Suffice it to say we only survived because we had each other's backs, just as you must learn to protect your fellow sisters."

"Well said," added the Temple Captain.

"Now," said Charlaine, "you must excuse me. I have much to do." She urged Stormcloud on, riding towards the head of the column.

Verushka waited on the road, the column temporarily halted. As was the custom, the companies maintained a distance of fifty paces between them while on the move. When they'd caught up with the lead elements, however, they'd halted with a gap of only ten.

"Trouble?" called out Charlaine.

"Yes, General. My scouts report troops blocking the road ahead." She waited until Charlaine was beside her before continuing. "Over that rise stands a group of warriors bearing what I can only assume are the King of Regensbach's colours. They're certainly not Temple troops."

"How many?"

Verushka called over one of her knights. "Tell the general what you saw."

The woman removed her helmet to be better understood. "I estimate close to three hundred men, General. They're poorly armed, for the most part, with a small core of better-equipped individuals. They've spread themselves across the road at a point where there is a thick forest on either side, making it difficult to avoid them."

"Do we attack?" asked Verushka.

"Are they aware of our presence?" replied Charlaine.

"Not as yet. I have two more knights keeping an eye on them. They'll let us know of any further developments."

"Sister…?"

"Rhea, General."

"Sister Rhea, be so good as to ride to the centre of the column and fetch Temple Captain Nicola for me."

"Right away, General."

Verushka watched her head off. "She's good, that one, full of initiative. A rare find these days. It was her idea to remain hidden while observing the enemy."

"I shouldn't like to consider them enemies just yet," said Charlaine. "We may be able to negotiate our way past them."

"We outnumber them significantly, and our armour is far superior to theirs."

"True, but fighting the men of Regensbach will do nothing to convince them our intentions are peaceful."

"We could parade before them and let our strength convince them to withdraw."

"I'd prefer not to use the threat of force if at all possible. However, if there are no other options, I will consider it."

"Shall you parley with them yourself?"

"I will," replied Charlaine, "but not until I've had a chat with Temple Captain Nicola."

"To what end, General?"

"If my attempts at reasoning with them fail, I should like to have something else prepared."

They waited in silence until Temple Captain Nicola appeared, along with Sister Rhea and Teresa, who'd taken it upon herself to ride to the front of the column.

"Ah, there you are, Nicola," said Charlaine. "I have a favour to ask, something I thought you might like."

"Do tell," replied the Temple Captain.

"Just up there are three hundred of the King of Regensbach's men blocking the road, which isn't ideal, considering our current circumstances. I intend to speak to their commander and try reasoning with him, but in case something goes wrong, I want you nearby."

"Nearby being defined as?"

"Select a dozen knights and work your way through those woods"—Charlaine nodded her head towards a group of trees—"so you can come at them from behind if needed. A dozen Temple Knights might not be seen as much of a threat, but..."

Nicola smiled. "You want it to give the impression there are more of us."

"Precisely, but only if completely necessary. We'll fight these men if we have to, but I'd much prefer a peaceful solution."

"How long do we have to get into position?"

Charlaine glanced up at the sky. "Can you be there by mid-afternoon?"

"That's cutting it a little close," replied Nicola, "but we can manage it."

"Good. Select your knights and get into position. I'll move up to engage them in negotiation, but I'll give your people enough time to get in place."

The afternoon wore on while Charlaine waited.

"Are you certain this is a good idea?" asked Teresa. "Couldn't we ride around them?"

"We could if we were familiar with the area, but we're more likely to get lost if we leave the road, and there's no guarantee the terrain gets any better than those forests."

"Do you really believe Nicola can get past those trees without being seen?"

"Time to find out. Let's have a chat with our friends from Regensbach." She urged Stormcloud forward and then looked back. "Are you coming, or are you going to sit there waiting?"

"Oh, I'm coming. I wouldn't miss this for the world."

They rode on, cresting the hill to get a good view of the men blocking the road. No more than ten stood ready, but at the sight of the Agnesites, those lounging to one side rose to their feet and rushed to form a line.

"Not the most disciplined of warriors," noted Teresa.

"Yet they still block our way. Come. Let's find out what their commander has to say for himself."

They rode closer, giving the men ample time to straighten their line. A fellow on horseback sat behind them, his position in the saddle giving him a clear view of the two Temple Knights.

"Greetings. I am Charlaine deShandria, Temple General of Saint Agnes. To whom do I have the honour of addressing?"

The mounted fellow cleared his throat. "Captain Willoughby Stern, servant of his Most Illustrious Majesty, King Seberg the Fifth."

"Might I ask, Captain, why your men are blocking the road?"

"We have been ordered to deny access to a group of renegade Temple Knights, my lady."

"I am a general," said Charlaine, "and a member of a fighting order. As such, I should be addressed as simply 'general'."

"My apologies, General."

"These renegades you speak of, have you a description?"

"Unfortunately not. We deployed in a hurry, and the instructions were less than precise, without any explanation of why such folk were in the area to begin with. Can you shed some light on the situation?"

"There is, I think, a group of Temple Knights of Saint Cunar operating in the area. Could these be the renegades you mentioned?"

The fellow hesitated, clearly unsure of how to proceed.

"How long have you been here?" continued Charlaine.

"We arrived just before noon," replied Stern.

"Is it possible they may have passed by earlier this morning?"

"I didn't think to ask if the locals saw any horsemen earlier in the day."

She moved closer, halting only a few paces shy of the line of warriors. "Perhaps I might be of some assistance."

"In what way?"

"If you stood aside and let us through, we could proceed down this road. If there are indeed renegade Temple Knights behind you, wouldn't it be far better for us to engage them?"

"How many knights have you?"

"Ten full companies."

All colour fled from the captain's face. "I shall order the road cleared at once, General." As she was about to wheel about, he added, "A question, if I might?"

"Of course. What would you like to know?"

"These Cunars, any idea of their numbers?"

"I'm afraid I have no specifics, although I imagine their numbers would be similar to our own."

"Thank you for your candour. You have been of great assistance." He ordered his men off the road.

Charlaine rode back to Teresa's position. "Tell Verushka to advance the column. The king's men have deigned to clear the road for us."

"You lied to protect us?"

"No. I let him make his own conclusions. Everything I said was the honest truth; I just neglected to provide the full details. Now, go deliver the news to Verushka. I'll remain here and keep an eye on our new friends. I shouldn't like them to have a change of heart."

Teresa left Charlaine to watch over Captain Stern and his men. They had cleared the road long before her Temple Knights topped the hill, but there was always the danger they might realize these were the very renegades they waited for.

Verushka appeared, leading the first company. As if in response, Captain Stern rode over to Charlaine, although his demeanour offered no clue as to his mood.

"I must admit," he said, "this is the first time I've seen Temple Knights of Saint Agnes up close."

"And your opinion?"

"I don't claim to be an expert in such things, General, but it seems to me they'd be the equal of any order in the Petty Kingdoms. Why, the horses alone would be the envy of most knights."

"Our order takes pains to acquire only the best of mounts. Are you a knight yourself, Captain?"

"Me? No. I'm a carpenter by trade."

"That begs the question of why you're here."

"Yes. I suppose it would. To raise an army on short notice, the king saw fit to empower a local militia. I don't suppose it's different from all the other Petty Kingdoms, but I'm told what makes ours unique is his insistence on employing militia officers, of which I am one."

"That's not so strange," replied Charlaine. "My father fulfilled such a position."

"Really? I had no idea others did that." He shrugged his shoulders. "I suppose that's what comes of not travelling much. People like me have a limited view of the world. Have you travelled much?"

"I have." She paused as the first company rode past, nodding at their salute. "I spent my first assignment on the coast of the Shimmering Sea."

"That must've been quite the sight."

"It was, though we didn't have much time to appreciate it. Such is the life of a Temple Knight."

"You must've had quite the storied career to make the rank of general at so young an age."

"Are you trying to flirt with me, Captain? If so, I must warn you we Temple Knights take an oath to remain free of such commitments."

"Saints, no," he replied, his cheeks turning rosy. "I merely meant to say that, from what I've read, most generals are far older than you appear to be. If I've insulted you in any way, I deeply apologize."

"I take no offence. As far as I know, I am the youngest Temple General to serve in any of the fighting orders, although I can't admit to spending much time researching the accuracy of that statement." The conversation was starting to get uncomfortable, so she shifted the focus. "You say you're a carpenter. Do you belong to a guild?"

"I do. Why do you ask?"

"In my former life, I was a member of the smiths guild."

"You were? I had no idea women could become smiths. What made you give it up?"

She kept her eyes on the second company, now riding past. "The necessities of life. You seem like a decent fellow, Captain. Would you mind if I offered you some advice?"

"Not at all."

"Your superiors sent you here with very little in the way of proper instructions. The renegades you spoke of earlier are highly trained and well-equipped. I would hate to see the results should your men be forced to fight them. If I were you, I would consider withdrawing and returning home, or at the very least, sending word to your superiors and asking for clarification. One can hardly be expected to do one's duty under such circumstances."

"That is a most excellent idea, General. I shall do as you've suggested." She nodded once more as the third company rode past. "Now, you must excuse me, Captain. I have duties to attend to. May the Saints watch over you."

"And you," replied Stern.

Charlaine trotted Stormcloud out onto the road, taking up a position beside Temple Commander Ursula, who was following her company.

"Trouble?" the woman asked.

Charlaine smiled as the sun broke through the clouds. "Not today, thank the Saints."

36

THE RIVER

SUMMER 1107 SR

"I must say, this is most disappointing." Temple Commander Amalia stared down at the Silver River, careful not to step too close to the steep cliff face.

"It's still running so fast," noted Charlaine. "I was hoping this far south, we'd find a place to cross."

"Perhaps there's a bridge nearby?"

Charlaine shook her head. "It appears we cannot cross into Menzen, which forces us to remain here, in Regensbach. I'm not ready to give up just yet, so we'll continue south in hopes of finding a ford or bridge. Are any of our knights from this area?"

"I don't know," replied Amalia, "but I can ask around."

"Do so, and if you find someone, bring them to me. It could well mark the difference between success and failure." Charlaine moved closer to the cliff, peering at the rubble down by its base. Even if they wanted to try crossing the river, there was no way they could get their horses down there.

She wandered back to the camp, taking her time in an attempt to organize her thoughts. It had been days since their escape, and with summer finally here, their thirst would only increase.

She was starting to think it had been sheer folly to escape the Antonine. Had they remained, the order would've been disbanded, but all these women would at least still be safe. With the prospect of starvation hanging over their heads, she had to seriously consider whether she'd made the right choice.

A young knight timidly approached. Charlaine halted, watching the woman gather her courage to speak.

"You wanted to see me, General?"

"Sister Genevieve, isn't it?"

"It is."

"What can I do for you, Sister?"

"I was told you're looking for someone familiar with the area."

"That I am," replied Charlaine. "Are you from this part of Regensbach?"

"I was born in the village of Silver Vale."

"Is that close?"

"Close enough. A few days to the south. It sits astride this very river, hence the name."

"Are there any fords or bridges nearby?"

"There's a ferry south of us, but other than the bridge in our village that leads to Kingshaven, you'd have to go all the way to the border with Amaria."

"A ferry, you say? Could we use that to cross into Menzen?"

"I doubt it. The ferry is small, barely large enough to take a farmer's cart. Warhorses like ours could only cross two at a time."

"I find that very disappointing, as Amalia is wont to say. What's on the other side of the river hereabouts?"

"Mostly wilderness."

"Yet someone built a ferry here. There must be a reason why?"

"Those on the Menzen side are closer to Silver Vale than any of their own villages. At least that's what I've been told."

"Have you ever been to Kingshaven?"

"Yes, many times. It sits across the bridge from Silver Vale, although I wouldn't claim to be an expert on it. Why?"

"It's a little difficult to plan a route to Hadenfeld when I don't have a map of the region. How many people live in Silver Vale?"

"No more than a hundred, assuming you count the farmers living on the outskirts."

"Is there a garrison there?"

"There used to be a small contingent of king's men to enforce trade regulations, but other than that, no."

Charlaine absently rubbed her chin. "If that's the only way across, they'll be expecting us. We'd likely arrive to find Cunars waiting there."

Genevieve shrugged her shoulders. "There's little choice if you want to head west. You could go all the way to the border with Amaria, but that won't get us to Hadenfeld."

"Then we shall cross at Silver Vale. Fetch Temple Captain Nicola, will you? And make sure you return with her. She'll likely have more questions for you."

"For me?"

"You did say you were from the area."

"Yes, General. Right away." She ran off as if the very legions of the Underworld nipped at her heels.

Charlaine sought out a stick, then walked over to a bare patch of dirt and began sketching out a rough map, which is where Temple Captain Nicola found her.

"You wanted me, General?"

"Yes. I know we didn't end up using you back when we encountered those men of Regensbach, but the tactic was sound."

"And?"

"I thought we might try it again, though with an added twist this time around." She nodded at the ground, pointing as she talked. "We are here, with the Silver River running to the west. There's a ferry up ahead, but it's much too small for the entire army to cross over on."

"Let me guess," said Nicola. "You want my group to cross there and parallel you on the other side of the river."

"That's the general idea, yes, though I have no idea if there'll be any roads for you to use. Your objective will be to reach the outskirts of the village of Silver Vale, which should lie somewhere down here." She poked with the stick. "Sister Genevieve is from there and tells me a small detachment guards the bridge."

"Word of our escape would've reached them by now, likely along with a considerable increase in the garrison."

"That was my thought as well," replied Charlaine. "I'm hoping your presence on the other side of the river might give them the impression that many of us have already crossed. I know it's a gamble, but anything you can do to weaken their defence of that bridge will be of immeasurable help."

"You can count on me, General."

"I was hoping you'd say that."

"How far to this ferry?"

Charlaine nodded at Genevieve.

"Two days," the knight replied, "perhaps a little less if you keep a steady pace."

"And Silver Vale?" asked Nicola.

"On this side of the river, a further day. I cannot speak for the western bank."

"We shall be on our way before nightfall, General."

"Once you arrive," said Charlaine, "remain out of sight. You'll know when we've been sighted, but until then, I don't want you putting your people in danger."

"Understood."

"Genevieve, you'll ride alongside me for the next couple of days. Your knowledge of the area may prove decisive."

After a hunger-ridden three-day march, the main complement of Temple Knights rested while Charlaine lay on a hilltop alongside Teresa and Genevieve.

"That's the Temple of Saint Mathew," said the young knight. "They ring the bell at noon, three, and then again at nightfall."

"A strange custom," noted Teresa. "Might I ask why?"

"Noon, so the workers out in the fields know it's time to eat."

"And at three to tell them it's time for a rest?"

"Yes, Captain."

"Any Temple Knights there?"

"No. Only lay brothers and a Holy Father."

Teresa looked through squinted eyes. "All I see is a lot of men in grey. It appears the Cunars beat us here, General."

"That's to be expected," replied Charlaine.

"How long until Nicola is in position?"

"If the terrain on the other side of the river is any indication, I'd say another day, possibly even two."

"It would help if we knew how many knights they had down there."

"I could go into the village and find out," offered Genevieve. "I'd have to wear the clothes of a commoner, but that shouldn't be too hard to arrange."

"Really?" said Teresa. "Did I miss a dressmaker's shop somewhere?"

The young knight chuckled. "There are several farms in the area where I can arrange to borrow some clothes."

"Do it," said Charlaine, "but don't take any chances. If you're discovered, they'll lock you up. Your presence would also serve to put them on alert, making our job even more difficult."

"I know the innkeeper, and I've yet to see a knight who didn't partake of the odd drink or two. If there's news to be had, that's where it'll be found."

"I don't like the idea of you going in there alone."

"I'll go with her," offered Teresa.

"Are you certain?"

"You can't go. You're needed back here to keep an eye on the army."

"And if they discover you're not locals?"

"I doubt a group of Cunars will know everyone from the village. They take a vow of celibacy, remember? That means they'll be actively avoiding women. Besides, if we do get into trouble, I can use my magic to extricate us."

"By healing your way out of the village?"

Teresa barked out a laugh. "Is that all you think a Life Mage can do? Trust me, I have all sorts of spells at my beck and call."

Charlaine spent most of the day watching over Silver Vale. The villagers went about their business, ignoring the Cunars, while the grey-clad Temple Knights practiced fighting in the field to the east. Everything looked so peaceful, Charlaine began to worry if Teresa and Genevieve had even made it as far as the inn.

The waiting, at least, gave her time to consider her options. The village was her ultimate goal; seize that, and they could use the bridge unimpeded. She only needed a way to neutralize the Cunars. A direct attack was an option, but the strength of her command lay in mounted troops. The Cunars could easily make the houses in Silver Vale into fortifications, requiring her knights to go in on foot.

From her viewpoint, it appeared the Cunars had a couple of companies, more than enough to defend the village should it come to that. Her best choice was to wait, hoping Nicola would arrive soon and draw some of the Cunars west into Kingshaven, weakening their garrison. Could Charlaine do something similar on the eastern side of the river?

She had a core of experienced knights, but the majority of her command were new to the order, having only completed their training before they escaped from the Antonine. It was too much to ask them to ride into battle without a little more seasoning.

Temple Commander Ursula moved up to stand beside her general. "Quite the view from up here."

Charlaine welcomed the interruption. "Yes. It gives us a clear view of the entire village."

"Have there been any developments?"

"There's no sign that they've discovered our people, if that's what you're asking."

"You should get back to the camp, General. Your presence has been requested."

"By whom?"

Ursula hesitated, an action that didn't go unnoticed.

"Out with it," urged Charlaine.

"Some of our newer commanders are nervous. They're afraid the longer we remain in place, the greater the likelihood we'll be discovered."

"They're not wrong."

"True, but without guidance, their fear grows unabated."

Charlaine was about to respond when movement caught her eye. Two women were making their way out of the village, heading east. She smiled, knowing she would soon have the information she needed. "Call for a meeting of the Temple Commanders and assure them we have things well in hand."

"Do we have things in hand?"

"Yes. Why? Does that surprise you?"

"To be perfectly honest, yes. Would you care to explain what our strategy is?"

Charlaine smiled. "Not yet, Ursula. You'll have to wait until all the commanders are assembled. In the meantime, go and fetch Temple Captain Mila. I need someone here watching the village while the rest of us prepare."

"Yes, General."

An out-of-breath Teresa entered the camp with Genevieve at her side, the younger knight acting like she had been out for a casual stroll as she announced their findings. "We know their numbers," she said, her excitement adding strength to her words. "There are three companies stationed in Silver Vale."

"Three experienced companies," added the Life Mage. "All under the leadership of a Temple Commander by the name of Quintilius. Have you heard of him?"

"I can't say that I have," replied Charlaine. "Is he from Thalemia, by chance?"

"He is. How did you know?"

"Centuries ago, Thalemia was a great maritime rival to Calabria. My father used to mock them to no end, claiming their names were too grandiose."

"This Thalamite sounds like he has some experience under his belt," said Teresa. "There are even rumours he served at Alantra aboard one of the Holy Fleet's ships."

"Not the flagship, I hope?"

"I couldn't say. That wasn't the type of thing we could bring up in conversation without raising suspicion. Still, it proves he's seen battle."

"That works against us, but we'll have to take that in stride."

"I know that look," said Teresa. "You have a plan."

"I do. Now, let's go and talk to the commanders, shall we? It's time we begin making preparations."

"Preparations?"

"We can't just saunter in and throw our weight around. What would Saint Agnes think?"

The Temple Commanders stood, staring at Charlaine expectantly. She'd addressed knights on many occasions, but this time, she saw their fear threatening to break through.

"I have a plan," she began, "but it has an element of risk. As you no doubt realize, we cannot remain here for long, or else the enemy will learn of our location. To that end, I mean to seize that bridge."

"A direct attack?" said Amalia. "Are you certain that's wise? We'd have to dismount."

"You're correct. We'd have to fight on foot, which is not the best use of our strength. That's why I intend to lure the Cunars away from the village. Now, before you start asking questions, let me continue."

She took a breath, trying to calm her nerves. "Teresa and Genevieve have provided us with an accurate account of the enemy's numbers, as well as an assessment of their capabilities. The garrison is close to a hundred and fifty in strength and led by an experienced commander, so when it comes down to the actual fighting, we need to concentrate our numbers whenever possible."

"For this to work," continued Charlaine, "Temple Captain Nicola needs to be in place, so I want someone down at the riverbank, watching for any sign of her."

"Excuse my ignorance," said Gerda, "but how will we see her if she's meant to stay hidden?"

"Nicola knows what's at stake here. She'll send someone down to the riverbank on their side to attempt to signal us. Once they've told us they're ready, things will develop quickly, so listen carefully."

She paused, ensuring she had everyone's rapt attention. "The plan calls for our two most experienced companies to make a demonstration east of the village, then flee south, down the road. Hopefully, the Cunars will follow, stripping Silver Vale of all but a token garrison, and that's where Nicola comes in. She'll lure the defenders to the western end of the bridge by making her presence known. Once they've done that, the remainder of our army will ride into the village. With a bit of luck, we'll surround them and avoid a lot of bloodshed. If not, we'll have to overwhelm them with numbers."

Temple Commander Katinka cleared her throat. "With all due respect, General, how do we know the bulk of the garrison will take the bait? Wouldn't it make more sense for them to remain in the village?"

"It would, indeed," replied Charlaine, "but the Cunars are a proud order, consisting of men who were trained as knights long before they became Temple Knights. I think they'll see our presence as an affront to the Church and react accordingly." She smiled. "They also believe themselves superior to us in every respect, so I doubt they'll hesitate, and therein may lie a problem. If they are too ardent in their pursuit, it might lead to actual fighting."

"Could we not send more companies to help? Two seems an awfully small contingent."

"Perhaps, but if we send too many, it may not have the desired effect. Even the most impassioned Cunar won't go chasing after the enemy if they're at risk of being outnumbered. The man in charge, Temple Commander Quintillius, has seen battle, so we can expect him to be cautious."

"These companies who'll be luring them away," said Katinka, "how are they to get across?"

"They'll take a circuitous route, doubling back to the bridge after the rest of us cross. I'll admit it's risky, but if we don't get across that river in a timely manner, our pursuers will catch up to us."

"Who will lead that group?"

"I volunteer," said Verushka. "And I'd like Katinka's company, if there's no objection."

"Might I suggest a third?" added Scyllia. "Not to lure them away, but to lie in wait, in case they're needed?"

"Very well," said Charlaine. She looked around, taking in their faces, knowing this might be the last time she saw some of them. "See to your companies, Sisters. We ride to battle!"

37

SILVER VALE

SUMMER 1107 SR

Upon confirmation that Nicola was in position, the small Agnesite contingent set out, riding east to avoid detection by the garrison at Silver Vale. They then turned south, travelling for some time before cutting west to pick up the road that led them back to the village.

Charlaine rode at the head of her knights, Verushka's company behind her, followed by that of Katinka's. They approached at a trot, wary lest the Cunars rush to the attack. Charlaine slowed as the first challenge came, halting Stormcloud a few paces farther on, where she could be sure of being heard.

Cunar Temple Knights scurried around the village, rushing to don their armour. Those on duty manned the crude defences, a row of boxes and barrels, along with an overturned cart. Charlaine smiled, for the Temple Knights of Saint Cunar shunned the use of missile weapons, considering them cowardly, which meant she could remain where she was free from the dangers of a crossbow bolt.

"Who commands here?" Charlaine called out. She knew the answer, but to betray that knowledge would give away that she'd sent someone in amidst them.

"My Lord, Temple Commander Quintillius," came the reply. The knights took to talking amongst themselves, Charlaine's sudden appearance being the most likely subject of their discourse.

"Then fetch him so that he and I might parley."

"Oh yes? And who do you think you are?"

"I am Charlaine deShandria, Temple General of Saint Agnes."

The knights behind the speaker raised their voices in concern. Unlike the men of Regensbach, these warriors knew the whole story.

"You are ordered to surrender yourself in the name of the Primus."

"Such matters are best discussed with those in charge. Now fetch your commander."

A heated argument arose amongst the defenders, and then one stomped off towards the inn.

The first speaker continued talking to her. "I suggest you lay down your arms, General, while we're in a mood to take prisoners."

"Tell me, Sir Knight. Is it the practice in your order to speak thus to a superior officer?"

He did not reply, and then all those around him quieted. Charlaine couldn't figure out why until she heard Verushka's company coming to a halt several paces behind her. Some of the Cunars pointed while others drew their swords, although there was plenty of time for the rest to prepare should the sisters advance.

The Cunar Temple Commander exited the inn, the gold lace on his surcoat glittering in the noonday sun. He advanced on the barricade, but instead of standing behind it, he climbed onto a barrel to make himself more visible. Words were exchanged with one of his men, obviously getting caught up in the situation, then he turned to face Charlaine.

"Good morning, General," he said at last. "I hear you came to discuss the matter of surrender?"

"I have indeed," she replied, "but any discussion on that matter would require addressing the fate of prisoners."

"I assure you that your fellow sisters will be clapped in irons and taken to rot in the dungeons of the Antonine. You, on the other hand, will be hanged before the Council of Peers as an example."

"I'm impressed. You have a vivid imagination, but I'm afraid you've mistaken my intent. I am not here to discuss our surrender; I am here to discuss your own capitulation."

"Are you, now? And what, might I ask, could we expect of you in terms of treatment, should we agree?"

"Your men will be disarmed and stripped of their armour."

"And then?"

"Then they would be expected to march back to the Antonine."

He laughed. "You accuse me of having a vivid imagination, but yours is clearly far superior. Why in the name of the Saints would I surrender to you?"

"My two companies of Temple Knights are ready to attack."

"And I have three and hold a fortified position. It may not look like much, I grant you, but we are more than capable of standing our ground."

Charlaine noted the horsemen assembling in the centre of the village. They would ride out soon, and she must be ready to give the impression of a panicked flight.

"I assume you do not intend to abandon the village?"

"That would be correct."

She smiled, an act that appeared to annoy him. "Then I wish the joy of the day to you, Commander." She turned around, riding back to Verushka's company.

"That was it?" asked Verushka. "I was expecting a response."

"And you shall have it," replied Charlaine. "They intend to pursue. Did you not notice the knights forming up in the village?"

"I must confess my attention was elsewhere. What's our next step?"

"We withdraw, as planned, and head south."

"At a gallop?"

"No, a trot. We don't want to lose our pursuers."

The second company, under Katinka, wheeled about, now leading the retreat while Verushka's followed along behind. Charlaine remained at the rear, glancing back from time to time for signs of pursuit.

Someone blew a horn off in the distance, the familiar sound calling on the Temple Knights of Saint Cunar to prepare to advance. It was the first command that all the fighting orders taught, and it revealed to Charlaine that their enemy was not charging recklessly in pursuit. Instead, they would follow at a more sedate pace, likely until they found terrain more favourable to a charge.

She spurred on Stormcloud and galloped to the head of the column. "Keep up the current pace," she said to Katinka. "I'll ride ahead and ensure Scyllia is in position."

With a nod from the Temple Commander, Charlaine went tearing down the road, giving Stormcloud a chance to show off the speed her breed was known for.

Under the command of Temple Commander Scyllia, the third company had taken up a position to the east of the road, the west being occupied by the Silver River. The terrain sloped up as it drew farther from the riverbank, offering Scyllia's company a place to conceal themselves from the approaching Cunars.

Charlaine joined them, slowing her horse as she drew closer. "They're coming," she said. "You know what to do?"

"Fear not, General. My knights will do their part."

"Then may the blessings of Saint Agnes guide you." With that, Charlaine turned around, heading for the road.

Katinka's company appeared, riding in a tight column. As they advanced, their commander raised her sword, waved it around, then used it to point eastward. The riders dutifully changed course, leading the column onto a flat area.

Charlaine found herself sweating, not due to the heat but because of nervousness. Luring the Cunars away had not been without risk, and she chided herself for not counting their numbers. Now, all she could do was wait to see if her strategy would prove successful or if it would be a costly blunder.

She'd first led others in Ilea, then honed her leadership skills in Reinwick before defeating the Halvarians in Arnsfeld, but this somehow felt different. When she defeated the empire, she'd commanded an army, including horse, foot, and bow. Their opponent had been disciplined, which had been evident from the start, but she'd trusted in her training to see her through to victory. Here, she faced men who'd trained all their lives to fight on horseback, led by a commander experienced in the very same tactics as herself.

The second company broke left, then turned around, facing north, creating a line of riders ready for the enemy. The company under Verushka's command filed to the west, taking up a position between the already formed Agnes knights and the river. It was a bold move to wait for the enemy to ride straight into them, as the Cunars excelled at charges.

The Temple Knights of Saint Agnes completed their manoeuvres and then waited. Charlaine heard the enemy before she saw them, for the road, like the river it paralleled, often twisted as it made its way south.

The lead riders finally came into view with their commander out front, giving orders. She couldn't hear his exact commands, but the results were obvious. The Cunars spread out on either side, forming a double line of battle, indicating their intention to engage in a charge, but then again, what else could they do?

A sense of calm swept over Charlaine. The enemy had come and done precisely what she'd hoped. Now, it all came down to timing. Her gaze flicked east to the hill, but Scyllia had seen fit to keep her knights hidden. Doubtless, someone was up there keeping an eye on things, ready to signal when the timing was right, but that was beyond Charlaine's control.

The Cunars took a moment to dress their ranks before they advanced in a classic approach, beginning with a trot, then increasing in speed as they drew closer to their target. One hundred grey-clad Temple Knights advanced on them, confident that though their numbers were equal, their experience and training would prove superior.

They reached the halfway point, keeping the pace deliberately slow. This was where they would speed up, the horses' hooves becoming a wave of thunder, drowning out any chance of giving orders. They were the might of Saint Cunar, the finest warriors of the Holy Army, ready to destroy their enemies!

Scyllia's knights crested the top of the hill unnoticed. Although it wasn't a steep slope, the rise just enough to hide their presence, they broke into a gallop as they made their descent, for the Agnesites needed to make contact with their adversaries before they realized they'd been flanked.

Hidden by the noise of the Cunars' own charge, the attack took them entirely by surprise. Charlaine waited until the moment of impact to sweep her sword down, the signal to advance. A hundred sister knights moved as one, increasing their pace, not quite reaching a full gallop before they hit the front ranks of Cunars.

Finding themselves attacked, the rear line of the Temple Knights of Saint Cunar abandoned their charge, turning their horses to engage the new threat. As highly disciplined warriors, they might've won had the front line not already closed range with Charlaine's forces.

The battle quickly deteriorated into a series of individual melees. The Cunars fought with a vicious ferocity, but the Agnesites were trained to work in teams rather than as individuals, and their numerical superiority began to take its toll on the Cunars.

Charlaine found herself embroiled in a gigantic brawl, swords doing little against plate armour. It became a test of stamina to see who could wear down their foe's strength first. She fought defensively, using her shield and saving her strength for later when it could be put to greater use. All around her, her fellow sister knights did the same, knowing this was a test of endurance rather than strength.

Knights went down on both sides, some merely unhorsed, others knocked senseless from repeated blows to the head. Cunars bred large horses to put weight behind their charges, but these same mounts tired quickly in the heat of the summer and the exertion of battle.

As the power of Charlaine's opponent's blows weakened, she recognized her chance, attacking with a renewed vigour, smashing her sword repeatedly into his shield and buckling it. He tried to strike back, but as their swords met, his snapped in two while Charlaine continued on, smashing against the side of his head. He tossed aside his broken weapon, holding his hands up in surrender.

All around her, others did the same. She struggled to understand why, then spied the body of Temple Commander Quintillius lying on the ground, his armour bearing witness to his fate—trampled by iron-shod hooves.

A grey-clad Temple Captain approached her, his helmet discarded, his sword held out, hilt first. "We surrender," he declared, "trusting to the Saints that we shall be treated with honour." He paused, struggling to catch his breath. "You fought well, General. I commend you on the quality of your knights."

"We fought because we had to, Captain."

"And we fought because the Temple Commander ordered it. With his death, command now falls to me, and I shall not continue with this madness."

"Madness?" said Charlaine.

"Is it not the very definition of insanity to fight amongst ourselves when the entire Continent is at risk? We should be fighting the Halvarians, not a fellow order."

"I couldn't agree more."

"You have our surrender. What will you do with us?"

"You shall surrender your weapons. I must also insist you and your men take an oath not to attack any member of our order in future."

"And that is all?"

"Your weapons and horses will be left in Silver Vale. You may collect them there once you've walked all the way back to the village."

"There is still a garrison there," warned the captain. "Unfortunately, they will not let you pass unscathed, and you cannot use the same trick there as you did here."

"Nor would I want to," replied Charlaine. "Order your men to dismount and surrender their weapons."

"Of course, General."

Charlaine remained off to one side as the weapons were collected. Katinka oversaw the entire affair, her knights carrying the blades off to the side of the road where they were stacked like so much kindling.

Verushka made her way over to Charlaine. "It worked," she said.

"Did you doubt it would?"

A wry smile crossed the Temple Commander's lips. "I must admit I had some reservations. Individually, the Cunars are the best warriors on the Continent."

"That's what they always tell us," replied Charlaine.

"You don't agree?"

"They were defeated in the east despite their reputation for ferocity. I suspect the influence of the empire has somewhat diminished their effectiveness."

"Perhaps, but they're still Temple Knights."

"Temple knights, who, by their own admission, failed to intervene in any struggles within the Petty Kingdoms save for their own crusades. From whence stems their reputation?"

"Are you suggesting they've become less effective?"

"Complacent might be a better description. For decades, they've fed off their reputations, but aside from the Holy Fleet, when was the last time they distinguished themselves in battle? We, on the other hand, fought the empire on three separate occasions, although there were only a few of us at Alantra. Make no mistake, Verushka, they're stronger than us physically, but they have become so enamoured of their renown that they forgot how to fight effectively."

"So now they're weak?"

"Individually, no, but I fear the rot plaguing their order has led to their senior officers being selected for their loyalty rather than their abilities."

"You mean loyalty to the Primus?"

"Precisely. We know the depth of his treachery, but up until now, I didn't realize how far his reach extended. He's cleaned out any senior officers resistant to his ideas, hence the demotion of Admiral Marius to the rank of Temple Commander. And let's not forget his cohort in crime, Father General Gilbert, who, even now, is systematically destroying what remains of the Holy Fleet."

"True," said Katinka, "not to mention how he's destroyed the rest of the fighting orders."

"Not quite destroyed," replied Charlaine. "We Agnesites haven't been crushed, and some of the Mathewites seek places of haven."

"And the others?"

"I have no doubt the Ragnarites will continue their work, driven underground by the need for secrecy. I assume they will be ignored, for they pose no military threat to the Halvarian Empire."

"And the Ansgarites?"

"I fear they are gone, for what need has the Church for their services now that the other orders are disbanded? The Cunars stand as the sole fighting order of the Church, just the sort of thing the enemy needs to ensure they don't interfere in the next invasion."

"Saints save us."

"It won't be the Saints who save us; it will be people like us who are willing to put their lives at risk for others."

It took some time to distribute the Cunar weapons amongst the Agne-sites, and then the three companies under Charlaine's command rode north, leading the Cunars' horses by their reins.

The battle had not been without its losses, for three sisters had perished, with another ten wounded, but she had hopes Teresa's magic could help the latter. She must now put the fight behind her and concentrate on the next step: seizing control of the village of Silver Vale.

38

THE BRIDGE

SUMMER 1107 SR

The people of Silver Vale went about their business in the hot afternoon sun despite the region's politics. The presence of grey-clad knights was the only indication that anything was out of the ordinary.

Charlaine had returned to the rest of her army halfway through the afternoon and now stood watching the distant village, waiting for Nicola to make her move. Behind her, the Agnesite army was poised within easy call, ready to descend on the place. To ensure success, she waited for the diversion that would draw the defenders westward towards the bridge that crossed into Kingshaven.

Her strategy was designed to minimize danger to the villagers by drawing the remaining Cunars to one location. Then, the Agnesite Temple Knights would attack from horseback, giving them a tactical advantage. It was a gamble, for the Cunars might remain mounted, but defending a bridge is much easier when afoot, especially if one can take cover behind a barricade. Fortunately for her, the barricade faced the wrong direction to protect the Cunars from them, something she intended to take full advantage of.

Charlaine's eyes started to droop and then snapped open as she spotted movement off to the west on the far side of the river. She thought at first she was mistaken, but then a group of Agnesites emerged from the trees, heading straight for the western end of the bridge.

Shouts of alarm rang out as the Temple Knights of Saint Cunar rushed to take up positions behind a series of crates and barrels. It was much the same strategy they'd used on Charlaine's first encounter with them, but this time, they only needed to protect the narrow end of the bridge.

Nicola halted, exchanging words with the defenders. Charlaine half expected the Cunars to mount up and chase after the scarlet-clad sisters, but whoever was in charge down there appeared hesitant to take action.

It dawned on Charlaine that Nicola's numbers worked against her, for a dozen knights might be powerful when employed against untrained warriors, but they did not pose much in the way of a threat to these Temple Knights of Saint Cunar.

Nicola rode back to her small command, remaining for a moment, likely discussing this turn of events, and then the entire group turned around and rode westward, deeper into Kingshaven.

The Cunar captain remained at his post. After Nicola's retreat, he'd sent a runner back into the village, disappearing near a larger residence. Charlaine stared a moment longer, trying to decide if this was the time to react, and then a group of mounted knights rode out from where they'd been hidden behind a building. The Cunars had taken the bait after all!

She counted ten knights riding in a two-wide column, trotting towards the bridge. As they grew closer, those on foot moved barrels aside, opening a gap in their makeshift defences through which their comrades rode.

Knowing her command needed time to ride from their encampment to the village, Charlaine waited, silently counting to a hundred. She needed to be sure the Cunars crossing the bridge were far enough away so they wouldn't abandon the pursuit if they heard the village was in danger.

When she determined the time was right, she rose, rushing back towards the camp, where Teresa sat on her horse, Stormcloud's reins in hand. Charlaine mounted in one smooth motion, then drew her sword and pumped it into the air, the signal to attack. The column advanced, moving at the trot, continuing at this pace until the village came into sight. As they reached the edge of the village, the knights split into smaller groups, heading to secure any houses the Cunars might otherwise attempt to fortify.

The buildings obscured their sight of the bridge, but Charlaine pressed on, knowing the Cunars had no more than forty men remaining.

She rode with Ursula's company directly through the village towards the bridge. The defenders came into view, their backs towards the Agnesites. One Cunar knight turned, calling out a word of warning, but it was too late. The Temple Knights of Saint Agnes were amongst them, using the weight of their horses to force the grey-clad knights into isolated pockets of resistance.

The Cunars put up a valiant defence but were unable to form disciplined ranks, succumbing to the superior numbers of the Agnesites. Charlaine sought out the Cunar captain but saw no sign of him. She spotted Ursula, who'd led the charge on the bridge and rode over.

"Have you seen their captain?" she called out.

"He was ordering his men into line when we struck, but I've not seen him since."

"I have," called out Anthea. "He's over there." She pointed to the north.

"I don't see him," said Charlaine.

"Our horses forced him back, and he went over the edge of the bridge into the water. I suspect his armour would've dragged him down to the bottom." She shivered. "What a horrible way to die."

"The only nice way to die is in bed at the end of a long and rewarding life."

Anthea moved to the foot of the bridge, peering into the river. "It looks deep here. Still, I can't say I'm sorry. At least his death put an end to the Cunars' defiance. They surrendered soon after."

"Speaking of which," said Ursula. "What do we do with the prisoners?"

"Divest them of their arms and armour," replied Charlaine. "We'll lock them up in the Temple of Saint Mathew for now and post a guard on them. Where's Amalia?"

"Over here, General." The Temple Commander drew closer. "My company are unscathed, and the village is secure."

"Glad to hear it. I'd like you to ride over to the west end of the bridge and secure it. There are still ten Cunars out there chasing down Temple Captain Nicola, and they'll soon grow tired of the pursuit. When they decide it's time to return, I want them to realize there's no point in attacking."

"Yes, General."

"You have company," said Ursula. She nodded back towards the village, where a delegation of villagers approached, leading a wagon.

Charlaine dismounted, handing Stormcloud's reins off to a waiting Temple Knight. "We mean you no harm," she said, moving closer. "Our dispute is with the Temple Knights of Saint Cunar, not you."

"That we understand," replied their leader, a man dressed in brown robes.

"You're a Holy Father?" she asked.

"That I am. Father Reamon, at your service."

"I'm surprised you would say that, considering all that's happened these last few weeks. Are you familiar with our falling out with the Church?"

"I am, as is my flock, but that doesn't change the essence of who you are and what you do, does it?"

"No," said Charlaine. "Not in the slightest."

"Then all is as it should be."

"Might I ask what you carry in that wagon?"

"Food," replied Reamon. "Donations from the village to feed your knights. You have a long trip ahead of you and will require sustenance."

"What would you know of our trip?"

"Only that you seek to flee the Antonine, or rather the forces sent to arrest you." He smiled. "The people hereabouts might be rustic, but they're not ignorant of what has happened, particularly as the Cunars proved so eloquent in cursing your order. The townsfolk welcome your success, General, and wish you well; hence, the food."

"I'm afraid you're not free of the Cunars just yet. The hundred who left earlier today will return, though it'll be some time before they arrive. Others will come in greater numbers, determined to chase us down."

"They'll get no help from us."

"I don't doubt it for a moment," replied Charlaine, "but if they suspect you aided us, your people could be treated harshly."

"That is our burden to bear, not yours."

"We've stripped the prisoners of their weapons and armour, but I'm afraid I shall have to ask you to lock them up in your temple, at least for the short term. You can release them once we're out of sight."

"There was a rumour amongst the Cunars that the Holy Army was nearby, and they will not be so easily persuaded to leave you alone."

"I know. Though it pains me to say, we'll be destroying the bridge. It's the only way to guarantee we won't be followed."

"It is a sturdy construction," warned Reamon.

"Yes, which is why we'll have to burn it. To that end, I ask your people to turn over any pitch or tar they might have at hand."

"I shall have them gather it at once. I assume you'll be leaving us soon?"

"Yes," said Charlaine. "My Temple Knights will begin crossing immediately. Once the last of us is across, we'll set the bridge ablaze. I advise you to keep your people well back from the fire, and you might also want to evacuate those buildings nearby in case stray embers set fire to their roofs. It is not my intent to cause undue hardship, but fire can be fickle, and I'd hate to see anyone injured."

"You are most gracious, General." He glanced back at the wagon. "Will you take the food?"

"Yes, but not the wagon. It would prove difficult should we find ourselves needing to avoid the roads. I'll distribute the food amongst our knights instead."

"Then allow me to volunteer to hand it out on your behalf. It will serve to speed you on your way. Not that we don't appreciate your presence, but as you said earlier, the Cunars are bound to reappear at some point."

"Thank you, Father Reamon. May Saint Mathew look kindly upon you."

"And you, General."

Nicola returned as the last of the Temple Knights crossed the bridge and immediately reported to Charlaine.

"You managed to avoid the Cunars chasing after you?"

"We did, though they proved most stubborn in their efforts." She waved her hand westward. "They're back there, somewhere, meandering around the thickest part of the woods. I doubt they'll trouble us anymore, not when we have a whole army at our beck and call."

"You've done well, Captain," said Charlaine. "Now, I need you to lead the column."

"Why? Where are you going?"

"Don't worry. I'll be along shortly, but I must remain here to see to the destruction of the bridge. And yes, before you ask, I've selected a suitable group of knights to keep me safe."

"Good," said Nicola, "because I have no clue where we're going."

"Yes, you do—to Hadenfeld."

"I'm fully aware of that, General, but that's a far cry from knowing how to get there."

"Head west. Sooner or later, you'll hit the river that forms the border. This road heads in the general direction, and I'll catch up to you long before you run out of road."

"I'll lead, although I'm curious why you want me, a simple Temple Captain when you've got so many Temple Commanders close by."

"I trust you, Nicola. And more importantly, I know I can depend on you. That's not to say I can't trust my commanders, but their hands are full taking care of their companies. Now, head to the front of the column and have Teresa give you something to eat."

"Are you suggesting we actually have food?"

"Yes," replied Charlaine. "Compliments of the villagers of Silver Vale. It won't last all the way till Hadenfeld, but we won't starve in the next few days."

She turned, watching Anthea and Magda pour the last remaining oil onto the heap of combustibles on the bridge. The hope was that the fire would catch hold of the wooden planks, turning the entire thing to ash, but Charlaine had to admit she was no expert in such things. Had she the time, she would've considered taking axes to it, but with the Cunars due to return soon, she didn't want to risk being caught before they completed the job.

She called the knights over, taking a lit torch from Mariele, who'd been waiting for just this opportunity. The young woman looked disappointed that she would not be lighting the fire, but Charlaine felt it more appropriate for her to perform the task herself.

Her thoughts drifted to what had brought her here. Could she have done something different to avoid this fate? Had her actions ten years ago doomed the order, or was the forcible disbanding of the Temple Knights a foregone conclusion? She shook her head. No, she knew there was nothing more she could've done, yet it still pained her to think of all the suffering this entire situation would bring to women across the Petty Kingdoms.

Charlaine struggled to settle her thoughts. Doubtless, a small handful of kingdoms would still welcome their order, but discovering which would be difficult. The truth of the matter was she didn't even know if they'd be welcome in Hadenfeld. She certainly hoped they would, but Ludwig was now a king and must base his decisions on the welfare of his people. It might be better for him to apologize to the Church and beg for forgiveness rather than remain as a kingdom they openly spurned.

Even as the thoughts came to her, Charlaine knew them to be false. Ludwig was a man of honour who'd made the right decision when he refused to let the Cunars build a commandery within the borders of Hadenfeld. He would not apologize to the Church. He would stand up for what was right and just.

She'd loved him once and still did, but it was now of friendship rather than intimacy. The two had spent one night together, and that night led them each to their respective careers, her to join the Temple Knights and he to assume the responsibility that marked a member of the nobility.

She tossed the torch atop the pile of oil-soaked timber and watched the flames shoot upward. She stepped back as the fire spread, popping and crackling as more and more wood caught.

Before long, it was blazing skyward, a beacon of light alerting all within range that the Temple Knights of Saint Agnes were in the area. She had no doubt that, come morning, the place would be crawling with Cunars. Even now, she could see the hundred Cunars she'd defeated earlier in the day making their way north, paralleling the river as they approached. Charlaine had promised that their weapons and horses would remain for them to recover, and so she'd done just that, leaving their mounts in a field to the east, and their weapons stacked in the centre of Silver Vale. Would she be remembered as an honourable woman or be vilified for daring to challenge the might of the Church?

"General?"

Charlaine turned to see Anthea, Magda, and Mariele staring at her expectantly. "Our work here is done," she told them. "It's time to go." She led them past the end of the bridge, where their horses waited under Teresa's watchful eye. Stormcloud nuzzled up to her, and then she climbed into the saddle.

"Will it be enough?" asked Teresa.

"We shall have to trust in the Saints that it will," replied Charlaine. "We can remain here no longer. The Antonine is now behind us, as is Regensbach."

"What about the King of Kingshaven? Will he welcome us?"

"I don't know, but it's too late to ask for permission. We'll try to avoid marching too close to the larger towns of the realm and stick to the countryside."

"And if he does seek to interfere?"

"Then we'll appeal to his wisdom. We didn't ask for this war, nor did we actively seek it, but now that we've been thrown into the fray, we must do whatever we need to protect ourselves. If that means fighting the ruler of a Petty Kingdom, then so be it."

"On the brighter side of things," said Teresa, "the bridge behind us is now useless, making pursuit impossible."

"Not impossible, merely more inconvenient, but I doubt that will overly trouble the leaders of the Cunars. We'll see them again before we reach the border of Hadenfeld; of that I'm certain."

"How can you be so calm about all of this?"

Charlaine lowered her voice. "I'll let you in on a little secret. I'm as worried as you are; I just don't show it."

39

LAST STAND

SUMMER 1107 SR

The next few days were peaceful for the most part. The column continued westward, following a road that meandered north and south on occasion, passing by several villages where they found no signs of opposition. The people of the region were glad to see them, offering food from their meagre stocks.

The Temple Knights of Saint Agnes bore the burden stoically, and soon, a new name emerged for their band of exiles: The Five Hundred. It wasn't an exact count, but it caught on, and before long, even Charlaine found herself using it.

It became a source of pride that they, alone, had undertaken this difficult task, a trial of sorts, marking them as the founders of a new order or at least a new future. As they drew closer to the border with Hadenfeld, their morale improved. Their new home approached, giving them hope, though Charlaine knew the eastern extents of the kingdom were thick with forest and woefully underpopulated.

The thought of having to cross the river that formed the border between Kingshaven and Hadenfeld drove Charlaine to distraction. She had no knowledge of eastern Hadenfeld and feared another great river like that of the Silver might bar their way, forcing them to once again seek out a bridge or ford, which would undoubtedly be guarded.

One afternoon, Nicola and a few knights had ranged out ahead along the road to ensure the way was safe. Not long after, the Temple Captain came galloping back, her horse in a lather.

"Stop the column," she called out. "We have a problem."

Charlaine's call for a halt was repeated by each Temple Commander in turn. She waited until the entire column stopped before turning back the Temple Captain. "I'm guessing you discovered someone waiting for us?"

"How did you know?"

"I can think of nothing else that would cause you to wear your horse to exhaustion in such a manner. Give me the details."

"The village up ahead, a place called Nettle Green, told us of a large host assembled to the north."

"Is there a bridge there?"

"No. There's a ford, which, according to the locals, is the only way to cross into Hadenfeld."

"Have we any idea of the composition of this army?"

"I never said it was an army," replied Nicola.

"You'd hardly be concerned if it were only a dozen riders."

"You make a good point. I'm afraid the descriptions we received varied tremendously, making it difficult to estimate numbers, let alone composition. They did, however, mention some were the king's men."

"That's disappointing," replied Charlaine. "I had hoped he'd stay well clear of all this."

"He's said to be a devout worshipper of the Saints, which means he'll consider us traitors to the Church." Nicola shook her head. "It's frustrating. We were so close I could almost taste it."

"I assume you've already made enquiries about what lies to the south?"

"I have, and it's not good news. The river gets much wider, and there's no place to cross within a week's march. I'm afraid if we want to get across, we have to fight that army."

"We can't do anything until we assess their strength. To do otherwise would be folly." Charlaine turned in the saddle. "Temple Commander Verushka, you're in command until I return."

"Where are you going?" she called back.

"Nicola and I are riding up the road a ways. It will likely be late by the time we return. In the meantime, you can set up camp and post sentries."

"Yes, General."

Charlaine turned back to Nicola. "Are the rest of your people still in the village?"

"They are."

"Find yourself a fresh horse, and we'll ride up the road and meet them."

"And then?"

"Then we'll look at this army of theirs and try to work out our next move."

. . .

They passed through the village of Nettle Green and continued on to the Durwick River, the border between Kingshaven and Hadenfeld. The road they were on ended as it met one that paralleled the eastern bank of the river.

Charlaine paused by the running water, trying to determine whether it might be possible to float her troops across on rafts, but without someone who had the expertise to build them, it would be a difficult and time-consuming enterprise. She soon gave up on the idea and turned north, ready to see for herself what awaited them.

They proceeded slowly, having only gone a mile or so, when Nicola spotted a pair of sentries up ahead. They quickly left the road, finding a spot some distance back where their horses wouldn't be overheard. From here, Charlaine and Nicola went forward on foot, leaving the rest of the group ready to ride to the rescue should it prove necessary.

The sentries stood beneath a large oak tree, seeking respite from the sun's heat. With no sign of horses nearby, one of them would have to run back to camp to warn of any attack. Charlaine decided to get closer to gauge the strength of the threat before she launched her attack.

They went west to the riverbank, wading through shin-deep water, a copse of trees hiding their presence. The swift current forced them to take their time as they paralleled the road, staying hunched down to avoid discovery. Eventually, they left the river, moving in amongst the under-brush while still continuing north.

The sounds of a large camp drifted towards them. Somewhere up ahead, a blacksmith pounded on a blade or a horseshoe while horses whinnied. They heard talking and froze, worried someone was coming closer, but no one approached. They continued, finally pushing aside some foliage, exposing an army camp spread out before them. The King of Kingshaven's gold-and-blue banner caught the rays of the setting sun.

"How many, would you say?" asked Charlaine.

"We haven't the best view," replied Nicola, "but I don't think His Majesty would march with anything less than a thousand, and that's not including the Temple Knights." She pointed, indicating the Cunars' familiar grey banner. "I was hoping we wouldn't have to deal with them again."

"We knew they might beat us here," said Charlaine.

"We could turn south instead. Granted, it wouldn't take us to Hadenfeld, but at least we could avoid facing that lot."

"And go where? Our entire strategy was to find safety in Hadenfeld. No other kingdom on the Continent would dare resist the Church."

"What kingdom lies south of Hadenfeld?"

"There are two," replied Charlaine. "Mirantha, in the east, and Hollenbeck to its west, but that's too far for our purposes."

"Would Mirantha consider helping us?"

"I know next to nothing about the realm, but it is said to be very small. I doubt it would dare risk offending the Primus."

Nicola sighed. "It's looking less and less like we have any choice."

"So it would seem."

"Could we use the same strategy we used back in Silver Vale and lure them away from the ford?"

"We were lucky then. I doubt it would work again. Our position is also different. There, the bulk of our troops stayed to the north while we lured the Cunars south. This time, everyone is south, with no hope of getting past the king's men to draw the Cunars away. Or did you forget the sentries on the road?"

"Oh no," replied Nicola. "I didn't forget them. I'm trying to suggest we dispatch them before they can give a warning."

"I'd need a better view of their camp."

"How do you suggest we do that—walk right in?"

"That's an excellent idea."

"Pardon me?"

"If we wait until dark, then remove our tabards, there'll be nothing marking us as Temple Knights, or women. Our armour would hide who we are."

"I suppose it would, as long as we don't interact with anyone. I don't know about you, but my voice isn't very masculine."

"Nor is mine," replied Charlaine, "but I think it worth the risk, don't you?"

"We might as well give it a try."

They discarded their tabards and walked directly into the enemy camp. They'd left their visors down, obstructing their vision somewhat, but it gave them the ability to get much closer. Even though darkness had descended, dozens of campfires lit their way. Men gathered around the fires, discussing the affairs of the day, while others tended to horses or cooking.

The warriors of Kingshaven differed greatly from the army Charlaine had seen in Ardosa. These were well-equipped men, giving the appearance of some experience, although she was unfamiliar with their history. All of this worried her, yet not nearly so much as the presence of the Cunars, for they were present in alarming numbers.

Charlaine remained silent to avoid her voice betraying her ruse. They wandered for hours, finally making their way back to where they'd first entered the camp, confident they had an accurate assessment of numbers. They recovered their tabards and headed towards the river, wading along its eastern bank to avoid discovery by their sentries.

The moon had been high in the sky for many an hour by the time they returned to their camp. Most of her command were asleep, but Verushka had taken pains to post sentries lest the enemy make an unexpected appearance. Charlaine sent for her Temple Commanders so they could discuss their coming strategy. With a few yawns and blankets wrapped around their shoulders, they all gathered in a rough circle, their eyes locked on Charlaine.

"I'll start with the bad news," she began. "The Army of Kingshaven, supported by Temple Knights of Saint Cunar, blocks our way into Hadenfeld."

"How many?" asked Amalia.

"By our estimates, the Army of Kingshaven numbers over eight hundred, with at least an additional three hundred Cunars."

"At least?" said Katinka. "Are you suggesting there may be more?"

"Their camp was spread out across a field, and lingering any longer would have put us at further risk of discovery. They could have more camped farther north, but trees blocked our view."

"Not the best of news," noted Verushka. "Their army outnumbers us by more than two to one. Were the king's men mostly militia, like those back in Regensbach?"

"I'm afraid not," replied Charlaine. "We are dealing with an experienced army of professionals, including footmen, archers, and cavalry. Whoever's in charge organized their camp into distinct sections, the mark of a disciplined army, and that's before we include the Cunars." Their faces fell with the news. Now that Hadenfeld lay within spitting distance, it crushed their spirits to learn their way was blocked.

"You'll find us a way through this," said Ursula. "We have faith in you."

"Faith won't help defeat a numerically superior enemy. For that, we need some sort of strategy."

"And we don't have much time," said Nicola. "They've secured the ford, and I suspect it won't be long before they start sending scouts out looking for us."

"Do we withdraw back to the border with Regensbach?" asked Amalia.

"I wouldn't suggest that. It puts us between two armies."

"Nicola's right," added Charlaine. "The last thing we need to do is give them even more of an advantage than they already have."

"Could we draw them off?" asked Gerda. "It worked once. Why not again?"

"We aren't dealing with only cavalry this time. Even if we did draw off their horse, it's unlikely they'd send their foot after us, which still leaves us outnumbered. We must also bear in mind this is a ford, not a bridge, so we can't destroy it once we've crossed. If we don't deal them a crushing blow, they will pursue."

"But wouldn't they be risking war with Hadenfeld if they did?"

"The eastern extents of the kingdom are wild and untamed," replied Charlaine. "I doubt King Ludwig would be aware they'd crossed the border. Even if he was, it's not as if he'd consider them a threat to the realm."

"Could we build our own bridge?" pressed Gerda.

"Who amongst us has the experience to do that? And even if someone did, how long would it take? We'd have to hew timber, not to mention get to the other side to anchor it. It would take weeks, if not months, and that army up there is not going to sit by and ignore us."

"What about rafts?" asked Ursula. "Could we float our people across?"

"That would certainly be faster, but I fear the Durwick's current is too swift for such an endeavour."

"We'd still have to cut down trees," said Nicola, "and while I'm certain we could convince the locals to lend us axes, it would create a lot of noise, further increasing the risk of discovery."

"There has to be a way to get across!" insisted Amalia. "If we put our minds to it, I'm certain we'd come up with a solution."

"That's an excellent suggestion," said Charlaine. "Think it over, everyone, and we'll discuss this matter tomorrow morning when we've all had a good rest. And some prayers might be in order. You're all dismissed."

Charlaine couldn't miss the disappointment on the faces of the commanders as they walked back to the bedrolls. The pressure of command weighed heavily upon her shoulders this night. She was their general, the person to whom they gave their unwavering loyalty. There must be something she could do.

She lay down and tried to sleep, but her mind wouldn't stop, so she rose, wandering the camp until she was amongst the horses. She brushed down Stormcloud, a familiar ritual that helped her focus.

Fighting was not the answer, nor was a ruse aimed at luring away some of the enemy army. The only other option was to avoid them altogether, but for the life of her, she couldn't work out how.

Charlaine closed her eyes. "Oh blessed Saint," she prayed out loud, "stand by me in this time of need that I might feel the warmth of your compassion and the clarity of your mind. Help me find a safe haven for these women, that they might continue to serve in your name." She let the thought linger. "Saints be with us."

"Saints be with us all," came a voice.

The words startled her. She turned around to behold a man standing some five paces away, watching her intently. Something about him set her at ease, although she couldn't put words to it.

"My pardon," he said. "I didn't mean to startle you."

"Who are you?"

"My name is Messick, Messick Oakwind."

"I'm Charlaine-"

"deShandria. I know."

"I'm afraid you have the advantage of me. Have we met before?"

"We have not, but your name is known to me."

"I don't mean to be rude, but why are you here?"

"You prayed for help, and while you didn't call on my goddess by name, she heard your pleas."

"Your goddess?" said Charlaine. "Would that be Akosia or Tauril?"

"Akosia. She has heard your pleas."

"You mean you heard my pleas."

"It amounts to the same thing."

"I'm curious why you would take an interest in us. It's not as if we worship the Goddess of the Sea."

"Your Temple Fleet was blessed in her name, which led to an increased awareness of her powers."

"How do you know all this?"

"Those of us who preach the old religion are a tight-knit group. There are also ways of spreading the word that mere mortals wouldn't comprehend."

"You speak of magic. I might not be a mage, but I still understand the concept."

He smiled. "You are wise beyond your years, Charlaine deShandria. I do, indeed, refer to the mystical arts. Some believe such power comes from within, but we know better. It is the gift of the Gods, or in this case, the goddess Akosia."

"How do you happen to be here at this precise time?"

"I've been searching for you. When we learned there'd been a rebellion in the Antonine, we knew at once that you were involved. Our brethren have been scouring the countryside for your people."

"I am no worshipper of Akosia."

"But you follow the true teachings of your Saint, teachings that preach you should live in peace and harmony with followers of the old Gods. You honoured those teachings in the north, and now we've come to your aid as a way of giving thanks."

"I'm honoured, though I'm at a loss of how you might be of assistance."

Once more, he smiled. "Now, that's an interesting tale in itself…"

40

THE DURWICK

SUMMER 1107 SR

Verushka knitted her brows. "Are you absolutely certain about this, General? We're about to engage in battle with an army which vastly outnumbers us." She looked north, up the road that led up to the enemy encampment.

"You must have faith," replied Charlaine.

"Faith I have in abundance. What I don't have is clarity. Why are we deliberately antagonizing our enemy?"

"If we cross the Durwick and do nothing to oppose that army, they'll use the ford to follow us."

"We want to draw them after us?"

"Precisely. We don't need the entire army, mind you, only the cavalry."

"Foot can still follow."

"True, but our horses can easily outpace them."

"That's assuming we can get across that river," said Verushka. "You're putting a lot of faith in this Messick fellow. Are you that confident he can do what he promised?"

"Absolutely," replied Charlaine. "Are you familiar with the campaign in Arnsfeld?"

"Only the basics."

"The border between Arnsfeld and Halvaria is a river much like the Durwick. How do you suppose they crossed it?"

"With boats?"

"They tried that, but a river serpent caused a great loss of life."

"Then how did they get across?"

"A trio of Water Mages lowered the level of the water."

"I didn't know such a thing was even possible."

"Neither did I," replied Charlaine. "If I hadn't seen it with my own eyes, I might still have difficulty believing it. Magic is capable of doing so many things."

"Agreed. Sister Teresa is a prime example of that. It's a pity mages don't do more to benefit others."

"Have you ever met a mage?"

"Other than Teresa, no," said Verushka.

"I wouldn't be so quick to dismiss them. Back in Arnsfeld, a woman named Orlina Day helped us. Without her preparation of the battlefield, we would've been defeated."

"Really? None of that was mentioned at the Antonine."

"Does that surprise you, given all that's happened?"

"No," said Verushka. "I suppose not."

Charlaine's gaze drifted off down the road that led to the Cunar sentries. Once she and her contingent rode far enough ahead to be seen, the rest of the plan should take care of itself.

"You should join the column, General. You're too valuable to risk here."

"I cannot ask my fellow sisters to risk their lives if I'm not willing to do the same. My presence will serve as an additional incentive for the army to pursue us."

"And the crossing?" asked Verushka.

"Katinka is more than capable of handling that."

"I'd still feel better if we weren't dependent on the actions of an outsider. There's also the matter of timing. Get that wrong, and we'll arrive when only half the column is across."

"You must put your faith in your fellow knights and concentrate on the task at hand."

"Yes, of course. Sorry, General."

"Don't apologize for confessing your fears."

Charlaine urged Stormcloud into a trot, and the thought crossed her mind that she should order those behind to follow, but then she heard the telltale clopping of hooves.

When the road turned slightly, the king's sentries noted their arrival. At first, they stared, not moving, perhaps not believing the audacity of the Agnesites. Then, shouts of alarm erupted, with a few of them running off to give warning to the enemy camp.

"Shouldn't take long now," said Charlaine. "I expect the Cunars will respond first. They'll be eager for revenge, especially after the drubbing we gave them in Silver Vale."

"You're not worried?" asked Verushka.

Charlaine laughed. "Worried is my natural state of late, but I've learned to hide it. My main concern now is that they'll be too quick to pursue. If that happens, we have to find some way of delaying them."

"And if they're too slow?"

"That means we can take our time getting back to the crossing." They rode past the point where the sentries had stood watch, the king's men now having completely abandoned their post. Horns sounded in the distance.

"Here we go," said Charlaine. "It's time to start things rolling."

"Didn't we do that the moment those scouts spotted us?"

"Now that you mention it, yes." She held up her sword, pointing it to her right.

The portion of Verushka's company directly behind her headed in that direction, with those following copying their manoeuvre until they stretched out into a long line. Then, they all turned left, forming a solid front, facing the enemy.

The king's men arrived on the field first, hastily forming into companies of foot, with the archers behind them while the cavalry was held back as a reserve, ready to exploit any potential weakness. The Temple Knights of Saint Cunar, who were camped farther north, took longer to appear, but when they did, they were already formed into a tightly packed column.

"My," said Verushka. "Don't they look grand."

Temple Commander Scyllia's company fell into line behind that of Verushka's.

"Time for a little demonstration of what we're capable of," said Charlaine. "You may initiate the charge, but remember you're to break off before contact."

"Yes, General." Verushka gave the command to advance, then joined the left end of the line.

Charlaine watched as the Temple Knights of Saint Agnes approached the enemy, increasing their pace, their hoofbeats echoing off the trees like drumbeats. The men of Kingshaven wavered, and then one company broke, streaming northward away from the thunderous approach of the sister knights.

Another company wavered, and then a barrage of arrows flew into the air, falling in amongst the knights, sounding for all the world like hail as they struck armour. Charlaine could see no sign of injury to her knights, although a few horses went down.

Verushka's knights came within twenty paces of the enemy line, then veered off, racing westward, clearing the way for the company behind. From the defender's point of view, their respite was short-lived as a second wave bore down on them. Two more companies broke, the threat of so many armoured opponents too much to bear.

The king, or whoever commanded his men, acted quickly, ordering their knights into the fray. Two hundred Royal Knights moved up to fill the void.

Verushka's company returned to their starting point as Scyllia's commenced their charge. Bolstered by the presence of their own knights, the men of Kingshaven held their positions. A second volley of arrows flew forth, creating another hailstorm, and then the Agnesites turned to the west as their sisters had, riding along the front of the enemy line without making contact. Charlaine played a dangerous game, and she feared the Royal Knights might take exception, but it appeared they were content to hold their positions.

If she harboured any reservations about why they were waiting, the grey-clad knights approaching in one large, well-formed column put them to rest. Charlaine estimated how long it would take them to get into position at the end of the Kingshaven line, and then gave the signal to withdraw.

Verushka's company responded first, turning left and changing from line to column in preparation to march off the field. Scyllia, still returning from their faux charge on the enemy line, was too busy to see the signal and continued riding back to their starting point.

Charlaine expected the Cunars to halt and dress their ranks once they'd reached their position, but instead, they surged forward, a horn sounding a charge. Caught unawares, Scyllia's company could not maintain their formation while they turned to meet the threat. The area became a mix of grey and scarlet as the two orders clashed. Charlaine held her breath, willing Scyllia and her knights to disengage, but the fighting had become too chaotic to even consider such a thing.

Verushka saw the danger, turning her own command and leading a charge to rescue her sisters. They closed quickly, joining the fray and adding to the cacophony of battle. It would have ended in disaster had the king's knights joined in, but it appeared they had no stomach for it. Charlaine could only assume they had no wish to interfere in a Church matter.

Her knights fell. It couldn't be avoided, but out of the carnage burst a host of scarlet as the Temple Knights of Saint Agnes tried to disengage from the melee. Charlaine rushed forward to rally the fleeing knights. She briefly considered returning them to the melee, but the Cunars had gained the upper hand. With a heavy heart, she ordered them to retreat and ride south towards the remainder of The Five Hundred.

She paused to look back on the battle, finding no sign of Scyllia, but she spotted Verushka surrounded by a sea of grey. Charlaine knew their sacrifice would haunt her for the rest of her days, yet she had no choice but to honour their lives by getting what remained of her command to safety.

The water level was unusually low as she reached the eastern bank. The bulk of her army was already across, thanks to the efforts of Messick, and only Amalia's company remained on this side of the river. The Water Mage stood midstream, his shoes discarded in favour of being barefoot in the ankle-deep waters of the Durwick.

She found the concept difficult to grasp, for the water had to go somewhere, yet here they were, crossing what amounted to a stream where, this morning, a raging river had flowed.

Teresa appeared at her side. "Are you injured?"

"No, but many of my knights are." Charlaine glanced over her shoulder. "The Cunars are close behind us. We must hurry across."

"I'll take care of the wounded once they're on the other side." Teresa glanced up the road. "Verushka?"

"Lost, I'm afraid, as is Scyllia. They were caught out in the open by the Cunars."

"Should we wait?"

"No. Do that, and we put our entire exodus in jeopardy. We must save those we can. Take command of these knights and get them across that river while I watch for those Cunars. I doubt it will take them long to follow our trail."

Teresa ordered the survivors into the river, then followed at a sedate pace, watching lest any of the injured fall from the saddle.

Charlaine remained where she was, a growing sense of foreboding threatening to overwhelm her. They'd fled the battle, racing down the road to reach safety, but the Cunars were not warriors who'd be willing to let them go.

She quickly glanced at Messick, his eyes closed, his hands held up in the air as if he were physically holding back the water. Her thoughts turned to Reinwick, where she'd met Elsbeth Fel, a Sacred Mother of Akosia, who embraced friendship and acceptance with the Temple Knights of Saint Agnes, even going so far as to bless each vessel of the Temple Fleet in the name of the Sea Goddess. Was she the one responsible for sending Messick to aid them in their time of need?

The thundering sound of hundreds of hooves from the north drew her attention to the road. Her knights were still crossing, the last now entering the knee-deep water as the first of the grey-clad riders appeared.

Charlaine drew her sword, then advanced several paces, placing herself between the two orders. "Halt, in the name of Saint Agnes!" she cried out.

The Temple Captain leading the Cunars raised his hands, halting his column before he trotted his horse forward, stopping only a few paces shy of her.

"I admire your courage, General, but I'm afraid it's misplaced. I have no idea how you found a ford, or why our scouts missed it, but it matters little. Flee if you must, but know we will soon be on your heels."

"Across that river is the Kingdom of Hadenfeld," said Charlaine.

"What of it? Do you think the threat of a heathen realm will dissuade us from our service? We shall cross this ford just as you have, and then your pathetic excuse of an order will be wiped out and erased from history."

She sheathed her sword and gripped Stormcloud's reins. "You think you can cross that river and not suffer any consequences?"

He stiffened in his saddle. "Do not dare to lecture me on what I can and cannot do!"

"I do not recommend you follow us, Captain, but if you insist, there is little I can do to dissuade you. Consider yourself warned." She turned Stormcloud and made a rush for the river.

Charlaine didn't watch the Cunars; instead, she focused on navigating her way across the river to where the last of her knights now climbed onto the western bank, the Water Mage, Messick, with them. Stormcloud was a swift runner, but the river's rocky bottom made for treacherous footing, so Charlaine slowed her pace. Behind her came the splashing of hooves as the first of the Cunars entered the water.

Her eyes locked with those of Messick for a brief moment. "Now!" she shouted. "Release the water before it's too late!"

He nodded, lowering his arms. The area went eerily quiet, save for the horses behind her, and then a distant roar grew from the south, building in intensity.

A great wall of water smashed into Stormcloud's feet, pushing them northward. The Calabrian mount was knocked sideways, losing her footing as the water pushed Charlaine from the saddle, the fierce current threatening to drag her under.

She clung to the reins with a desperate strength, and then they went taut as Stormcloud dragged her against the current, pulling her from the river. A group of sister knights rushed to her aid, and she collapsed on the riverbank, vomiting water. Behind her, the raging water washed the sounds of screaming horses northward.

Teresa kneeled over her, slapping her on the back.

"I—I-I'm fine," Charlaine spat out. "We must get moving before the Cunars recover and cross at the ford."

"I don't believe there's much chance of that," replied the mage. "Look." She pointed.

Charlaine sat up. The Durwick had returned to its regular depth, the water rushing past. A couple of riderless horses struggled to gain the eastern riverbank, but the only Cunars left within sight were those few standing on the far bank, their tunics thoroughly soaked.

"They were swept away, all except the ones closest to the eastern side."

"My apologies," added Messick, approaching the two knights. A thin trail of blood dripping from his nose revealed the extraordinary draw this feat had been upon his power. "My spell held back the river, but all that water had to go somewhere. When I released it, it came in one great wall." He looked northward, where, even now, the river raged, ripping trees and bushes from its banks. "It may cause some flooding downriver, but that's what comes of trying to control nature."

Charlaine got to her feet. "I must thank you," she said. "Without your aid, we would've faced certain defeat."

"The goddess has embraced you as a champion of the old religion."

"Even though I'm a devotee of the Saints?"

"Can you not be both? Your actions in the north benefited worshippers of both faiths, and unlike your grey-clad brothers, you work to unite people rather than divide them."

"The Saints tell us to accept those of other faiths, for we share many of the same beliefs."

He bowed. "You are gracious in victory, a trait that is to be greatly admired."

"What will you do now, Father Messick? Will you accompany us to the capital of Hadenfeld, or return home?"

"My part in this is complete. I must return to my role of watching over the waters of this land in the name of Akosia. I wish you well, General, for although this part of your journey is over, I fear there are still difficulties ahead of you."

"Farewell."

The Water Mage turned, making his way southward along the banks of the Durwick.

"I don't understand," said Teresa. "How would Akosia know where we were, and how did Messick know what you got up to in the north?"

"The rivers of the Petty Kingdoms run for hundreds of miles," replied Charlaine, "and water is her domain."

"Are you suggesting the goddess is real?"

"Does it matter? To her followers, she exists. Who are we to claim any different?"

Teresa shook her head. "He is a Water Mage, nothing more. The Petty Kingdoms have many such individuals."

"Yet he knew all about me. There are things in life that remain a mystery. Perhaps it's better we leave it as such?"

41

LOST

SUMMER 1107 SR

The oppressive heat forced the knights to travel in their cassocks rather than their plate armour to avoid exhausting themselves. It made for a strange sight as each Temple Knight carried a large bag filled with armour slung over the back of their saddles.

Safe from pursuit, the column slowed to preserve the strength of their horses while they picked their way through the unyielding thick woods filled with heavy undergrowth.

Days passed as they weaved north or south to maintain their westward progress. The forest provided plenty of fodder for the horses but little for the sister knights, save the occasional patch of berries, hardly enough to sustain them. Their stomachs growled with hunger.

It had been a week since the encounter at the river, and Charlaine called for a rest. A nearby stream offered fresh water, and a few sisters tried to tease some fish from the river to complement the edible plants they'd found along the riverbank.

Charlaine sat on a log, her gaze roaming the camp. Everyone was tired and hungry, but a spark of resistance remained in their eyes, one that said they would continue with these trials until they reached their destination. It was faith at its finest, yet faith alone would not suffice to fill an empty stomach. Before long, they'd be too weak to continue.

Teresa slumped down beside her. "By the Saints, it was hot in Ilea, but nothing like this." She pulled at the neck of her cassock. "I feel as though I've been swimming."

Charlaine chuckled. "And here I thought you were afraid of water."

"You can thank the Elves for curing me of that fear."

"And how did they manage that?"

"By teaching me how to swim. Clean mountain streams fed the water on the island, making for a refreshing dip. I wouldn't say the water around here could be described in that manner, would you?"

"No," replied Charlaine. "But then again, there are no mountains in this part of the Continent."

"How much longer till we reach civilization?"

"I don't really know. My experience with Hadenfeld was mostly confined to the city of Malburg."

"Yes, but you must know something?"

"The kingdom's eastern extents are said to be nothing but wilderness."

"But you've been in correspondence with the king, haven't you?"

"Not for some time, and now that he's sitting on the Throne, he's far too busy to send me any letters."

"I doubt that's the case. From how you've described him, he sounds like an honourable man."

"He is, but ruling a kingdom is a great burden, one that he would take very seriously."

Teresa let out a sigh. "So many trees. Is the entire kingdom like this?"

"No, not at all. Malburg is mostly open, although there's a large forest east of Verfeld, Ludwig's land before he became king."

"And when we arrive, how do you think he'll greet us? With open arms or with drawn swords?"

"The presence of hundreds of Temple Knights in his lands will cause some alarm. We must also consider the capital, Harlingen, lies in the western part of the kingdom."

"Meaning?"

"Any response will likely be led by one of his nobles. That being the case, we can't necessarily count on a friendly reception."

"Will they listen to reason?"

"I hope they would," replied Charlaine, "but I expect a few are unhappy with him seizing the Throne. They might view this as an opportunity to begin another war."

Teresa nodded. "Once a kingdom falls into the chaos of civil war, it's difficult to climb out. If he can't unify the factions, it'll likely fall into war yet again."

"Are you an expert in politics now?"

"To a certain extent. The Sea Elves kept records of Human history, and our politics were of great interest to them."

"Why so?"

"I think they feared an invasion. Keeping an eye on what Humans were up to was their way of watching for any signs of potential hostility on our part. How much do you know about the Successor States?"

"They came about after the defeat of Therengia, although I suppose we should now call it the First Kingdom of Therengia, considering there's a new one in the east."

"What you say is true, but it was also a dark time for Humans. The alliances that worked together to defeat Therengia soon broke apart, and then they were at each other's throats. It devolved into a series of bloody and brutal wars the Elves reckoned were so bad, the number of Humans on the Continent diminished."

"And from all that carnage came the Petty Kingdoms, though I can't claim they're any less prone to war. I don't know what that has to do with Hadenfeld."

"As the Elves are so fond of saying, 'History has a way of repeating itself.' Humans are, by nature, aggressive and territorial, and many, particularly the wealthy, are drawn to power and control."

"Ludwig's not like that," said Charlaine. "And if he ever showed such tendencies, I'm certain Charlotte would say something."

"Charlotte?"

"The queen, and before you ask, she was crowned alongside him, so she's not just a consort."

"You know her as well?"

"I attended their wedding."

"And?"

"She was a most delightful woman, well-suited to someone of Ludwig's temperament."

"You still love him, don't you?"

"Yes, but not in the manner you would expect. We are friends, perhaps even confidantes, but there is no romance between us. Our relationship is based on mutual trust and respect."

"And he feels the same?"

"I cannot claim to know his inner thoughts, but I believe he does."

"So I suppose the only question remaining is how long before we find our way out of this forest."

"That was a very abrupt change of subject," said Charlaine.

"What can I say? My mind wanders on occasion. Have you an answer, or are we doomed to ride in circles forever?"

"I suspect it'll be a while before we clear these woods. Hadenfeld is one of the larger Petty Kingdoms, and if the east is anything like the west, we'll have hundreds of miles to traverse before we reach any signs of civilization."

"Then we'd best pick up the pace," said Teresa. "We won't find it sitting around here."

The days of wandering through the woods continued, but thankfully, food became more plentiful. Small clusters of berries gave way to occasional groves and more streams teaming with fish. On these occasions, they'd rest half a day to gather food and conserve their strength.

Each day, six knights rode out in front, searching for a path they could navigate. They were sometimes forced to backtrack to find a better route, but they didn't rest until the column made some progress.

They were closing in on nearly two weeks since they'd crossed the Durwick as Charlaine sat on a rock, with Stormcloud drinking from a small stream. Sister Anthea approached nervously.

"Something on your mind?" asked Charlaine.

The young knight stepped closer, speaking in a quiet voice. "I...I think we're being watched."

"What makes you say that?"

"The woods will grow quiet all of a sudden."

"It could be an animal."

"I didn't mean to suggest it wasn't, merely that someone, or some thing, is watching us."

"You're not trying to suggest a monster, are you?"

"We are in an unexplored region," Anthea replied, "or at least I assume it's unexplored. Who knows what's lurking behind all those trees."

"This quietness," asked Charlaine. "When did you first notice it?"

"Yesterday, when we were bedding down for the night, the entire forest grew quiet."

"And did anyone else remark on this?"

"No. I mentioned it to Temple Commander Katinka, but she dismissed it, saying it was only natural with all of us knights parading through the forest."

"She makes a convincing argument," noted Charlaine, "but that doesn't necessarily mean it's correct."

"Does that mean you believe me?"

"I have seen my fair share of unusual things."

"You have?"

"I saw a river serpent in Arnsfeld, and that's not something you soon forget, so I'm willing to believe something strange could be lurking out there." She rose from her seat. "Just to be safe, we'll post extra guards, and if you notice it again, come see me at once."

"Yes, General."

"Anything else?"

"No, General." The young knight's stomach growled, a loud gurgling noise that seemed to echo off the trees.

Charlaine couldn't help but laugh. "Don't worry. You're not the only one whose stomach is protesting."

"Will there be food once we reach Hadenfeld?"

"We're in Hadenfeld."

"I meant once we reached civilization."

"That largely depends on where we emerge from this forest. I don't imagine a small village has enough food for five hundred knights."

"We have less after that large fight." Anthea cast her gaze down. "Sorry, General. I didn't mean to correct you."

"No. You have the facts right. Our count has fallen beneath that number, but I doubt history will care. I fear we shall be known as The Five Hundred forever more. It will matter little in the long run; those of us who made this trip will be forever enshrined in the history of our order, providing we survive."

"Do you seriously think we won't?"

"There's no guarantee Hadenfeld will welcome us, and even if they did, supporting this many knights is an expensive proposition. We can't rely on funds from the Church anymore, which means we'll have to pay for everything ourselves."

"We will survive," said Anthea. "We have to."

"Much as I admire your faith, we cannot rely on that alone to survive."

"Then we shall become settlers, working the land to feed ourselves."

"A noble sentiment," said Charlaine, "but how do you propose we continue the order without fresh recruits? Or are you suggesting we all settle down and have children? If so, I must tell you about how that is accomplished, for you don't seem to realize we have no men."

Anthea's blush ran contrary to her words. "I'm well aware we need men to procreate. I merely meant that in the short term, we could feed ourselves."

"It's a good plan and one I'll consider once we've found ourselves a home."

"Could we not claim land here, in the forest?"

"Your parents were farmers, weren't they?"

"They were, although they mostly raised livestock."

"Then you are aware this many trees are difficult to clear if you want to plant seeds. There's also the matter of having something to plant."

"Trees can be cut down, and stumps cleared."

"I understand, but we lack the basic tools needed to do any of that."

"Sorry, General. I should've realized that."

"Don't apologize for speaking your mind. If more did that, there'd be a lot less strife in the world."

A shout of alarm interrupted their conversation, followed by a call to arms. Knights rose, gathering weapons and retrieving their horses. Before long, the entire army was armed and ready to fight, although it remained to be seen who or what had alarmed the sentries.

Katinka approached, along with Sister Rhea. "We bring news, General," said the Temple Commander. She turned to her knight. "Tell her what you found."

"I was on sentry duty," explained Rhea, "and heard movement in the underbrush. Moments later, an arrow flew forth, striking my shoulder, though it did no damage. Whoever it was then fled deeper into the forest." She held up an arrow. "I found this after they left."

Charlaine took it, examining its head. The fine steel tip seemed out of place in the depths of the forest. The shaft, too, was well-made and dyed green, making it difficult to see.

"Could it be Orcs?" asked Katinka. "I hear the Therengians employed them in the east."

"I remember finding Orc prints back near Verfeld, but that was years ago. To my knowledge, there's been no interaction with them in the last few decades. This arrow also looks to be the work of a skilled smith."

"Could you check for a maker's mark?"

"Without knowing any in the region, what use would it be? Besides, we can't blame a fletcher for the use of his arrows. It would be like blaming a swordsmith because one of his customers used his creation to kill someone."

"But this tells us someone is out there."

"It does," replied Charlaine. "I was just discussing that very thing with Anthea. Have you sent people to search the area?"

"I have," said Katinka, "but they turned up nothing. Whoever's out there is a skilled hunter."

"Yet foolish enough to loose off an arrow at hundreds of Temple Knights. This was no attack; it was a warning. Someone doesn't like us being in the area."

"What do you propose we do about it?"

"We have no choice but to continue. From this point forward, I want all sentries working in threes. That ought to be enough to discourage this hunter. Scouts, too, for that matter. The last thing we need is to take more casualties. Oh, and from now on, all knights are to be armoured despite the heat."

The individual responsible for loosing the arrow must have fled. Either that, or they settled for watching the Temple Knights, as there were no further attacks on their scouts.

Late the next day, word came that a great river blocked their progress. Charlaine halted the column and rode forward with Teresa to determine how much of a problem it would cause. Although the river was as wide as the Durwick, the current was not quite as strong. It did, however, look deep.

"It doesn't appear we'll be crossing here," said Teresa.

"Interesting," replied Charlaine. "The water here is running south rather than north."

"It likely flows into the Shimmering Sea."

"I'm not so convinced of that. Unless I'm mistaken, the southern border of Hadenfeld is defined by the river Hollen. This must flow into it."

"Does that mean we're close to civilization?"

"I couldn't say for certain. The eastern baronies were part of a separate kingdom when I lived there. I believe they were sparsely populated, but once we get across, there's a much better chance of finding a road."

"Was there a river near Malburg?"

"There was, but it flowed north, so this can't be it."

"What do we do now?"

"Set up camp and send riders north and south, looking for a place to cross. We'll still keep a watchful eye out for our visitor; it could well be that he's gathered friends and is waiting to ambush us as we attempt to cross."

"I don't like this," said Teresa. "If Messick were still with us, it would be different, but that river is wide. I can't imagine a ford being anything other than treacherous."

"We've faced worse."

"I'll grant you, fighting the Cunars was difficult, but at least we could see them. This is completely different. An entire army could be lurking in the woods on the other side, ready to pick us off like flies as we cross."

"It would take a skilled archer to penetrate our armour."

"True, but our horses lack barding. Kill them, and the knights will be stranded, or worse, swept away by the current."

"You make a good point," said Charlaine. "However, if someone wants to deny us access to the other side of the river, there must be something over there worthy of being protected."

"Like a village?"

"Precisely. And villagers tend to be reasonable folk. I'm certain we could convince them we mean them no harm."

"Assuming they allow us the opportunity to speak."

"I'll see to that. Now, let's concentrate on finding a place to cross first. There's no sense in worrying about anything else till we discover if it's even possible. For all we know, we may be several days away from a ford or bridge."

Teresa nodded. "I shall pass on your orders."

"Oh, and Teresa?"

"Yes?"

"Thank you."

"For what?"

"For making me think through things."

"Danica's not here, so someone has to do it."

"True, but not everyone has your gift. You're easy to talk to."

"I shall take that as a compliment."

"As it was meant."

"Now, can I be on my way?" said Teresa. "I'd like to get people out searching before it gets dark. Who knows, there could be a ford only a stone's throw from here."

Charlaine laughed. "You're ever the optimist, Teresa. You may carry on."

42

PARLEY
SUMMER 1107 SR

"Well? What do you think?"

Charlaine dismounted, moving to the river's edge to dip her hand in the water. "Seems safe enough. Have you tested the depth?"

"I have," replied Nicola. "I rode to the other side and back, and it was never more than waist deep. There's also only a gentle current, which is a nice change."

"And no signs of our recent visitor?"

"No arrows flew at me, if that's what you're asking. That could also mean they're waiting for us to cross in greater numbers so they can do more damage."

"There's not much choice if we want to get to the other side. It's not as if we found any other suitable crossings."

"So we'll cross here?"

"Let's take this one step at a time," said Charlaine. "We'll bring everyone up to the riverbank, then send an advance party across to scout out the other side. I don't suppose we have anyone who can search for tracks?"

"No," said Nicola. "They're all knights, not hunters."

"In the future, we should look at other disciplines."

"Meaning?"

"Yes, we are knights, first and foremost," said Charlaine, "but without a Holy Army to support us, it would be useful to have other skill sets available within the order."

"Such as hunting?"

"Well, woodcraft is certainly one that would be useful, as well as archers."

"We have a hard enough time recruiting knights."

"True, but we don't necessarily have to recruit women to act as archers; merely have them available to support us when we march to war."

"You make it sound like we're about to fight."

"The Halvarians will no doubt take advantage of the schism in the Church to launch their invasion. I'd like to be prepared when that time comes."

"We haven't even found a home yet. What makes you think we'll be in any position to fight?"

"We're knights, Nicola. It's what we do, and now that we're no longer under the control of the Church, we'll need to prove our worth."

"I'm not certain I understand."

"We'll be outsiders wherever we end up, and that's going to sow a lot of distrust. To win over the people of the Petty Kingdoms, we'll need to demonstrate we're not afraid to fight."

"By recruiting archers?"

"Not only archers. We'll need foot soldiers, too."

"And where do we find the funds to pay for all this?"

"I'm still working on that," replied Charlaine, "but it's definitely something that's been on my mind."

"Does anyone else know about these plans?"

"No. You're the first I've mentioned them to. Why?"

"You might want to keep it to yourself awhile longer, at least until we've found a more permanent home."

"Good advice. That's why I need you to be my aide, providing you have no objection?"

"None at all, although I'm a little surprised."

"Why?" asked Charlaine. "You served the grand mistress for years."

"I did, but I'd have thought you'd want to chart your own course."

"You sound like Danica."

"I assume that's a good thing?"

"Yes, very good. And as for your background, your service to the grand mistress means you're intimately familiar with how the order operates. You must have run across plenty of inefficiencies over the years; think of this as an opportunity to clear away the cobwebs."

"Very well, I accept. Now, as my first official act as your aide, may I recommend we retrieve the others so we can get across that river?"

It took half the morning for all the Temple Knights to arrive at the crossing point. They couldn't assemble in one place, thanks to the thick underbrush, so they formed a single immense line stretching well back into the forest.

Temple Commander Amalia entered the water first, halting as she reached midstream, where she waved the rest of her command forward. Her knights advanced into the water and were halfway across when a hail of arrows flew from the opposite bank.

Most struck armour, for the Temple Knights had seen fit to protect themselves against just such an ambush, but Amalia slumped over, silently slipping from her saddle. Her horse bolted with an arrow protruding from its shoulder, galloping for the eastern side of the river.

Charlaine dismounted, rushing into the water to save the fallen Temple Commander. When she'd gone no more than five steps, another burst of arrows flew from the other bank. She kept her head low, trusting in her armour to keep her safe.

Amalia lay on her side, an arrow protruding from her neck, the blood staining the river crimson. Charlaine turned her back on the attackers, placing one arm under the Temple Commander's back and the other beneath her legs. Whoever was opposing them must have recognized the act of mercy, for the arrows ceased. She carried Amalia to the eastern bank, where their healer waited to use her magic.

Teresa uttered her strange words, and then her hands began to glow. She nodded at Charlaine, who yanked the arrow from the fallen knight's neck. Blood gushed forth as Teresa placed her hands on Amalia's shoulders. The light leaped into the fallen knight's body, flowing towards the wound, her neck glowing brightly. When the light faded, the wound was no longer visible.

"Remarkable," said Charlaine. "I've seen healing magic before, yet it never ceases to amaze me. You truly have a gift."

"A gift I shouldn't have had to use," replied Teresa. "Why won't they let us cross?"

"I intend to find out." Charlaine stood, then turned to face their attackers. She couldn't see them while they hid in the underbrush, but there could be no doubt that they still watched. With her visor open and her arms out to either side, she walked back into the water.

"I mean you no harm," she called out but received no answer. She kept going until she stood in the middle of the river, then removed her helmet. "I am Charlaine deShandria, Temple General of Saint Agnes. We come in peace."

"Should that name be known to me?" came the reply, though the language was clipped and foreign-sounding. She tried to work out why and came to the conclusion this wasn't the speaker's native language.

"Are you not Human?" she asked.

No one responded. Charlaine began to wonder if they'd all left when a tall, lithe figure dressed all in green stepped into the open, revealing a flash of silver beneath their cloak. "You must excuse the delay." The voice was less stilted, with a definite feminine quality to it. "Your language is difficult for us to understand."

"You speak it well enough."

"Only with the aid of magic. May I come closer?"

"By all means."

The person stepped into the water, keeping their head bent forward, watching their footing as they navigated to the halfway point. When they removed their hood and helmet, Charlaine was shocked to see pointed ears and an elongated face.

"You're an Elf!" she said.

"How astute of you to notice. My name is Fariel, Talon of Nethendril." She bowed with a flourish.

"I was under the impression these lands were part of Hadenfeld."

"That kingdom lies west of us. You are currently trespassing in the Goldenwood."

"We come seeking sanctuary under the rule of King Ludwig."

"Sanctuary, is it? How strange that you travel in such a well-armed group. Is it common for your Church to trespass in such great numbers, Temple General?"

"We no longer serve the Church."

The Elf looked shocked by Charlaine's words. "Your situation is not something I can judge. My duty is to keep the Goldenwood safe, and your army threatens that safety."

"Then take me to your ruler, and I'll explain how we find ourselves in this circumstance."

"Do you expect me to lead over four hundred armed warriors to Nethendril? I am no fool, Temple General."

"Nor did I take you for one. I am honest in my desire to find a peaceful solution, Talon. I ask only that my companion Teresa and I be given the opportunity to speak to your leader."

"And why would I allow that?"

"Having lived amongst the Sea Elves, she is fluent in their language. I assume that also holds true of your own?"

"The Sea Elves? This is most curious, indeed. I will agree to take you and your companion to meet our high lord, but the rest of your people must remain on the eastern side of the Erlen, as you Humans call it."

"I need a moment to retrieve my horse."

"You may take all the time you wish," replied Fariel, "but you and your companion must leave your weapons behind."

Charlaine turned, heading back to the eastern bank. Amalia looked much better, although still pale. "You heard?"

"I did," replied Teresa. "Are you certain this is wise?"

"Wise? Perhaps not, but we must do something. Those Elves aren't going to leave us alone so long as they perceive us as a threat."

"And what of everyone else? Are they to starve while we go to this city of theirs?"

"I shall see if I can arrange for them to supply food."

"You think they will?"

"It's either that or they let us hunt, and I can't imagine them being happy with Temple Knights riding all over their forest, can you?"

"No," said Teresa. "I suppose not."

Charlaine unbuckled her belt and handed her weapons to Amalia. "Keep an eye on these. I'll need them in the future. Temple Commander Katinka is in charge while I'm away."

"Yes, General," replied Amalia.

"Ready, Teresa?"

"As ready as I'll ever be."

Charlaine climbed into Stormcloud's saddle, waiting as her companion mounted her own horse. They trotted into the middle of the river where Talon Fariel waited.

"My people require food," said Charlaine.

"I anticipated your request," replied the Elf. "You may rest assured no one will starve in your absence."

"How far do we have to travel to reach your city?"

"Three days, perhaps four. It largely depends on your ability to traverse the Goldenwood's thick forests."

"Then let us waste no more time."

Fariel nodded, then turned, leading them towards the western bank. They exited the river to discover half a company of Elves, each armed with the longbows they were said to favour. Charlaine had watched them in action back at the Battle of the Brinwald, but this was the first time she'd experienced them up close.

The Elf talon noticed her staring at the bows. "I see you have an interest in our weapons."

"I've seen them before. They were most effective in defeating the Halvarian cavalry."

"They are even more effective here, where we can use them from a place of concealment. Our arrows can pierce even the thickest of armour at short range."

"I'm surprised we didn't suffer more casualties."

"Casualties? Those arrows were meant to warn you off, not injure you. Had we intended otherwise, your people would have died."

"Yet one of those arrows drew blood."

Fariel shrugged. "Even the best-laid plans sometimes go awry. Now, come. We have much distance to cover before nightfall." With that, she was off, rushing through the forest, barely making a sound.

The thick forest canopy cut out both the sun and moon, resulting in a gloomy trip. As darkness fell, their hosts built a campfire and then passed around some food and drink, sharing with their newfound companions.

"Who rules in Nethendril?" asked Charlaine.

"The High Lord, Sindra."

"Are you on friendly terms with Hadenfeld?"

"We have an agreement to come to each other's aid should we find ourselves invaded."

"A mutual defence pact? Ludwig made no mention of it."

"Ludwig?" said Fariel. "You know the king?"

"I've corresponded with him for years."

"I am sorry. I do not understand. The spell of tongues gives me only a basic understanding of your language."

"*Allow me to translate,*" said Teresa, slipping into Elvish. "*The general knew the king many years ago and has remained in contact through letters.*"

"*I find that surprising yet also interesting. Is he aware of your current circumstances?*"

"*We do not believe so. Things developed quickly in the Antonine, and although we sent word through private means, the letters are likely still in the process of being delivered.*"

Fariel returned to speaking in the common tongue. "The king, in all likelihood, wanted to hide his agreement with us to avoid diplomatic consequences. He believes some in his kingdom would seek to use it against him."

"I understand," replied Charlaine.

"I am not an expert in reading the faces of Humans, but it looks like something is troubling you."

"It is. Years ago, I promised never to return to Hadenfeld."

"Then why have you sought to bring your knights here?"

"To plead they be given sanctuary. If I must leave, then I shall, but only after I ensure their safety."

"I sense much has happened to bring you here, but such things are, I think, best left until you are before the high lord."

Charlaine nodded her understanding. "Perhaps you might be able to answer a question?"

"I shall certainly try. What would you like to know?"

"You called yourself a talon. Is that a rank or a title?"

"A rank," replied Fariel. "I believe you Humans would call me a captain."

"Are there many talons in Nethendril?"

The Elf smiled. "You are full of questions, General. I shall not answer that particular one until I have been given leave to do so by the high lord. I trust you understand?"

"I do," said Charlaine. "What can we expect when we meet your high lord?"

"She is wise, as all rulers should be, and does not rush to judge others. Be frank and honest with her, and you will find her more sympathetic to your cause."

"I have so many questions," said Teresa, "but I understand we have to gain her trust first."

"She will be most interested in you," replied Fariel. "The Sea Elves are our distant cousins. For centuries, all we have heard of them is rumour and speculation. Do they truly thrive?"

"They do."

"And how did you learn their language—our language?"

"I spent time amongst them while Master Gwalinor taught me the healing arts."

"I do not know the name, but that is to be expected."

"I just had a thought," said Charlaine. "Fariel, when you discovered our presence, did you send word to Ludwig?"

"I sent word to Nethendril, but by the terms of our agreement with King Ludwig, the high lord would have been honour-bound to inform him of your incursion. I expect a rider is even now rushing west. Why?"

"If I were a king, and I heard of a large group of armed strangers in my lands, I would mass an army and send it to investigate. I'm afraid our very presence here may have inadvertently given the impression this was an invasion."

"It matters little," said the Elf. "If Ludwig sends an army, that is his right as king. A ruler who ignores such things invites calamities."

"A truer word was never spoken," replied Teresa. "However, in our case, it would be more beneficial if Ludwig were slow to take action."

Charlaine shook her head. "He won't be. He's never been one to sit back and do nothing. If he believes the threat is genuine, he'll send everything he's got."

"Yes, but will he lead it himself or send a general to lead his men?"

"Why does it matter?" asked Fariel.

"Depends on the general." Teresa looked at Charlaine. "Who commands his army?"

"I'd assume he would, though now that he's king, it might've changed."

"Then who is he likely to appoint as general?"

"I couldn't say for certain. Back in Reinwick, he travelled with a large fellow named Sigwulf, whom he served with as a mercenary. It might be him."

"I doubt that," said Teresa. "Most kings wouldn't trust their army to a foreigner."

"Whomever he chooses, you can be certain of two things."

"And those are?"

"He'll trust them implicitly, and they'll be very competent at what they do. I'm still hoping he'll come himself; it would make things much simpler, but I've given up worrying about what I have no control over."

"You Temple Knights are a strange breed," said Fariel. "You are dedicated to fighting, yet at the same time, you help the sick and poor."

"It sounds like you've met our brother order, the Temple Knights of Saint Mathew."

"I have, in Eisen. They have a garrison there, although I am led to believe they intend to move to the capital at Harlingen."

"Eisen?" noted Teresa. "I don't believe I'm familiar with that name. Is that an Elven city?"

"No, a Human one. It used to be the capital of Neuhafen. During the recent war, we Elves defended it on behalf of Ludwig, allowing his warriors to be used in the campaign to seize the Throne."

"Do you maintain a garrison there?" asked Charlaine.

The talon shook her head. "All our warriors returned home, save for those serving in the court of King Ludwig. Now, enough of this talk. You must rest. There are still many miles to go before we reach Nethendril."

43

NETHENDRIL

SUMMER 1107 SR

"There it is," said Fariel. "Nethendril, capital of the Goldenwood."

Charlaine surveyed the city that sat on the other side of a river. The towers were spaced evenly along its high walls, but the most striking feature was the hill in the centre of the place, for a massive tree grew out from it, with golden boughs that soared over everything.

"Remarkable," she said. "How old is the tree?"

"It predates the coming of Humans. We were once a realm so vast, an Elf could travel for months and still remain within our borders, but the Great War saw an end to that."

"Great War?"

"A conflict between Elves and Orcs waged more than two thousand years ago. It scattered the Orcs while leaving us so diminished in numbers that we were unable to resist the expansion of Humans."

"And so you sought solitude in the forests of Eiddenwerthe?"

"Had we not, we would have been overrun by your kind."

"But Humans must have wandered into your lands from time to time. How did you keep its existence a secret?"

"Up until recently, it was death for any outsider who dared to enter the Goldenwood."

"How recently?" asked Charlaine.

"Just over three years ago, a Prince of Hadenfeld came here seeking those who had vanished."

"You mean Ludwig?"

"Yes."

"How in the name of the Saints did he get you to change your policy regarding outsiders?"

"One of our talons captured his group and brought them to Nethendril in violation of our laws."

"I can't imagine that went over well."

"It did not, but Elonin held some influence at court."

"There's got to be more to the story than that."

"There is," replied Fariel, "but such things are best left for the high lord to explain, should she wish it."

They crossed the river where it was shallow, continuing on towards a massive gate. "You are not the first Humans to set foot in Nethendril, though you are the first not to arrive as prisoners but as guests."

"That's very decent of you," said Teresa, "though we're guests who've been denied their weapons."

"Would you take your weapons before a king of the Petty Kingdoms?"

"In some cases," said Charlaine, "although I'll admit it's not a common practice."

"My glade warriors are more than capable of keeping you safe."

"Glade warriors?" said Teresa.

"Elves trained in guarding the Goldenwood."

"Are all your warriors glade warriors?"

"No. Only those proficient at woodcraft. The bulk of our army is what you would consider more traditional warriors, though I am led to believe we have more archers than would typically be found amongst your people."

"And have you cavalry as well?"

Fariel laughed. "Would you have me reveal all our military secrets?"

Upon seeing the talon, the gate guards stepped aside as the gates swung open. The buildings therein were similar to those found across the Petty Kingdoms, with thatched roofs or shingles protecting them from rain, while the streets were covered in planks of wood so dark as to appear almost black.

Charlaine noticed them immediately. "Is this shadowbark?"

"It is commonplace in the Goldenwood, although I understand it is rare amongst Human realms."

"This street alone would have cost thousands were it built in a Human city. Have you ever thought of exporting it?"

"Wealth is not our primary concern. We are more interested in maintaining the security of our kingdom."

The path led them past many buildings, shops of one type or another, while every step brought them closer to the centre of the city, where the great tree rested upon the hill, dominating the skyline. At its base stood an enormous wooden building, oak panels forming the walls, with the roof shingled in yet more shadowbark. The entire structure looked like it belonged in the midst of a forest, as if it had grown from the earth itself.

"The high lord resides within," said Fariel. "From this point forward, you must be on your best behaviour."

"We shall," replied Charlaine. "I promise you."

The talon ordered her command to halt and advanced to the door, where two Elf guards stood. They recognized her immediately, offering a salute, then opened the doors and stepped aside.

"Come," she said. "It is time you dismounted. It is not proper for you to meet High Lord Sindra while on horseback."

The entrance hall led to a second set of doors flanked by yet more guards. Charlaine dismounted, passing off Stormcloud's reins, waiting as Teresa did the same, and then they entered the building.

"Beyond this door," said Fariel, "lies the council hall. Within, you will find the high lord and those she deems worthy of offering advice." She nodded to the guards, who opened the inner door.

A sunken floor filled the centre of the room, with a raised throne standing alone at the far end. On either side, there were steps that would, presumably, be used as seats, though today, these were empty.

Upon the throne sat Sindra, High Lord of Nethendril, dressed in green and gold. Her long hair hung in elaborate braids down the front of her tunic. Behind her stood a warrior in bright silver mail one would liken to fish scales.

Fariel paused a few paces from the throne, then bowed deeply, speaking in the Elven tongue. *"Your Eminence, I bring you Charlaine deShandria, Temple General of Saint Agnes."*

Sindra looked down at them, showing no emotion. "And the other?" she answered in common.

"Temple Captain Teresa," replied Charlaine.

"Why have you entered the Goldenwood?"

"We came here out of necessity, Eminence, after escaping the Antonine."

"That place is unfamiliar to me."

"The head of the Church of the Saints resides there."

"Ah, yes. The Church of the Saints. This I have heard of. I fought along-side the Temple Knights of Saint Mathew some years ago."

"You did?"

"Yes. We came to the aid of Hadenfeld when their northern neighbour invaded." The warrior behind her stepped forward, and they exchanged words in hushed tones, then the high lord turned back to Charlaine. "I believe you know it as the Kingdom of Zowenbruch?"

"I do, Eminence."

"Had you arrived a few years earlier, you might have all been put to death."

"So I'm led to understand."

Fariel cleared her throat. "She claims to know King Ludwig, Eminence."

"Does she, now? How curious. Is he aware you entered the Goldenwood with over four hundred knights?"

"I cannot say for certain. We sent word some time ago but do not know if it was delivered."

"Why is that?"

"Our flight was conducted on short notice, necessitating us to travel cross-country. A courier would need to take a more indirect route to reach Harlingen."

"You present me with a difficult choice, General. You have violated our borders with a large force of armed knights, yet you claim to know the King of Hadenfeld, our ally."

"There is more," pressed Charlaine. "I bear news of the greatest import to King Ludwig."

"To Humans, everything is of great import. I suppose that is what comes of being so short-lived."

"Hadenfeld is in terrible danger. The Church means to declare a Holy War against it."

"Why would they do that?"

"Ludwig refused the offer to house the Temple Knights of Saint Cunar."

"And for this, they take offence?"

"The order is corrupt, Eminence, and under the influence of the Empire of Halvaria." Charlaine waited, but there was no hint of surprise on the Elf's face. "You already know of them."

"I do. I learned of their presence well before I agreed to this alliance with Hadenfeld. As to this order of Temple Knights you speak of, that is something else. Are you certain the empire controls them?"

"I found proof back in the Antonine," said Charlaine, "but it was too late. The damage had already been done. All the Temple Knights were ordered disbanded, save for the Cunars, and we chose to flee rather than submit."

"A brave choice or a foolhardy one, I have yet to decide which. How do I know I can trust you, General?"

"*Temple Knights don't lie,*" said Teresa in the Elvish tongue.

"*You speak our language?*" The high lord's eyes bored into those of Fariel. "*Why did you not see fit to inform me of this?*"

"*My apologies, Your Eminence. You were deep in discussion before I had a chance to mention it.*"

"What is to become of us?" Charlaine interjected in her native language.

The high lord addressed Charlaine's question in the common tongue. "My father would have executed you for invading our territory, but this is a new age, and with it comes new ideas."

"I assure you we mean no harm. We wish only to live in peace."

"Yet you come armed. And even if you hadn't, war is looming. Are you trying to tell me you would sit back and allow your new home to suffer invasion?"

"No, Eminence."

"And if this Church of yours does invade, on whose side would you fight?"

Charlaine straightened her back. "That of Hadenfeld, without a doubt."

"I find it difficult to judge the sincerity of Humans, but I have no reason to doubt you, so I accept you at your word. Tell me more about this threat you spoke of."

"The man who heads the Church, the Primus, was incensed Hadenfeld refused his offer to house Temple Knights of Saint Cunar and, as a result, decided to use other means to secure the kingdom."

"Why would he want these Temple Knights in Hadenfeld to begin with?"

"I believe he wanted them present to oppose any move made by King Ludwig to counter a Halvarian invasion of the Continent."

"I think you give them far too much credit. How could one group of knights hold an entire kingdom hostage?"

"It would be difficult to march to war with a hostile force within one's borders."

"I concede the point," said Sindra. "You have given me much to consider." She turned to Fariel. "See them to guest quarters. We will talk more once I have spoken with my advisors."

"Yes, Eminence."

The Elf talon led them back outside. "I shall take you to guest quarters where you may rest and partake of a meal."

"*A question, if you please,*" said Teresa, switching to Elvish. "*Do you believe that went well?*"

"*I think you have given the high lord much to consider. If it is any consolation, she did not order you imprisoned like the last Humans who visited.*"

"*King Ludwig was imprisoned?*"

"*He was indeed; though, to be precise, he was not yet a king, merely a prince.*"

"*And what does an Elvish prison look like?*"

"*It was not a prison,*" said Fariel. "*It was a cage that hung suspended from a tree. A cage, I might add, that held no room to stand or to lie properly.*"

"*Then I'm happy we're to be treated as guests.*"

Fariel halted by a door. *"These are your rooms. Ensure that you remain within. Someone will be by later with food."* She left without another word.

"What was that all about earlier?" asked Charlaine.

"Nothing important," replied Teresa, switching back to the common tongue. "I was expressing my admiration for the treatment we're receiving."

"Really? It didn't sound like it."

"Oh? Can you understand Elvish now?"

"No, but your mannerisms tell me otherwise. You tensed during your conversation with Fariel, a sure sign something was amiss, and when you tried to explain it away, your voice sounded a little strained."

"I suppose I should've expected you to catch that, considering you're so good at reading people."

Sunlight flooded the room as Charlaine threw the shutters wide open. The breeze coming through the window was filled with a humidity that left her clothes clinging to her, the heat of the early morning already threatening to become unbearable. A knock on her door drew her attention. "Come," she called out.

The door opened to an Elf bearing a tray of food. "This is for you," he said with a slight bow, then placed it on a small table off to one side. "The talon will see you shortly," he added before he backed out.

Charlaine approached the tray that held a goblet of water accompanied by an assortment of nuts, berries, and other fruits, a far cry from the porridge common in most commanderies.

Teresa poked her head in through the doorway. "Are you up?"

"I wouldn't be standing here if I wasn't. Have you eaten?"

"I have." The healer moved to the window to peer out. "Your view is much better than mine. You can see that gigantic tree so clearly." Teresa waited for Charlaine to respond, but when nothing was forthcoming, she turned to her companion. "What's troubling you?"

"I've been thinking about our situation here, and it doesn't bode well. I made a mistake bringing us through the Goldenwood."

"You couldn't have known it was claimed by Elves. It's not as if they had signposts up warning us not to trespass."

"True, but in my ignorance, I may have doomed the order. There's every possibility the high lord will order us to leave the Goldenwood and return to where we came from."

"If we do that, we'll be marching straight into the arms of the Holy Army."

"That's what worries me."

"Won't your relationship with King Ludwig save us?"

"I'm not certain that helps. The Elves of Nethendril may have an alliance with him, but that doesn't mean they're friends. It's more likely an agreement built on mutual necessity. The Elves need Hadenfeld to stave off invasion, and Ludwig needs allies to help bolster his defences in case of an attack." She fell silent, picking away at the fruit.

"What can we do about it?" asked Teresa.

"Nothing. Trust me, I spent half the night trying to come up with a plan, but I could think of nothing that would help us. At least our knights are being fed."

"So we've been told, but do we know that's true?"

"What are you suggesting?"

"They could be driving our sisters back towards Kingshaven while we're here, trying to secure our future."

"You spent ten years amongst the Elves," said Charlaine. "Are you suggesting they can't be trusted?"

"Elves are like Humans in certain aspects. Yes, they live longer, but deep down, they're driven by the same desires and petty jealousies as we are. Gwalinor once claimed any position of power corrupts the soul and stated the ruling council of Eloria was no exception."

"Did you see that for yourself?"

"No," replied Teresa. "The only person I met even remotely close to that level was what we'd call the local mayor, although the Elvish term is more akin to master of the city."

"I understand your reticence to trust these Elves, but my experience has been somewhat different from yours. Back in Arnsfeld, the Elf leader of Mythanos came to our aid, even though we didn't ask. I have a hard time believing she did so out of her own selfishness."

"You are a trusting person, Charlaine, and I applaud you for that, but I feel I must give you fair warning. Elves do not always think like Humans. Yes, they are similar in many ways, as I said earlier, but their immortality makes them less inclined to make quick decisions. We may find it takes weeks, perhaps even months, for them to decide what to do about us."

"That's good," said Charlaine. "The longer it takes, the better the chance my letter will reach Harlingen."

"And when it does, will the king come to our rescue?"

"Rescue may not be the right term, but I think we could expect a response."

"I thought you were worried about the Elves, but it's Ludwig, isn't it? You don't think he'll welcome us."

"He wants to do what's best for Hadenfeld, and giving us sanctuary may not accomplish that goal. Doing so puts him in firm opposition to the Church, a Church that's already committed to punishing him for his temerity in refusing the Cunars."

"If they are intent on resisting the Church, wouldn't it be better for eight companies of Temple Knights to be on his side?"

"That's the question I keep asking myself, but there are other matters to consider."

"Such as?"

"Let's assume he gives us sanctuary," said Charlaine. "What then? Where do we live? We can't send all our Temple Knights to Harlingen. How would they eat or pay for fodder for their horses, let alone themselves? The Church cut us off, which means we no longer have the funds to pay for necessities."

"We have the strongbox we brought from the commandery in Saint Agnes."

"We do, but that will only carry us so far. We still need to re-establish contact with all the other commanderies in the Petty Kingdoms, and the Cunars will be on the lookout for any signs of where we might have fled."

"But they know where we fled," said Teresa. "They were there when we crossed into Hadenfeld."

"They were, which begs the question, who will Ludwig have to fight first, the Church or Halvaria?"

44

THE THREAT

SUMMER 1107 SR

Sindra looked down upon the two Temple Knights she'd summoned to stand judgement, revealing no sign of what was to come. Charlaine waited as one of the high lord's advisors cast a spell, and then, to her amazement, she discovered she could understand what the Elves were saying.

"There," said the high lord. "*Now, we can carry on this discussion in a manner the Lords of Nethendril understand.*"

There must've been at least thirty Elves in attendance, all lavishly garbed, but Charlaine's gaze remained on Sindra. "*You have had time to ponder our predicament, Eminence. What is your decision?*"

"*I would consider myself a compassionate individual, but as high lord, I must judge you on the threat you pose to the Goldenwood and the Realm of Hadenfeld, who are now our allies. Your presence here, indeed your presence anywhere, is a weight of swords that will tip the balance of military power to an extraordinary degree. I fear if you were to be accepted in Hadenfeld, you would draw the ire of this Church of yours, causing no end of conflict.*"

"*The Church will attack whether we're here or not,*" replied Charlaine. "*King Ludwig has a better chance of fending them off if we fight alongside him.*"

"*That is not my decision to make. We sent word to Harlingen the moment we detected your presence, and though we have heard nothing in reply, you may rest assured King Ludwig will not sit idly by while such an army exists so close to his border. There is also the matter of our alliance. You have threatened the Golden-wood, and the treaty between our two peoples requires him to send an army to assist in our defence.*"

"*But we are no threat to you.*"

"I hear your words, but Humans can be capricious at times. How do I know your followers will not turn on us?"

"My followers are Temple Knights. Each one has taken an oath to serve the order and is highly disciplined. To even think they could act in such a manner is insulting."

Sindra leaned forward on her throne. *"Your sisters are surrounded by my glade warriors. Were I to command it, they would all be slain before they even realized they were under attack."*

"With all due respect, Eminence, we both know that statement is false. I have borne witness to the emptiness of the streets here in Nethendril, and I seriously doubt you have the numbers to take on so many Temple Knights. I say this not to cast aspersions on your people, merely to illustrate I will not tolerate such deceit."

The high lord sat back, her eyebrows raised. *"So you have a backbone after all. Were I to let you leave the Goldenwood, General, where would you go?"*

"To Hadenfeld," replied Charlaine, *"as I already stated."*

"Even though their army comes to bring an end to your journey?"

"My people need a home. If that means we must disband the order and live as commoners, then so be it."

"You have passion, which does you credit, but let me make this perfectly clear. You will not be allowed to remain in the Goldenwood, and should you choose to return to it without my leave, you do so under sentence of death." The high lord paused, taking a moment to regain her composure. *"My glade warriors will escort you to the western edge of our lands. From there, you will be on your own, but should you find yourself in distress, know your way east is blocked."*

"And if the Army of Hadenfeld insists we leave their lands?"

"Then go south, or north, if you must. It matters little to me."

"Might I ask where we are to emerge from the Goldenwood?"

The warrior behind the high lord leaned forward, whispering. Sindra kept her eyes on Charlaine the entire time, nodding briefly, then sitting up straighter. *"You will emerge near the town of Tongrin. Are you familiar with it?"*

"No," replied Charlaine. *"I'm afraid not."*

The warrior stepped forward. *"It is a smaller barony and ruled by one of King Ludwig's loyal supporters. There has been much turmoil in Hadenfeld these last few years, and the Baron of Tongrin helped put Ludwig on the Throne. As such, I would expect him to have significant influence with the king. He is also likely to take great exception to the sudden appearance of over four hundred knights in the middle of his lands."*

"And you are?"

The warrior stiffened. *"I am Elonin, Talon of Nethendril."*

"And marshal of my army," added Sindra. *"You would do well to remember*

that, for if you choose to return to the Goldenwood, it will be her warriors you would face."

Charlaine bowed. *"I accept your terms, Eminence, though I am at a loss why you display such anger towards us. We have never taken up arms against your people or ridden through your lands with the intent to damage or destroy. We are refugees, seeking only a place to call our own."*

"Refugees adorned in heavy armour who come to us mounted on beasts of war. Your intentions may be honourable, but from our point of view, it is difficult to expect you would deal with us fairly when you come in such large numbers."

"We are no threat to you!" insisted Charlaine.

"Your mere presence is a threat!" Sindra took a deep breath. *"This realm has stood for more than two thousand years. I will not see its borders defiled by Human warriors."*

"Yet you are in an alliance with Hadenfeld."

"Look around you, General. Other than yourselves, do you see any Humans in this room? My court is ruled by Elves, not Humans, and while we have taken an oath to help protect Ludwig's lands, that does not allow him unfettered access to this court."

"Are the warriors of Hadenfeld not bound by treaty to come to your aid if threatened?"

"Only if we request it. I have said my piece. It is time for you to be returned to your people."

Charlaine looked at Teresa, who appeared nervous. "We will get through this," she soothed in the common tongue.

The Life Mage forced a smile. "I've faced worse."

"This way," said Fariel, who'd remained by the door. She led the Temple Knights outside, then halted. "You have drawn the ire of the high lord, not an easy thing to accomplish."

"Is there something we're not aware of?" asked Charlaine. "She was a lot more antagonistic today."

"She met with her advisors this morning. Their opposition to the Hadenfeld alliance was strong, and many Elven lords wanted her to take a harder line against intrusions. Although the position of high lord is hereditary, if there were doubts about her ability to do what's best for the realm, she would soon find herself deposed."

"Tell me," said Teresa, "did she speak the truth when she said they would prevent us from fleeing, or was that merely a threat?"

"She was deadly serious. If you knew anything about us Elves, you would understand we do not threaten unless we are ready to act."

"That was not my experience in Eloria."

"Ah, yes. The famed Sea Elves. Understand this, Temple Captain; those who fled before the Great War do not bear the scars that cut so deeply into our people."

"I'm not sure I follow," said Charlaine. "What scars?"

Fariel looked around, ensuring no one else was within earshot. "The Great War placed a tremendous burden on us, one from which we never fully recovered."

"By your own reckoning, that was more than two thousand years ago."

"It was, but as your friend knows, we forest folk do not die from natural causes."

"That still doesn't explain the venom behind your high lord's threat."

"The war with the Orcs raged for more than a century, involving long campaigns waged across the length and breadth of the Continent. We Elves learned how to harness incredible magic during that time, including using the magic of the earth to transport warriors over great distances."

"And?"

"It turned out to be our undoing. We defeated the Orcs, but it was a hollow victory. By the end, we were so depleted, our population had shrunk tremendously."

"This I understand," said Charlaine, "but surely, in the intervening years, you've managed to build back your numbers?"

"That's just it; we can't. The very magic that brought us victory denied us the ability to bear the next generation. No new Elves have been born in almost two thousand years. Instead, our population slowly dies off, not from old age, mind you, but we can still pass to the Afterlife due to sickness or war. So you see, the very notion of fighting to prop up the rule of the King of Hadenfeld is problematic."

"But so would fighting us!"

"Admittedly, it would," said Fariel, "but it would also prove our military prowess, something many of the Lords of Nethendril feel is lacking under the current high lord."

"Was this not the same high lord who helped repel an invasion from their northern neighbour, Zowenbruch?"

"Many considered that a waste of our resources. The invaders had no designs on the Goldenwood, only Eisen. Sindra's support of Ludwig, who was only a prince then, was viewed as her way of rewarding him."

"For what?" asked Charlaine.

"For saving her life. Her uncle killed her father, then tried to usurp the Throne and murder her. Had Ludwig not been here, it would have ended in disaster. Having said that, some think her uncle might have made a more capable ruler."

"So she's torn between her desire to do the right thing and appeasing these lords you mentioned?"

"Now you understand the path she walks and why so many nobles attended today's meeting. One stray step, and she could easily find herself displaced."

"Thank you," said Charlaine. "You've given me a much better understanding of the politics of the Goldenwood. Might I ask what happens now?"

"We shall retrieve your horses and escort you to your command. After that, you'll cross the Erlen and make your way towards Tongrin, but my people will only guide you to the edge of our realm. The rest is up to you."

Fariel set a blistering pace at the beginning of their trip back to The Five Hundred despite being on foot. Stormcloud was more than up to the challenge, but the same could not be said of Teresa's mount. It lagged behind, and no amount of cajoling on the Elves' part convinced it to do otherwise, forcing them to slacken the pace.

Charlaine talked little, her mind occupied with the endless possibilities of what the future might hold. Would the Elven Lords of Nethendril win over their high lord and convince her that the Temple Knights should be attacked, or would they be allowed to leave in peace as Sindra promised? The politics of the Petty Kingdoms were full of deceit and treachery. Would the same prove true with the Elves?

Her only dealings with the forest folk before this had been in Arnsfeld, and while Bethiel, the leader of Mythanos, was cordial and polite, she'd talked little. Charlaine had read that some scholars believed an Elf's mind was remarkably different from that of a Human's, but Charlaine had doubts. Sindra's change of behaviour shocked her, but it made perfect sense in light of Fariel's explanation.

That brought her to her own plight. As Temple General, she was responsible for the survival of the entire order, not just The Five Hundred. Would she be forced to bow to political pressure and compromise her beliefs? This gave her a new appreciation for those who ruled, which, in turn, brought her thoughts to Ludwig.

Would her appearance in Hadenfeld help or hinder the king's ability to rule? Would his nobles oppose the presence of the Temple Knights? The realm has seen much bloodshed in the past decade, and for Hadenfeld to survive, Ludwig must navigate a fine line between punishing those who stood against him and embracing them as valued members of the nobility.

A not so dissimilar situation from the narrow path High Lord Sindra walked.

The days wore on, and the closer she drew to her people, the more she became convinced they must prepare for battle.

Fariel and her glade wardens led them halfway across the Erlen River, then came to a halt.

"This is it," she said. "I do not expect you to march on such short notice, so I give you the rest of today to make preparations. Come first light, however, I expect your people to be ready to cross."

"I understand," replied Charlaine. "I promise we shall be ready to march at first light."

"My glade wardens will be waiting on our side of the river to escort you. Two will remain within your sight at all times, while the rest will be in the woods. Your guides will lead you out of the Goldenwood and then point you in the direction of the Human village of Tongrin."

"Will we see you again?" asked Teresa.

"It is doubtful," replied Fariel, "but should we find ourselves in each other's company in the future, I hope it will be as friends."

"A feeling we share," said Charlaine. "Good day to you, Talon, and may the Saints look down on you with kindness." She urged Stormcloud on, splashing her way to the eastern bank where a familiar face waited.

"Sister Anthea," said Charlaine. "You look like you've seen a ghost."

"My pardon, General. You'd been gone so long we thought you were lost to us."

"Did you think I would so easily abandon the order?"

"No, General. Of course not," the Temple Knight blurted out.

"Come and help me gather the others. There is much to discuss."

Addressing everyone would've been too impractical, given they were deep in the forest, so she called for only the officers of the order to meet by the river. They arrived there first, talking amongst themselves while they waited. At her approach, all conversation stopped.

"No doubt you have many questions," Charlaine began, "and I shall get to them in due course, but first, there is the matter of where we go from here." She paused, looking at those around her. "Tomorrow morning, we will resume our march. The Elves have graciously allowed us passage through their lands, but I'm afraid it's a one-way trip. Should we fail in our endeavours, there will be no turning back." She paused again while she worked out how to phrase their current predicament.

"It has come to my attention that the King of Hadenfeld may not take kindly to the presence of so many Temple Knights in his lands. Over the past few years, the kingdom has undergone two civil wars and likely still suffers from very deep divisions. Some of his nobility may urge him to forbid us entry, for not doing so would invoke the wrath of the Church."

"Too late for that," said Elliana. Everyone looked at her, and she blushed at all the attention.

"The Temple Captain is correct," continued Charlaine. "The Church has already declared Hadenfeld as heretical, but the news may not have reached the king yet. The Elves sent word to Harlingen when they originally discovered us, so all he knows is that a force of mounted warriors entered the Goldenwood. I'm expecting to find a Royal Army waiting for us when we clear these woods in a few days."

"Are we to face battle?" asked Ursula.

"I shall do everything in my power to avoid that, which brings me to my next point. To survive, we may be required to surrender our arms and disband the order." Everyone talked at once, forcing her to raise her voice to be heard.

"I'm not finished!" she shouted, waiting for the noise to die down. "A battle is not guaranteed, and surrender is only one possible outcome—there are others. My intent is to negotiate with the king or whomever he has sent to command his army. If he is aware of the Church's stance towards his kingdom, then we have a chance to remain knights if we agree to help defend this realm. If not, then we must rely on the king's good character and plead our case on humanitarian grounds.

"I know this is not what you wanted to hear," she continued, "but when I accepted the rank of Temple General, I swore to protect all of you to the best of my ability, which is precisely what I intend to do, no matter the risk. I promise you we will get through this, but we need to stand together one more time to see it through to the end."

45

TONGRIN

SUMMER 1107 SR

The Five Hundred reached the edge of the Goldenwood six days later. Beyond, lay a small town nestled in a gap between hills and yet more trees. Of greater concern, however, was the mass of warriors blocking their way.

Charlaine rode to the front of the column as soon as word reached her. The Temple Knights halted, waiting on her commands before taking action. Still too far away to pose any danger, the distant army raised the alarm, forcing hundreds of men to form into a line of battle.

"Not the most heartening of sights," noted Nicola. "I wonder who commands them?"

"Not the king," replied Charlaine. "There's no sign of a Royal Pennant."

"There's no sign of any pennant. Could this be the local baron's garrison?"

"With that many people? I doubt it. According to the Elves, Tongrin is one of the poorer baronies, yet I see more than a thousand souls."

"Closer to twelve hundred," offered Teresa. "And they appear to have knights."

"What's your assessment, Nicola?" asked Charlaine.

The Temple Captain's gaze wandered across the opposing army. "I see no evidence of militia, and their footmen look to all be in mail; not the best of signs from our point of view."

"That's to be expected. King Ludwig will have wanted a well-trained army to discourage anyone from ousting him."

"What's our response?" asked Nicola.

"We'll form up in two waves, four companies wide."

"Do you think we'll have to fight?"

"It's certainly a possibility, but I'll try talking to them first. If things go bad, though, I want our knights prepared to fight." Charlaine tore her gaze from the Army of Hadenfeld to look at her aide. "Send my compliments to the Temple Commanders and tell them to prepare for battle."

"Yes, General." Temple Captain Nicola rode off while Charlaine studied the army before them.

"I wonder who's in charge over there," said Teresa.

"Let's find out, shall we?"

"Shouldn't we wait until everyone is in position?"

"It will take us a considerable amount of time to close the range. Our people will be ready long before we get anywhere near that army. Now, are you coming or not?"

"Me?" said Teresa. "I'm a healer, remember."

"Yes, and a trusted confidante. I'll need an honest appraisal of whoever leads that army over there."

"You don't think it'll be the king?"

"If he were there, his standard would be flying." Charlaine chuckled. "Not that he's overly concerned with such things, but his nobles would insist on it. Remember, he sits on a Throne he seized through battle; he won't want to appear weak."

Behind them, orders were shouted, and The Five Hundred began moving into position. It was a glorious sight, with the scarlet of their tabards mixing in with the bright silver of their plate armour. At any other time, it would've been a spectacle worth watching, but Charlaine had to face the hard truth that it might just be the last time anyone would see the sight.

She closed her eyes, saying a silent prayer. A breeze blew in from the west, sending a stray strand of hair across her face. She briefly considered lowering her visor, but then pragmatism got the better of her. "Helmets off, I think."

"Are you certain?"

"We are about to plead for our lives. As such, I shouldn't like to be misunderstood. Come on, Stormcloud. Let's see who commands this lot, shall we?" She urged her mount onward, keeping a modest pace.

Teresa fell in beside her. "What do you know about King Ludwig's army? Are they experienced?"

"He defeated an invasion from Zowenbruch, then took those same men and seized the Throne. I suspect he kept them under arms to maintain order."

"How long ago was this?"

"Back in oh four. Why?"

"That's almost three years ago. Surely he would've secured his rule by now?"

"Civil wars have a way of bringing out the worst in people, with those on the losing side often bearing grudges for years."

"So, who commands here? Someone loyal to the king or a person with a score to settle?"

"We'll know soon enough. Teresa, if this doesn't go the way we want it to, I need you to promise me something."

"Yes?"

"If possible, make your way to Temple Bay. Danica will look after you there."

"With all due respect, I'm not about to abandon the order. I've also taken an oath to help the injured. I could never abandon wounded in need."

"I knew you'd say that," said Charlaine. "It's what comes of serving under Sister Giselle."

"You're a lot like her."

"Who, Giselle? I'm surprised to hear you say that."

"Why? You both put the needs of the order above all else, and you have that… I don't know, that undefinable thing that makes such a great leader. You inspire others to be better versions of themselves. Such qualities are rare, and I've had the good fortune to serve under two women so gifted." Teresa halted suddenly, surprising her companion.

"Something wrong?" asked Charlaine.

"I just had a thought. What if Ludwig has been replaced? Hadenfeld has had two civil wars. Why not a third? The Church might've instigated an uprising after sanctioning the kingdom, and we've had no news for months."

"I hadn't considered that, but if it were true, don't you think the Elves would have mentioned it?"

"Yet here we are facing a potentially hostile army. If Ludwig were still on the Throne, wouldn't he send a delegation instead of an entire army?"

"The last time Ludwig wrote to me, he made no mention of trouble."

"Did he mention the Elves?"

"No, but there's doubtless a good reason for that."

"That being?"

"The smiths guild carried our correspondence," replied Charlaine. "An organization run by Dwarves. As such, the mountain folk would have access to anything he wrote."

"But you trust them to carry our letters?"

"True, but what if the Elves of the Goldenwood have some animosity towards the Dwarves, and he picked up on that."

"You make a good point," said Teresa. "And I may know why. According to Fariel, the Elves suffered huge losses during the Great War. Think how much better off they would have been if the Dwarves joined them."

"Was there discord between the Sea Elves and the mountain folk?"

"That's difficult to say. They rarely spoke of outsiders, and when they did, it was usually with an air of superiority, but most of their ire was directed at Humans. We did replace them as the dominant race on the Continent."

"I'm not certain all this speculation helps us at this precise moment," said Charlaine.

"You're right. We should be concentrating on that army over yonder." Teresa urged her horse into a trot.

Stormcloud, sensing it was time to get moving, did the same. They rode on, the enemy army now solidly formed into a line of battle.

"The archers are in the second rank," noted Charlaine. "Not what one usually does with poorly trained warriors."

"Agreed," added Teresa. "But their cavalry is waiting in the rear, ready to deploy as needed. How much experience did you say Ludwig has?"

"Plenty. But once again, he's not in command here."

"Look. Someone's approaching."

A trio of riders broke through the lines, waiting as one of their group unfurled a banner.

"Do you recognize the colours?" asked Teresa.

"It's the flag of Hadenfeld, if I'm not mistaken."

"What's that supposed to mean? Surely you recognize their flag?"

"I spent most of my time in a smithy, not the place you'd see a flag."

"But you must have seen Royal Troops at some point?"

Charlaine shook her head. "No. Only those belonging to the Baron of Verfeld, and his colours were said to be different from those of the king."

A gust caught the banner, allowing it to flutter in the wind.

"It's blue," said Teresa. "Does that help?"

"To a certain extent. Blue is reserved for those with Royal Blood."

"So, is it Ludwig?"

"We'll have to wait and see."

The riders continued, the banner bearer following behind the other two.

"Strange," said Teresa. "I would've thought whoever led this group would be a noble, yet they wear common mail, not plate."

"That definitely settles the matter—it's not Ludwig."

"I'm getting a bad feeling about this."

The riders advanced, then halted ten paces away, the Temple Knights doing likewise.

What they assumed to be the leader, an immensely tall individual, moved closer by a horse length. "You are Temple Knights of Saint Agnes," he said, his voice deep and resonant. "Why have you come here?"

"I am Charlaine deShandria, Temple General of Saint Agnes, and I brought my sister knights here to bring warning to His Majesty, King Ludwig of Hadenfeld."

"Temple General?"

"A recent promotion."

He removed his helmet, revealing a thick beard. Something familiar about his features left Charlaine struggling to place him. "I know you," she said. "I saw you at the wedding of Lord Ludwig and Lady Charlotte. Aren't you Sigwulf?"

The fellow grinned. "I am, indeed, General. Sigwulf Marhaven, one of the king's trusted advisors. I believe you may have heard of Cyn?" He waved his shorter companion forward, who then removed her helmet.

"Greetings," the woman added. "I don't believe we've met, but His Majesty has told us all about you. Welcome home, General."

A wave of relief flooded through Charlaine. "Thank you. It's been a difficult journey."

"Sorry about all of this," said Sigwulf, waving his arm towards the waiting army. "When the Elves informed us someone entered their lands, they didn't see fit to relate you were Temple Knights. Then again, they've had no contact with your particular order prior to this."

"Is the king well?"

"He is, although the queen has been ill of late. He would've come himself had we known it was you, but I'm afraid other events have proved most troublesome." He glanced behind Charlaine to see the Temple Knights formed up for battle. "Just how many do you command?"

"Four hundred and thirty-five," replied Charlaine. "You should be made aware the Church disbanded our order."

"And you came here instead? What prompted such a move?"

"The Antonine has taken great offence at Ludwig's refusal to allow the Temple Knights of Saint Cunar to build a commandery in his lands."

"I warned him that would happen," said Cyn, "but you know Ludwig, always wanting to do the right thing."

"And he did," replied Charlaine. "We've learned the Church has been corrupted by agents of the Halvarian Empire."

"This is news, indeed," said Sigwulf. "Have you proof?"

"Only my word and that of my sister knights. We fled here, seeking refuge from the wrath of the Church. Will the king grant us what we seek?"

"I believe he will, although there will doubtless be details to work out."

"Of course he will," said Cyn. "His Majesty is a practical fellow, and having close to five hundred knights to help secure his lands would be of great benefit. The question we need to deal with is where do we put them? We can't march them all the way back to Harlingen."

"A good point. Tell me, General, have you many supply wagons?"

"None," replied Charlaine.

"None? And you made it all the way through the Goldenwood?"

"The Elves fed us, though only after we'd wandered for weeks on end."

"Tongrin is much too small to support so many. I think it's best to take you to Eisen. We can house some of your Temple Knights in the Royal Keep there, while others would need to be billeted in the city until we arrange some alternate means of housing them. How long does it take to build a commandery?"

"Years," replied Charlaine. "And if it were built like all the others, we would need ten."

"So you'll need something larger, then."

"The commandery in the Antonine housed us all," added Teresa.

"And you are?"

"My apologies," said Charlaine. "This is Temple Captain Teresa. She commands the Sisters of Mercy."

"I'm afraid I'm not familiar with them."

"Nor would I expect you to be," replied Teresa. "We are a new faction within the order, dedicated to the healing arts."

"Healers?" said Sigwulf. "How interesting."

"Not just healers," said Charlaine. "Teresa is a Life Mage."

Cyn grinned. "This keeps getting better. Might I ask how many Sisters of Mercy there are?"

"I am the only one trained so far, but I've already identified several sister knights capable of learning magic. Their training will commence once we've found a suitable home."

"Have they any restrictions on who they might heal?"

"No. Although in battle, the priority would be given to the sisters of the order."

"You spoke earlier of the Elves. Did you, by chance, meet Galrandir, their Life Mage?"

"I did not," replied Teresa.

"Between you and me," said Cyn, "the Elves leave much to be desired as hosts. They did, however, come to our aid to repel an invasion, so I shouldn't speak ill of them."

"A good point," said Sigwulf. "Eisen is close to the border of the Goldenwood. I hope that won't be a problem?"

"Not for us," said Charlaine. "My knights are highly disciplined and will not cause any trouble."

"And if the kingdom should be invaded?"

"That largely depends on our status here, but I can't imagine we would stand by and allow that to happen without some sort of intervention. You may relay that to His Majesty at your earliest convenience."

"Oh, you'll be able to do that yourself."

"How?"

"Once we get your people to Eisen, you'll accompany us to the Royal Court at Harlingen. You're welcome to bring any advisors along with you." He glanced back at his army. "There's no sense all of us standing around here ready to fight. I'll stand my people down, and then you can bring your Temple Knights to join them. Would that be acceptable?"

"It would. Thank you."

"I had best get to work, then." With that, Sigwulf turned his horse around, heading back towards his men. His bannerman followed, but Cyn remained behind, grinning from ear to ear.

"I sense this is a momentous occasion," she said. "You may very well have saved Hadenfeld." She paused to look at all the Temple Knights assembled to the east. "It's also nice not to be the only woman in armour for a change."

"Were you always a warrior?" asked Teresa.

"Yes. My father commanded a mercenary company. That's not a problem, is it?"

"Not at all," replied Charlaine. "I'm merely trying to ascertain where you and Sigwulf stand in relation to the Crown."

"We're both ranked as generals," said Cyn, "though some nobles took umbrage at that." She chuckled. "Umbrage. Look at me, getting all fancy with my words. I suppose court life has been rubbing off on me. Have you spent much time at court, General?"

"More than I care to admit."

"I hope that means we can expect to learn more about you?"

"You seem to know a lot about me already."

"What can I say? The boss speaks of you fondly, as does the queen, for that matter."

"The boss?" said Teresa.

"Sorry. Old habits die hard. I should have said, His Majesty, but if you know the king, you know he wouldn't take any offence."

"Nor do I," replied Charlaine. She smiled. "I don't suppose I could convince you to join the order?"

"Who, me? No. I'm too set in my ways, but I'd have no objection to fighting alongside more Temple Knights."

"More Temple Knights?"

"Yes. Didn't you know? We have a company of Mathewites billeted in Eisen. They helped put Ludwig on the Throne."

"Yes. He wrote to me about their involvement, but I've been so distracted by other matters, I hadn't considered what happened to them. I feel I should point out that when word gets out we've taken refuge here, you're likely to see a lot more."

"Why is that?"

"The Church disbanded their order, and all their knights were to swear service to the Temple Knights of Saint Cunar."

"I can't imagine that going over well."

"It didn't. A significant portion rebelled, as we did. Even as we speak, they'll be scouring the Continent for kingdoms willing to offer them a home."

"The more the merrier, I always say, though where we'll end up putting them is anyone's guess."

Sigwulf halted, turning in the saddle to call back to his companion, "Cyn, are you coming?"

"I'll be right there," she replied, then leaned in to speak with Charlaine. "I must go. He's lost without me." With that, she turned her horse around, galloping off to catch up with Sigwulf.

"This has all been a great relief," said Teresa. "What did you make of those two? Do we take them seriously?"

"They haven't realized it yet," replied Charlaine, "but it's people like them who hold the future of the realm in their hands."

EPILOGUE
AUTUMN 1107 SR

As the *Redoubtable* slid down the ramp, a wave of water sloshed over the dock. The vessel still required installation of the masts, along with all the rigging necessary to support the sails, but for now, it floated alongside its sister ships, ready to begin life as a member of the Temple Fleet.

"Remarkable," said Erika.

Danica chuckled. "That would've been a good name for a ship."

"How many does that make now?"

"*Redoubtable* is the fifth of her class, although, ironically, she was the first to begin construction."

"Yet the others are already afloat. How did that come about?"

"We made improvements to the design during her construction, allowing us to incorporate them into the other ships of the class from the keel up, but they were a bit more complicated to bring to *Redoubtable*."

"And now there are five, not to mention the other ships of the fleet."

"We have more being built, but they'll take time."

"Will we have enough, do you think?"

"The future is uncertain," said Danica, "and a war is looming, but rest assured, the Temple Fleet will do its part."

<<<<>>>>

Please Review Temple General

ON TO THE SERIES FINALE: WARRIOR KING

If you liked *???* then *Servant of the Crown,* the first book in the *Heir to the Crown* series awaits.

START SERVANT OF THE CROWN FOR FREE

CAST OF CHARACTERS

PEOPLE AND PLACES

PEOPLE:

ORDER OF SAINT AGNES
  Kaylene Gantzmann - Grand Mistress, the Antonine
  Julianne Rydel - Matriarch of Saint Agnes, the Antonine

TEMPLE COMMANDERS OF SAINT AGNES
  Amalia - Officer in training, the Antonine
  Charlaine deShandria - Regional Commander, Main character
  Florence - Arnsfeld
  Gerda - Officer in training, the Antonine
  Gianna - Commandary Commander prior to Charlaine, the Antonine
  Hjordis - Disgraced, the Antonine
  Katinka - Treasurer, the Antonine
  Nina - Training Commander, the Antonine
  Raphaela - Commandant, Training Academy, Eidenburg, Talstadt
  Scyllia - The Antonine
  Ursula - Officer in training, the Antonine
  Verushka - The Antonine

TEMPLE CAPTAINS OF SAINT AGNES
  Bernelle - Lidenbach
  Danica Meer - Admiral of the Temple Fleet
  Elliana - Officer in training, the Antonine
  Erika - Officer in training, the Antonine
  Georgia - Neburg,
  Giselle - Ilea
  Lysela - Torburg, Erlingen
  Marlena Falkenberg - Arnsfeld
  Mila - Duty Officer, the Antonine
  Nicola - Aide to the Grand Mistress, the Antonine

TEMPLE KNIGHTS OF SAINT AGNES
  Anthea - Initiate, the Antonine
  Aurelia (Deceased) - Served in Ilea with Charlaine and Danica
  Cordelia - Served in Ilea with Charlaine and Danica

Enna - Lidenbach
Genevieve - Initiate, the Antonine
Grace - Captain of *Redoubtable*
Grazynia - Captain of *Vigilant*
Helena (Deceased) - Served in Ilea with Charlaine and Danica
Iris - Initiate, the Antonine
Kiara - Torburg
Lucille - Initiate, the Antonine
Maeve - Lidenbach
Magda - Initiate, the Antonine
Mariele - Initiate, the Antonine
Rhea - The Antonine
Teresa (Missing) - Served in Ilea with Charlaine and Danica
Wilhemina - Ilea
Zivka - Captain of *Illustrious*

ORDER OF SAINT RAGNAR
Aiden - Temple Knight, Ilea
Carodoc - Temple Knight, the Antonine
Casimiro - Temple Knight, the Antonine
Jarak - Kurathian Life Mage, Ilea
Julius - Temple Knight, the Antonine
Torlin - Temple Knight, the Antonine

ORDER OF SAINT MATHEW
Gatan - Temple Knight, Lidenbach, Arnsfeld
Gideon - Holy Father, Angvil
Jamarian - Temple Captain, the Antonine
Reamon - Holy Father, Silver Vale, Regensbach
Thorley - Archivist, Lay brother, the Antonine
Walda - Temple Captain, the Antonine

ORDER OF SAINT CUNAR
Gilbert - Temple Commander, Krieghoff
Guthrie - Temple Captain, Angvil
Leamund - Temple Captain, naval architect, the Antonine
Marius - Temple Commander, Former Admiral, Holy Fleet
Quintillius - Temple Commander, Regensbauch
Roydin - Temple Knight, Angvil
Talivardas - Temple Commander
Wilmar - Primus, the Antonine

Aeldred (Deceased) - First King of Therengia
Akosia - Ancient Goddess of the Sea
Baldric (Deceased) - Mercenary, Grim Defenders
Casimo Venucci - Vintner, Ilea
Cynthia 'Cyn' Hoffman - General, Hadenfeld
Ecke (Deceased) - Captain, Grim Defenders
Edun - Royal Guard, Zeinhoffen, Ardosa
Elsbeth Fel - Sacred Mother of Akosia, Reinwick
Galrath (Deceased) - Knight of Paledon
Garadino Boniface - General, Ardosa
Lloyd - Bandit, Erlingen
Messick Oakwind - Worshipper of Akosia, Kingshaven
Nathan (Deceased) - Knight of the Sceptre
Orlina Day - Sacred Mother of Tauril, Earth Mage, near Braunfel
Oskar - Soldier, Galoran
Quentin - True name of Lloyd, murderer, Erlingen
Raynald - Knight of the Sceptre
Reiser - Captain, Ardosa
Rurlan - Dwarf courier for the smith's guild
Sigwulf Marhaven - General, Hadenfeld
Spirit (of the Sea) - Danica's horse
Stormcloud - Charlaine's horse
Tauril - Ancient Goddess of the Forest
Tomas deShandria (Deceased) - Master smith, father to Charlaine
Willoughby Stern - Captain, Army of Regensbach

PLACES

PETTY KINGDOMS

Abelard - Kingdom, east of Reinwick
Amaria - Kingdom south of Regensbach
Andover - Kingdom, north of Erlingen
Angvil - Duchy, east of Arnsfeld and Rudor
Ardosa - Kingdom known as the heart of the Petty Kingdoms
Arnsfeld - Kingdom, Northern coast, adjacent to Halvaria
Corassus - City State, Southern Coast, Holy Fleet
Deisenbach - Kingdom, north of Hadenfeld
Erlingen - Duchy, south of Andover
Galoran - Kingdom, north of the Antonine
Gotfeld - Kingdom, Northeastern border of Halvaria

Hadenfeld - Central Kingdom, birthplace of Charlaine
Holstead - Duchy, eastern Petty Kingdoms
Ilea - Kingdom, Southern Coast
Kingshaven - Kingdom, east of Hadenfeld
Krieghoff - Duchy, eastern Petty Kingdoms
Langwal - Kingdom, Great Northern Sea
Menzen - Kingdom, near the Antonine
Neuhafen - Former kingdom, now part of Hadenfeld
Novarsk - Kingdom, eastern Petty Kingdoms
Oberfeld - Kingdom, northeastern border of Halvaria
Parzen - Kingdom, north of Galoran
Regensbach - Petty Kingdom, where the Antonine is located
Reinwick - Duchy, northern Petty Kingdom
Rudor - Kingdom, south of Arnsfeld
Salovia - Kingdom, eastern Petty Kingdom
Talstadt - Duchy, west of Hadenfeld
Ulrichen - Kingdom, southeast of Erlingen
Zalista - Kingdon, eastern Petty Kingdom
Zowenbruch - Kingdom, north of Hadenfeld

Cities/Towns

Agran - Capital, Deisenbach
Alantra - Capital, Calabria
Anshlag - Town, Duchy of Erlingen
Braunfel - Barony, Arnsfeld
Caerhaven - City, Duchy of Krieghoff
Carlingen - City, Kingdom of Carlingen
Clearwater - Town, the Wildlands
Dubrow - City, Arnsfeld
Ebenstadt - City, Therengia
Eidenburg - City, Duchy of Talstadt
Eisen - City, Kingdom of Hadenfeld
Galmund - City, Duchy of Erlingen
Gessen - Capital, Galoran
Harlingen - Capital, Hadenfeld
Herani - Holy City, Coast of the Shimmering Sea
Korvoran - Capital, Duchy of Reinwick
Kurtzenberg - City, Arnsfeld
Lidenbach - Port, Capital of Arnsfeld
Malburg - City, Hadenfeld
Meirshoff - City, Arnsfeld

Mitterling - Barony, Ardosa
Mythanos - Elven settlement/city, Arnsfeld
Neiburg - Capital, Angvil
Nettle Green - Village, Kingshaven
Regnitz - Barony, Erlingen
Reichendorf - Capital, Regensbach
Rizela - Capital, Ilea
Silver Vale - Village, Regensbach
Sternhelm - Village, Angvil
The Antonine - The Holy City, within the city of Reichendorf
Torburg - Capital, Duchy of Erlingen
Verfeld Keep - Town, Hadenfeld
Zeinhoffen - Capital, Ardosa
Zienholtz - Capital, Andover
Zurkirk - Village, Erlingen

OTHER PLACES

Calabria - Kingdom, Shimmering Sea, occupied by Halvaria
Dun-Galdrim - Dwarf city, destroyed by the Halvarians
Durwick River- River forming the eastern border of Hadenfeld
Eiddenwerthe - The world in which everything exists
Eloria - Island kingdom, Sea Elves
Erlen River - River running through Hadenfeld
Five Kingdoms - Ardosa, Galoran, Menzen, Kingshaven, Regensbach
Grand Sanctum - Oldest building in the Antonine
Great Northern Sea - North of the Petty Kingdoms
Grey Spire Mountains - Mountain range, east of Galoran
Halvaria - Large empire west of the Petty Kingdoms
Hollen River - River defining the southern border of Hadenfeld
Hollenbeck - Kingdom, south of Hadenfeld
Lithandor - Sea Elf City, Eloria
Mirantha - Kingdom, South of Hadenfeld
Neuhafen - Former rebel kingdom, now part of Hadenfeld
Ostrova - Eastern Petty Kingdom
Rasfeld River - River forming the western border of Erlingen
Ruzhina - Kingdom, east of the Great Northern Sea
Shimmering Sea - South of the Petty Kingdoms
Silver River - River separating Ardosa from Galoran
Successor States - Formed after the Old Kingdom of Therengia
Temple Bay - Town, Island of Patience
Thalemia - Kingdom, formerly empire, Coast of the Shimmering Sea

The Forge - Agnesite training academy, Eidenburg
The Hopping Frog - Roadside Inn, Ulrichen
Therengia - Kingdom, East of the Petty Kingdoms
Therengia (Old Kingdom) - Ancient kingdom, destroyed 500 years ago
Zaran - Unexplored region, east of the Great Northern Sea

BATTLES

Battle of Alantra (1096 SR) - Ilean/Holy fleet defeats Halvarian Navy
Battle of Chermingen (1095 SR) - Erlingen defeats Andover invasion
Battle of Erhard's Folly (1104 SR) - Ludwig defeats King Morgan
Battle of Lidenbach (1103 SR) - Temple fleet defeats Halvarian Navy
Battle of the Brinwald (1103 SR) - Arnsfeld defeats Halvarian invasion
Battle of the Wilderness (1104 SR) - Therengia defeats Cunar Knights

THE CHURCH

Council of Peers - Ruling council of the Church of the Saints
Order of Saint Agnes - Protector of women
Order of Saint Ansgar - Internal investigators of the Church
Order of Saint Augustine - Guardians of the Holy Relics
Order of Saint Cunar - Primary warriors of the Church
Order of Saint Mathew - Protectors of the poor and sick
Order of Saint Ragnar - Dedicated to eradicating Death Magic
Temple Knight - Holy Warrior
The Primus - Ultimate Church authority elected by Council of Peers

SHIPS

Constance - captured Halvarian Cog, Ilea
Fearless - Double-masted warship, Flagship, Temple Fleet
Illustrious - Double-masted warship, Temple Fleet
Redoubtable - Three-masted warship, Temple Fleet
Valiant - Single-masted, Temple Fleet
Vanguard - Single-masted, Temple Fleet
Vigilant - Single-masted, Temple Fleet

THINGS

Afterlife - Where deserving individuals go after death
Easterlings - Therengian descents, east of the Petty Kingdoms
Great War - War between Orcs and Elves, 2000 years ago
Grim Defenders - Mercenary company
Knight of the Sceptre - Knightly Order, Duchy of Erlingen
Necromancer - Death Mage

Old Kingdom - Ancient realm of Therengia
Phoenix Ring - Set of rings for secure correspondence, Smiths guild
River Serpent - Large aquatic creature with a dragon-like head
Shadowbark - Heavy dark-coloured wood
Underworld - Where undeserving individuals

A FEW WORDS FROM PAUL

Before I began this series, I knew it would ultimately result in the collapse of the Church of the Saints, or rather, the centralized control that the Antonine held over the entire Continent. Make no mistake; this whole thing was organized by the Halvarian Empire, who wanted the fighting orders rendered useless prior to the launching of their Great Dream: the subjugation of the entire Continent. With the church distracted by internal struggles, the Petty Kingdoms are left to face the invaders alone.

Charlaine has reached the highest rank possible in the Temple Knights of Saint Agnes, but with that rank comes the terrible burden of ensuring the survival of the order. Unlike the other stories in this series, she finds herself in a position where she must refrain from fighting whenever possible rather than embracing it, a difficult task considering all she's up against.

Danica is the luckier of the two, for now, as she returns to command the Temple Fleet as they resume their war against the empire.

What of their future, you ask? Their stories aren't over yet. Charlaine rides again in Warrior King, while Danica next appears in Saviour of the Crown, Book 14 of Heir to the Crown.

There are many people to thank for this book, but as always, it is my wife, Carol, to whom I owe the greatest debt. Her perseverance as editor, promoter, and inspiration allows me to focus on creating the world of Eiddenwerthe and the characters found therein.

I would also like to express my gratitude to my children, Stephanie Sandrock, Amanda Bennett, and Christie Bennett, for their support, along with our gaming friends, Brad Aitken, Stephen Brown, and the late Jeffrey Parker.

Valuable feedback was also supplied by our BETA team, so thank you to Rachel Deibler, Michael Rhew, Phyllis Simpson, Don Hinckley, Charles Mohapel, Debbie Reeves, Susan Young, Anna Ostberg, Joanna Smith, Lisa Hanika, Keven Hutchison, Brad Williams, Lisa Hunt, Brad Williams, Barbara Raue, Charles Mohapel, Kari Fredlund, Jan Weinmann, Lia Diana Elliot Braddi, John Henniger, Steve Filson.

Last but certainly not least, I must thank you, my reader, without whose interest and support none of these tales would have seen the light of day. I hope you've enjoyed Charlaine's journey so far and that you look forward to completing the series with Warrior King.

ABOUT THE AUTHOR

Paul J Bennett (b. 1961) emigrated from England to Canada in 1967. His father served in the British Royal Navy, and his mother worked for the BBC in London. As a young man, Paul followed in his father's footsteps, joining the Canadian Armed Forces in 1983. He is married to Carol Bennett and has three daughters who are all creative in their own right.

Paul's interest in writing started in his teen years when he discovered the roleplaying game, Dungeons & Dragons (D & D). What attracted him to this new hobby was the creativity it required; the need to create realms, worlds and adventures that pulled the gamers into his stories.

In his 30's, Paul started to dabble in designing his own roleplaying system, using the Peninsular War in Portugal as his backdrop. His regular gaming group were willing victims, er, participants in helping to playtest this new system. A few years later, he added additional settings to his game, including Science Fiction, Post-Apocalyptic, World War II, and the all-important Fantasy Realm where his stories take place.

The beginnings of his first book 'Servant to the Crown' originated over five years ago when he began running a new fantasy campaign. For the world that the Kingdom of Merceria is in, he ran his adventures like a TV show, with seasons that each had twelve episodes, and an overarching plot. When the campaign ended, he knew all the characters, what they had to accomplish, what needed to happen to move the plot along, and it was this that inspired to sit down to write his first novel.

Paul now has four series based in his fantasy world of Eiddenwerthe, and is looking forward to sharing many more books with his readers over the coming years.